"The task of transforming the events of the 1916 Irish Rebellion into coherent fiction would terrify most writers. Llywelyn, however, has produced a thunderous, informative read that rises to the challenge. . . . Battle scenes are both accurate and compelling. The betrayals, slaughters, and passions of the day are all splendidly depicted as Llywelyn delivers a blow-by-blow account of the rebellion and its immediate aftermath. The novel's abundant footnotes should satisfy history buffs; its easy, gripping style will enthrall casual readers with what is Llywelyn's best work yet."

—*Publishers Weekly* (starred review)

"A timely and gripping novel. . . . The historical characters are woven into a masterful plot."

—*The Irish Times*

"The politics and factionalism behind the Rising are a tangled web indeed, but Llywelyn unravels them skillfully. Even those who know the story well will be surprised and rewarded by the way she brings back to life a group of brave men who went nobly to their deaths."

—*The Philadelphia Inquirer*

"Llywelyn tells her tale with gusto and a respect for the facts; a good deal of both bizarre and somber history shines through the fictional fustian of its likable characters."

—*Kirkus Reviews*

"Llywelyn's *1916* is a work of true creative genius. People and events have been brought vividly to life. This novel, swift and exciting in its pace, will captivate those who love Ireland and are stirred by heroic virtue in the fight for human freedom."

—William M. Bulger,
president of the University of Massachusetts

have a keen vibrancy that makes the Rising a reality for today's readers. Llywelyn's deft pen is a creative sword."

—The Irish American Post

"In my judgment Morgan Llywelyn is a preeminent author of the twentieth century—and the preeminent insofar as I am concerned. *1916* is a great historical novel."

—Senator Jesse Helms

"*1916* is the most compelling novel of the Irish Troubles I've ever read. When you've finished the book—when you have experienced it from beginning to end, as I have—you will know the meaning of 'a terrible beauty.' "

—Parke Godwin

"*1916* is indeed an important work. . . . Morgan Llywelyn has done more than anyone to bring the rich history of Ireland to life. In fact, Morgan Llywelyn has radically changed the public perception of the past as it regards Ireland and her people."

—John P. Flaherty, Chief Justice of
the Supreme Court of Pennsylvania

" 'Twas a chequered journey for Ireland from Clontarf to the GPO. . . . Here, Llywelyn has made the long journey complete. And she's done it with consistency. . . . Whether writing about the Celts of antiquity or their intrepid descendants who marched out to fight for an Irish republic, Morgan Llywelyn's prose career has been enriched by an almost tactile feel for both Irish history and Celtic legend. Best of all, Llywelyn's painstaking research gives this novelist an uncanny credibility when she suggests the must-have-beens of the chronicle of Ireland. Those qualities, added to her extraordinary prose, make *1916* a must-read. It borders on genius."

—Terence Folan, author of
The Gold Sun Book of Irish Freedom

THE PROCLAMATION OF
POBLACHT NA H EIREANN.

THE PROVISIONAL GOVERNMENT
OF THE
IRISH REPUBLIC
TO THE PEOPLE OF IRELAND.

IRISHMEN AND IRISHWOMEN: In the name of God and the dead generations from which she receives her old tradition of nationhood, Ireland, through us, summons her children to her flag and strikes for her freedom.

Having organised and trained her manhood through her secret revolutionary organisation, the Irish Republican Brotherhood, and through her open military organisations, the Irish Volunteers and the Irish Citizen Army, having patiently perfected her discipline, having resolutely waited for the right moment to reveal itself, she now seizes that moment, and supported by her exiled children in America and by gallant allies in Europe, but relying in the first on her own strength, she strikes in full confidence of victory.

We declare the right of the people of Ireland to the ownership of Ireland, and to the unfettered control of the Irish destinies, to be sovereign and indefeasible. The long usurpation of that right by a foreign people and government has not extinguished the right, nor can it ever be extinguished except by the destruction of the Irish people. In every generation the Irish people have asserted their right to national freedom and sovereignty: six times during the past three hundred years they have asserted it in arms. Standing on that fundamental right and again asserting it in arms in the face of the world, we hereby proclaim the Irish Republic as a Sovereign Independent State, and we pledge our lives and the lives of our comrades-in-arms to the cause of its freedom, of its welfare, and of its exhaltation among the nations.

The Irish Republic is entitled to, and herby claims, the allegiance of every Irishman and Irishwoman. The Republic guarantees religious and civil liberty, equal rights and equal opportunities to all its citizens, and declares its resolve to pursue the happiness and prosperity of the whole nation and of all its parts, cherishing all the children of the nation equally, and oblivious of the differences carefully fostered by an alien government, which has divided a minority from the majority in the past.

Until our arms have brought the opportune moment for the establishment of a permanent National Government, representative of the whole people of Ireland and elected by the suffrages of all her men women, and provisional Government, hereby constituted, will administer the civil and military affairs of the Republic in trust for the people.

We place the cause of the Irish Republic under the protection of the Most High God, Whose blessing we invoke upon our arms, and we pray that no one who serves that cause will dishonour it by cowardice, inhumanity, or rapine. In this supreme hour, the Irish nation must, by its valour and discipline and by the readiness of its children top sacrifice themselves for the common good, prove itself worthy of the august destiny to which it is called.

Signed on Behalf of the Provisional Government.

THOMAS J. CLARKE

SEAN Mac DIARMADA. THOMAS MacDONAGH.

P.H. PEARSE. EAMONN CEANNT.

JAMES CONNOLLY. JOSEPH PLUNKETT

TOR BOOKS BY MORGAN LLYWELYN

1916

Morgan Llywelyn

TOR ®

A TOM DOHERTY ASSOCIATES BOOK
NEW YORK

This is a work of fiction. All the characters and events portrayed in this book are either products of the author's imagination or are used fictitiously.

1916

The poetry of Pádraic Pearse, Joseph Plunkett, and Thomas MacDonagh quoted in the book is taken from *The 1916 Poets*, edited by Desmond Ryan, published by Gill and Macmillan Ltd., Dublin, 1995.

"We Saw a Vision" ("Rinneädh Aisling Dúinn") is printed by permission of the author, Liam Mac Uistín.

A Tor Book
Published by Tom Doherty Associates, LLC
175 Fifth Avenue
New York, NY 10010

www.tor-forge.com

Tor® is a registered trademark of Tom Doherty Associates, LLC.

ISBN 978-0-8125-7492-0
Library of Congress Catalog Card Number: 97-29838

First Edition: April 1998
First Mass Market Edition: March 1999

Printed in the United States of America

0   9   8   7   6   5   4   3

For
Tom Doherty

O WISE MEN, RIDDLE ME THIS: WHAT IF THE DREAM
COME TRUE?
WHAT IF THE DREAM COME TRUE, AND IF MILLIONS
UNBORN SHALL DWELL
IN THE HOUSE THAT I SHAPED IN MY HEART, THE
NOBLE HOUSE OF MY THOUGHT?
LORD, I HAVE STAKED MY SOUL, I HAVE STAKED THE
LIVES OF MY KIN
ON THE TRUTH OF THY DREADFUL WORD. DO NOT
REMEMBER MY FAILURES,
BUT REMEMBER THIS MY FAITH.

PÁDRAIC PEARSE, 1915

Dramatis Personae

Major Fictional Characters

Edward Joseph Halloran (Ned)

Kathleen Halloran Campbell

Alexander Campbell

Síle Duffy

Henry Mooney

Father Paul O'Shaughnessy

Mary Cosgrave

Ursula Jervis (Precious)

Secondary Fictional Characters

Patrick Halloran and Theresa Daly Halloran, Ned's parents

Francis Patrick Halloran, Ned's older brother

Lucy and Eileen Halloran, Ned's younger sisters

Aunt Norah Daly

Daniel Duffy

Thomas and Janey Devlin

Father Hagerty

Bridie Lynch

Louise Kearney

Mrs. Flanagan

Alderman and Mrs. Claffey

Eliza Goggins

Della Thornberry

Neville Grantham

Sister Concepta

Des and Ina Cahill

Historical Characters

(*Those who were executed for their part in the Rising are shown in bold type.*)

Aloysius, Father. Capuchin priest

Asquith, Herbert Henry. Prime Minister of Great Britain, 1908–1916

Astor, Vincent. American millionaire whose father, John Jacob Astor, died aboard the *Titanic*

Beauchamp, Robert H. Dublin solicitor

Birrell, Augustine. Chief Secretary for Ireland

Bowen-Colthurst, Captain J. C. British army officer at Portobello Barracks

Burke, Frank. Student at Saint Enda's who became its last headmaster

Brugha, Cathal (Charles Burgess). Born in Dublin, Ireland, in 1874. Second-in-command to Eamonn Ceannt at the South Dublin Union. Killed in 1922 during the Irish Civil War.

Carson, Sir Edward. Leader of the Irish Unionist Party

Carney, Winifred. James Connolly's secretary

Casement, Sir Roger (1864–1916). Born in County Dublin, Ireland. Former British consul; gained an international reputation as an investigator of human rights abuses. Treasurer of the Irish National Volunteers.

Ceannt, Eamonn (Edmund Kent) (1881–1916). Born in County Galway, Ireland. Musician; clerk with Dublin Corporation. Member of the Military Council, IRB. Director of Communications, Irish Volunteers, and Commandant of the Fourth Battalion, Dublin Brigade.

Clarke, Kathleen Daly. Tom Clarke's wife, member of Cumann na mBan

Clarke, Thomas James (1857–1916). Born on Isle of Wight, grew up in Dublin. Emigrated to America in 1880. In New York joined Clan na Gael, was arrested on a mission to England, served fifteen years in prison. Returned to Ireland in 1907. Member of the Supreme Council, IRB; and of the Military Council, IRB.

Colbert, Con (1893–1916). Born in Limerick, Ireland. Organizer of the Saint Enda's branch of the Fianna. Assigned as Pádraic Pearse's bodyguard during the Rising.

Collins, Michael (1890–1922). Born in County Cork, Ireland. Aide-de-camp to Joseph Plunkett during the Rising. Commander-in-Chief of the Free State Army during the Irish Civil War.

Colum, Pádraic. Writer, poet, and folklorist

Connolly, James (1870–1916). Born in Edinburgh, Scotland. Socialist, labor leader, and journalist. Spent seven years in America studying the trade union movement. Commandant-General of the Dublin Forces during the Rising.

Daly, Edward (1891–1916). Born in County Limerick, Ireland. Kathleen Clarke's brother, Commandant of the First Battalion, Dublin Brigade.

D r a m a t i s   P e r s o n a e

de Valera, Eamon (1882–1975). Born in New York of a Spanish father and an Irish mother. Grew up in Ireland. Mathematician and teacher. Commandant of the Third Battalion of the Dublin Brigade. Became President of the Irish Free State in 1932.

Devoy, John. Leader of Clan na Gael in the United States

Dillon, John. Nationalist Member of Parliament

Flanagan, Father. Curate of the Pro-Cathedral in Dublin

Franklin, A. S. Vice President of the White Star Line

Fitzgerald, Desmond. Member of Headquarters Company in the G.P.O.

Friend, Major-General Lovick Bransby. Commanding officer of British forces in Ireland, 1914–1916

Gifford, Grace. Artist; Joseph Plunkett's fiancée

Green, Alice Stopford. Historian; widow of J. R. Green, author of the *Short History of the English People*

Grenan, Julia. Nurse in the G.P.O.

Griffith, Arthur (1871–1922). Journalist and publisher of *Sinn Féin*

Guest, Ivor Churchill. Baron Wimborne, Lord Lieutenant of Ireland during the Rising

Hanrahan, Michael (d. 1916). Quartermaster-General of the Irish Volunteers

Heuston, Seán (1897–1916). Captain of Na Fianna Eireann; Company Leader, D Company, First Battalion, Dublin Brigade

Hobson, Bulmer. Secretary of the Irish National Volunteers

Hyde, Douglas (1860–1949). Cofounder of the Gaelic League

Joyce, Brian. Former student at Saint Enda's who fought in the Rising

Kelly, Tom. Alderman of Dublin

Kent, Thomas (d. 1916). Officer with the Volunteers in County Cork

Kitchener, Horatio Herbert. First Earl, British Secretary of State for War

Larkin, James (1876–1947). Founder of the Irish Transport and General Workers Union

Little, Patrick J. Editor of *New Ireland*

Lowe, Brigadier-General W. H. M. Accepted Pearse's surrender.

Lynn, Kathleen Florence. Physician; medical officer for the Citizen Army. One of the first women in Ireland to take a degree in medicine.

MacBride, John (1865–1916). Born in County Mayo; husband of Maud Gonne; second-in-command to Thomas MacDonagh at Jacob's Factory; father of Seán MacBride, who won the Nobel Peace prize in 1975.

MacCarthy, Rev. Eugene. Prison chaplain at Kilmainham

Mac Diarmada, Seán (Seán MacDermott) (1884–1916). Born in County Leitrim, Ireland. National Organizer for Irish Republican Brotherhood. Member of the Military Council, IRB.

MacDonagh, Thomas (1878–1916). Born in County Tipperary, Ireland. Poet, university professor, editor of the *Irish Review*. Became a member of the Military Council, IRB. Commandant of the Second Battalion, Dublin Brigade.

MacDonnell, Thomas. Music and Dancing Master at Saint Enda's

MacNeill, Eoin (1867–1945). Cofounder of the Gaelic League; university lecturer and historian. President and Chief of Staff of the Irish National Volunteers.

MacRory, Michael. Head gardener at Saint Enda's

Mahony, Lieutenant. British surgeon who helped in the G.P.O.

Markievicz, Constance (1868–1927). Daughter of Sir Henry Gore-Booth, Baronet. Wife of Count Casimir Markievicz. Cofounder with Bulmer Hobson of Na Fianna Eireann. Member of Cumann na mBan and the Citizen Army. Second-in-command to Michael Mallin in Saint Stephen's Green. Later, while in an English prison, became the first woman to win election to the British Parliament although she never took her seat there. Subsequently served in the new Irish Parliament as the world's first Minister of Labor.

Martyn, Edward. Playwright

Maxwell, General Sir John Grenfell. Commander-in-Chief of British forces in Ireland in 1916

Nathan, Sir Matthew. Under-Secretary for Ireland

Norway, Arthur. Postmaster-General of Ireland and father of novelist Nevil Shute, author of *On the Beach*

O'Brien, Lucius. Lord Inchiquin

O'Farrell, Elizabeth. Nurse in the G.P.O. who carried the surrender message

O'Grady, Standish. Novelist

O'Kelly, Seán T. (1882–1966). Aide-de-camp to Pádraic Pearse during the Rising, subsequently envoy to Paris Peace Conference to promote recognition of Irish independence. President of Ireland 1945–1959.

O'Rahilly, Michael Joseph—"The O'Rahilly" (1875–1916). Born in County Kerry, Ireland. Emigrated to America, returned to Ireland in 1909. Member of the Gaelic League central executive. Director of Arms for the Irish Volunteers.

Otter, Richard. Merchant from Liverpool who died on the *Titanic*

Pearse, Margaret Brady. Pádraic Pearse's mother

Pearse, Margaret and Mary Brigid. Sisters of Pádraic

Pearse, Pádraic (Patrick Henry Pearse) (1879–1916).
Born in Dublin, Ireland. Headmaster of Saint Enda's. Writer,
editor, poet, playwright, educationalist. Degree in Law from
University College, Dublin, and King's Inns; practiced briefly
as a barrister. Member of the Military Council, IRB.
Commander-in-Chief during the Rising.

Pearse, William James (1881–1916). Born in Dublin, Ireland. Art and Drawing Master at Saint Enda's. Noted sculptor;
obtained a Distinction from the Metropolitan School of Art,
Dublin.

Plunkett, George Noble. Hereditary papal count, Director
of the Museum of Science and Art, father of Joseph Plunkett

Plunkett, George and Jack. Brothers of Joseph Plunkett

Plunkett, Geraldine and Philomena. Sisters of Joseph Plunkett

Plunkett, Joseph Mary (1887–1916). Born in Dublin, Ireland. Poet, cofounder of the Irish Theatre with Edward Martyn, editor of the *Irish Review*. Member of the Military
Council, IRB. Director of Military Operations during the Rising

Redmond, John. Leader of the Irish Parliamentary Party

Rossa, Jeremiah O'Donovan (1831–1915). Fenian

Ryan, Desmond (1893–1964). Former Saint Enda's student
and secretary to Patrick Pearse. Journalist and historian who
subsequently wrote a number of books dealing with the Irish
struggle for independence.

Sheehy-Skeffington, Francis (1878–1916). Socialist, pacifist, feminist. Registrar of University College, Dublin.

Walsh, William F. Archbishop of Dublin

Yeats, William Butler. Poet and playwright, later winner of
Nobel prize for Literature

1916

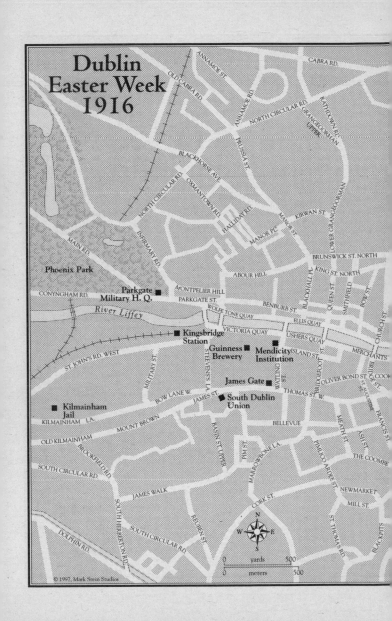

Dublin Easter Week 1916

ANNAMOE ST.

CABRA RD.

OLD CABRA RD.

ANNAMOE RD.

NORTH CIRCULAR RD.

RATHDOWN RD.

GRANGEGORMAN UPPER

BLACKHORSE AVE.

PRUSSIA ST.

OXMANTOWN RD.

KIRWAN ST.

HALLIDAY RD.

MANOR PL.

MANOR ST.

LOWER GRANGEGORMAN

NORTH CIRCULAR RD.

INFIRMARY RD.

BRUNSWICK ST. NORTH

MAIN RD.

ABOUR HILL

KING ST. NORTH

BLACKHALL PL.

QUEEN ST.

SMITHFIELD

BOW ST.

CHURCH ST.

Phoenix Park

CONYNGHAM RD.

MONTPELIER HILL

■ Parkgate
Military H. Q.

PARKGATE ST.

WOLFE TONE QUAY

BENBURB ST.

ELLIS QUAY

River Liffey

VICTORIA QUAY

USHERS QUAY

■ Kingsbridge
Station

STEEVEN'S LANE

Guinness ■
Brewery

■ Mendicity
Institution

ISLAND ST.

MERCHANTS

ST. JOHN'S RD. WEST

MILITARY ST.

BRIDGEFOOT ST.

OLIVER BOND ST.

ST. AUGUSTINE ST.

FRANCIS ST.

BRIDE ST.

BOW LANE W.

JAMES ST.

■ James Gate

WATLING ST.

THOMAS ST. W.

■ Kilmainham
Jail

KILMAINHAM LA.

MOUNT BROWN

◆ South Dublin
Union

BELLEVUE

MEATH ST.

ASH ST.

PIMLICO

ARDEE ST.

OLD KILMAINHAM

BASIN ST. UPPER

PIM ST.

THE COOMBE

BROOKFIELD RD.

SOUTH CIRCULAR RD.

JAMES WALK

MARROWBONE LA.

CORK ST.

NEWMARKET

MILL ST.

ST. THOMAS RD.

BLACKPITTS

DOLPHIN RD.

SOUTH CIRCULAR RD.

REUBEN ST.

SOUTH HERBERTON RD.

N
W   E
S

0   yards   500
0   meters   500

© 1997, Mark Stein Studios

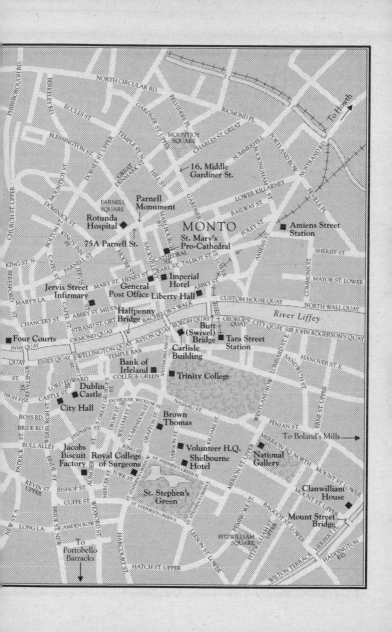

PHIBSBOROUGH RD.

NORTH CIRCULAR RD.

BERKELEY RD.

ECCLES ST.

BLESSINGTON ST.

BELVEDERE PL.

RICMOND PL.

To Howth

GARDINER ST. UPPER

MOUNTJOY SQUARE

CHARLES ST. GREAT

SUMMERHILL

BUCKINGHAM ST.

PORTLAND ROW

NORTH STRAND RD.

SEVILLE PL.

16, Middle
Gardiner St.

LOWER KILLARNEY

RAILWAY ST.

MONTO

Amiens Street
Station

PARNELL
SQUARE

Parnell
Monument

Rotunda
Hospital ◆

75A Parnell St.

St. Mary's
Pro-Cathedral

SHERIFF ST.

AMIENS ST.

FOLEY ST.

MAYOR ST. LOWER

COMMONS ST.

Jervis Street
Infirmary

General
Post Office

Imperial
Hotel

Liberty Hall ■

CUSTOM HOUSE QUAY

NORTH WALL QUAY

Halfpenny
Bridge

BACHELOR'S WALK

River Liffey

Four Courts ■

Butt
(Swivel)
Bridge

Tara Street
Station

GEORGE'S QUAY, CITY QUAY, SIR JOHN ROGERSON'S QUAY

ORMOND QUAY

INNS QUAY

QUAY

ESSEX QUAY

WELLINGTON QUAY

ASTON QUAY

BURGH QUAY

Carlisle
Building

TEMPLE BAR

Bank of
Ireland ■

COLLEGE GREEN

Trinity College ■

WESTMORELAND ST.

Dublin
Castle ■

City Hall ■

CASTLE ST.

LORD EDWARD

NASSAU ST.

Brown
Thomas ■

To Boland's Mills →

FENIAN ST.

WESTLAND ROW

LINDSAY ST.

SANDWITH ST.

HANOVER ST. E.

MERRION SQ. NORTH

Jacobs
Biscuit
Factory ■

Royal College
of Surgeons ■

Volunteer H.Q. ■

Shelbourne
Hotel ■

National
Gallery ■

St. Stephen's
Green

ST. STEPHEN'S GREEN N.

ST. STEPHEN'S GREEN S.

Clanwilliam
House ◆

MOUNT ST. LOWER

MOUNT ST. UPPER

Mount Street
Bridge

To
Portobello
Barracks

HATCH ST. UPPER

FITZWILLIAM
SQUARE

PEMBROKE ST.

LEESON ST. LOWER

WILTON TERRACE

HADDINGTON RD.

HERBERT ST.

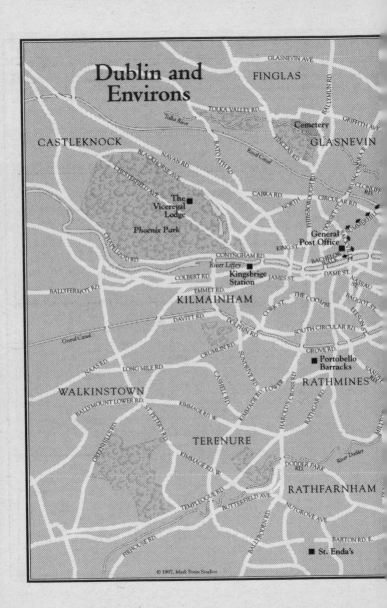

Dublin and Environs

GLASNEVIN AVE

FINGLAS

TOLKA VALLEY RD.

BALLYMUN RD

Tolka River

GRIFFITH AVE

Cemetery

CASTLEKNOCK

Royal Canal

GLASNEVIN

NAVAN RD.

RATOATH RD.

FINGLAS RD.

DRUMCONDRA RD

BLACKHORSE AVE

CLONLIFF RD.

CHESTERFIELD AVE.

CABRA RD.

NORTH CIRCULAR RD.

DORSET ST RD.

The Viceregal Lodge

FITZROROUGH RD.

SUMMERHILL

Phoenix Park

General Post Office

CHAPELIZOD RD.

CONYNGHAM RD.

KING ST.

River Liffey

BACHELOR'S WALK

COLBERT RD.

Kingsbridge Station

JAMES ST.

DAME ST.

EMMET RD.

NASSAU ST.

BALLYFERMOT RD.

KILMAINHAM

CORK ST.

THE COOMBE

BAGGOT ST.

LEESON ST.

DAVITT RD.

DOLPHIN RD.

SOUTH CIRCULAR RD.

Grand Canal

CRUMLIN RD.

SUNDRIVE RD.

GROVE RD.

Portobello Barracks

NAAS RD.

LONG MILE RD.

CASHELL RD.

HAROLD'S CROSS RD.

RATHMINES

SANDY

WALKINSTOWN

BALLYMOUNT LOWER RD.

KIMMAGE RD. W

KIMMAGE RD. LOWER

BATHGAR RD.

GREENHILLS RD.

ST PETER'S RD

TERENURE

KIMMAGE RD. W

DODDER PARK RD.

River Dodder

RATHFARNHAM

TEMPLEOGUE RD.

BUTTERFIELD AVE.

BALLYROQUE RD

NUTGROVE AVE.

FIRHOUSE RD.

BARTON RD. E.

St. Enda's

© 1997, Mark Stein Studios

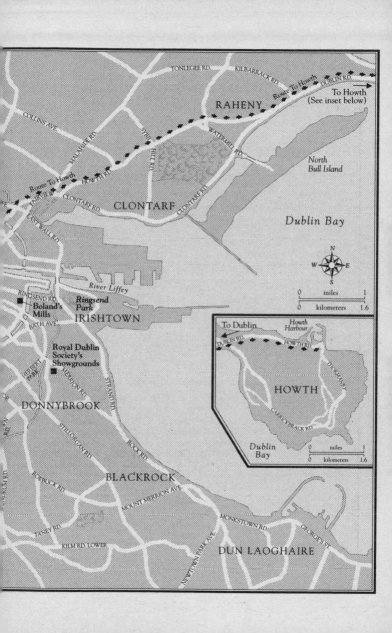

TONLEGEE RD. KILBARRACK RD.

Route To Howth

DUBLIN RD.

To Howth
(See inset below)

RAHENY

COLLINS AVE

MALAHIDE RD.

SPIER HILL RD.

WATERMILL RD.

North
Bull Island

Route To Howth

HOWTH RD.

FAIRVIEW

CLONTARF RD.

CLONTARF

CLONTARF RD.

Dublin Bay

EAST WALL RD.

N
W   E
S

0   miles   1
0   kilometers   1.6

River Liffey

RINGSEND RD.

Boland's
Mills

Ringsend
Park

IRISHTOWN

BATH AVE.

Royal Dublin
Society's
Showgrounds

To Dublin

Howth
Harbour

DUBLIN RD.

HOWTH RD.

HERBERT
PARK

MERION RD.

THORMANBY RD.

HOWTH

STRAND RD.

DONNYBROOK

STILLORGAN RD.

CARRICKBRACK RD.

ROCK RD.

Dublin
Bay

0   miles   1
0   kilometers   1.6

ROEBUCK RD.

BLACKROCK

MOUNT MERRION AVE.

TANEY RD.

MONKSTOWN RD.

GEORGE'S ST.

KILM RD. LOWER

NEWTOWN PARK AVE.

DUN LAOGHAIRE

Chapter One

NED awoke with a start.

The atmosphere in the darkened cabin was warm and close, smelling of lavender wax and fresh linen. A goose down pillow cushioned his head; his pajamas were crisply ironed. But something was wrong.

That evening the dinner menu in the second-class dining saloon had included such exotic items as curried chicken and rice, roast turkey with cranberry sauce, cocoanut[1] sandwich—and American ice cream! "Can I have a bite of everything?" he had asked hopefully. The waiter stifled a smile, but Mama frowned.

Ned was only fifteen years old, however, and this was the adventure of a lifetime, so at last she agreed. Mrs. Halloran could deny her children nothing.

By the time he returned to his cabin the boy was suffering from a stomachache. He undressed and crawled into bed without even washing his face in the basin, trusting a night's sleep to put matters right. The last thing he remembered was a muffled throb like the beat of a giant heart lulling him into sleep . . . until a jolt and a peculiar grinding noise startled him awake again.

He lay still for a few moments, disoriented. Then he sat up. The whisper of breeze through the open porthole of his cabin had ceased, as had the rhythmic creaking of a ship in motion. Instead there was silence.

The muffled heartbeat had stopped.

Ned swung his legs over the side of the berth and groped on the floor with his bare feet, searching for his shoes—highly polished, store-bought shoes instead of his customary country brogans. At the same time his fingers reached for his woolen bathrobe, also new, lovingly sewn by his Aunt Norah and lined with red flannel from one of her old petticoats.

He had no intention of opening the cabin door until he was decently covered. Mama would be mortified.

Theresa Halloran continually worried about other people's opinions. Her guiding precept was not the strict morality of her Catholic faith but "What will the neighbors think?" When the tickets arrived she had found one pretext after another to call on every family she knew, up and down the country lanes of Clare. "My daughter Kathleen's fiancé is bringing us out to America for their wedding," she would announce during her visit, casually producing the tickets to show around while teacups clattered and slices of fruitcake were reduced to crumbs. "He has a very important position with the shipping line, so he does."

The entire family would not be going. Passage for only three was being provided by Kathleen's fiancé. "Is it not mean of him?" Theresa had complained to her husband in the privacy of their bed. "Sure an important man like himself could send for us all!" She sat up and pounded her pillow with a doubled fist.

"Be grateful for your blessings, love," Patrick Halloran had advised. "And while you're about it, would you ever get us another quilt?"

The couple had decided to take their second son. "As Frank is the oldest, he will be needed at home to mind the farm and his little sisters," Patrick had explained.

When Ned heard he was going to America he could hardly believe his good fortune. He was even to have his very own cabin on the ship! All his life he had shared a bed with Frank, who invariably fell asleep first and snored. Rushing out of the house, Ned turned cartwheels in the muddy Ennis road; a tall, wiry boy with an unruly mop of black curls, celebrating the prospect of a great adventure and the first concession to his burgeoning manhood.

That had been two months ago. Now, three days out of Queenstown, Harbor he sat on the edge of his berth in the dark, listening to silence.

His skin prickled with an atavistic warning.

"Wisha, lad, don't be letting your imagination run away with you," Mama would say; Mama, who heard banshees on the wind and shrieked aloud if someone brought whitethorn blossoms into the house.

Ned swallowed hard. Some intuition whose existence he had never suspected was ringing alarm bells in him. Yet at the same time he felt a curious thrill.

If the ship was in trouble . . .

Perhaps the liner had been boarded by pirates!

If there were pirates they might have drugged the crew with the help of accomplices. Or they could be holding the captain at gunpoint.

Suppose some daring young man was able to sneak up behind the pirates and take them by surprise . . .

Where could he find some sort of weapon? A pitchfork, for example; pitchforks were invaluable in times of trouble. But there would be no farm tools on a passenger liner. Guns, though . . . there might at least be a gun. In the captain's cabin? Where would that be in relation to Middle Deck F?

Ned struggled to recall what he had learned about the ship's layout. His was an insatiable mind that absorbed information as readily as his mother's soda bread absorbed buttermilk. The huge steamship was eleven storeys high, four city blocks long, and was carrying some thirteen hundred passengers. She even made her own electricity. There was no electrification in rural Ireland, so a ship glowing with unflickering light was a vision of heaven to Ned.

The vessel was like a small city, with a fully fitted gymnasium, a swimming pool and Turkish bath, even a replica of a Parisian sidewalk café for "the young set." Unparalleled comfort and luxury were provided. The Grand Staircase was five stories high. First-class suites were decorated with valuable antiques and boasted electric heaters. Second-class had crystal light fixtures and elevators with wrought iron grillwork.

From the moment Ned saw the liner he had loved her. A sovereign of the seas, serene and assured, she encompassed everything a human could desire.

Ned's cabin on Middle Deck F was small by comparison to the more costly suites. Yet it contained a single mahogany-framed berth set against one wall with lockers over the bath, an upholstered couch on the opposite wall, another locker with fitted drawers, and a highly polished mahogany wash-stand with mirror, basin, and a concealed chamber pot. Robe hooks and soap dishes and drawer handles and porthole fittings were all of polished brass.

In that cabin Ned had felt like an egg-bound chick that had finally broken out of its shell into a larger and finer world. If the wonderful ship was in danger now, he, Edward Joseph Halloran, meant to fight for her!

But first he had better get fully dressed. One could hardly cut a heroic figure in a bathrobe, even a new one lined with red flannel.

THE long white corridor was dimly lit. Through closed cabin doors he could hear the sound of voices, but there was no one in the passage. Ned looked left and right to be sure, then glanced at his parents' door. Should he knock and go in to them?

If he did, Papa would never let him go looking for pirates.

Ned set off down the corridor.

A white-jacketed steward emerging from a side passage startled him. "I'm after hearing something strange," Ned explained hastily, "and then there was a sort of jolt."

The man flicked him a distracted glance. "Everything's all right." Even as he spoke they heard a clanging crash somewhere below.

"It's nothing to worry about," the steward insisted. Brushing past Ned, he hurried on. At the far end of the corridor he knocked on a door and murmured something, then went to the next door.

The corridor seemed to have grown very cold.

As if carried on an invisible current, Ned resumed walking. Others were feeling the current too. First one cabin door and then another opened. People put out their heads and looked around, or emerged in varying degrees of undress. A stocky man wearing trousers and braces and a half-unbuttoned boiled shirt stepped from his cabin so abruptly he collided with Ned. "What's happening?" he demanded in a Liverpool accent.

Ned had noticed the Englishman earlier in the second-class dining saloon. A waiter had addressed him as "Mr. Otter"; the name seemed comical then. Faced with the size and solidity of the man in the narrow passage, however, there was nothing amusing about him.

"I'm sure I don't know, sir," Ned replied with reflexive humility. "Be meek in the presence of your betters" was the motto drummed into Irish bones from birth to the grave.

The Englishman scowled into a pair of black-lashed green eyes that looked as if they had been put in the boy's face with a sooty thumb. "You're Irish, aren't you?" He made it sound like an accusation.

"I am, sir. From Clare, sir."

"Then what are you doing here? You belong in steerage."

Ned's chin lifted, displaying the *scoilt*, the inherited Halloran cleft. "I do not," he replied before he could stop himself. "My family has second-class passage. Bought and paid for."

"Is that so?" The man sounded skeptical. "You should go back before you're found out. Your people aren't allowed on this deck."

"I told you, we're traveling second-class. My father works for Lord Inchiquin," Ned offered as additional credentials.

"Never heard of 'im. You think that gives you the right to ape your betters?"

The boy's face flamed. "I have the right to be here."

"Your sort are always trying to act above their station. Did I not see you earlier with some other rascal from steerage, a redheaded lout? The two of you were sneaking into the second-class library."

"He's my friend," Ned argued, surprised at his own temerity, "and we were not sneaking. I invited him. I just wanted him to see all those books."

The Englishman's complexion mottled with anger. "You can't 'invite' steerage here! I'll have you both—"

But whatever he intended to say was interrupted by a shout echoing down the corridor. "They're uncovering the lifeboats!"

Suddenly the passage was filled with men and women milling in confusion, asking one another questions no one could answer. Stewards' bells began to ring throughout the ship.

"What's happening?" Otter repeated irritably. "Bloody nuisance, middle of the night . . ." Turning away, he stumped off down the corridor like a man determined to set things to rights.

For all his unpleasantness, Otter was an adult and English and therefore doubly a figure of authority. Ned followed him.

They made their way up the second-class stairs and emerged on the portside boat deck. More passengers were gathering there, but no one seemed interested in getting into the lifeboats. On a bitter cold night in the middle of a vast ocean, it would be insane to leave the safety and comfort of a ship known to be invulnerable.

Ned's breath was a miniature version of the clouds of steam being exhaled from the four huge smokestacks towering above the deck.

Overhead glittered the indifferent stars. The sky had never looked so deep. From the lounge the sound of the ship's orchestra began to drift out over the water; they were playing a song Ned did not recognize.

Though the ship was dead in the water no one appeared alarmed. The mood was one of curiosity and amusement, as if an entertainment were being presented. The passengers were paying for the finest care in the world and expected nothing less. A few members of the crew circulated among them, making guesses as to the cause of the delay which were no better informed than those of the passengers themselves. A purser suggested the ship had lost a propeller. In reply to an irascible question from Mr. Otter, a junior officer claimed she had hit ''some floating ice, but we'll be under way again soon.''

Neither possibility seemed as dramatic to Ned as pirates, but the hope of seeing an iceberg sent him to the rail. He leaned as far out as he could and peered into the Atlantic night. No mountainous berg could be seen from his vantage point, but there were strangely glimmering islands floating on the black water. The air was shimmering with ice crystals and so dry and cold it burned the membranes of his nose.

A voice shouted, ''There are huge chunks of ice on the starboard boat deck!''

''Let's go get some!'' cried a young man. Several passengers set off at once, challenging one another to an impromptu hockey game. Ned trotted after them with a vague notion of finding Dan Duffy.

The adventure would be more fun with a friend.

Chapter Two

NED had met Dan on the dock at Queenstown as his family waited to board the ship. Beneath her best woolen cloak, Mrs. Halloran was attired in her first "traveling costume"—a tailored skirt that covered her instep, a peplum jacket with puffed sleeves, and a linen blouse foaming with Limerick lace. Atop her head was pinned a broad-brimmed hat with a large white plume. The wind blew filaments from the plume into her eyes, and whenever she moved her new corset creaked.

Her husband was equally uncomfortable in a thigh-length frieze coat, spotted waistcoat, and high-collared shirt that scratched his wind-reddened neck. In place of his familiar cords were wide-legged trousers that let cold drafts blow up his legs, and he missed his cap. His wife had been very firm about this: "You are not going to America wearing that filthy old Scarriff hat you inherited from your father. You shall have a new black top hat, like a proper gentleman."

Ned was to begin the voyage in a Norfolk suit of black-and-white Donegal tweed, which at least was warm. Privately he thought he looked ridiculous, and he hated the knee britches, but his mother had saved to buy the fabric and he did not dare complain. While his parents were preoccupied with making arrangements about their baggage, he ducked under a barrier and joined those waiting to embark as third-class passengers. As Irish people, the Hallorans were very much in the minority in second-class. Those who would be traveling steerage had Irish faces. Young faces.

Their clothes, though clean for the most part, were entirely homemade, patched and mended. Men and women alike wore boots. They had no baggage to be stored in the steamship's capacious baggage rooms; the few possessions they carried with them were in cloth bundles or pasteboard boxes fastened with string. Grandchildren of the Great Famine, theirs was the most recent generation of exiles from a depopulated land.

Among them were several startlingly pretty girls. One in particular had a high, rounded bosom and swaying hips.

One shy glance was all he had dared. Even that gave him the unsettling feeling of an extra layer of heat beneath his skin. He could almost hear Father Hagerty warning against sins of the flesh, erecting the pillars of guilt that supported a Catholic conscience. Regretfully, Ned had dragged his eyes away only to have his attention caught by a redheaded boy flashing a jaunty grin. When Ned grinned back, the other beckoned him forward. "Ain't she a wonder?" the boy had asked. At first Ned thought he meant the girl, but he was indicating the waiting ship. "Did you ever know there was anything in the wide world like that?"

"I never did," Ned had answered truthfully. Side by side, the two had stood gazing at the great liner in openmouthed admiration.

That was how he had met Dan Duffy, a rawboned, freckled youth a year or so older than himself, with merry brown eyes and work-callused hands. By a happy coincidence Dan was also from County Clare. Anyone from your home county became a friend when met in a strange place.

Now, as he searched for Dan aboard the stalled liner, Ned recalled their first conversation. The redhead had explained, "I'm one of too many Duffys. Our holding at Ruan has been divided so many times among so many sons over the generations that it's all stone walls now, with hardly enough earth left to grow a tattie. It'd make a cat laugh if it weren't so sad.

So I'm off to Amerikay to make me fortune.''

"How are you going to make your fortune?''

"There's gold in them streets.''

"You're not believing that.''

Dan had chuckled. "Perhaps not. But there's jobs sure. I'm strong, so I am. Could be I'll work on a railroad, or dig a canal. What about yourself?''

"My sister Kathleen went out two years ago. My mother has cousins in Boston who visited us in '09. Kathleen went to visit them the next year; she'd been talking of nothing else since the day they went back. My mother was worried, but Kathleen appealed to Papa and he found the money for her passage. Kathleen always could get her way through Papa. She's a real beauty, with dark curly hair like mine and a dimple in her chin instead of a cleft. All the lads in Clare were after her.''

Dan nodded absently, his mind more beguiled by Kathleen's destination than by a catalog of her charms. "Amerikay,'' he breathed as one invokes the promised land.

"Kathleen loves everything about America,'' Ned said. "Not long after she arrived she wrote us about a man who works in the offices of the steamship company, someone called Alexander Campbell. By the next letter they were walking out together. It happened so quickly Mama was scandalized, but Kathleen says America moves at a different pace.

"Now we're going out for the wedding—imagine our Kathleen marrying an American! He must be someone important; he paid for passage for the three of us.''

"That's all you have in your family?'' Dan asked incredulously. "There was sixteen of us—same as me age. That's counting me brothers and sisters in Heaven, of course.''

"Oh, I have an older brother and two younger sisters, but they're staying home with my Auntie Norah.''

"And where would home be?''

"A farm near Clarecastle.''

"I thought people in Clarecastle starved to death during the Famine.''

"Many did,'' Ned agreed. "People in Newmarket-on-

Fergus were so desperate they ate the blighted potatoes and died of the illness. But my great-grandparents were tenants of Sir Lucius of Dromoland, who later became Baron Inchiquin. His Lordship fed people from his own stores.[1] During the worst of the hunger he even set up a soup kitchen between two ash trees; they're there to this day. The trees, I mean.

"The Hallorans survived the Famine on bacon and meal from Dromoland, and since then we've done our best to repay the kindness. My father works for the present Lord Inchiquin as his land bailiff."

Dan made a face. "Sure and there's never an end to repaying the bloody English."

"Lord Inchiquin's an O'Brien, a descendant of Brian Boru, so he isn't really English."

"Anglo-Irish, then. The Ascendancy," Dan retorted, spitting out the term. "They think they're better than we are because they surrendered to the English and married English-women and learned to talk with their noses all stopped up. I know about your Lord Inchiquin. Amn't I from Ruan, less than a day's walk from Dromoland Castle? The O'Briens turned Protestant so the English would let them keep their lands. Better Irishmen held on to the true faith and lost everything they had," he added sourly.

Loyalty dictated Ned's reply. "If the O'Briens had not kept their lands, who'd have fed my family during the Famine? The Hallorans would have starved or emigrated. Instead, in '04 we finally were able to buy land of our own. Now we even have a tenant ourselves."

"Your Da's a strong farmer, then," mused Dan, using the common term. He ran his eyes appraisingly over Ned's Donegal tweeds. The redhead's own clothing was homespun and threadbare, his boots tied on with string.

Ned had the grace to be embarrassed. "We've been lucky."

"God's been good to you," Dan corrected him.

Ned had smiled. Mama often said the same thing.

He smiled now, remembering.

The ship, which had listed slightly to port throughout the voyage, now had a slight list to starboard. The temperature seemed to have dropped since midnight passed.

As Ned hurried on, scanning passing faces for a familiar, merry grin, another conversation came back to him. Dan had said almost with disbelief, "You'll be coming back to Ireland?"

"After the wedding? Kathleen will stay in America with her husband, of course. Papa thinks that's one of the reasons she's marrying him, so she can be an American too. But we'll come home surely."

Dan had given a slow, fatalistic roll of his shoulders. "It took all me parents could raise just to buy the one ticket over, they even sold the pig. They're counting on the money I'll be sending back but I won't be coming back meself. Before I met you I never knew anyone who was coming back." His irrepressible grin resurfaced. "But it's not so bad. They were after giving me a wake when I left. An American wake, they call it."

"As if you were dead?"

"Young 'uns who go out to Amerikay are as good as dead to the ould 'uns at home," Dan had replied. "So I enjoyed meself, I drank poitín and danced with all the girls. Made the most of every opportunity and didn't tell the priest," he added with a meaningful wink, digging his elbow into Ned's ribs. "There's nothing like a merry wake!"

Dan Duffy was a true son of the peasantry, while Ned Halloran belonged to the emerging Irish middle-class. "Strong" farmers, shopkeepers, and tradesmen now formed a social order quite apart from either the truly poor or the Anglo-Irish gentry.

But Ned was more comfortable with Dan Duffy than with the other passengers of Middle Deck F, and on this April night he wanted to be with his new friend to share whatever adventure might befall them.

Meanwhile bells continued to ring throughout the ship. There was a sound of running feet and voices began shouting orders.

On the dock at Queenstown, Ned and Dan had agreed to meet again once they were aboard ship. This had not proved easy; third-class was strictly quarantined, as if poverty were contagious. But within hours of sailing Dan Duffy had joined Ned at the rail of the second-class promenade.

"How did you get here?" Ned had asked in astonishment.

The redhead winked. "Och, I have me little ways. I've had plenty practice ducking and dodging."

In the April twilight the two boys had leaned on the rail together, watching Ireland fade into the distance.

"If I had me choice," Dan had remarked after a time, "I would stay in Ireland, ye know. If I had me choice."

Ned was surprised by the passion in his voice.

They had met several times after that; on each occasion it being the resourceful Dan who came to Ned. Now Ned must reverse the process and find Dan. Ned had his parents, but Dan—with an independence Ned had formerly envied—was traveling alone. "Me berth's above the place where they put the motorcars," he had said with a strange pride.

That meant he was somewhere forward. As Ned searched for a way to get to him he heard the first creaking of the lifeboat davits.

The obvious way forward along the boat deck was blocked by the barrier that separated the first-class promenade from second-class. In spite of increasing congestion people were keeping to their own spaces, with first-class in the middle of the ship and second-class farther back. Third-class was held to the stern or to the well deck near the bow.

Dan Duffy would not accept such segregation.

Of course! Dan was probably trying to get to him, and if they were both searching they could easily miss one another.

Best stay where he was, then, Ned told himself. Or go below—Dan knew the number of his cabin anyway—and be certain his parents were all right.

He turned and made once more for the second-class stairs, only to run into a solid wall of people. Encouraged by crew members, a few were putting on life jackets, fumbling with the straps and teasing one another about how fat the jackets made them look. They still seemed calm, but by now it was a superficial tranquillity, that of people determined to carry on as usual.

The crew was giving orders now. To Ned it looked as if they were directing a new sort of game, arbitrarily choosing players for the sides. First-class passengers were winnowed out and ushered toward the boats with grave courtesy; second-class passengers were also directed toward the boats, but with, Ned thought, a degree less politeness.

What about those like Dan? he wondered. Who is looking after third-class?

Overhead a white light flared. Startled, he looked up. A giant shooting star blazed into the sky, then burst into thousands of sparks that blended with the ice crystals dancing in the air.

"They're firing off rockets," a woman said in a wondering voice.

Foreboding turned to alarm. Ned forgot about Dan Duffy. *Mama!*

He began to run, thrusting his way between people with rude elbows. Someone caught at him. "Here now, lad, don't—"

But Ned whirled away and was gone.

April 15, 1912

TERRIBLE LOSS OF LIFE AS *TITANIC* SINKS

April 16, 1912

MORE THAN 1,500 LOST IN GREATEST
SHIP DISASTER EVER

Chapter Three

Iɴ Boston, Kathleen Halloran had been preparing for the trip to New York to greet her family when Alexander Campbell arrived at her door. Her fiancé's eyes were troubled, and beneath his graying hair his blunt-featured face, usually so ruddy, was pale.

"Are you alone, Kate? Is there not someone here with you?"

"Please don't call me that, Alexander," she replied with a smile to soften her words. "I've told you I don't like the name."

"But are you alone here?"

"My cousins are paying their calls. I was invited to go with them, but I wanted to lay out my frocks for New York and . . . Why? What's wrong?"

He tried to speak again but the words caught in his throat. Silently, he handed her the newspapers.

Kathleen would never be able to remember much about the frantic trip to New York. Alexander had wanted her to stay in Boston with her cousins and await news there, but she would not have it.

The train was cruelly slow, held up on one siding after another with various excuses. The American efficiency that she admired failed when she needed it most. Alexander patted her hand and said "There, there" whenever he could, but as a representative of the White Star Line he felt obligated to circulate through the coaches, offering what reassurance he could to other worried next of kin making the trip for the same reason.

When he left her side, Kathleen stared bleakly out the smudged train window, seeing nothing.

Although the majority of passengers had no connection with the *Titanic,* news of the disaster was the principal topic of conversation on the train. One stout woman swathed from neck to ankles in black bombazine announced for all to hear, "It is God's judgment on John Jacob Astor and all those decadent aristocrats."

The wizened man sitting beside her looked embarrassed and buried his face behind his newspaper.

At last the train pulled into the steel-ribbed majesty of the new Pennsylvania Station. Kathleen was indifferent to the dazzle of light from the corrugated glass roof arches and domes, the vaulted magnificence said to be a replica of the Caracalla Baths. The world seemed as dark around her as if she were in a tunnel.

Alexander wanted her to wait at the hotel while he went directly to the office, but she refused. "I have to know," she kept saying. "I have to know. I'm staying with you."

Looking at her white face and stubborn chin with the dimple he found so beguiling, he relented. "Come with me, then."

The red-brick building at 9 Broadway that housed the White Star offices was under siege. Police had been compelled to set up barricades to hold back the crowds. When intimations of trouble had first reached New York, A. S. Franklin, vice president of the line, had declared unequivocally, "We place absolute confidence in the *Titanic.* We believe that the boat is unsinkable."[1]

Subsequently, the *Evening Sun* announced that there had been a collision but all were saved, and the city had breathed a collective sigh of relief. Soon enough, however, wireless operators listening in on Atlantic ship traffic began overhearing disturbing transmissions. Then confirmation arrived from the *Titanic*'s sister ship, the *Olympic*.

The unsinkable liner was lost. The *Carpathia* was returning to New York with 675 survivors aboard.

For a time White Star tried to downplay the scale of the disaster, but by the time Alexander and Kathleen reached 9 Broadway it was obvious that a death watch had been mounted. No list of survivors had yet been posted.

Followed by Kathleen, Alexander shouldered his way through the crowd and was admitted into the building. A man at the door tried to turn Kathleen aside, but she shoved past him. "You would not dare lay hands on a lady!" she hissed. Her blazing blue eyes drove him back, abashed.

Alexander found a small cubby-hole with a rolltop desk and a pair of red leather chairs and left her seated there, twisting her handkerchief, while he went in search of information. Beyond the frosted glass door Kathleen could hear quick footsteps on polished floors, tense voices, frenetic clatter. After a time a worried-looking young man appeared at the door and gave a discreet cough by way of seeking admission. He carried a pot of tea and two cups—bearing the White Star emblem—on a tray, which he set down on the small table between the two chairs. Then he departed as gently as he had come.

Kathleen poured a cup of the steaming beverage, but her hand was shaking too badly to carry the cup to her lips. With a rattle of china she replaced it in the saucer.

The wait seemed interminable.

When Alexander at last returned, his expression was somber. "The worst is confirmed, Kate. The *Titanic* is lost, but we'll have no details until the *Carpathia* arrives. That won't be until Thursday night or possibly even Friday, although she will be sending the list of survivors on ahead. In the meantime, let me take you back to your hotel and—"

She glared at him. "I'm here and I'll stay here until we know about my family." Lifting the cup, she drank the stone-cold tea and then poured herself some more, establishing territorial rights to the chair and room.

She was still there at ten-thirty, when Vincent Astor arrived and was personally ushered into the vice president's office, only to emerge shaken and weeping.

The first survivor list was posted. No Hallorans were on it.

"There will be more coming," Alexander assured Kathleen.

At the White Star booking office, the names were read aloud by a chief clerk standing on top of the counter while the crowd surged back and forth.

The world seemed to be holding its breath, waiting.

At last, overcome by exhaustion, Kathleen let Alexander escort her to the hotel where rooms had been booked for her family from Ireland. They had been meant to rest there for a few days before going on to Boston.

The windows were closed against the chill of the April night, but that did not explain the faintly acrid smell.

A large arrangement of flowers on the table—a tribute from Alexander to his future in-laws—inexplicably had begun to wither.

THE *Carpathia* sailed into New York Harbor on Thursday night, arriving in an icy rain. Tens of thousands lined Manhattan's western shore from the Battery to Fourteenth Street to see her come in. Countless flashbulbs, like fitful lightning, followed her progress, but there was no cheering. The massive crowd was mute.

Kathleen Halloran joined the throng of relatives waiting at Pier 54. She carried a priority pass that Alexander had arranged, and had his own strong body beside her. Never had she been more thankful for him. For his sake she would face the storm that was bound to come when her parents learned . . . if her parents learned . . . if they were on board the *Carpathia*, as she hoped and prayed.

Surely there were survivors whose names were not on the lists!

It seemed an eternity before the tugs nudged the *Carpathia* into her slip, and another eternity before the gangplank was lowered. In unspoken courtesy, the regular passengers of the *Carpathia* stood aside and let the *Titanic* survivors leave first.

Some tottered wearily down the gangplank; others marched head up, as if from a normal voyage.

But every face looked strained and haunted.

Standing on tiptoe, Kathleen scanned each one in turn. When at last she saw him, a lifetime's training in reticence deserted her. "Ned!" she screamed. "Thank God!"

DURING the cab ride from the docks his sister refrained from asking him any questions. The conversation to follow was best held in privacy. Kathleen and Alexander sat together with Ned facing them, but they had the curious impression he did not really see them. His gaze was inward.

For a time there had been no coherence to his memories. Lacking a linear narrative, they appeared instead as bits and flashes; vivid, unconnected scenes surrounded by darkness. Try as he might, he could not penetrate the blackness on either side of some stark image. Was that, Ned wondered, what life was like, bracketed between the state of being unborn and that of being dead?

SOMEONE had removed the withered flowers, but no fresh ones were in their place. Mechanically, Kathleen unpinned her hat and laid it on the table. Alexander Campbell hovered beside her while Ned shrugged out of a coat he had been given aboard the *Carpathia*, then gazed apathetically around the small suite.

He did not really see the hotel rooms. Over them like an obscuring shadow lay a memory of the cabins of the *Titanic*.

"Mama and Papa . . ." Kathleen began.

Ned nodded but did not meet her eyes. "Mama and Papa. Our steward from the *Titanic* told me he'd seen them. He tried to direct Mama to a lifeboat but she . . . but she . . ."

Kathleen, who knew her mother, finished for him. "She would not leave Papa."

"Women and children first," Alexander Campbell interjected. "It is the rule, of course."

The boy nodded again.

"Were they found at all?" the white-faced young woman asked.

Ned's husky whisper filled the silent room. "They're with the *Titanic*."

He had had four days to absorb the blow, but it struck Kathleen as if her parents had died moments before. Her knees buckled. With an effort of will she straightened and made her way to a chair, where she sat stiffly upright.

Alexander ordered tea. A porter brought a tray, and the familiar ritual of pouring and drinking provided a brief respite. Cups clattered in saucers, napkins were pressed to lips. Alexander ate a few of the sugared cookies arranged on a paper doily.

Ned could not even look at them. He had taken little food since the *Titanic* sank. It seemed monstrous to him that he still needed to eat and drink when his parents were dead.

Kathleen turned again to her brother. In a voice that was—almost—steady, she asked, "How did you get off the ship?"

Ned knew she really meant, How did you manage to survive when our parents did not?

He had asked himself the same question and found no answer. Any thought of his parents stirred up a storm of emotion within him. There were times when he passionately wished he had been with them—and other times when he was guiltily thankful to have escaped their fate. He could not express either feeling. The first seemed like being ungrateful to God for the gift of his life; the second was deeply humiliating.

His sister was waiting; he had to say something. "By the time I realized the ship was in danger there was such a great roolya-boolya, Kathleen! People scarpering about, shouting . . . it was enough to shake the brains out of me head. Mama and Papa were still in their cabin, so I tried to go back down to them. But there was such a clatter of people coming up the stairs I couldn't get through. I was pushed back to the boat deck, and then an Englishman called Mr. Otter caught hold of me and thrust a life jacket into my hands. 'Take this, you young fool,' he said."

Ned paused and cleared his throat, blinking back tears. "That life jacket . . . He saved my life, I think.

"I put on the jacket anyway and then I went on looking for Mama and Papa again. I was shouting their names, but everyone was shouting. By that time I could feel the tilt in the ship and all sorts of things were sliding down the deck. She was going down at the bow. That beautiful ship . . ."

He paused again, balled his fists, and continued. "They were putting women and children in the lifeboats, but some men were getting in them, too. The first boats went away half empty, though."

Kathleen gasped.

"Go on, lad," urged Alexander Campbell.

"People didn't want to leave the ship; they insisted it couldn't sink. I had a bad feeling, though. I was that desperate to leave, so I was, but not without Mama and Papa. But I couldn't find them. I kept searching and searching and couldn't find so much as the dust from their clothes. I would have saved them if I could.

"Then everything began to happen very fast. There was a terrible crashing below as if the boilers were breaking loose, and a crowd from third-class came bursting through one of the barriers. They were wild with fright. Most all the boats were gone by then except the last collapsible. Some men were trying to get it free and launch it, but the water was coming up . . ." Ned closed his eyes for a moment as if he could still see the cold green water surging up the deck toward him.

"Men began jumping from the rail. An officer shouted that the suction of the ship would pull them down, but they jumped anyway. Most people were scrambling toward the stern, though, to stay out of the water as long as they could. You can't imagine the *sounds.* The screams and cries, the roaring of the ship like an animal in pain, and . . . I know you won't believe this, but the orchestra kept playing and playing . . . I wanted to shout at them to stop, it was madness, but . . . suddenly the whole ship reared up and *broke,* somehow. Buckled and broke. One of the smokestacks came crashing down almost on top of me and I just . . . I just jumped.

"The next thing I knew I was in the water. The ship seemed almost to stand on her head. The stern was like a huge black mountain towering over me. I just knew I would die then, so I did. She hung there for a terrible long time. Then she began to slide down into the sea with people still crowded into the stern, clinging to the rails and each other, screaming. . . .

"The suction did not pull me down; they were wrong about that. All I felt was the terrible cold of the water. Mr. Otter's life jacket kept me afloat, and then there was one of the collapsibles, overturned but close enough, with men climbing onto it. A man reached into the water and took my hand and pulled me up. I looked back, then. I saw her . . . saw her go . . ." Bowing his head, Ned let the tears come at last.

Chapter Four

NED knew no words for the experience he had endured. It was not only the death of his parents which tormented him but the size of the total loss.

The death of the ship was a tragedy encompassing all others. For Ned the *Titanic* had represented the heights man could aspire to: wealth and beauty, security and certainty.

And then she was gone.

Just like that. As if an arbitrary God had snapped His fingers and wiped away the best that man could do.

Nothing would ever be certain again.

But how could he explain these things to anyone else? How could he describe the impact on his young mind of an entire floating city vanishing, taking with it fifteen hundred souls? The loss of the *Titanic* had left a hole in Ned's view of the world for which he had no language.

His shoulders heaved.

Kathleen flung her arms around the boy and drew him close, burying his face in the starched linen ruffles of her shirtwaist. Bending over him, she murmured repeatedly, "Ah Ned, what happened?" As if she had heard nothing he said— "What happened?"

It was a question he had already been asked time and again, and would be asked for years to come.

All Ned knew was that existence had treacherously shifted its borders. The solid surface he had taken for granted had been stripped away to reveal chaos beneath, an unguessed ocean of lightless water into which one could sink without a trace. How could he make anyone understand what he did not understand himself?

Aboard the *Carpathia* in the four days that elapsed between being plucked from the Atlantic and arriving in New York, Ned had struggled to come to terms with the tragedy. Strangers patted him awkwardly on the shoulder. "You're a lucky lad," some said.

"How did you feel when the *Titanic* sank?" others wanted to know. But he could not answer. He struggled under a burden of unarticulated horror.

After he had searched through the survivors, peering with fading hope into every face, he had been forced to admit Mama and Papa were lost. A conversation with their steward from the *Titanic* had only confirmed what he already knew in his heart. No vacuum had pulled him under with the sinking ship, but a great vacuum existed now, a howling void within him where Mama and Papa had been. His polestars, his security. *The people he loved most.* Agonizing memories of Mama's loving smile and Papa's strong hands kept flashing through his brain. His belly was full of hot tears that felt like blood.

In a futile effort to distract himself he had searched the *Carpathia* again, for Dan Duffy. But he had already seen all the survivors—with the exception of Bruce Ismay of the White Star Line, who had secreted himself in the surgeon's cabin with liquor and sedatives.

The bony redhead from Clare was somewhere two miles down, with the *Titanic*.

To his load of grief, Ned must add the loss of his newfound friend. How Dan had looked forward to a new life in America! "There's gold in them streets," he had said. For one so young and full of energy to end his life in an icy ocean far from home and loved ones . . . "There's nothing like a merry wake," Dan had said.

Those words tormented Ned.

Sleep proved to be his only escape. At first he feared sleeping, terrified he would have nightmares. But the nightmares were in the daytime. When exhaustion overcame him aboard the *Carpathia* he sank into a muffled darkness where no memory intruded and no voices rang out across the water, begging for rescue after the ship vanished, screaming in terror when the lifeboats refused to come back for them.

In New York he resorted to sleep again as an anodyne. He curled up in the hotel bed with the covers over his head and stayed there twelve, eighteen, twenty hours at a stretch. Mama's Daly cousins came down from Boston, reporters gathered at the front desk and sent up their cards begging interviews, and still Ned slept. A worried Kathleen called the hotel doctor in to examine him, but the man assured her the boy was basically healthy. "It's nervous prostration, my dear. Give him time; he'll recover."

Time, indeed. Kathleen was not so sure. This was Ned's first great wound; he had no experience of the ability of time to blur the edges and soften the center. He thought the intensity of his pain would continue undiminished to the grave.

Alexander Campbell spent as much time with the boy as he could, his employers having suggested that he make an effort to gain Ned's confidence and get him to talk about his experiences. Worried about the investigation to come, White Star was hoping to have as many survivors as possible testify on behalf of the shipping line.

When he finally dragged himself out of bed, sodden with too much sleep, Ned found it difficult to talk to anyone. Alexander Campbell was a man of calculated silences that waited, like deep pools, for words to be dropped into them. He was always there, encouraging Ned to remember.

After a few days the boy began to open up to him. Campbell was a virtual stranger, which made it easier. Ned knew little about him and so far had no curiosity, had not even taken a close look at the man. He could not really see anyone or anything but the ship, and the night, and the sea.

In answer to Campbell's quiet urging, he began recalling

details that had lain buried beneath layers of shock. He spoke
of the third-class passengers being held back by barriers and
denied access to the boats. Most of the rich and privileged
survived, but no one seemed to care about third-class. Irish
steerage passengers like Dan Duffy were left to die.

"No room in the lifeboats—oh, no," Ned said bitterly.
"No room for our kind."

He did not notice the look on Campbell's face.

"The *Titanic* was an unlucky ship from the start," Ned
claimed the first time Campbell took him out of the hotel for
a walk and a breath of air, "and divvil a thing anyone could
do about it. On the *Carpathia* later, people were talking about
a near collision that was after happening when the *Titanic*
was still in harbor, before the voyage even began. Others said
there was a coalfire smoldering below decks when we left
Queenstown and the crew knew about it but kept it a secret
from the passengers."

New York City on a warm spring afternoon. Beams of but-
tery light streamed through the leaves of young trees planted
along the curbs. High-stooped brownstone row houses—
which would have been called "terraced houses" in Ireland—
stood solid and secure. Small dogs trotted importantly along
cement sidewalks. The streets were thronged with motorcars,
a sight that would have amazed and delighted Ned only a few
days before. Now he did not even notice them.

He saw only the night and the sea. "I'm thinking the *Titanic* had a curse on her," he said in a haunted voice.

"Put that notion out of your mind, lad," Alexander Campbell replied brusquely. "And you would be well advised not
to tell others the foolish things you have said to me. They
would only be taken as ignorant Irish superstition."

"Are you not superstitious?" Ned turned and looked
sharply at his sister's fiancé for the first time. "With a name
like Campbell—surely you're a Scot."

"I'm an American, born and bred here. My father was an
Ulsterman from Belfast, though. Of Scottish descent."

The first thoughts not directly connected to the sinking of
the *Titanic* were beginning to float to the surface of Ned's

brain. "An . . . Oh. Does that mean you're a . . ." He paused in confusion, uncertain how to phrase the question without causing offense.

"Protestant. Scots Presbyterian."

Ned stared. "Did Kathleen know when she promised to marry you?"

"Of course she did."

"And she agreed anyway?"

"Obviously." Since forward progress seemed halted for the time being, Alexander took a cigar from the pocket of his jacket and went through the elaborate ritual of lighting it. He squinted at Ned through the smoke. "There is no prejudice against Protestantism in America, and Kathleen wants very much to be an American."

Without replying, Ned continued to study him. In the bright sunlight, he realized Campbell was considerably older than Kathleen. A gray-haired, middle-aged man. And a *Protestant*.

Had Mama and Papa known? Surely not; that unwelcome surprise had been waiting for them once they arrived in America. Ned could imagine their shock and the scene that would have followed. Kathleen had been clever, putting them under obligation to her fiancé before they ever met him. But why had she agreed to marry Alexander Campbell in the first place?

As if reading Ned's mind, the older man said, "Your sister's an exceptionally beautiful young woman, but I have a lot to offer, too. I have an excellent position with White Star and mean to go much higher in the company. The firm will not sink with the *Titanic*, I assure you. As I told Kate, I can give her a very good life here, much better than she could have back in Ireland."

"You don't know what she could have in Ireland."

"I've been to the Harland and Wolff shipyards in Belfast more times than you've had hot dinners, Ned. I know Ireland. It's a sad, poor country, and there's no future there, as I've pointed out to Kate many times."

Anger rose in a slow, hot wave through Ned's being. This man—this smug, self-satisfied *stranger*—had lured Kathleen into staying in America by denigrating Ireland to her. But for that, Mama and Papa would be alive today and safe at home. Home.

County Clare . . . green fields and gray limestone, the fiddle music and the cuckoo's call, the black Cliffs of Moher rising sheer from the sea to defy the Atlantic itself.

"I want to go home," he announced to his sister as soon as they returned to the hotel.

"Ah, surely not, Ned!" She had lost so much; the idea of his returning to Ireland seemed almost like another death to her. "Stay here with us. Alexander can get you work, or we could—"

Ned jutted his chin at a stubborn angle that reminded Kathleen of their father. "I want to go home."

She threw a beseeching look to her fiancé. "Alexander? Convince him to stay."

"Your parents are gone, lad," Campbell responded dutifully. "You have a place here with us, but there's nothing for you in Ireland now."

"There's the farm!" Ned cried, shocked that anyone could consider land to be nothing. "And my brother Frank and my two little sisters and I want to go back to them. Right now!" Ned knew they thought him unreasonable, but he did not care. He longed for the familiar green island in the uncertain sea, an image he clung to as a drowning man might cling to a lifeline.

In the end it was Alexander, rather than Kathleen, who told him, "We have decided to postpone our wedding for a year out of respect for Kate's parents. She'll live with her cousins until we are married, then she'll move into a new house here in New York with me. In the meantime, the White Star line is sending *Titanic* survivors home with all expenses paid, and I can arrange a berth for you on the next liner heading east if that's what you want."

Ned felt he owed it to his sister to make her understand. "Your life is here, but mine's not, Kathleen. We were only coming for a visit; no one meant to stay."

"Millions dream of emigrating to America," she reminded

him. "Don't be throwing away your chance."

An image rose in his mind of Dan Duffy, and of all those like Dan Duffy. *If I had me choice,* Dan had said in the April twilight, with the green land fading away astern, *I would stay in Ireland.*

Ned shook his head. "I choose Ireland," he told his sister resolutely.

Kathleen gave him a long, thoughtful look. There was something in his eyes that spoke to her of little fields like patchwork, and lacy stone walls with bits of sky showing through. She threw her arms around him and held him close. Even his crisp black curls seemed, in her imagination, to smell of Clare earth.

The body in her arms was lanky and boyish but possessed a wiry strength. Deep in Ned Halloran was steel. His determination was proverbial in the family. Everyone knew that once he had set himself upon a course, there was no hope of changing him.

"I'll write," she promised, struggling to get the words past the lump in her throat. "And you write, too, Ned. Tell me how things are . . . at home."

May 1, 1912

CANADA ANNOUNCES *TITANIC* DEAD TO BE
BURIED IN NOVA SCOTIA

May 28, 1912

WASHINGTON D.C. INQUIRY RETURNS
VERDICT OF NEGLIGENCE IN *TITANIC* DISASTER

Chapter Five

T HE last thing Ned Halloran wanted was another ocean voyage, but it was the only way to get back to Ireland.

Realizing that survivors returning to Europe might have misgivings about setting foot on any ship, White Star tactfully arranged passage on vessels as unlike the *Titanic* as possible. No one would have to sail on her sister ship, the *Olympic,* for example. White Star had also chartered two cable ships to scour the site of the sinking for bodies. Some three hundred had been found. Those that could be identified were embalmed and sent on for burial; the rest were buried at sea with full rites.

Theresa and Patrick Halloran would never be found. Nor would Dan Duffy.

When the day came for Ned to depart, Kathleen accompanied him to the pier. Forcing himself to walk up the gangplank was an effort. The steward who accompanied him cast him a solicitous glance. "It will be all right, sir," he assured Ned. "After all, you have survived the *Titanic*. Nothing else can harm you now."

A few minutes later Ned stood at the railing, looking down at the crowd below. His eyes searched out his sister's slender form. She looked very small and far away. He waved and she stood on tiptoe to wave back, but his gaze was already turning toward the horizon.

I *have* survived, Ned thought. He let the full meaning of the words sink in and repeated them to himself like a talisman. *I have survived the* Titanic.

Thus armed, he could survive anything.

HIS welcome was muted by mourning for his parents. Black crèpe was hung on the door, but otherwise the house a few hundred yards from the Ennis road looked the same. Built of local stone, the original four rooms had been altered and added to over the years and now boasted two stories with a steeply pitched slate roof, a cluster of outhouses, and a walled yard. No Irish person would have called it a cottage, which the English in Ireland had given a derogatory connotation. The Halloran home was a farmhouse, plainly if sturdily built, and sited to catch the sun.

When she had entered her new home as a bride twenty years earlier Theresa Daly Halloran had confided to her many sisters, "I'm going to make something of this place, so I will." Although she would never say so aloud, her model for domestic perfection was the Big House, the country mansion of the Anglo-Irish gentry.

From that day forward she had swept and polished and garnished, but the rough bones of the Halloran house stubbornly resisted her attempts to turn it into anything grander than it was. Yet she persevered, and when she acquired a servant girl, Janey Devlin's life was dedicated to the same cause.

Theresa's love for her home was equaled only by Patrick Halloran's love for his farm. His forty-seven acres "had the grass" of eighteen cows, and also supported half a dozen pigs, two plow horses, and a pony for the cart. On the blue-black marshlands of the Fergus he grew corn for the market, while a large kitchen garden kept his family supplied with potatoes, cabbages, carrots, and turnips. Hens and geese in the yard furnished eggs for the table and stuffing for pillows and feath-

erbeds. The orchard hummed with bees, and in a good summer the high meadow was golden with hay.

Below the meadow was a half acre and a limewashed cabin
that Patrick rented to Thomas Devlin of Clonroad. Devlin was
a brawny, taciturn man who paid the rent with farm labor
while his unmarried sister, Janey, served in the Halloran house
as maid-of-all-work. The tidiness and prosperity of the holding was due in no small measure to their devotion over the
years.

Seeing his mother's house, his father's fields, hit Ned like
a blow to the heart.

But his brother's face shocked him. Although he was only
three years older than Ned, Francis Patrick Halloran seemed
to have turned into a middle-aged man in two short months.
Deep pouches had formed beneath his blue eyes. His brown
hair lay lank across his forehead, his shoulders drooped beneath the weight of burdens they were unprepared to bear.
Once he had made the countryside ring with his whistled rendition of the new Percy French tune, "The Darlin' Girl from
Clare." But the music was dead in him now.

Norah Daly was doing her best to maintain a home for
her sister's orphaned children, but the strain was evident on
her as well. A plump, soft woman, with thick brown hair—
graying now—scraped back into a knot, in her youth she had
been the beauty of the Daly clan. The family home on Abbey
Street in Ennis had seen its share of young men trying to court
Norah, and not just for her dowry. But she had refused them
all, becoming instead the devoted spinster aunt to a horde of
nieces and nephews.

When the locals wondered among themselves at her failure
to marry, only Patrick Halloran had never joined in the speculation.

Now Norah Daly stood in the Halloran doorway to welcome Ned home, as the two little girls, Lucy and Eileen,
peeped shyly around her skirts. "Wisha, Ned, you're wearing
your father's face!" was Norah's greeting to him. Then she
burst into tears.

• • •

NED'S mother had been so proud of her parlor. The walls were decorated with holy pictures and the windows were hung with lace curtains that Janey Devlin starched four times a year with potato water, but Norah and Frank bypassed the parlor and went straight to the kitchen. Ned followed. In rural Ireland people invariably gathered in the kitchen.

A massive stone hearth dominated one end of the room. The chimney breast was coated with a tarry residue from countless fires. Within the mouth of the fireplace was a spit for roasting meat, and an iron crane with a projecting arm braced to hold pots and kettles. Sides of bacon hung from hooks above, curing in the smoke. Similar fireplaces had been the hearts of Irish homes for hundreds of years.

Beside the hearth stood a creel: a large, square basket made of hazel rods and piled high with blocks of turf. Since the island had been denuded of its timber in the sixteenth century, turf cut from peat bogs had become the ubiquitous fuel. The achingly sweet smell of Ireland's burning earth was as much a part of Ned as the color of his eyes.

A note of modernity was provided by an iron cooking range. Here food could be prepared by a woman standing upright, and smoothing irons could be heated without being coated in ash. So this new household god, lovingly blacked and polished, was much venerated by the womenfolk. It, too, depended on turf, however.

In the center of the flagstone floor was a large deal table surrounded by *sugán* chairs with straw-rope seats. Other furnishings included a tall flour bin with a sloping lid, a wooden kneading trough, and a pine dresser displaying the 'delph'— glazed pottery in blue and white and speckled brown. A half door opened onto the yard; strings of onions hung drying beside a curtainless window. The kitchen smelled of fresh-baked bread and muddy boots.

On the mantelpiece next to the clock was a dog-eared book of poems in a faded leather binding, the sort of slim volume

Patrick Halloran had always carried in his pocket, even when working in the fields.

At first no one knew what to say. Norah blew her nose on a handkerchief; Frank rummaged in his pockets. The ticking of the clock was the only sound in the room as the surviving members of the Halloran family looked at one another.

Ned wished his mother were there. She always had something to say.

"I'll poke up the fire and put fresh water in the kettle," Norah said abruptly. "Lucy, Eileen—you had your tea already. Be off and play now, let your brother catch his breath. He'll have time for you after."

Two sets of small arms wrapped themselves around Ned's neck, hugged hard, then reluctantly loosened. The bottom of the half door slammed.

"I'm sorry my sewing things are all over the table, I was cutting patterns," Norah went on, speaking too fast. "But here, we'll put the tea on this." She unfastened a hinged tabletop that was held to the wall by a wooden turnbuckle. When it was let down and its two folding legs were lowered into place, the "falling table" provided additional eating space for the extra laborers hired at the hiring fair to help with the harvest. It served other functions as well; the surface was deeply grooved as a result of being used for cutting up pig carcasses after slaughtering.

Ned felt as if he were visiting the house for the first time. He had grown up in this place and never before questioned either its style or its substance. He was astonished at how primitive it seemed to him now.

"Would you like bread and jam?" Norah asked as she spread an oilcloth over the table. "There is black currant or gooseberry."

In his mind's eye Ned could see his mother and the servant girl as clearly as if they were in front of him, ladling the hot, jewel-toned jam from the kettle into the jars. The smell had filled the kitchen, so thick and sweet it coated his throat and flooded his mouth with saliva. And Mama looked up, flush-faced from the heat, and smiled. . . .

"I'm not hungry," he managed to whisper.

"You're as thin as a lath; there's not a pick o'meat on you. You will eat, I'll see to it." Suiting deed to word, Norah began placing food in front of him. A Blue Willow platter was piled high with "boxty," cakes made of raw grated potato mixed with flour, then flavored with sugar, caraway, and cinnamon and cooked on a greased griddle. A second platter was heaped with thick slices of bacon, pork steak, and black pudding. A bowl held boiled eggs; another contained creamy pot cheese. Wedges of soda bread still warm from the oven were slathered with sweet butter, and scalding hot tea— "strong enough for a mouse to trot across," just the way Patrick Halloran had liked it—was poured into Ned's cup.

"Eat," his aunt commanded. "You too, Frank."

They obeyed. As was the custom with country women, their aunt would wait until the menfolk were finished before taking anything for herself.

"White Star's disclaiming further financial responsibility," Frank told Ned while they ate. "They seem to think they've done enough just sending you home. So with Papa gone, it's up to me to support us until the girls are old enough to marry."

Ned glanced out the window toward his two sisters, playing in the yard. Lucy, at age nine, was already a sober little girl, with heavy eyebrows and a sallow complexion. She had none of her older sister Kathleen's beauty. Five-year-old Eileen was fair and chubby, with dimpled hands and a gurgling laugh that caused Lucy to scowl and shake her head.

Ned could not make out what the older girl was saying, but it was surely some admonition to remember their parents were newly dead.

"I'll help," Ned said, turning back to his brother. "You won't have to do it all yourself."

"Work on the farm, you mean?"

"I do of course. I've been working on this farm since I was five years old, same as yourself."

Frank said, "Lord Inchiquin wants to do something for you

to make up for what you've been through. He suggests sending you away to school.''

"I'm after having my schooling, I don't need any more. I went to National School until I was twelve.''

"Your father always said you had a great turn for the books, Ned,'' interjected Norah. "So His Lordship would like you to have a proper education. To equip you for the larger world, as he says.''

"I won't go, so I won't! I'll stay here and do my share of the work.''

His aunt was watching him with an intent gaze, struck anew by his resemblance to Patrick Halloran. "Would you not do something other than farming, if you could?''

"Farming was good enough for my father.''

An expression Ned could not interpret flickered in Norah's eyes. "Your father did what he had to. That was his way. But it is possible he wanted something else, might have yearned all his life for . . .'' She bit her lip.

"How would you know what my father wanted?''

Her face closed, hiding secrets behind locked doors. "Just tell us, Ned. You love books like your father before you, and you always say you never get enough of them to read. Would you take more schooling if it was on offer?''

Before the *Titanic* he would have answered no with a shrug and a laugh. What need had a County Clare farm boy for a "proper'' education?

Now the *Titanic* was gone, but the horizons she had opened in his mind had not shrunk. Yet too much had happened in too short a time; he was mentally and emotionally exhausted.

Later Frank and Norah discussed the matter out of Ned's hearing. "We have to stay here, Frank, though everything we see reminds us of our loss. But the boy is different. Like his father, he . . . Oh, let us give him this chance! Down deep he wants it, I know he does. He's trying to do his duty. Can we not be generous and let him follow his heart instead?''

In an Irish household the senior male's word was law—but the women knew how to legislate. Frank made only a token objection before giving in to his aunt. Ned was duly sent up to Dromoland for an interview with Lord Inchiquin.

Chapter Six

AFTERWARD he wrote Kathleen:

> I had never been inside Dromoland Castle before and
> it is very grand. The air inside is so still, you would never
> know there are lots of servants about. There is a library
> with hundreds of books. Lord Inchiquin said he had not
> read them all. I would read them if they were mine. He
> has a kind face with a nose on him as long as a wet
> winter. I could tell he felt sorry for me. I do not like it
> when people feel sorry for me. He talked about my father
> and said what a hard worker he was, and Her Ladyship
> gave me some sweet biscuits with pink icing on them. I
> just et one and brought the rest home to Lucy and Eileen.
> Lord Inchiquin has promised to send me up to Dublin to
> school. We are going to ask Father Hagerty to recom-
> mend a Catholic one. When I next write I hope to have
> good news.
>
> Your loving brother, Ned.

There was one duty he felt honor bound to perform. On a
cold gray day when the wind blew in off the Atlantic like
death's own voice, Ned took the pony and rode to Ruan to

pay a call on Dan Duffy's family. He hardly knew what to say to them, but he had to go.

As the pony trotted along the winding roads he saluted with a countryman's nod the other travelers he met, and called out to laborers in the fields, "God bless the work!" They grinned and waved back; none were strangers in Clare.

When Ned reached the village of Ruan a white-haired, weather-beaten post "boy" on a bicycle directed him to the Duffy holding, which proved to be a dilapidated *bothán scóir* at the end of a rutted lane. Tiny, stony fields growing a meager crop of potatoes and turnips surrounded a rectangular cabin built of rocks and mud and roofed with reeds. The hovel was like a pustule erupting from a sea of mud.

Ned noticed that someone had made an effort to bring a touch of beauty to this particular hovel. There were wildflowers in a jug on the sill of the only window.

Liam Duffy met Ned at the door. His resemblance to his dead son gave Ned a physical jolt. Ned stammered, "I was . . . I was on the *Titanic*."

A moment later he was inside and the hospitality of the house was being pressed upon him. It was only cold potatoes and buttermilk, but the best they had. He could not offend them by refusing. While he forced down a few bites the senior Duffys watched him avidly, hungry for any comfort to which they could cling. Their remaining children gathered around them, staring at the stranger. The noses of the younger ones were running. They wiped them on their sleeves, if at all.

Ned glanced around the cabin. As was common when one structure must serve as both house and barn, a drain running across the hard-packed earthen floor marked the division between human habitation and animal byre. Sleeping accommodations consisted of one small recess containing a rickety bedstead with a mattress of woven straw, a sleeping loft above reached by a ladder, and a lean-to accessed through a hole knocked in the wall. There was no real fireplace, merely a few turves smoldering on a slab.

"And was he brave at the end?" Liam Duffy kept asking. "Was me lad brave at the end?"

"As brave as Brian Bóru," Ned assured him.

Mrs. Duffy said, "Is there no chance he could have survived? He would not have been easy to kill, our Dan." She thrust her face into Ned's, every line and seam and broken vein telling a tale of struggle.

Ned longed to hold out hope, however slim. But the heartbreak of future disappointment would be more cruel than telling the truth now. "Dan went down with the *Titanic*," he said.

Though his voice was pitched low, the words cut the smoky air like a butcher's knife.

Mrs. Duffy threw her apron over her face and turned away. Her husband stood solidly, feet planted wide apart, and absorbed the blow without flinching. "So," he said. "Sure, don't we all have one foot in the grave and the other on its edge anyway."

Ned stayed only as long as good manners dictated. Conversation was limited: Ned spoke of going away to school; Mr. Duffy complained of his "rheumatics." The older children watched silently; the younger ones sniffled and fidgeted.

When Ned rose from his broken stool and said his goodbyes, one of Dan's sisters came forward and pressed his hand. " 'Twas good of you to come, so."

She was a year or two older than he and almost as tall, with creamy, freckled skin. Eyebrows and eyelashes were purest cópper; her rust-colored hair was like raveled rope. Her eyes were slanted like a cat's. She was not beautiful, her features were too strongly modeled. But her bosom was magnificent.

Ned's hand felt burned by the touch of hers.

"Síle!" her father said, "be letting go of the lad's hand now, he'll be wanting to be on his way before dark."

The girl released him, but held his gaze. "Someday," she said softly, "I'm going to leave, too. There's nothing for me here, no dowry to get me a husband." Her mouth twisted. "Perhaps I'll go to Dublin like you. Watch for me there, you never know."

Then she threw back her head and laughed.

On the way home Ned kept thinking about her. He was surprised she had such an old-fashioned name. People of his class christened their children with English names, or at least anglicized the Irish. Síle—*Sheila*—would have been changed to Cecilia.

And none of the Irish girls he knew would have taken his hand the way she did, or met his eyes so boldly.

June 19, 1912

IRISH HOME RULE BILL ONCE MORE
BEFORE PARLIAMENT

September 30, 1912

RUSSIA MOBILIZES 245,000 TROOPS AS
TENSION MOUNTS IN BALKANS

Chapter Seven

THE parish priest, Father Hagerty, was an energetic little man with the veinous nose of an alcoholic and a tendency to slur his speech on occasion, though his parishioners swore he rarely touched "a drop o' the crayture." His political views were in no doubt, however. Home Rule and the Gaelic League commanded his passionate loyalty, to the distress of his bishop. Pat Hagerty wanted Ireland to be ruled by its own parliament in Dublin and speak its own language everywhere. He was an Irishman to his toes.

"There's a school in Dublin that would be the very place for yon lad," Father Hagerty told Frank Halloran. "Mind you, he might be a bit old, but I could have a word with a cousin of mine who's married to one of the Bradys. The headmaster's mother was a Brady from County Meath."

Frank Halloran nodded. He understood the complex network of familial relationships by which most arrangements in Ireland were made.

"This school, Saint Enda's," the priest went on, warming to his subject, "was established in 1908 to acquaint Irish boys with their native language as well as give them a thorough education. They don't teach our own Irish history in the National Schools, but Saint Enda's does—and the Irish language, too. If the lad has a good mind he'll do well there."

"Is it very expensive?" worried Frank. "And do you think His Lordship would object to paying the tuition for a school that teaches . . . Irish?"

"The Lords Inchiquin may be anglicized, but in the heel of the hunt they're still O'Briens underneath," Father Hagerty replied stoutly.

True to his word, Father Hagerty made the arrangements. On a warm autumn day Frank prepared to drive Ned to the train station. Ned insisted on harnessing the pony to the trap himself, giving the animal a fond rub between the eyes as he adjusted the bridle.

Norah and the girls stood at the door to bid him good-bye. Norah gave him a smothering hug, then turned away. Lucy also hugged him, the embrace hard and abrupt, swiftly broken off.

But little Eileen followed him to the road and stood beside the wheel of the trap. She held up her dimpled arms. "Please, Neddy. Please!"

He leaped out and squeezed her to him until she gasped for breath. This time it was Ned who wept.

As they drove away he dared not look back.

On the train for Dublin he sat with his pasteboard suitcase on his lap and tried to ignore the itching caused by his new woolen trousers, a gift from Dromoland. He felt certain that Mama would somehow know if he scratched himself in public.

Reminded of her, he removed his cap—his father's beloved old Scarriff hat—and held it on his lap with the suitcase until he noticed that other passengers were heaving their luggage onto racks above the seats.

A few moments later a deep voice asked, "Is the seat beside you taken?"

"It is not taken," Ned assured the stranger standing in the aisle.

The man introduced himself as Henry Mooney, and the two shook hands before he sat down. Mooney was of medium

height, with rounded shoulders and brown hair. A heavy jaw
dominated his face, but laugh lines bracketed his clear blue
eyes.

At first their conversation was limited to an exchange of
names and family connections. The trip was a long one, however, and soon they were chatting companionably. "I've been
working as a reporter for the *Limerick Echo*," Mooney told
Ned, "but now I'm going to Dublin to look for a job with
one of the city papers. It's my ambition to write feature articles. Something pungent and witty, perhaps," he added with
a chuckle.

Beyond the window a green blur of landscape swept by,
foaming with billows of golden gorse—a plant always to be
found in bloom somewhere in Ireland, no matter what the
season. The newspaperman idly quoted, "When the gorse is
out of bloom, kissing is out of fashion," then was surprised
to see his young companion blush.

Was I ever that young and innocent? Henry Mooney wondered as he lit a cigarette. I'm not yet thirty, but he makes
me feel ancient.

"Look out the window there, lad," he said, leaning across
Ned and enveloping him in a cloud of cigarette smoke and
bay rum. "We're in Tipperary now. See the signpost for
Clonmel? The Irish Labor Party was founded here just this
past June."

"What do you know about them?" Ned asked as he peered
through the smoke-grimed window. "Are they anything like
Mr. Parnell's Home Rule Party was?"

His seatmate smiled. He had taken an instant liking to the
lad; there was a country softness in Ned's speech, a country
shyness in his gaze. But there was something proud in him
as well, a set to his shoulders and a lift to his chin.

Henry Mooney discoursed, with humorous asides, on the
labor movement as seen from the Limerick perspective. Ned
listened with gratifying interest. Mooney spoke next of the
recent death of Dublin-born Bram Stoker, the author of *Dra-
cula*, then moved on to the protest staged by British suffragettes in Dublin, the high cost of tobacco, and the recent riot

in Belfast between Protestant and Catholic football supporters. He seemed to know something about everything.

"Where were you schooled, sir?" the boy asked admiringly.

Mooney gave a hearty guffaw. "Schooled? Why, most of what I know I found out for myself, lad. That's how anyone learns anything. I went to the Boys' National School at Killaloe with my cousins, the Reddens—don't suppose you know them?—and then to Michael Walshe's Intermediate until I realized there was more to the world than anyone was teaching me out of books. So I set out to find it."

On impulse, Ned confided, "I've seen something of the world. I was on the *Titanic*."

Mooney turned in his seat to stare at him. "Are you serious?"

"I am serious. My mother and father . . ." His words ground to a halt.

Mooney already had his notepad out and was scribbling furiously. A *Titanic* survivor! Providence had dropped the boy into his lap.

Ned regretted having spoken. He had grown wary of a river inside himself, a river of memories he kept dammed lest they flood through him and sweep him away. Staring fixedly out the window, he replied to the reporter's questions with monosyllabic answers.

"You really don't want to talk about this, do you?"

"I'm not bothered," said Ned, but the older man recognized the polite lie. It was a deeply ingrained Irish trait, this business of telling people what they wanted to hear whether it was true or not.

He put his notepad away and tactfully changed the subject. "So now you're going up to Dublin. That's a journey many Irish people never make in a lifetime. What do you know about the place?"

"Not very much."

"The most important thing to remember," Mooney said in a confidential tone, "is that it's a foreign city. Always has been."

"Sir?"

"Dublin was founded by the Vikings, overrun by the Normans, and now is English to the core, from Dublin Castle to the Viceregal Lodge. When you enter the Pale you leave Irish Ireland behind you."

"You know Dublin well, sir?"

"Well enough to convince me it's the place for a journalist to be now. Things are happening, my lad. Stirrings in the wind." Mooney gave a wink and a nod but for once did not elaborate.

When Ned's stomach began to rumble he produced a packet of bacon sandwiches his Aunt Norah had prepared for him and offered to share them with his seatmate. Mooney laughingly refused. "I don't like to eat on an empty stomach." Instead he withdrew a battered tin flask from his jacket pocket and took a deep pull.

The train lurched and shuddered on. Ireland sped past the windows.

"We'll be in the Big Smoke before long, Ned," Mooney said at last. "Is someone meeting you at the station?"

"No one is meeting me, but I am to go straightaway to . . ." The boy dug into a trouser pocket and produced a scrap of pasteboard. "To this address."

Mooney took the embossed calling card and saw Lord Inchiquin's name, then the name and address scrawled below: "Robert H. Beauchamp, solicitor, 25 Fitzwilliam Square South." He gave a low whistle. "Very posh. I expect you will be well looked after, my young friend. But here . . ." He turned the card over and scribbled something on the back. "I shall be staying with a widowed cousin of mine, Louise Kearney, at number sixteen Middle Gardiner Street. She lets rooms to bachelors like myself. If you need someone to show you around the city, or if you're simply lonely for a West of Ireland accent, call on me."

"That's very kind of you; I shall. But how do I find Gardiner Street?"

"Same way you find anything in Dublin; same way you find anything down the country, come to that: ask at the nearest public-house. Use Nelson's Pillar as your landmark; Gardiner Street is but a short walk away. Where will you be lodging? Not with a solicitor in Fitzwilliam Square, surely.''

"I'm to be a boarding pupil at Saint Enda's. It's run by a man called Patrick Henry Pearse."

"Pearse? Don't know that I've heard of him."

"You will," Ned assured Mooncy. "My parish priest says he's going to revolutionize education in Ireland."

KINGSBRIDGE Station, headquarters and terminus of the Great Southern and Western Railway Company, possessed an imposing sandstone facade in the style of a Renaissance palazzo. The colonnade was thronged with people. More spilled out into the roadway, competing for the horse-drawn hackney cabs lined up at curbside.

Ned was immediately conscious of being out of place, "up from the country." His tweed jacket had a rustic cut he had not been aware of before. When he sought to engage a hackney cab the driver gave him a look that measured his age, his ignorance, and his ability to pay in one swift glance before signaling him to climb aboard.

The back of Ned's neck burned red.

The blinkered bay mare trotted across Stevens' Lane and headed east along the quays that lined the river Liffey. The street was paved with cobbles; iron horseshoes struck sparks from embedded tram tracks.

Ned almost choked on a cloying, yeasty aroma that struck him like a blow to the stomach. "What's that smell?"

The driver chuckled. "Hops and grain to make Guinness, boyo. Mother's milk. That's the brewery wall there to yer right. Ye couldn't begin to count the barrels of export stout ferried from James's Gate to the ships on Custom House Quay. Once ye've had Guinness and oysters at the Red Bank ye can die in a state o' grace."

As they whirled along the quays, the smell from the brewery was replaced by the pungent odor of the river with its load of sewage and industrial waste. The day darkened. A misty rain made the streets glisten and conferred a deceptive softness on the scene. Throughout Dublin lights winked on like stars.

A "foreign city"? Perhaps it was. Certainly one of the bridges spanning the dark waters of the Liffey was exotic. The cabby volunteered, "That's the Wellington Bridge there, but we call it the Metal Bridge or the Ha'penny. Foot traffic only and a ha'penny to walk across it.[1] See the tollgate on this side?"

The humpbacked bridge was surmounted with ornate curves of lacy ironwork forming arches reminiscent of cupolas in a Victorian garden. "It's beautiful," Ned breathed. "Like something out of a fairy tale."

The driver flicked his whip at the mare, who slanted one ear back at him but continued to clop along at the same steady pace. "I can show ye much better sights than that, young fellow-me-lad. Only cost ye a . . . shilling, say?"

The man must take me for a fool, thought Ned. A shilling indeed, when a penny would buy a packet of Lyons' Tea or a pint of paraffin oil for the lamp. "Just Fitzwilliam Place, thank you."

The driver shrugged.

Ned felt a pleasurable stir of anticipation. Since the *Titanic*, he had been aware of a numbness, an echoing hollow at the center of his being. He had been too dazed to appreciate New York properly. But the numbness was beginning to wear off. Perhaps it had begun when Síle Duffy touched his hand. Unconsciously, he smiled.

Chapter Eight

THE cab threaded its way among countless bicycles and horse-drawn vehicles of every description, while an occasional Humber or Panhard testified to the increasing prominence of the motorcar. At the widest of the bridges spanning the Liffey a number of electric trams converged, bells clanging, beneath a spiderweb of overhead cables. Showers of sparks flashed from the trolley heads as the heavily laden transports swung and swayed. A massive Daimler with goggled chauffeur cut out of the traffic and sped past with hooting horn, only to find its way blocked by a motorized Argyll delivery van.

There were not thirty automobiles in all of Clare; seeing even one had been an event. And as for double-decker electric trams . . . ! To a boy from the west of Ireland, Dublin was as alien as New York.

Ned observed that Dublin men dressed in suits ranging from Saville Row tailoring to charity castoffs. The prosperous sported shiny top hats. Most of the others, even laborers replacing stone cobbles in the street, wore bowlers.

Ragged barefoot boys scurried from one corner to another, delivering laundry baskets almost larger than themselves or trying to cadge pennies from pedestrians. Adult peddlers

shouting colorful slogans pushed hand barrows selling everything from fish to clothing.

Fashionable women wore long narrow skirts, and no costume was complete without an eye-catching hat and pristine
gloves. The poorer classes dressed in shabby secondhand
goods, often layering their entire wardrobes over their bodies.
Among them were the traditionally garbed women known as
"shawlies," who looked much as their great-grandmothers
had.

Faces from every social class bore mute testimony to the
ravages of smallpox, while over all hung an effluvium composed of coal fires and horse manure, public abattoirs and
private slaughterhouses.

As the cab progressed through the city, they encountered a
Scots Guards band piping its way in advance of a small detachment of troops. A handful of small boys strutted along
behind in irreverent imitation.

Ned had never seen so many uniformed soldiers before.
They were everywhere. Not content to parade in the streets,
they strode the footpaths of Dublin as if it was their town.
The citizenry gave way to them with lowered eyes. Ned recalled something Father Hagerty had once said under his
breath, as if afraid the bishop would overhear him: "The army
of occupation . . ."

The driver drew up with a flourish. "Ho, Bella! Twenty-
five Fitzwilliam Square," he announced.

Ned looked up to find himself in front of a handsome five-
story Georgian house, one of a terraced row built of cut stone
with polished brass door knockers, classical fanlights, and pel-
metted draperies visible through tall windows. Each house
staked its claim to individuality by painting its front door a
different color.

There could be no mistake; this was an enclave of the gentry.

Ned exited the cab in an undignified scramble and stood
holding his cap in his hand while the cabdriver set his suitcase
on the pavement.

The man cleared his throat.

Ned's cheeks burned as he dug into his pocket, seeking coins. Then he hefted his case and started up a flight of well-scrubbed marble steps. Behind him, the driver called, "Gee up, Bella," and cracked the whip, but Ned did not look around. His eyes were fixed on the door, which was painted a glossy dark red and bore a discreet brass nameplate reading "R. Beauchamp."

Tentatively he fingered the lion's head knocker. Before he could hit the striker plate the door opened and a spare, elderly man gazed out at him. "Sir?" He managed to inject both courtesy and chilly dignity into the single syllable.

"I'm here to see Mr. Beauchamp."

One eyebrow lifted fractionally. "May I have your name?"

"I am called Ned . . . er, Edward Halloran."

"And your business, Mr. Halloran?"

Ned felt a trickle of sweat run down the back of his neck. "Lord Inchiquin sent me," he claimed as he fumbled for the bit of pasteboard that could identify him. He could not find it.

His inquisitor waited impassively.

One last, frantic dig in his jacket pocket produced the precious card. Ned held it up with a flourish. "Here!"

At once the butler relieved him of his suitcase and took a half step backward. "This way," he said, drawing the boy inside with a sweeping gesture of his free hand.

EVERYTHING has a price, Ned. The price of your education was your parents' lives, if you want to look at it that way," said Robert Beauchamp later that afternoon as they sat beside the fire in his high-ceilinged drawing room. The solicitor, a heavyset man in his mid-fifties whose buff waistcoat strained across his ample paunch, frowned when the boy flinched at his words. "Forgive me, I am a blunt man. I find it saves time. I appreciate the same quality in others, though it is in rare supply in this benighted land.

"My lord Inchiquin fortunately shares my view to some extent. He sent me only the briefest of missives concerning you, but that was quite sufficient to allow me to make the necessary arrangements. I am to pay the school direct for the cost of your tuition and books, and you are to receive a small personal allowance every month so you will have a few coins to jingle in your pocket. I trust you appreciate my lord's generosity.''

"I do sir," Ned said hastily.

Beauchamp went on. ''You will spend the night here with us, then tomorrow my coachman will take you to Saint Enda's. They are expecting you. Though why Lucius O'Brien is willing to fund an education in such an establishment is quite beyond me.''

"It was my family's choice, sir," the boy replied.

"But surely there are more appropriate schools. You *are* Church of Ireland, I assume?''

Ned met his eye squarely. "I'm not a Protestant, sir; I'm a Catholic.''

"Ah. I see." Beauchamp leaned back in the satin-striped wing chair and tented his fingers. ''Lucius did not bother to explain that in his letter. It makes all the difference, of course. No Trinity College for you then, and a school in England is quite out of the question. Saint Enda's it is. First thing in the morning.''

"Is it not a good school, sir? I was told—"

"Oh, I'm certain it's quite good enough," Beauchamp assured him.

The unspoken qualifier hung in the air between them. Ned could hear it. Good enough for an Irish Catholic.

Within the solicitor's drawing room the fire crackled cheerfully, but outside a cold rain fell. It drummed against the windows with relentless fingers until a parlor maid came and closed the brocade draperies.

That night Mr. and Mrs. Beauchamp held one of their ''musical evenings,'' an occasion that included dinner for a select group of friends, followed by a piano performance in the drawing room. Ned was not invited. He ate his supper in the servants' hall under the stern eye of the cook, then went to bed in a small bedroom on the top floor. As he lay sleepless he could hear the music drifting up to him and found himself missing the sound of Frank's snoring.

The next morning he was driven to Saint Enda's by the Beauchamps' coachman. A bobtailed gray gelding, its head drawn unnaturally high by a check rein, was harnessed to the solicitor's sidecar. Once Mr. Beauchamp had used the sidecar for business around the city, but he now preferred his Peugeot. He liked to drive himself and had no compunction about parking the motorcar on footpaths and blocking pedestrian traffic.

Ned wondered what Mama would have said if she could see her son traveling like gentry with a liveried coachman.

Then Beauchamp's words came back to him: *The price of your education was your parents' lives . . .*

The city dwindled behind them. In the distance rose the gentle shoulders of the Dublin mountains. Black-and-white sheepdogs sat guardian beside cottage gates, cats slumbered on windowsills, cows grazed in fields beside the road. Ned and the coachman chatted; rather, the coachman talked and Ned listened attentively.

"Rathfarnham up ahead," said the man, interrupting a rambling tale about himself, his brother, and a three-legged dog.

Rathfarnham was no great distance from Dublin geographically, but miles away in atmosphere. Though it boasted paved roads, a variety of shops, and even a tram station, like other villages ringing the urban center it was still a country town. People greeted the sidecar with a wave or a friendly nod.

The previous day's rain had continued through the night, but now autumnal sunlight bathed the scene. The air was heavy with moisture, as cool and sweet as fruit juice on the tongue.

A mile beyond Rathfarnham the coachman gestured toward a pair of large gates set close to the road. "Here we are."

Thanks to Father Hagerty, Ned knew that Saint Enda's had been established four years earlier at Cullenswood House, in the suburb of Ranelagh. The school had already outgrown its first home. It now occupied the Hermitage, a leased country estate at the foot of the Dublin mountains.

Father Hagerty had not prepared Ned for its beauty.

The sidecar passed between a pair of granite pillars pierced by arched gateways. "The Hermitage" was carved on the pillars, but the open gates themselves bore the proud blazon "Scoil Eanna." Beyond them a graveled drive canopied with ancient trees curved gently to the left. The horse trotted up the drive between borders of flowering shrubs and dense green laurel. Birdsong competed with the crunch of wheels on gravel. From somewhere nearby came the sound of boys shouting and laughing at some game on the grassy lawns.

Ned caught his breath at the sight of the house. It stood three stories high, a square, perfectly proportioned eighteenth-century country mansion built of granite, with a classical portico supported by massive Grecian columns. Low curving walls extended from either side like embracing arms to define the graveled forecourt. The overall impression was of solemn elegance gilded by the autumn sun.

"I'm to live *here*?" the boy whispered in disbelief.

The horse had barely halted when the tall double doors opened and a slight young man with flowing hair came hurrying down the steps. "Welcome to Saint Enda's! You must be our new lad from Clare."

Ned felt suddenly shy. "I am from Clare," he said through dry lips. "My name is—"

"Edward Halloran, of course you are. And I am William; the boys call me Willie. Willie Pearse, resident art and drawing master."

"I was told to present myself to Mr. Patrick Pearse."

"Pawd-rig?" He gave the name its Irish pronunciation, a fact not lost on Ned. "He's inside. Is that your luggage? Let's have it then, and come on."

Willie Pearse waved the coachman aside and lifted Ned's case out of the sidecar himself, talking all the while. "We have fifty boys here now, more or less. All boarders; we lost our day pupils when we moved out of the city. But it was worth it for the air and the views, would you not agree? You'll be in the Senior School, of course. There's Junior and Infants as well, and we used to have a girls' school, Saint Ita's, but unfortunately the economics—" He interrupted himself to dismiss the coachman with a few courteous words, then led Ned up the broad steps.

A comfortable-bosomed woman with gray hair was standing just inside the fanlighted doorway. "I'm Mrs. Pearse," she said with a smile so warm Ned forgot his shyness and smiled back. "I'm the headmaster's mother. Come in; he's waiting for you in his study. You can leave your case with me and I'll have it carried up to your dormitory."

Ned stepped into a square, bright entrance hall. There was no furniture aside from a table and a coatrack. Facing the front doorway was a tiled fireplace with a large painting hanging above, depicting a radiant child with arms extended to either side.

Willie knocked at a righthand door, then beckoned Ned to enter.

The study was a handsome, high-ceilinged room lit by casement windows framing views of the forecourt and surrounding gardens. Books were everywhere, overflowing bookcases, stacked to a precarious height on tables, heaped on windowsills. The air smelled of leather and ink. As Ned came through the doorway Pádraic Pearse, Headmaster of Saint Enda's, rose from behind a desk piled high with more books. Removing the pince-nez he used for reading, he came forward to greet his new pupil.[1]

Pearse was taller than average and well built, though beginning to develop the softness around the middle common to men in sedentary occupations. He wore a black academic's gown over a black broadcloth suit, which made him seem older than his thirty-three years. He had a broad forehead, a rounded jaw, and deep, profound eyes with a slight cast in one.

Ned hardly noticed the blemish. The eyes themselves held him transfixed.

"*Failte romhat go Scoil Eanna,*" said the headmaster, holding out his hand.

Ned's face burned crimson. "My Irish isn't very good, sir."

"We shall remedy that," Pearse promised with a kindly

smile. "I just said, 'Welcome to Saint Enda's.' In a few weeks you too will be able to converse in your native tongue. You need not worry about understanding what is said to you in the meantime, however; we don't use Irish exclusively. We are a bilingual school because Ireland has two vernacular languages.[2] We believe Irish should be central to the education of an Irish person, however, so most lessons are given through that medium. We share with the Gaelic League the conviction that language defines a people. Are you familiar with the Gaelic League, Ned?"

Thanks to Father Hagerty, he was able to answer, "The league was founded around the turn of the century to preserve the Irish language. The Christian Brothers teach some Irish in their schools, but I went to a National School."

"Where your native language was never mentioned," Pearse rightly concluded. "Did you know that your parish priest wrote me your letter of reference in Irish?"

Ned stared down at his shoes. "I didn't know that, sir."

"Nothing to be ashamed of," Pearse said brusquely. "Look up. Be proud. The Irish are a separate and distinct race with a right to their own language and customs. Both have developed over two thousand years and reflect the Celtic, rather than the Saxon, character."

Pearse's formal phraseology was that of an educated man who demanded precision of himself. He spoke slowly and with a measured cadence that made his voice unusually compelling. Only later would Ned learn that these speech habits were the results of a lifelong effort to repress a stutter.

"In addition to teaching Irish," Pearse went on, "at this school we promote an active reverence for the virtues of decency, honesty, fortitude, and kindness. Our philosophy is to encourage gentleness towards the weak and courtesy and charity to all. The only boy ever expelled from Scoil Eanna was guilty of cruelty to a cat. Our goal is the development of decent Irish men who will possess self-reliance and a sense of social duty."

Willie whistled. "Don't give him all that at once, Pat! It's too much for the lad to take in; he'll have mental indigestion.

He can read it later in the prospectus if he likes."[3]

Ned turned from one to the other. There was a marked family resemblance, though Willie's face was longer and narrower, with a sweet, rather melancholy expression.

But it was not Willie who drew Ned like a magnet. All his attention focused on the man with the glowing eyes of a visionary.

Chapter Nine

KATHLEEN looked up as Alexander entered the parlor of their brownstone house off Madison Square, and waved a sheaf of closely written pages at him. "This is from Ned at last!"

"So I see." But Alexander was not looking; he was gazing into the bowl of his pipe with an expression on his face as if he smelled something unpleasant. "It's about time the boy wrote you to apologize for not coming to our wedding."

"He has nothing to apologize for, and I won't hear you say a word against him. He couldn't take so much time from his schooling."

"I was prepared to arrange his passage," Alexander Campbell grumbled. "He simply chose not to come. He doesn't approve of me any more than your parents would have approved of me."

Her eyes flashed. "That's not true, Alexander. Once they got to know you, they would have loved you as I do."

But though they had been married for only two months, already he had some doubts about the nature of her love. Even making allowances for her virginity, the ardor Alexander had expected to awaken in his Irish bride was curiously lacking. He refused to believe Kathleen was cold. Her Irish temper betokened a passionate nature. Yet in his arms in the marriage bed she was docile, obedient—and dull.

Alexander Campbell was a robust man. He wanted more from a woman than mere acquiescence.

Their first real argument since the wedding had not been about sex, however, but about servants. With every good intention, he had engaged an Irish girl, Bridie Lynch, to be his new wife's housemaid. He could hardly have anticipated Kathleen's response.

"I won't have one of my own on her knees in my house, scrubbing my floors."

Alexander had been nonplussed. "But Kate, did you not tell me your mother had an Irish servant girl in her house?"

"That's different. She and her brother are tenants on our farm and pay their rent in labor. In Ireland there's no one to do menial work *but* the Irish. In America, however . . . surely we can find someone else."

"You're being irrational. Everyone we know employs Irish domestics. Immigrant Paddys are honest and hardworking."

"Don't call them that! Am I not an immigrant Paddy, too? You must find someone else, Alexander. Tell Miss Lynch I'm sorry and help her find employment elsewhere."

She could fight, could Kathleen; for a cause. It was only in bed that he found her passive. From the set of her chin he could tell she was prepared to fight now, though Ned was not the issue. Something deeper was involved.

In the sixteen months since the deaths of her parents, Ireland had loomed ever larger in Kathleen's thoughts. She who originally had loved America with the passion of the newly converted was now dreaming of the land she had left behind. She equated it with her own lost innocence, the not-altogether-pleasant change in her life formally marked by her wedding night.

While Alexander watched she bent over her letter again. Her hungry eyes devoured the words as she spread out the pages on a golden oak table in front of the settee. He had furnished the house himself before their wedding. What little Alexander knew about interior design had been acquired through association with transatlantic steamships and leaned toward the ostentatious.

Brown velvet draperies with ball fringe hung at the windows, where the light was further obscured by thick lace curtains. The new electrified chandelier of which Alexander was so proud could barely dispel the gloom. Most of the available floor space was crowded with brocaded settees, upholstered chairs, footstools, tables of various sizes, and a velvet-covered divan with satin pillows, so that a path must be carefully chosen to get from one side of the room to the other. Sentimental paintings of florid children set in heavy gilded frames lined the walls, alternating with equally sentimental lithographs of Newfoundland dogs. The oak table gave pride of place to one of Alexander's favorite ornaments, a large glass dome containing a pair of stuffed mallard ducks that he had shot himself. They stood rigidly amid a spray of lacquered cattails, their lifeless shoe button eyes ignoring the pages of Ned Halloran's letter, spread out beside them.

Kathleen was poring eagerly over her brother's letter. Frank, busy with the farm, was not much of a correspondent, but Ned's words brought Ireland into the room.

Dear Caitlín,

I have now spent almost a full school year at Saint Enda's. I apologize for not writing you a long letter sooner. We are encouraged to write frequent letters home, but the time has flown by since last autumn. At first it was not easy to get back in the habit of school, and I have had to work as hard as I ever worked at plowing or threshing.

Saint Enda's is in a beautiful setting. Lord Inchiquin himself does not have a lovelier one. It's hard to believe all this is for Irish boys. There are almost fifty acres of parkland, with formal gardens, orchards, bridges, grottoes, a dolmen, a miniature stone fort, several meadows, and a wooded glen with a little rushing stream. We go on nature walks in the nearby Dublin mountains, and nature studies such as botany and geology are very much a part of our curriculum. Mr. Pearse says God's creation is our best teacher.

In everyday conversation I speak Irish; we all do. Our main subject is the Irish language as taught through a modern, rather than classical, literary program. We study the English language as well, and read the great writers to improve our vocabulary and usage. My other courses include algebra, Latin, Greek, mathematics, geography, Christian doctrine, both world and Irish history, nature studies, and Irish dancing.

The headmaster's widowed mother is both matron and cook at Saint Enda's. She is a jolly woman who enters into our pranks with good spirit, even when she's not quite certain what we're up to. In many ways she reminds me of Mama. Mrs. Pearse is careful to leave by the door she enters, and I've seen her put out a bowl of milk for the ''Good People'' when she thought no one was looking.

The headmaster's brother, Willie, is a talented sculptor who has exhibited at the Hibernian Academy, and has also been an actor and stage manager at the Dublin School of Art and the Abbey Theatre. In manner he is rather nervous, but he is as staunch as the Cliffs of Moher. He is good at handball, too, and coaches us in a wooden handball court beyond the house.

The physical drill here is very challenging. We concentrate on Gaelic games. I am good at hurling, though not so good as Frank Burke, who is already a national champion. Even in the middle of a hard-fought match, however, we halt at noon and kneel to observe the Angelus. We also have morning and evening prayers in the school chapel, and are never allowed to miss Mass. Mama would be relieved to know my spiritual needs are being taken care of.

In addition to hurling and football, we are taught to fence, box, wrestle, shoot, and swim. In fact, the Saint Enda's pupils have won any number of athletic awards, so you know I am not becoming too bookish! I have grown at least two inches this term, I believe, and gained a stone in weight. When I look in the mirror I hardly know myself.

"Caitlín?" queried Alexander, reading over his wife's shoulder.

"It's the Irish for Kathleen," she said absently. "He's studying Irish now."

Her husband cleared his throat in a way she had learned indicated disapproval. "Ned is a subject of the British Empire; he has no need for another language."

Her eyes flashed again but she said nothing, merely resumed reading her letter:

I'm saving the best till last. The headmaster is a remarkable man. Mr. Pearse took Bachelor of Arts and Bachelor of Law degrees at university and was called to the Bar,[1] though he now professes contempt for lawyers. He writes poetry and plays and short stories, his articles on education are very well received, and he edits both Gaelic and literary journals. Added to that, he is surely the gentlest, most patient man I have ever met. His family simply dotes upon him.

At first I thought him austere, but much of that is shyness and the fact that he is always so busy. He is forever seeking ways to enrich our minds. Many of the subjects we study are not part of ordinary schooling at all. For example, we are learning to grow fruit and vegetables, and to make tools, and how a house is built—we're constructing small scale models and even weaving fabric for the drapes and carpet.[2] Most of all, we are learning to think and to have confidence in ourselves. Mr. Pearse says instilling his pupils with moral courage and personal integrity is the best way to prepare them for life.

We boys admire him tremendously. "Live up to your finest self," he tells us, and takes for granted that we will. So we make our best effort for his sake. He is very fair and shows no favoritism, yet manages to make each

of us feel that he is special. I have never known a teacher
to be so well-liked by all his students.

Well, not quite all. There are a couple of "bold boys"
here who do not like him. (And isn't it odd that when
we say "bold" in Ireland we mean "naughty," but when
Americans say "bold" they mean "brave"? I wonder
why they are the sort of lads who do not like anyone
who makes them work hard. They only want to show off
and cause mischief. I used to be a bit like that myself,
but not anymore, I think.

In reply Kathleen wrote:

Thank you, my darling boy, for your good letter. Already
your education shows! I have taken so long to answer
because every thought of Ireland fills me with longing.
If I had known I would be so homesick, I might never
have come here.

It was safe to write such sentiments to Ned. He was three
thousand miles away.

Of course, I love America. [She hastened to assure her
brother:] This is a splendid country, full of opportunity.
An Irish man who lives just next door to us has recently
become an alderman, which carries much responsibility
in New York City. Anything is possible for us here.

Yet I miss Ireland in the most desperate way, Ned.
Ever since Mama and Papa died my thoughts have been
full of home, and of the family and friends I left behind.

Last night I dreamed of dancing. Not the formal Irish
dancing you are learning at Saint Enda's, but the way
we used to dance at the crossroads, the lads coming with
fresh-scrubbed faces to meet the girls and everyone shy
and laughing at the same time. I can almost hear the
fiddle once more, and taste the sweet dust of the road in
my throat. How the priests disapproved! They called it a
sin, those dry old men. But it was no sin, Ned. It was

joyous, innocent fun, and there is little enough of that in the world.

Do write again soon and let me know what you are doing, and that you are happy.

Ned answered her letter with more descriptions of his life at Saint Enda's:

There is a wonderful big study hall almost like a theater, with a fireplace set at the back of an elevated stage where we perform plays. At one end are the doors to the school's own oratory, which has leaded windows set with stained glass. One or another of the staff and students can often be found praying there. The atmosphere is so peaceful.

Six classrooms and the refectory are in a separate building, which is connected to the house by a covered veranda. The dormitories are in the house itself and are named for Irish saints. I am in Saint Brendan's, which is encouraging me to study all about him and his voyage to America. My bed is narrow and quite hard, and the room is cold. Mr. Pearse says we need to be hardy. Some of the Dublin boys complain a lot, but I don't. Down the country we are used to unheated bedrooms.

The views from the windows are magnificent. To the east is the sea, with Howth and Ireland's Eye, and on the other side of the house are the mountains with Three Rocks and the Hellfire Club. I would like to know more about the Hellfire Club but nobody will talk about it. It must be very wicked.

Ned's letters expressed a deep and growing happiness. The Saint Enda's philosophy made learning a privilege rather than an obligation, and cherished the boyhood in students while developing the manhood. Every fortnight a *céili* was held after the last class of the day. These were a combination of informal concert and dancing exhibition, giving the students a chance to demonstrate their skills. Debates, which usually took place around the stove in the refectory, were also a much-enjoyed feature.

Ned's special delight was in playing parts in school theatricals. Under Willie Pearse's direction, mythic figures from the Irish past such as Cuchulain and Fionn MacCumhaill were brought to life. The performances were fund-raisers for the school, which was always in need of additional finance. But there was more to be gained from the dramas.

"We are made to feel," Ned wrote Kathleen, "that the achievements of noble heroes are not beyond our own abilities, but are an inherent part of our heritage. As I stood on that stage, Caitlín, I felt as if I *was* one of the Fíanna. I was not acting; I was *living.*"

Closing her eyes for a moment, Kathleen saw Ned in the costume of another time, a young warrior with his sword and his spear and a bright light shining on him. He stood alone on a stage above a sea of people, and there was something extraordinarily proud and joyous in his face.

"Mr. Pearse says we are to concentrate on becoming good men rather than learned men," Ned's letter continued. "But he also means us to be truly educated rather than merely qualified to pass examinations. That is a very important distinction, which I am beginning to appreciate. I ask a lot of questions, but he never seems to mind; he encourages them. The headmaster is slow to chastise but quick to praise and treats us all with respect and dignity."

Kathleen put down the letter and gazed thoughtfully into space. Respect. Dignity. Was that not what she—and so many others—had hoped to find in America? Even for the daughter of a strong farmer, respect from the British ruling class was in short supply in Ireland. Only the Anglo-Irish were accorded any measure of dignity, though she suspected that was begrudged. She recalled her father relating a comment Lord Inchiquin had once made to him: "In Ireland I am resented as English, while in England I am looked down upon as Irish."

In refusing to employ an Irish servant, Kathleen instinctively was rejecting the centuries-old assault on Irish dignity. She would have liked to explain this to Alexander, but he had no interest in philosophical conversations. He had married her for her beauty. She was to be an ornament to his life and his house; for intellectual companionship he looked elsewhere.

From the earliest days of their marriage he had absented himself two nights a week, Tuesdays and Fridays, returning very late and reeking of cigar smoke. When she inquired where he went he simply replied, ''Out, my dear. I have business.''

At first Kathleen accepted this with no further question. Business was, after all, part of that male world from which women were excluded in order to protect them from the harsher realities of life. Then a casual comment revealed certain ''meetings'' that Alexander attended; meetings of a society to which he belonged. An all-male society, of course. And so secret he did not even tell her its name.

In Ireland such meetings could have only one purpose— political.

The Halloran home had been apolitical, carefully occupying neutral ground between Lord Inchiquin's anglicized views and those of the simmering rebel element in Clare. The 1903 Land Act, which had allowed Patrick Halloran and others like him to buy their holdings from the landlords by a system of annuities, had not overcome the ancient bitterness that festered in the county and was exacerbated by undying memories of the Famine.

While the Hallorans had not converted to Protestantism, they had otherwise done whatever they could to guarantee a future for themselves, just as Lord Inchiquin's family had once secured its own future by espousing the English cause against the Gaelic Irish. In a poor country, such accommodations were a matter of survival.

But there were many in Clare who would never be able to accept that their land was a vassal state governed by a foreign power. The demand for Home Rule continued to grow. Its advocates insisted the Irish should be allowed to govern themselves in their own country. Moderates would be willing to settle for having an autonomous Irish parliament functioning as a respected partner in the British Empire. Nationalists argued that Ireland herself must belong to the Irish, must be free and independent as she had not been since the twelfth century.

There were a lot of nationalists in Clare.

Kathleen's father had never attended the meetings held in back rooms and barns where such matters were discussed. If he was aware of them he never mentioned them at home. Yet somehow his family had known. Everyone in Clare knew.

The longing for freedom was like fine pollen blown on the wind. Though unremarked, it pervaded the atmosphere of the county. Secret societies flourished. Names like the Fenians were mentioned in a whisper.

Now Kathleen had learned that her own husband belonged to a secret society in America. It must be dangerous, she reasoned, else why would it be secret? She began to imagine her husband being brought home to her injured—or worse. Such things had happened in Ireland.

But when she tried to talk to Alexander he brushed her aside.

"You've no need to concern yourself, Kate, with matters you could not possibly understand. I assure you I am perfectly safe; this is not your barbarous Ireland. Forget your foolish imaginings. Soon, I trust, you will have a family to keep you occupied and can devote yourself to those things which are appropriate for women."

He smiled at her but she did not smile back. She was annoyed for two reasons. In Ireland women deferred to their husbands in public, but within the walls of the home the real power lay with them. She would not have Alexander dismiss her so casually. And she resented the fact that, in spite of her protests, he continued to call her by a nickname she disliked. Yet he insisted that his full Christian name be used even in their most intimate moments.

She raised the issue of his meetings again and was denied again. Her frustration grew. The couple began bickering, at first playfully, then with increasing rancor. Alexander was determined not to lose control of his wife, and annoyed that she was more inclined to spend her passion on domestic arguments than in bed.

Kathleen began to feel the need of more than a confidante in Ireland. She required an ally closer to hand.

Chapter Ten

I don't want to make my husband angry, but I am worried about him," Kathleen admitted to the priest from Saint Xavier's, the Roman Catholic church four blocks from their house. Before their wedding Alexander had agreed that any children would be raised in the Catholic faith. Yet she was increasingly aware of his silent disapproval of her religion. Going to Mass had become almost an act of defiance. Fortunately, she liked Saint Xavier's; it was very much a neighborhood church in a neighborhood that had few Catholics.

It made her think of home.

"Have you learned the name of this secret society he belongs to?" Father Paul asked as she sat with him in the parlor of the presbytery. He thought the church dark and rather gloomy at the best of times, so he encouraged parishioners to speak of their problems in the more relaxed atmosphere of the priests' residence.

At that moment the housekeeper appeared carrying a tray with hot coffee and tiny cakes arranged on a lace doily. Kathleen took a cup of coffee and a cherry cake, then waited until the woman left the room. "Freemasons."

The priest inhaled sharply.

Father Paul was a lean, well-proportioned man in his thirties. In dramatic contrast to his fair hair he had dark, swooping

eyebrows like ravens' wings. A second-generation Irish-
American, he was the sort of man of whom women said,
''What a pity he's a priest!'' But if celibacy weighed heavily
upon him he gave no indication.

''Are you certain your husband's a Freemason, Kathleen?''

''I am, though he didn't tell me.''

''Then how did you find out?''

''From my next-door neighbor, Alderman Claffey's wife.
She thought I already knew. She said I should be glad Alexander is a Freemason because they support one another po-
litically; that's how her husband became an alderman. She
gave the impression that it was almost like joining a church.
I believe there are Freemasons in Ireland, though I know nothing about them.''

Father Paul's blue eyes darkened as if someone had turned
off a light behind them. ''In spite of its arcane philosophy
and symbolism, Freemasonry is not a religious institution.
Most Masons are strongly Protestant, however. I must tell
you, the church does not approve of Freemasonry. Pope Clem-
ent banned the society in the eighteenth century for being anti-
papist, but it has continued to flourish.''

''Is it dangerous? To my husband, I mean?''

''Not dangerous in the physical sense. Is that what you
were worried about?''

She nodded.

''Then I can put your mind at ease on that score.'' When
Father Paul smiled, the ravens' wing eyebrows lifted and his
eyes sparkled. Kathleen found herself smiling back at him, a
smile so radiant the priest caught his breath.

Leaning forward, he put his hand over hers. It was intended
merely as a solicitous gesture, but a vein suddenly began
throbbing above his temple.

Kathleen could not help noticing.

Like every good Irish girl of her time, she had come to her
marriage bed a virgin. Alexander had done nothing to awaken
her. Her husband was vigorous but single-minded. When in
the throes of passion he seemed barely aware of her except
as a stimulus and receptacle. Afterward, he acted almost em-

barrassed, turning away and falling asleep without speaking.
Always with his back to her.

In the intense gaze of Father Paul she read hints of a far
different nature, tightly held in check but simmering beneath
the surface.

When she left Saint Xavier's she walked for a long time
before returning to the brownstone. Only two years before she
had thought herself the luckiest girl alive. A devoted fiancé,
a new home in America, prosperity and a bright future; how
wonderful those things had seemed from the outside.

Now she was inside, and nothing was as it had appeared.
And Alexander was talking about a family. Was she ready for
babies, ready to lose herself in the nursery and the endless
rounds of pram pushing and talking with other young mothers
about colic and teething?

In Ireland she would have accepted such a life as inevitable.
But there was something different in the air in America, a
sense of possibilities even for a woman.

Her heels pounding against the pavement, Kathleen scolded
herself for being ungrateful. She had so much by comparison
to women her age back home in Ireland. Why was it not
enough? If she voiced her reservations about motherhood to
her priest, what would he say?

Why did Father Paul's touch disturb her so?

In her next letter to her brother at Saint Enda's, Kathleen
sought to reveal nothing of her personal feelings. Ned occupied a world that seemed far distant now, receding into mist
and memory.

She wrote:

My dear brother, I hope everything is well at home.
Frank is a hopeless correspondent, and Norah is far too
busy to put pen to paper, though I write her regularly. I
rely on you to keep in touch with them and let me know
if there is anything they or the girls need. Times are
always hard in Ireland, I know.

Oh, Ned, I do wish you were here, and I'm not just
being selfish. Under the circumstances you had no

chance to appreciate America on your first visit, but this is the best possible place for young people. Anyone who wants to can find work, I am told. There is so much to do, concerts and museums and various other entertainments available every day of the week. It's a far cry from home and a Saturday night *seisún* in someone's parlor with local boys playing tin whistles and a fiddle.

You say you are developing a fondness for theater. If you were in New York now I could take you to see Laurette Taylor in a play called *Peg O' My Heart,* which has received glowing reviews in the papers. Or we could go to the Astor Theater. An eight-reel motion picture called *Quo Vadis* is showing there to capacity crowds. Just imagine! I would love to see it, but of course a lady cannot go without an escort, and Alexander is not interested in such fads.

When he read Kathleen's letter Ned thought it sounded a bit too wistful, as if she was trying hard to convince herself how wonderful everything was.

July 15, 1913

IRISH HOME RULE BILL AGAIN DEFEATED IN HOUSE OF LORDS, 302–64.

Chapter Eleven

IN his narrow dormitory bed at Saint Enda's, Ned dreamed of the *Titanic*—not as he had last seen her, broken and dying, but as she had first appeared to him, a sovereign of the seas, dynamic and complete, offering everything a human might require.

She had seemed invulnerable then.

As he ran down the hurling field with the *camán* in his hands and his teammates in their white jerseys and knickers shouting encouragement, he would have a sudden, flashing memory of the deck games aboard the *Titanic*. Passengers laughing and carefree in their sporting togs.

The dark sea waiting.

ONCE he got over his initial shyness Ned had no difficulty making friends at Saint Enda's. He did not talk much about himself for fear of uncovering memories he could not bear to face. But he listened to others with a flattering intensity of interest that soon made him popular with students and staff alike. Even the headmaster's busy mother found time to reminisce with him.

Margaret Brady Pearse did not see her elder son as an authority figure. To her he was still the little boy who shyly brought her flowers every May Day. "Pat was such a grave, sweet child," she told Ned.[1] "But he had a hot temper, too; he would not be laughed at or tolerate bullying. From the beginning Willie idolized him and wanted to do everything his older brother did. They're still devoted to each other, you know. Pat would kill for Willie and Willie feels the same about him.

"When Pat was old enough we sent him to the Christian Brothers' school because it was the best education we could get for him. The brothers had a reputation for preparing students for the Intermediate examination no matter what it took. Everyone knew they could be brutal to boys, though, and I worried for Pat. But one of his teachers, Brother Maunsell, was a native Irish speaker from County Kerry,[2] and once Pat started studying Irish he was happy enough. He always loved the hero tales."

"So did I!" exclaimed Ned. "When I was haying in the fields I used to pretend I was Cuchulain attacking Maeve's warriors with the scythe."

Mrs. Pearse said, "My boys never worked in the fields; they are city boys, born and bred. Their late father—he was an Englishman, you know—was a fine sculptor. The churches 'round the city competed for his stonework. He provided well for us, though since his death we have put all our money into Pat's school. Yet I suppose the Irish love for the land is in the blood."

"Were your people farmers?"

She shook her head. "Not at all. Both my parents were Dublin born. My grandfather farmed, but he had to move to the city during the Famine. His sons drove hackney cabs here, and his daughters went into service. When I married James Pearse—he was a widower, and a good catch—I was living in a tenement near the North Strand. Now we're surrounded by fields and woods, and Pat even keeps a tiny cottage in Connemara to be closer to what he calls 'the real Ireland.' "

Ned laughed at the irony. "And to think, I came up to the city to get away from the real Ireland!"

• • •

In the classroom Ned devoured knowledge as if making up for lost time. Sometimes he crept from his bed after the other boys in his dormitory were asleep and, with a paraffin lamp in his hand, made his way to the inner hall to sit hunched over his books until dawn streaked the eastern sky.

With amazement he read of the wealth of natural resources Ireland had once possessed, the lure that had brought the looters.

All gone now. Taken away, with only the potato as recompense.

At one time the Irish had been forbidden by English law to educate their children, to own a horse worth more than five pounds, to play the Irish pipes, to wear the color green . . . the list went on and on. Most of the oppressive statutes were no longer enforced, but the shamed submission they had engendered remained.

Ned's initial surprise at Ireland's former prosperity became a sense of outrage over her humiliation. He studied more, worked harder, strove to understand what had happened to this land, this people.

Ned's scholastic progress was duly reported to Robert Beauchamp. "The boy appears to have a good mind," the solicitor grudgingly admitted in a letter to Lord Inchiquin. "He may make something of himself some day—within certain limitations, of course."

In fine weather lessons were taught in the open air after the custom of the Socratic school.[3] The teachers assembled the boys around them on the grassy lawn and stood to lecture, or sat among their pupils for more informal discussion. At first Ned was homesick for the rolling fields of Clare, the Atlantic wind as reliable as a shoulder to lean upon, the wide high sky. He hated being shut up in the classroom, and was thankful that Pádraic Pearse gave his young charges all he could of sun, wind, freedom.

That was a word often spoken at Saint Enda's. *Saoirse.* Freedom.

The Hermitage was both school and family home. The Pearses were close-knit and loving, with pet names for one another. Family and friends referred to Pádraic simply as "Pat." But Mrs. Pearse called Willie "Little Man," and her elder daughter, Margaret, was nicknamed "Wow-wow."

Sensible, reliable Margaret ran the preparatory school and taught Junior French. Her younger sister, the temperamental Mary Brigid, assisted Thomas MacDonnell, the resident music and dancing master. One of the Brady cousins also helped at the school, and other teachers were recruited through the Gaelic League. Even so, there was a perpetual shortage of staff, and senior boys were called upon to supervise the younger ones.

Discipline was no problem. As Ned wrote to Kathleen:

At Saint Enda's we boys are on our honor. We are not spied upon. If a boy misbehaves he is called to the head-master's study and given to understand that he has done something shabby; he has let down Mr. Pearse as well as himself. A reproachful glance from the headmaster can hurt worse than a caning.

Until I came to Saint Enda's I thought being beaten was a normal part of education. In the National School I had my share of the cane, the strap, and the ash plant. It seemed as if I was the one who always got caught.

But other boys have suffered worse. A couple of the lads in my dormitory here still have nightmares from treatment they endured in Christian Brothers' schools. One will go to his grave with terrible scars across his back.

There is nothing like that at Saint Enda's. Corporal punishment is very rare, and always mild.[4] Mr. Pearse knows boys are full of mischief, but he has such faith in our inherent (I just learned that word) decency that we strive to live up to that ideal, and for the most part we do.

He gave no details of his own first encounter with Saint Enda's discipline. One of the "bold" Dublin boys had smuggled a dozen cigarettes into the school, and Ned and his friend Brian Joyce were among those who sneaked out into the woods to try them. The smuggler lit up and inhaled with ostentatious pleasure. The other boys watched enviously as he blew smoke rings. His eyes dared them to join him. Brian hesitated, but Ned lit a cigarette as if he had been smoking for years, and took a deep drag.

He thought he would die.

Someone was ripping out his lungs and setting them on fire. He could feel Brian pounding him on the back, but it did not help. He managed to get back to the house, only to have his half-digested breakfast come boiling up into his mouth and spew out right in front of Margaret Pearse.

I'm the one who always gets caught, he thought bitterly.

Soon he was facing Pádraic Pearse across the headmaster's desk, trying to ignore the smell of vomit still clinging to his clothes. Pearse shook his head reproachfully. "Ned, Ned. I thought better of you than this."

The embarrassment of that encounter would stay with him a lifetime. He had only to smell tobacco smoke to bring it all back.

LIKE his ideals, Pearse's enthusiasms were infectious. When he lectured a class, speaking in either English or Irish and swaying gently from side to side as was his habit, he held his listeners transfixed.

"In this very room," Pearse would say, gazing into the past with his visionary's eyes, "young Robert Emmet often sat. Perhaps with his elbow propped on that windowsill. In our walled garden is a vine from which he plucked grapes. You boys eat grapes from the same still-living vine. Emmet and his sweetheart, Sarah Curran, walked together beneath our trees. Her favorite horse is buried in these very grounds.[5] Here she and Emmet shared their joys and sorrows and pledged

their troth. If you exercise your imaginations you might catch
a glimpse of them still.''

Brian Joyce leaned toward Ned and whispered behind his
hand, ''Did you know the headmaster had a sweetheart
once?[6] She was a university student who drowned. Mary Brigid told me—she thought it was aw'fly romantic. The headmaster wrote a poem that goes: 'In love I got but grief that
withered my life.'[7] When he talks about Robert Emmet and
Sarah Curran I think he's remembering his own—''

Pearse frowned at the whispering boy, and Brian slumped
into his seat with a contrite expression. The lecture continued.
''Emmet was hanged by the British as a rebel, but in truth he
was a patriot who gave his life for his native land.''

As the months passed, Pearse and a variety of guest lec-
turers painted an increasingly alluring vision of an Ireland
restored and invigorated by its heroes.[8]

A sovereign nation, dynamic and complete, offering everything a human might require.

On the last Sunday in August, Ned decided to explore Dublin. Like many Irish people, the Pearse family routinely used
bicycles for transportation. Ned did not have a bicycle, so
after early Mass he walked into Rathfarnham and caught a
tram. The day was overcast, with a strange hard brightness
behind the clouds. Since there was no rain Ned rode on the
upper deck to enjoy the view.

He got off the tram at Nelson's Pillar, a towering column
surmounted by a statue of the British naval hero gazing im-
periously down the broad, cobbled boulevard of Sackville
Street. The Pillar shared the boulevard with the Parnell Monument at the top of the street and the O'Connell Monument
at its foot, but it was Nelson who dominated. His pillar was
the hub of Dublin's tramway traffic. On this morning, however, there was only a line of horse-drawn cabs and one or
two motor cabs waiting for fares.

Ned tilted his head back to look up at Lord Nelson. The
admiral ignored him. From a sea of fruit stalls at the foot of
the Pillar women shouted the praises of apples and oranges
and greengage plums. One of the fruit stall women caught

Ned's eye and made a rude gesture in the direction of the statue.

With only the vaguest of ideas where he was going, Ned set out to find 16 Middle Gardiner Street. He ambled along, stealing glimpses of himself reflected in shop windows. Splintered images of a lanky figure in a tweed jacket and cap. A young man of the city? Or a country boy trying to look as if he belonged?

It was no good asking directions in a pub; none were open on Sunday morning. But eventually he found his way, more by chance than design, to the cross at Summerhill, then left into Middle Gardiner Street. There he narrowly avoided being knocked down by a Guinness dray pulled by a huge team of Clydesdale horses. The drayman in his bowler hat cursed Ned and the horses impartially.

Number 16 was a double-fronted Georgian house built of red brick, five bays wide but only one room deep. The front door was surmounted by an ornate plaster relief, with lights to either side patterned with oval and diamond panes. An abundantly fleshed woman with a Limerick accent replied to Ned's knock, looked him up and down as if he were a chicken to be plucked, then led him to a reception room off the front hall. "Wait here while I see if Mr. Mooney is in."

Ned surveyed the parlor with interest. Though the horsehair upholstery had seen better days, gaslight fixtures and coal in the scuttle by the hearth promised comfort.

Ned was standing with his head cocked to one side reading the spines of books on a row of shelves when Henry Mooney entered the room.

"My young friend! How good of you to remember me. I thought you'd go back to Clare for your holidays. What brings you here?"

Ned took him literally. "I came in on the Rathfarnham tram, sir. As for Clare, I'm stopping at Saint Enda's this summer instead. Because of my farming experience Mr. Pearse asked me to stay on and help the head gardener. Michael MacRory's a native speaker, so working with him will improve my Irish. I mow fields, mend walls, that sort of thing—

but not on Sunday, of course. If it's not too late, sir, I'd like to accept your offer of a tour of Dublin."

He did not mention how his heart yearned for Atlantic sunsets and the hills of Clare. Yet after the decision to stay the summer was made, he had been strangely relieved. He could not imagine the farm without his parents; returning would have meant confronting ghosts.

Mooney grinned. "Say no more. I'm delighted you're here; by a happy coincidence I had nothing planned for this afternoon. And forget about 'sir,' you're to call me Henry from now on. Are we not fellow west-of-Ireland men?

"You were lucky to find a tram running, you know. Since Tuesday morning most of the drivers and conductors have been out on strike. There was a riot just yesterday and a police baton charge on Eden Quay. Of course, this is Horse Show Week, which is the height of the Dublin social season, and that only makes matters worse. The union chose its time well."

"Union?"

"I.T.G.W.U. The Irish Transport and General Workers Union, to you and me. But you didn't come to Dublin to talk politics today, did you? Let's go have a look at the city."

Henry ushered him back toward the front door, pausing only to select a cap from the hat rack. As the two men set out through the streets Ned asked, "Do you not go home yourself in the summer, s—uh, Henry? Do you not visit your mother? I recall you said she's a widow."

Henry gave a mocking laugh. "Visit my mother? Not if I can avoid it. She has my younger brothers and sisters to keep her company; they all live within a hare's leap of her—except for me. I'm the lucky fellow who got away."

Ned smiled, uncertain if this was a joke. "You don't mean that."

"Indeed I do. My mother and I have no real feeling for one another, though she would never admit it. Mam's a perfect example of the middle-class Irish, pinioned between English Victorian manners and Irish Catholic morality. She sends me weekly letters meant to make me feel guilty for my

dereliction of duty to her saintly self. But duty's not a sub-
stitute for love and my mother's not the Virgin Mary. Women
aren't, you know. They're just human beings.''

Ned was staring at him. Henry chuckled. ''Surprised you,
didn't I? Well, it's the truth. And I'll tell you another. Holy
Mother Church is not as perfect as she pretends to be, either.
As a newspaper reporter, I've seen enough to convince me
that this country of ours suffers no more from the British than
from a repressive Catholic morality that owes little to Christian compassion.''

Ned was so shocked he could think of nothing to say.

They walked through a typical Dublin streetscape. In front
of a handsome Georgian residence a little girl in a taffeta dress
and starched petticoats was rolling a hoop. Her shining ring-
lets were held with a freshly ironed ribbon, and her face was
rosy with health. A nanny in a starched cap glanced out the
window, keeping a fond eye on her charge.

In a service laneway beyond the house two ragged boys
were amusing themselves by slinging a dead pigeon in large
circles on a bit of twine. They could not have been more than
eight or ten years old, yet they had old men's faces. Their
clothes were an odd admixture of hand-me-down male and
female clothing. Their filthy feet were bare, their ankles
scarred with rat bites.

When they saw Ned and Henry watching, the larger one
made a rude gesture and shouted, ''Wot yiz gawpin' at? Pick
yer nose and eat boogers!'' Both boys cackled with laughter.

Henry remarked, ''They're lucky they have a dead bird to
play with; many children have less. I just wrote an article on
Dublin's poor for the *Irish Independent*. They published it
without a byline, but it won't make much difference. No one
wants to know.''

''I'd like to know,'' said Ned, as always an eager audience.

''To begin with—behind the homes of the gentry is another
world entirely. Look down that alley, lad. What do you see?
Smashed windows, a wall collapsing, part of a roof gone.
Desperately overcrowded tenements in shocking disrepair.
Dublin's slums are the worst in Europe for a city of its size.

Tuberculosis is endemic, not to mention typhus.

"A third of the population of Dublin is seriously malnour-
ished. In the worst tenements two tiers of people share one
bed. The first ones in lie on a filthy mattress if they're lucky
enough to have one, or on bare boards. Then a scrap of blanket is thrown over them and another layer of people sleeps
on top. The first person awake in the morning throws his
shoes ahead of him to frighten the rats away.

"The only water source is an outside pump. There may be
a common toilet in the yard, though many families must rely
on an overflowing cesspit. Dublin Corporation boasts of the
city's modern water-drainage system, but it's not available to
tenement dwellers. Meanwhile, the Irish poor are condemned
as filthy by the very people who keep them in such conditions.

"These people are always cold; always hungry. They have
no childhood—you saw those boys in the alley. They'll be
men at twelve and old at thirty. They will neither know nor
care what is going on beyond their own miserable hovels.
Everything is sacrificed in the struggle to live. Mind, heart,
and soul become concentrated in the starving belly.

"Dublin's working-class neighborhoods are literally ruins
and rubble, Ned. I could show you places in Linenhall Street
or Chancery Street that look like a war's been fought there,
and so it has. A war on poverty, long since lost."

Henry's words chilled Ned. Poverty was the most degrad-
ing sin. The worst victims of the Great Famine had been the
poorest peasants, those already forced to bare subsistence before the potato blight struck. An inarticulated shame lingered
among the people of Ireland from those terrible years, as if
their holocaust were their own fault. Had not the English repeatedly characterized them as lazy and improvident?

Pauper had become a pejorative in Ireland. Ned recalled
that the most dreaded place in Clare was not the cemetery but
the poorhouse.

"Do the tenements belong to foreign landlords, Henry?"

The journalist snorted. "Many of them do, but not all by
any means. A recent investigation showed that sixteen members of Dublin Corporation—that's the body entrusted with

the maintenance and improvement of the city—privately own eighty-nine tenements among them.⁹ They're profiting from the very slums they're supposed to clean up."

"Who lives in the slums?"

"The working-class Irish; unskilled laborers, for the most part. What you might call the urban peasantry. Porters, dockers, tramway workers, street menders, men who shovel coal or sluice down abattoirs. Women who work at the Jacobs' Biscuit factory. Deserted wives and children, widows who take in washing. Servants who work for the gentry but don't 'live in.' There's a sprinkling of struggling artisans as well, plus any number of drunks and rogues and layabouts. And prostitutes, of course."

"Prostitutes?"

Henry Mooney gave Ned an amused glance. "Have you not heard of prostitutes in the rarefied climes of Saint Enda's?"

Ned's cheeks burned with embarrassment. "Of course I have," he mumbled.

Senior boys occasionally whispered among themselves, but no one knew very much. The slightest reference to vulgarity or lasciviousness disgusted Pearse, to whom purity was a by-word. Though a few of the bolder lads speculated as to whether the headmaster and his dead sweetheart had ever been intimate, the consensus was that they had not. Pádraic Pearse's reverence for women was excessive.

Excessive but not unique. In rural Ireland, many a man went to his grave a virgin.

Secretly Ned prayed that would not be his fate.

"Monto lies that way," Henry said with a nod of his head. "The brothel district. Not eight minutes' walk from where we stand. It's roughly a triangle called after Montgomery Street, once known as World's End Lane.¹⁰ Dublin Corpo's been trying to clear it out for years, even renaming some of the streets to improve their reputation. But they can't erase Monto. The good people of Dublin prefer having their vice confined to one area, so they can pretend it doesn't exist, rather than spread throughout the city. Monto's said to be one of the most dissolute spots in Europe.

"At first customers were mostly British navvies coming in to Dublin port, but now businessmen and shopkeepers and even students go there. The higher-class kips—that's the local name for brothels—are patronized by politicians and gentry who arrive after dark in curtained motorcars."

Ned wanted to know more but was too embarrassed to ask. Henry understood. His own first visit to Monto was clearly etched in his memory.

"How old are you, Ned?"

"Sixteen . . . just."

"Almost a man, then. You could fight in a war."

"I could." Ned's eyes flashed as he recalled the headmaster telling his boys how they might one day fight for Ireland.

"When you're seventeen I shall take you to Monto myself. The girls who work there call it the Village.[11] I know the best places, the flash houses."

"You do?" Ned exclaimed, then reddened again.

Henry laughed. "It's part of a man's education in this city. But in the meantime there are other sights to see."

He guided Ned back to Sackville Street. The boulevard was more crowded than when Ned had first arrived, with a number of Dublin Metropolitan Police in their dark blue uniforms. The policemen were invariably Irish and invariably large, being chosen for towering height and a muscular physique. Armed only with regulation wooden batons, the men of the DMP were a familiar part of the city scene.

Henry was saying, "This is the heart of Dublin. Sackville Street is, of course, an Ascendancy name. It's been officially changed to O'Connell Street, but no one calls it that. See the monuments? Whose is tallest? Parnell and O'Connell were Irish; it's the English Lord Nelson who gets the Pillar."

A muscle tightened with indignation in Ned's jaw.

"Or consider the General Post Office down there," Henry went on, indicating a massive building beyond Nelson's Pillar. "Classical Palladian design with Ionic columns; nothing remotely indigenous. The only concession to Ireland is the name of one of the statues over the portico: Hibernia. The other two are supposed to represent Fidelity and Mercury. Although I must say, Mercury with his wingéd heels is a bit aspirational for our postal service."

Ned was showing more enthusiasm for the wares at a nearby street bookstall. Observing the object of his interest, Henry asked, "Do you like poetry, Ned?"

"I do like poetry, very much." He lingered over, then regretfully put back, a slim volume. "I can't afford this, though. Lord Inchiquin gives me a bit of pocket money, but he hasn't sent my allowance for this quarter yet."

Henry promptly purchased *The Golden Joy* by Thomas MacDonagh for himself. "This book is by one of the men who founded *The Irish Review*. I thought all copies of it had been destroyed, so finding one is like finding treasure."

"I actually know Mr. MacDonagh, Henry. He used to teach Irish and literature at Saint Enda's, and he still comes back to visit."

"How would you describe him?"

"He's a friendly, amiable little man. I've heard that he can be a severe critic but he's passionate about the things he believes in, like the Gaelic League and good literature. Occasionally he seems sad, but mostly he's cheerful and even"— Ned rummaged through his new vocabulary—"ebullient. That's it, ebullient. Everyone likes him. As we say at home, 'You wouldn't feel a long day passing in his company.'

"Mr. MacDonagh helped Mr. Pearse found the school but he won't take any credit for it. They say he once burned a lot of his poetry on a bonfire at the school because he felt it wasn't good enough."[12]

Henry said, "That's a pity. We Irish are too quick to be self-effacing. Poetry is the soul standing naked, an act of courage if ever there was one. We can't afford to feed good examples to bonfires."

Tucking the little book into his waistcoat pocket, the journalist continued his commentary. "Sackville Street's the finest boulevard in Europe, in my humble opinion. Consider its incredible width. The old Romans could hold their chariot races

here. And look at those elaborate lampposts! Dublin's called
the Second Capital of the British Empire, you know. They've
spent a lot of money on giving it an impressive public face.

"But there's more to Dublin than neoclassical architecture.
Let's walk down to the O'Connell Bridge; I want you to see
the Dublin Bread Company. It's crowned with a tower that
looks for all the world like a huge bread hamper. Then just
across the bridge on Burgh Quay is the Carlisle Building,[13]
containing the editorial and commercial offices of the *Irish
Independent*. Originally the paper was housed in Middle Abbey Street, along with the *Evening Herald* and the *Sunday
Independent*. But things got too crowded for the staff of all
three papers, so now some of us are across the bridge. I'd like
to show you where I work, and the south side of the city, but
we'll save that tour for another day. When you've seen the
best of the north side we'll go to the Pillar Café and I'll shout
you to a cup of tea."

Henry Mooney had been in Dublin long enough to think
of it as 'his' city, and took pleasure in showing off the place.
But he had another reason for encouraging Ned's friendship.
The boy was obviously someone to whom things happened.
The *Titanic*, and his choice of schools, proved that.

Since coming to Dublin Henry Mooney had learned quite
a bit about the headmaster of Saint Enda's. As they walked
down Sackville Street he cast a sidelong glance at his companion and wondered just how much Ned knew about the
other, increasingly perilous enterprises of Patrick Henry
Pearse.

The overcast afternoon had grown very hot and still.

There was a powderkeg feeling in the air.

Chapter Twelve

SEVERAL hundred people had gathered in front of the Imperial Hotel. Henry stopped with a frown and took out his pocket watch. "It's noon," he muttered. "But surely not . . . He wouldn't dare . . ."

A bearded old man in a wheelchair was trundled through the crowd and into the hotel.[1] Henry caught Ned's arm. "Look there! He can't fool me; that's Jim Larkin."

"Who's Jim Larkin?"

"The founder of the Transport Workers' Union. The labor movement's turned ugly because the employers are fighting back. There's been no end of trouble here this summer, with angry confrontations and brutal policing. Larkin's been giving strong speeches at Liberty Hall in Beresford Place all week. He was arrested once, but they let him out on bail—if he'd behave himself. He promptly announced a big rally in Sackville Street for today. It was officially banned, of course, but it looks like that won't stop Big Jim. And at Murphy's own hotel, too. What a brass neck! Come on, let's get closer." Tugging the boy after him, he waded into the press of bodies.

A few minutes later the man from the wheelchair appeared standing in a balcony window above the street. The outsized Crombie coat he wore failed to conceal his impressive height. As he pulled off his false beard a woman at the front of the crowd shouted, "Three cheers for Jim Larkin!"

Larkin thrust the beard into his pocket and raised his arms to call for silence. He had said only a few words when several policemen grabbed him from behind. A scuffle followed. Simultaneously more police swarmed into the street below, wielding batons to drive back the crowd.

Shouts of support for Larkin gave way to cries of alarm as a large company of mounted policemen came thundering up the boulevard. They were armed with more than batons.

A saber flashed in the air.

Some in the crowd were trying to fight back while others were running away. It never occurred to Ned to run. Had he not survived the *Titanic*?

Seeing a policeman lean from his saddle to slash at an elderly man, he threw himself forward and caught the booted foot in the stirrup. "Leave him alone!" he shouted. "He's doing you no harm!"

The policeman turned on Ned. Beneath his helmet his features were contorted with unmistakable glee.

In a moment of dreadful clarity Ned felt the shadow of the saber on his own face. Then its darkness expanded to blot out the sky.

THE ocean was roaring in his ears. His head hurt terribly. In fact, he hurt all over. But he would not allow himself to give in to the pain and sink down into the roaring ocean. He had survived the *Titanic*; the sea could not claim him now. . . .

He could feel horsehair upholstery prickling through the back of his shirt. With an effort, Ned opened his eyes.

A blurry figure leaning over him gradually came into focus. "He's coming around now," Henry said.

A second person moved into Ned's field of vision. "Here's more brown paper and vinegar," said a feminine voice. An acrid smell stung Ned's nostrils and he felt hands fumbling at his head, then something cool was spread across his forehead and the ocean closed over him again.

When he awoke a second time his head still hurt but his

vision was clear. He gingerly turned his head and looked around.

He lay on a black horsehair couch in the front parlor of Number 16 Middle Gardiner Street. There was no sign of Henry, but a young woman sat in a rocking chair by the nearest window, resting her chin on one hand and gazing out at the street.

He coughed politely to get her attention. Pain lanced through his head.

She got up at once and came over to him. "So you're awake. That's a good sign." In spite of the ugly bruise on the side of his face he was a nice-looking boy, Mary Cosgrave thought to herself. A very nice-looking boy. The cleft in his chin was intriguing, and now that his eyes were open, their thick-lashed green gaze made her breath catch in her throat. "How are you feeling?"

He could not see her face. She was only a silhouette against the light from the window. "I . . . sore. What happened?"

"You were hit on the head with the flat of a saber for trying to save my father," she replied angrily. "And then some of them beat you with batons as you lay on the ground."

When she bent closer he could make out her features: a perfect oval face framed by clusters of glossy brown curls. She wore a white muslin shirtwaist with a yoke of frothy lace. To Ned's dazed mind she looked like an angel.

"How is your f-father?" he managed to stammer.

"He'll be all right, thanks to you. I told him not to go, there was sure to be trouble, but he wouldn't listen. After they arrested Mr. Larkin, Mr. Mooney brought you both here. Then he sent for me. My father's resting upstairs now. He's a bit bruised too, but there's no real harm done; I've seen him come back from the pub with worse."

Ned's head had begun to pound with an insistent, compelling beat. He closed his eyes but did not lose consciousness, so he heard when Henry returned to the room. "How's my young friend doing, Mary?"

"He was awake a few moments ago."

"That's a relief. There's no sense taking him to hospital if we can avoid it; I wouldn't want it on the record that he was involved in a riot. Your father's feeling better now, too. Whenever you like I shall fetch a cab for you, Mary, so the pair of you can go home. I imagine your mother's very anxious.''

Ned did not realize he had fallen asleep again until he awoke to find the room gilded with gaslight. Henry was tugging at his shoulders. ''Up ye get, lad, and upstairs with you. Mrs. Kearney has fixed a bed in my room for you, and I'll take you out to the school tomorrow myself.''

''Where's Mary?''

''Mary Cosgrave, is it? You weren't as badly hurt as I thought,'' Henry said with a chuckle.

The next morning no trams were running, so Henry hired a motor cab to take himself and Ned to Rathfarnham. For a time Ned rode in silence. His head was throbbing, his ribs were sore, one arm was badly bruised. There was no way he could get comfortable.

The cab jolted on the cobblestones.

''I owe you an apology for yesterday,'' Henry said. ''I never meant to get you involved in anything like that. I didn't expect it; the rally was banned.''

''It's all right, it wasn't your fault.'' Yet I could have been killed, Ned thought to himself as the realization slowly dawned. *Me, dead.* Going down into the dark sea. Strangely, the possibility seemed more real than it had on the sinking *Titanic.*

''Of course, most of what happens in life is unexpected, lad,'' Henry went on. ''That's why we have newspapers—to report on things we never anticipated. As a result of that riot seven hundred people were sent to hospital. Most of them were just innocent passersby who got caught up in the riot. A man and a woman were killed outright and another man died this morning.

''Last night the police went berserk and broke into working-class homes all over the city, arresting men and smashing furniture while terrified women and children looked on. It's a damned shame,'' he added angrily. ''They're making a bloody police state of this city.''

Ned did not ask who "they" were. His head was throbbing.

"The DMP have no patience with unions," Henry continued. "It's been war between the workers and the police all summer. The hotel where Jim Larkin tried to speak is owned by William Martin Murphy. You could say he's my boss; he owns the *Independent*. But he's also a director of the Dublin Tramways Company, and Larkin called the tramway workers out on strike. Needless to say, Murphy's no friend of the union movement. He's leading the new Employers' Federation against unionism."

"Is that why you said Jim Larkin had a brass neck?"

"Exactly. Yesterday was an act of defiance and I commend his courage, but it went badly wrong. He's been arrested just when his union needs him most."

"Is Mr. . . . Cosgrave . . . a member of the union?"

Henry nodded. "A tram conductor. I know the family, I interviewed them for an article I wrote on the last strike. Had to handle it very carefully, as you can imagine. My sympathies are with the workers but I have to make a living.

"Cosgrave's a decent enough man, though some might say he bends the elbow too often. He married above himself—a sickly woman who's always ailing. But her father was a merchant who left her a good house in Dorset Street. Otherwise the family would probably be in one of the Church Street tenements.[2]

"The Cosgraves buried three little girls and have two grown sons working in England. Mary's the only surviving daughter; she works at Brown Thomas as a draper's assistant. Would you not say she's a very pretty girl?" Henry nudged Ned with his elbow.

Ned hastily changed the subject. "I appreciate your going to Saint Enda's with me, but should you not be at work?"

"I am at work. The riot was one story and meeting your Mr. Pearse just might provide me with another."

When they reached the gates of Saint Enda's, Henry gave a low whistle. " 'The Hermitage,' eh? Looks more prosperous than I expected."

"What do you mean?"

"I've heard the school is one step ahead of bankruptcy. Pearse may be a superb educator, but he's financially naive. He's put everything he has into this place. Lately he's become involved in the nationalist movement and that takes up a lot of his time and energy, too, so he's bound to be overstretched.

"Douglas Hyde's Gaelic League gives him philosophical support but a place like this costs more than a few shillings to run. Still . . . Ho, look there, Ned." As their cab drew up in front of the house, Henry drew Ned's attention to a large private motorcar behind them. Henry paid the cabdriver and had a brief argument with him about waiting, while Ned watched three men and a woman get out of the motorcar and mount the steps. They knocked and were immediately admitted.

Henry concluded his arrangements with the cabdriver, then turned to Ned. "Now, that's interesting. Did you get a good look at them? The young man in the dramatic cape was Joseph Mary Plunkett, who edits *The Irish Review*. His father's Count Plunkett, the director of the Museum of Science and Art."[3]

"Do you know who the woman was?"

"Indeed I do; you can't be in the newspaper business for long without recognizing her. That's Countess Markievicz."

"The founder of the Fianna?"

"The very same. Thomas MacDonagh—there's a coincidence for you, Ned—was the third of the party, as I'm sure you already noticed. And unless I'm mistaken the last one out of the car was Edmund Kent. He works in the City Treasurer's department of Dublin Corporation.[4] Rumor has it he's also a member of the Irish Republican Brotherhood—although they may not know that in the Corpo. Now what are those four doing here together, do you suppose?"

Henry Mooney had a definite gleam in his eye.

Mrs. Pearse opened the front door just as Pearse emerged from his study. "Thanks be to God you're back. We've been very worried about you!" His gaze fixed on Ned's bandaged head. "How were you injured? Is it serious?"

Henry interjected, "This lad came into the city yesterday only to be struck down during the riot in Sackville Street.

There's no lasting damage done, but he will have a few aches and pains for a while. He's a friend of mine, so I kept him at my place overnight to recover.''

Pearse's eyes swung to Henry. "I am in your debt, sir. And you are . . . ?''

"Henry Mooney, at your service. I write for the *Irish Independent*.''

"I have read some articles with your name on them, Mr. Mooney,'' Pearse replied. "They were well written and thought provoking. Please, join me in my study. Both of you.''

Pearse's guests rose to their feet when the newcomers entered. "These two were in Sackville Street yesterday,'' the headmaster told them.

Curly-haired Thomas MacDonagh greeted Ned with a smile of recognition. *"Failte isteach!''* With his high forehead, long nose and narrow jaw, MacDonagh was the very portrait of an academic. But there was nothing stuffy about him. The little man's enthusiastic nature endeared him to everyone who knew him. Although he was now an assistant lecturer at University College Dublin, he still visited Saint Enda's frequently and was a great favorite there.

Next, Joseph Mary Plunkett extended his hand. His fingers were laden with rings. In contrast to the others he was an exotic figure, wearing expensive clothing cut in the latest continental fashion. Behind thick-lensed spectacles his face was very pale, however, and his dark eyes were fever-bright.

Edmund Kent wore the type of nondescript gray suit favored by civil servants, but he had a luxuriant brown mustache. Well muscled for a man who worked indoors, he acknowledged Ned and Henry with a silent nod.

No sooner had Pearse introduced Constance, Countess Markievicz, than the woman exclaimed, "Those brutes! This child could have been killed.''

Suddenly Ned recognized that voice. *Three cheers for Jim Larkin!*

Constance Markievicz was a tall, lean woman in her middle years. Her features, though finely modeled, were sharp. Graying brown hair was twisted into a careless knot at the nape of her neck, and she wore an old cardigan long out of fashion.

Ned was staring at her bruised mouth. "You were there?"

"I most certainly was! Jim had borrowed my husband's coat as part of his disguise. After he was arrested, some drunken policeman hit me in the face."

"That's worse than hitting a child," Ned said indignantly. "I mean . . . I'm not a child, I'm almost seventeen."

Her expression softened into a smile and he realized she was beautiful. "I was sixteen myself many years ago," she told him. "It's a grand age. I apologize for calling you a child; you are obviously a fine young man."

With those few words she won his heart.

"I'm quite an admirer of your work," Henry was saying to Thomas MacDonagh. He cleared his throat self-consciously and quoted:

> There is no moral to my song,
> I praise no right, I blame no wrong;
> I tell of things that I have seen,
> I show the man that I have been
> As simply as a poet can
> Who knows himself poet and man.[5]

Then he fumbled in his pocket and produced the slim volume he had purchased the previous day. "I never expected to meet you here, but since I have, would you be so kind as to sign this for me?"

MacDonagh frowned at the proffered book. "There are two in this room who are much better poets than I. You should be collecting the works of Mr. Pearse and Mr. Plunkett instead of mine." But he took a pen from Pearse's desk, dipped it into a bottle of ink, and bent to inscribe a few words on the flyleaf.

Henry remarked, "Ireland is producing a full complement of bards in this generation." Then he added with deliberate casualness, "Do you also write, Mr. Kent?"

The quiet man shook his head. "Ceannt," he corrected, subtly changing the pronunciation of his name to its Irish equivalent. "Eamonn Ceannt, please. To answer your question, my enthusiasm is music. I play the pipes. I've written some articles in Irish for a literary journal Pat edits,[6] but you might say I am more of a physical person.''

Constance Markievicz barked a laugh. "You could say the same of me—though my sister Eva writes poems."[7]

"I confess to being perplexed," said Henry. "This is delightful company to find myself in, but I am curious as to what brings you together."

Pearse replied, "We share an enthusiasm for the Irish language and culture. Eamonn met Tom and me through the Gaelic League, and Tom taught Joe Irish."

"Is that all?" Henry asked.

The headmaster gave him a long, thoughtful look. "For taking such good care of our Ned, perhaps you do deserve a more complete answer. Besides, if I read you correctly, you share many of the feelings which unite us."

Ceannt took a step forward to lay a hand on Pearse's arm. "Are you sure, Pat? It's best to be careful."

Pearse turned to Ned. "Will you vouch for your friend?"

"Mr. Mooney may have saved my life. I trust him implicitly."

The headmaster nodded. "The faith of a Scoil Eanna boy is good enough for me. Your articles speak well for you, Mr. Mooney, and Ned has earned the right to hear what we are discussing; he paid for it with his blood. Please take seats and join us, gentlemen. You have come upon"—he smiled, though his eyes were solemn—"a conspiracy of poets."

September 5, 1913

50,000 ATTEND FUNERAL OF WORKER
KILLED BY POLICE

September 24, 1913

SERBIAN TROOPS MOBILIZE IN
THE BALKANS

Chapter Thirteen

Caitlín, *a chara*,

Some weeks ago I went into Dublin to meet my friend, Henry Mooney. While I was there we accidentally witnessed a riot involving Jim Larkin, the leader of the labor movement, and the police. Several innocent people were killed. It's now being called Bloody Sunday.

Ned felt no need to tell his sister of his own injury. Geographical distance, allowed a desirable blurring of certain details one would prefer not to share with family.

The next day we were present when a group came to discuss the current situation with Mr. Pearse. Like him, each of them feels a passionate commitment to make things better.

Among the group was a woman, Countess Markievicz. Her husband is a Polish count, but her maiden name was Gore-Booth and she comes from an Ascendancy family with estates in Sligo. She grew up in a big house and has a posh accent, but she's as Irish in her heart as Mr. Pearse. She was even arrested in 1911 for "revolutionary activities" during the visit of King George and Queen

Mary to Ireland—and she doesn't seem the least bit embarrassed about it!

In 1909 the countess and a man called Bulmer Hobson founded a youth corps called Na Fíanna Éireann after Fionn MacCumhaill's army. They wear uniforms and have parades and do all sorts of exciting things. She even teaches them to shoot. She is a crack shot and has her own rifles. The Fianna love the countess; they call her "Madame."

A young apprentice teacher at Saint Enda's, a fellow called Con Colbert who also works part-time as a bakery clerk, organized a company of Fianna here. After I met the countess I decided to join, and I'm proud to say I have been accepted. We go on maneuvers in the Dublin mountains with other companies. One of the friends I have made in the Fianna is a lad my own age called Seán Heuston. Seán has just come up to Dublin from Limerick and works in the Fianna headquarters in Hardwicke Street.

Seán has told me more about the countess. She has spent years trying to teach tenement dwellers basic health care. She is always fighting for the working class and the poor. That has made her unpopular in certain circles, as you can imagine. Seán says her husband calls her a "floating land mine."

She is a most remarkable woman, Caitlín, and not the least bit pretentious. She's full of fire and spirit like the Irish warrior-women in the old legends.

Full of fire and spirit. Irish warrior-women. Frowning, Kathleen folded Ned's letter neatly along its creases and put it back into her pocket. His phrases seemed to condemn her.

"In Ireland there are women struggling against poverty and injustice," she subsequently bemoaned to Father Paul, "but what have I done? I live in more luxury than most Irish people could ever imagine."

"Don't be so hard on yourself," counseled the priest. "You're a good wife and someday you will be a good mother.

What more do you think God asks of you?'' Yet something in his voice as he phrased these questions made her wonder if the conventional answer was the right one.

Kathleen had been raised to believe that priests were as sexless as angels. Since meeting Father Paul she had begun to suspect otherwise. Alexander had not awakened her, but awakening was as inevitable as the coming of spring.

In her next letter to her Aunt Norah she wrote:

> One thing I do not miss about Ireland is the hypocrisy. There is no sex in Ireland; the church forbids it. The babies of decent folk are the result of Immaculate Conception. Anything else is Original Sin. No wonder we go through life crippled by guilt and fear.
>
> I blame the priests, though they must suffer, too. Until recently it never occurred to me that they had bodies beneath their cassocks. Yet surely they have feelings like the rest of us, for all they try to deny them.

KATHLEEN blushed as she wrote the words, but she wrote them, digging the nib of her pen into the paper.

Her trips to the presbytery were becoming more frequent, always when she knew Father Paul would be there. He shared the house with two other priests, and kept a schedule as regular as the rising of the sun. ''May I speak privately to Father Paul? I have a problem and need his advice,'' she invariably said when the Irish housekeeper answered the door.

Clucking her tongue over Kathleen's unidentified problem, Mrs. Flanagan would usher the young woman inside and seat her in the parlor. Father Paul usually joined her within a matter of minutes. Then the ritual began: steaming coffee and soft-voiced conversation. Kathleen discussed everything with the priest from Alexander's Freemasonry to her worries about the family back in Ireland.

As the months passed she began to speak of even more personal matters.

In the most delicate of phrases she alluded to her dissatisfaction with the physical side of marriage. "Alexander is very good to me," she insisted, "and gives me whatever I ask for. But he is not . . . tender. He does . . . what is necessary for making babies, but . . ."

"But?"

"Afterward I feel, well, lonely. I know God tells us marriage is for procreation, but surely there should be other satisfactions, too. It isn't all just about having children, is it?"

Father Paul's blue eyes studied her face. "The institution of marriage was founded to protect the family," he said. "And in the broader sense, to safeguard property."

"Do emotions not matter?"

"Surely you love your husband."

"When we married I was quite certain I did, but now I think—I don't know what love is."

He struggled to recall the phrases so glibly learned in the seminary. "Love develops within the sanctity of marriage, Kathleen."

"But how?"

"You must be patient," he replied, knowing that was no answer.

As she lay in bed beside Alexander, with his back turned to her like a mountain, Kathleen found herself trying to visualize Father Paul without his clothes. The first time this happened she throttled her imagination and whispered a hasty Act of Contrition. But the next night she felt less guilty. And the next night . . .

He would be slender, she decided, but more muscular than he appeared in clerical garb. Unlike Alexander, he would have little body hair. As for his private parts . . .

A girl raised in the country could not be ignorant of male anatomy, but Kathleen had never seen her husband naked. A combination of tactile evidence and brief, embarrassed glimpses as he crawled into bed in his nightshirt informed her that his penis was stubby and thick even in repose, with ruddy, coarse-grained skin that reminded her of turkey wattles. He used an erection like a battering ram, as if both it and she were insensitive.

Paul would be different, she thought. His would be a spear, long and smooth and clean.

She did not notice that she had ceased thinking of the priest as Father.

In America, as in Ireland, the parish priest fulfilled a variety of roles from confessor to marriage counselor to surrogate parent. Paul O'Shaughnessy was second generation American, but still close enough to Ireland to understand the sense of the alienation many immigrants felt. He had cousins in both Galway and Dublin, and occasionally received letters from them which depicted a society quite different from America— so different he wondered how anyone ever made the transition.

At first he simply gave Kathleen the support he would have extended to any of his parishioners and took an innocent pleasure in listening to her lilting Clare accent. But as time passed, something changed. When he was serving Mass and Kathleen knelt at the altar rail with her hands folded and her eyes downcast, Paul was intensely conscious of her. Once he was privy to the problems in her personal life he should have discouraged any emotional attachment she might be transferring to him.

Yet he had not.

One morning she looked up and met his eyes as he held the chalice toward her. Through the miracle of Transubstantiation the liquid in the cup had become the blood of Christ, the ultimate sacrifice, but for one moment it was wine again, and he was offering it to the woman he desired.

The hand that held the chalice trembled.

For a young seminarian from a devout Catholic home, the celibacy the church imposed upon its priests had contained its own romance. Rejecting the sensual life in favor of the spiritual had been an act of love. Over the ensuing years he had suppressed the urges of his body like every other priest he knew, a lonely struggle taking place in the dark. Until Kathleen, he thought he had won.

Chapter Fourteen

Aᴜᴛᴜᴍɴ wind rattled the casement windows, but inside the classroom the air was warm and moist with the exhalations of two dozen boys. In spite of himself, Ned yawned.

At once he felt Pearse's eyes upon him. The headmaster did not speak, yet the weight of his gaze was enough to snap Ned to attention.

The subject, as so often, was duty. Pearse never described duty as an obligation, but as an opportunity. "Anything worth having," he was saying, "demands a sacrifice. It may be hard work, or it may be the last ounce of your heart's blood. But all life comes at a cost and at the end of life we die. How much better, then, to spend ourselves in a noble cause!

"I shall never have a wife and children of my own. You are the sons I would have loved and cherished, had God given me sons. Instead I educate and cherish the sons of other men. When the great opportunities come to us we must seize them, seize them with joy and never look back, never regret we did not take another path. Then when the sunset comes we can say, 'I did my best.'"

"I did my best," Ned whispered to himself in echo.

He began to daydream about devoting himself to some great cause. The labor movement, perhaps, like courageous Jim Larkin.

After Bloody Sunday the battle between employer and worker had intensified. Determined to break the unions, large firms refused to deal with members of the I.T.G.W.U. Thousands were thrown out of work in what came to be known as the Great Lockout.

Soon outright starvation was widespread in the tenements. Dublin union leaders attended a congress of British trade unions in Manchester and asked the members to support their Irish colleagues. The British unions refused a sympathy strike, but sent more than sixty thousand "family boxes" to feed Irish workers. When all the boxes had been given out a soup kitchen was set up in Liberty Hall, the union headquarters, and Constance Markievicz was among those who worked long hours providing food to Dublin's hungry.

The Great Lockout hardened and intensified something in Pádraic Pearse.[1] The gentle Gaelic scholar dreaming of ancient Ireland was transformed into an angry man outraged by current injustice. He wrote, "The tenement houses of Dublin are so rotten they periodically collapse upon their starving inhabitants, and if the inhabitants collect in the street to discuss the matter, the police baton them to death."

While Jim Larkin was in Mountjoy Prison the government let it be known that any association with him would be suspect. He was branded a dangerous troublemaker, and as a result no school in Dublin would accept his children. Yet Pádraic Pearse did not hesitate to take the older boys—Jim, Denis, and Finton—into Saint Enda's.[2] The baby, Barney, was too young, but Pearse assured Mrs. Larkin there would be a place for him too when he was ready. "Saint Enda's is not run by Dublin Castle," Pearse said simply. "We will be honored to have the boys here. Jim Larkin has done more in six months than the politicians and ourselves with all our talk."[3]

Pearse did not discuss contemporary politics in the classroom. Students at Saint Enda's were inculcated with patriotism and a love of country while being sheltered from the rough-and-tumble of current political reality. Yet the history Pearse taught his students was undeniably political history.

"For eight hundred years," the headmaster lectured one storm-swept morning, "this once-rich island has suffered from attempted conquest by her neighbor to the east. The Anglo-Normans, led by Strongbow, arrived in the twelfth century.

"Then in the sixteenth century England undertook what was called 'plantation,' giving huge tracts of Irish land to Englishmen loyal to the Crown. Through this method Queen Elizabeth rewarded her favorites such as Essex and Raleigh. The rightful owners of the land were driven from it by whatever means was deemed expedient.

"Naturally they fought back. But they could not withstand the growing military might of England. At the Battle of Kinsale in 1601 the Gaelic aristocracy was defeated and plantation began in earnest. In 1649 Oliver Cromwell, a fanatical anti-Catholic, undertook to punish the "rebellious" Irish, most of whom remained steadfastly Catholic, and bring them to heel once and for all. Using the twin weapons of gunpowder and terror, his army drove thousands from their homes and depopulated great tracts of land. Those who resisted were slaughtered outright.

"Ulster, the Ulster of Hugh O'Neill and Hugh O'Donnell, was arguably the most Gaelic part of Ireland, and it was the northeast that bore the worst of Cromwell's fury. Catholics in Drogheda were locked in their own church and burnt alive."

Pearse closed his eyes for a moment as if he could not bear to look upon that blazing memory.

Cold rain fell on Saint Enda's, drumming against the tall windows. Pearse roused himself and went on.

"By 1653 Ireland was subjugated. Almost the only land still under Irish control was the barren, stony soil of Connacht in the west. Cromwell had vowed to send the Irish 'to Hell or to Connacht,' and so he did.

"At the Battle of the Boyne in 1689 two claimants to the English throne fought—on Irish soil. The Dutch Protestant, William of Orange, defeated the Scots Catholic, James Stewart. Religion was not the real issue, however. As always, the war was about territory and the power that goes with it.

"As a result of the Orange victory, northeast Ulster in particular was given over to plantation. Protestant colonists were sent there to uphold English interest, English honor, and the Protestant faith against any and all resistance. In return they were granted not only land but extraordinary privilege. Superiority over the natives was taken as their established right."

As he listened to these words Ned felt an ancient anger come to life within him. The enforced subservience of centuries scalded his soul. He was gritting his teeth so hard his jaws asked.

Pearse went on, "With the domination of Scotland, England took on a new identity. She became 'Great Britain'; an empire was in the making. But the empire suffered a setback when in 1776 British colonists in America staged a revolt and won their independence.

"The French staged their own revolution only thirteen years later. The Bastille fell, republicanism was in the air and the universal cry was for freedom.

"Britain had been allowing the Irish at least a semblance of self-government with their own parliament in Dublin, but now resolved to bind them with chains of iron. The British had no intention of losing their nearest colony as they had lost America."

America, thought Ned. They got their freedom. Why not us? Pearse continued, "By the Act of Union in 1800 Ireland ceased to be a separate political entity. For good or ill, she was subsumed into the United Kingdom of Britain and Ireland. The parliament in Dublin was effectively dismantled and elected representation was transferred to Westminster.

"At about the same time, the Orange Order was organized to commemorate the triumph of the Protestant minority in Ireland. Around Belfast, as nowhere else in Ireland, the descendants of the colonists outnumbered the native race.[4] Understandably, Belfast became the stronghold of the Unionist Party.

"The Irish Parliamentary Party of today is little more than

a rubber stamp in the halls of Westminster, where British self-
interest always takes precedence. John Redmond, the current
leader of that party, began as a political moderate of the nationalist persuasion. He once said, and I quote, 'For us the
Act of Union has no binding moral or legal force. We regard
it as our fathers regarded it before us, as a great criminal act
of usurpation carried on by violence and fraud.'[5]

"Unfortunately, over the years Redmond has lost touch
with the people of Ireland and become anglicized. Thus has
this island been welded in a loveless marriage with Britain."

Ned wrote that last sentence in his copybook, then added,
"It is not a marriage of equals." The headmaster, walking
between the desks, looked down and read those words.

NED enjoyed his membership in the Fianna. Con Colbert,
who was a member of the Gaelic League, drilled the Saint
Enda's company three times a week. The uniforms were a
strange mixture of Celtic fantasy and Robert Baden-Powell's
recently formed Boy Scouts. The rank and file of the Fianna
wore kilts with double-breasted dark green tunics, but senior
officers had breeches and leather leggings.[6] Their hat was the
same as the Boy Scouts', their badge a gold sunburst with a
white pikestaff head on a green field. Mr. Pearse heartily approved of the uniforms, particularly the kilts.

Colbert designed their drills himself and issued his commands in ringing Irish. Under his tutelage the company became expert at marching in formation and reconnoitering
enemy positions.

For want of a better image, Ned imagined the enemy as
English.

Some "bold boys" who had once been troublemakers
found a new outlet for their adolescent energy in the Fianna.
Impudence and joie de vivre were the hallmarks of Madame's
army and were never discouraged, merely redirected.

But there were other "bold boys" outside the positive influence of the Fianna. Two strapping youths who lived at the
edge of Rathfarnham had taken to amusing themselves by

waylaying pupils from Saint Enda's as they made their way to or from the village.

The bullies were a year or so younger than Ned. But they were bigger. He prudently avoided them—until the day they thrashed one of the smaller students and left him with torn clothes, a black eye, and a copious nosebleed. Ned happened to encounter the victim as he returned to the school, valiantly trying not to cry.

"What happened to you, Gerry?"

"Those big lads. They were waiting for me in the road and . . ."

A muscle twitched in Ned's jaw. "Right. Go have Mrs. Pearse see to you, I'll be back soon."

The culprits were easy enough to find; they were strutting up and down the road only a few hundred yards from the front gate, hurling stones at trees. When they saw Ned coming toward them the taller one called out, "You looking for some of what we gave your friend?"

"You'd better go back," sneered the other. "We wouldn't want to be hurtin' you now."

Ned tossed his head to throw his curly dark hair out of his eyes. "Would you not? That's decent of you—considering I intend to hurt you mightily!"

For a moment they just stared at him. In that moment Ned had plenty of time to be afraid, and he was. His belly plummeted toward his feet and his skin prickled all over.

I've survived the Titanic, he forced himself to remember.

Ned danced toward them with both fists raised and a grin like the rictus of a corpse and landed two blows on the bigger boy before the other could defend himself, then whirled to punch the second bully square in the mouth.

"Ye mis'rable git!" the boy cried, fighting back with flailing arms. But he was not used to an opponent as fit as Ned. The physical drill at Saint Enda's had given the young man strength and reflexes that stood him in good stead now.

The first bully sprang forward and tried to knock Ned down with his shoulder, but Ned spun around and left him stumbling through space, cursing. The pair then tried to pin Ned between them while he skipped, ducked, dodged, and landed two blows for every one they inflicted on him. His breath was coming in harsh gasps and he knew he would be bruised in the morning, but he did not mind.

To his astonishment, he was having a wonderful time.

When he saw a crucial opening Ned drove his fist up from his hip to make a cracking connection with an unguarded chin. The bigger bully staggered backward and sat down hard. His eyes went perfectly blank.

After a moment's hesitation, his companion took to his heels and ran.

"Come dance with me at the crossroads any time!" Ned called after him.

He was sorely tempted to give the fallen bully a kick for good measure. But he could almost hear Mr. Pearse saying, "That would make you no better than he is." Regretfully, Ned shrugged and turned away.

As he walked back to Saint Enda's, whistling rather breathlessly, he kept playing the scene over and over in his mind. It *had* been fun. The pure unalloyed joy of releasing all his youth and strength—and frustration too—in one unrestricted explosion made him feel ten feet tall.

Yes! *Yes!*

A steady stream of visitors called at Saint Enda's. Bulmer Hobson came to discuss the school's financial situation, Douglas Hyde to exchange educational theories. William Butler Yeats, Standish O'Grady, Edward Martyn, Pádraic Colum, and the historian Alice Stopford Green were frequent visitors, eagerly glimpsed by the students as they arrived to discuss literature or the theater or Irish history.[7]

When Constance Markievicz came to conduct target practice with the Fianna, Mrs. Pearse always set out the best tea service in the drawing room so the countess could be properly entertained afterward. But Madame would as readily drink out of a chipped cup. Ideas and action interested her; material objects did not.

On one memorable occasion Eamonn Ceannt arrived complete with traditional Irish piper's costume—handmade by himself—and played his pipes, to the delight of the students, although some made a great show of putting their hands over their ears.

Joseph Plunkett and Thomas MacDonagh were always warmly welcomed to Pearse's study. For a time Mary Brigid Pearse had a crush on Joe Plunkett that she made little effort to conceal. Sometimes her behavior bordered on the outlandish, but he treated her with the same exquisite courtesy he showed everyone.

Aside from a love of Gaelic culture, neither the happily married MacDonagh nor the flamboyant Joe Plunkett, whose father was a hereditary papal count, appeared to have much in common with Pearse. Yet the three men were good friends. Plunkett teased the sober headmaster by calling him "Poor Old Pearse," and MacDonagh claimed, "Pat only founded this school so he could make all the speeches he wanted."[8] They deliberately made Pearse laugh, easing the lines of strain around his eyes.

"Being caught up in the Larkin riot has involved you in politics whether I approve or not," Pearse told Ned one day after class, "so it's time you had more understanding of the issues. Madame Markievicz is coming out tomorrow to discuss some recent developments in the labor movement; why don't you join us in my study?"

Ned was delighted.

He learned that the workers' revolt had broadened. Jim Larkin was the uncrowned king of the Dublin working man, and Larkinism had been condemned by the *Irish Times* as "intolerable tyranny."[9] But since his arrest new leaders were coming to the fore. There was much talk of James Connolly, a Scottish-born trade union organizer from Belfast who had been working with Larkin. "Frank Skeffington says he has the best mind in the labor movement," Constance Markievicz told Pearse.

Francis Sheehy-Skeffington, socialist and pacifist, had been the first lay Registrar of Trinity College, Dublin. A dedicated champion of women's rights, he had resigned after a dispute over allowing women academic status. He also had testified on behalf of Jim Larkin after Bloody Sunday and made an impassioned plea for his exoneration—a plea that fell on deaf ears.

Now Pádraic Pearse said of him, "Frank's opinions are always worth listening to, but I must reserve judgment on Connolly. I recently heard him quoted as saying, 'Ireland as distinct from her people is nothing to me.' "

Madame Markievicz smiled knowingly. "He wrote that in an editorial in the *Irish Worker*. But the rest of the quote is 'and the man who is bubbling over with love and enthusiasm for "Ireland" and yet can pass unmoved through our streets and witness all the wrong and suffering, the shame and degradation, wrought upon the people of Ireland without burning to end it is, in my opinion, a fraud and a liar in his heart.'[10] You have more in common with him than you think, Pat."

Eamonn Ceannt observed Connolly from a civil servant's perspective. In early October he reported that under Connolly's influence the labor movement was extending its energies in a widening ripple that lapped at the very walls of Dublin Castle. The Castle, headquarters of the government, was a fortress of British bureaucracy. The common people rightly claimed it was indifferent to their situation.

"But the problems of the working man are symptomatic of larger issues," Ceannt said, "and they can't be ignored any longer. We're hearing the rumblings even in that hole where I work. The strikes and the lockouts go on and on, and police brutality is getting even worse. As a result, in a few days James Connolly is going to lead four thousand workers in a march through the streets of Dublin. That will make the senior civil servants sit up and take notice!"

In November, Big Jim Larkin was released from Mountjoy and promptly went to England to drum up support for Irish workers among British trade unionists.

That same month, Ned was present when Pearse asked Thomas MacDonagh, "Did you read Eoin MacNeill's latest article?"

"The one calling for the formation of a volunteer corps to

counterbalance the UVF?'' MacDonagh's eyes danced. ''Indeed I did! And I heartily approve.''

''What's the UVF?'' asked Ned.

''The Ulster Volunteer Force, a Protestant militia founded last year by Sir Edward Carson's Unionist Party.'' Pearse explained. ''They are the only Irish political party with any real influence in Parliament. Their support is helping keep Prime Minister Asquith and his Liberals in power. The avowed purpose of the UVF is to prevent Home Rule, which unionists interpret as a threat to the special privilege Protestants to conform with republicans elsewhere have enjoyed here for centuries.''

Ned started to say ''I suppose no one willingly gives up being part of the ruling class,'' but then he thought of Madame Markievicz and changed his mind.

''If the UVF succeed,'' interjected MacDonagh, ''they'll make military force and the threat of armed violence the determining factors in relations between this country and Britain from now on. But you have to admire Carson in a way. Here's a man born in Ireland, same as us—and a Trinity College man, to boot!—refusing to be pushed around by the 'British government.' More than that, he's raised an army to give himself the power to stand up for what he believes in.''

Pearse nodded agreement. ''A few of us met with Professor MacNeill yesterday at Wynn's Hotel to discuss setting up a volunteer corps of our own in the south.[12] We're arranging an inaugural meeting on the night of the twenty-fifth in the Small Concert Room at the Rotunda.[13] Joe Plunkett has already agreed to come along. We can take you in his motorcar, Tom, there's plenty of room.''

''I'll certainly join, but I don't know if I'll be there on the night. Muriel hasn't been feeling well and I don't like leaving her and little Don alone. Why don't you take young Ned here?''

''Please, sir!'' Ned said so promptly that both men laughed.

ON the night of the twenty-fifth a crowd far in excess of anyone's expectations descended upon the Rotunda. The

Small Concert Room was inadequate to hold them and they overflowed into the skating rink. The majority were men, but many had wives and sweethearts with them.

Members of the Fianna were pressed into service as ushers.[14] As Ned was helping people find the last available spaces, Eamonn Ceannt arrived flushed and out of breath, carrying a pipe-bag. "Sorry to be late. Been playing music."

The first order of business was the election of officers. When the final ballot was taken Eoin MacNeill was confirmed as president and chief of staff of the Irish National Volunteer Corps, with Bulmer Hobson as Secretary. Pádraic Pearse was among those appointed to the Provisional Committee, the governing body of the new organization.

Once the elections were out of the way the speeches began. The new president was first to address the crowd. MacNeill was a highly respected historian and university lecturer. Three of his sons and a nephew had attended Saint Enda's.[15] MacNeill was a spare, erect man with ascetic features, whose northern accent betrayed his County Antrim birth. Throughout his life he had mixed with Protestants and Ulstermen, yet no one could doubt his devotion to Gaelic Ireland. Since co-founding the Gaelic League with Douglas Hyde in 1893, he had been a tireless campaigner for the native Irish language and culture.

During his speech MacNeill made a point of saying, "We do not contemplate any hostility toward the volunteer force in Ulster. The strength of that movement consists in men whose kinsfolk were amongst the most resolute in winning freedom for the United States of America. Many of them are descendants of those Ulster Protestants who protested in their thousands against the dismantling of the Dublin parliament in 1800.

"The more genuine and successful the local volunteer movement in Ulster becomes, the more completely does it establish the principle that Irishmen have the right to decide and govern their own national affairs. We have nothing to fear from the Ulster Volunteers nor they from us. We gladly acknowledge the evident truth that they have opened the way for the National Volunteer Corps."[16]

Not everyone in the crowd was pleased by MacNeill's moderate approach. For many, all that mattered was the last sentence. A national military force. An army of Ireland's own for the first time in centuries.

When Pádraic Pearse rose to speak, he began by saying, "Our relationship with Britain is not a marriage of equals." His eyes met Ned's over the heads of the crowd. "All the power lies with Britain. We have only the right to throw our votes into the vast and complicated machinery of British politics, where they are disregarded.

"The passage of the Home Rule Bill would be the first step toward redressing the imbalance. Ireland should be allowed to govern her internal affairs. Canada has had her own prime minister since 1867; Australia since 1901. Yet the unionists refuse Home Rule here.

"The UVF is already heavily armed. They claim to be supporting the British constitution by protecting four Ulster counties 'for the Empire.' Their real purpose, however, is to prevent Home Rule.

"If the Home Rule Bill is finally passed next year as we hope, there could be civil war. James Connolly is already commanding what amounts to a workers' army, organized by himself and Jim Larkin. They are holding drills at Croydon Park with the purpose of preventing further outrages such as Bloody Sunday. But that is not enough, my friends. What is needed, as Professor MacNeill has pointed out, is a counterbalance for the Ulster Volunteers."

Pearse drew a slow, deep breath, then raised his voice until it rang like a clarion. "If their object is to protect four counties for the Empire, should not the other twenty-eight counties dedicate themselves to the protection of Ireland? The *nation* of Ireland?"

The word hung in the air. Nation.

After a long moment, Eoin MacNeill spoke up. "It must be understood from the outset that we are to initiate no military action. The role of the Irish Volunteers is to be strictly a defensive one. Protection, as you say, and not aggression."

Pearse nodded. "I am sure I speak for all here when I say we wish no man harm."

"Even the bloody-minded Orangemen?" shouted a man at the back of the room.

Pearse fixed a cold eye on the speaker. "Do not condemn members of the Orange Order for the fervor of their religious belief. To do so is to serve them as badly as they have served Catholics in the past.

"My own father was raised in the Unitarian faith, though he subsequently converted to Catholicism.[17] Many northern Protestants were among the heroes of the Rising of 1798. And we must not forget Wolfe Tone, Robert Emmet, Charles Stewart Parnell . . . all men who gave this country the last drop of their blood and their devotion. All Protestants. Ireland would be a much poorer place without them.

"When Ireland becomes a republic there shall be no state religion. Every citizen shall be free to worship God according to his conscience. Perfect freedom of worship shall be guaranteed as a right and not granted as a privilege."

Only later did Ned learn that Pearse was quoting verbatim from the constitution of the Irish Republican Brotherhood.

At the conclusion of the meeting a stirring manifesto was read aloud, and elicted sustained cheering.[18] Men were clamoring to sign up. Before the night was over, there were four thousand Irish Volunteers.[19]

Ned felt an excitement he could hardly contain. "I want to join too!" he told Pearse.

"Not tonight, lad. It's enough that you are in the Fianna. A good and decent man is paying for your education at Scoil Eanna, and I cannot break faith with Lord Inchiquin by letting you give your studies less than your full attention."

"But I'll continue to study—"

"Indeed, you will," Pearse interrupted. "When the school year ends next summer you will have completed your formal education with us. Then if you still wish to join the Volunteers you may."

Next summer. Ned hugged that promise to himself.

In the first flush of enthusiasm the Irish Volunteers grew rapidly. Sir Roger Casement, the hero of the Congo, was prevailed upon by MacNeill to accept a position on the Provisional Committee as treasurer. Having a former member of the British consular service on the committee was considered a great coup.

Not everyone was pleased about the new organization, however. At his next visit to Saint Enda's, Plunkett reported, "Both Seán O'Casey and Big Jim Larkin are vocal in their antagonism to the Volunteers. Larkin has no interest in anything that doesn't actively espouse a shift from capitalism to socialism. As for O'Casey, he's made a career out of writing bitter plays that reject any seed of hope. It's typical Irish begrudgery." Wracked by coughing, he broke off while Ned ran to bring him a glass of water.

Joe Plunkett gave Ned a wrench of pain whenever he saw him. Flamboyant, romantic, and highly strung, he burned with a flame too hot to last.

Although Pádraic Pearse was increasingly preoccupied with the volunteers he continued to teach, exhorting his pupils, "Never be mediocre, always do your best." "Do nothing you would not do before the whole world." And most tellingly, "Faith without works is dead."

In the winter of 1913 Willie Pearse took the students of Saint Enda's to a performance of *Cathleen ni Houlihan* that left Ned emotionally shattered. When a tragic old woman in a long cloak was ultimately revealed as Ireland herself, the Ireland who had inspired countless bards and for whom untold thousands had died, he wanted to leap to his feet and shout, "Don't despair! I'll save you!"

January 1914

GREAT BRITAIN'S LLOYD GEORGE CALLS
BUILDUP OF ARMS IN EUROPE "ORGANIZED
INSANITY"

February 1914

H.M.S. *BRITANNIC*, SISTER SHIP TO THE
TITANIC, LAUNCHED IN BELFAST

Chapter Fifteen

Early in the new year Ned announced his intention to buy a birthday present for his Aunt Norah "at the best shop in Dublin." Kathleen in America unexpectedly had sent him a gift of money for his own birthday, and he had saved most of it for just such a purpose. Norah and Frank and the girls were very much on his mind. Although miles separated them, he wanted to do something for them, make some gesture that would show he was still connected to hearth and home.

On a cold Saturday morning he set out for Dublin's Grafton Street, a fashionable thoroughfare lined with dressmakers, tailors, furriers, jewelers, stationers, and similar establishments interspersed with cafés such as Mitchells and the Café Cairo. Although it was early traffic was already brisk. A veritable procession of ladies of wealth and privilege were making their way up toward Saint Stephen's Green or down toward College Green.

Ned's destination was the large shop that advertised itself as Brown, Thomas & Co., Silk Mercers, Linen Drapers, Haberdashers and Milliners. Broad glass windows displayed smart frocks together with frothing petticoats and swaths of silk stockings, all unmistakably first-class. One look was enough to make a farm boy blush.

But Mary Cosgrave worked in Brown Thomas.

Resolutely, Ned approached the front entrance. A "commissionaire" in top hat and frock coat bestowed a professional smile on him and held the door wide.[1] Out wafted the aroma of expensive fabric and costly scent.

For one moment Ned was back on the *Titanic*. Second-class.

No sooner had he entered the shop than he saw a floor-walker staring at him. The man's job was to welcome regular customers and discourage undesirables. His glance took in the cut of Ned's tweed jacket, then dropped to his shoes and expertly assessed their quality. His face closed.

As if Pádraic Pearse were speaking in his ear, Ned recalled the headmaster saying, "Since Elizabethan times the Irish have been taught to defer to English authority, no matter how unjust that authority might be. This has been drummed into us by those who believe themselves our betters in order to keep us herdbound and submissive. Thus, generations of contempt and condescension have robbed us of any sense of our own worth.

"To accept that judgment is to compound the error. Throw back your shoulders and stand tall in any company; remember that you are of the Gael, inheritors of a proud race. Do nothing but that which is noble and fine, and thus force others to recognize you as an equal."

Lifting his chin with the Halloran cleft, Ned looked the floorwalker in the eye. His heart was pounding but his gaze was steady.

The floorwalker blinked first. Then he turned his attention elsewhere.

Ned felt a momentary elation.

An inquiry at the nearest counter sent him deeper into the realms of privilege. Brown Thomas; clientele were elegantly dressed women whose skin glowed with health beneath the extensive electric lighting. Such diseases as the pox were simply not allowed through the doors. Mary belongs here, Ned said to himself. Protected and cherished.

Miss Cosgrave worked in Hats and Gloves, third floor. He fairly ran up the stairs to that department, only to be told by a sallow woman in steel-rimmed spectacles, "Sorry, but Miss Cosgrave isn't here today. She sent a note saying that her mother is ill."

How swiftly elation turned to despair! Burying his hands in his pockets, Ned slouched out of Brown Thomas and was back in Grafton Street before he remembered his aunt's birthday. But he had no desire to face the supercilious floorwalker a second time.

Knaggs Bros, at number 27, was advertising "Irish Bog Oak Jewellery." Ned gazed through the window at their wares, rubbed the cleft in his chin thoughtfully, walked on a few paces, then turned and went back. A female clerk helped him select a brooch made of glossy bog oak inset with silver wire and jet. "Your aunt will like this," she assured him. "The saints themselves would like this, so they would."

Ned tucked the paper-wrapped parcel in his jacket pocket and set out to explore the city south of the Liffey. He rummaged happily through P. S. O'Hegarty's Bookshop in Dawson Street, circumnavigated Trinity College, admired the classical facade of the former Irish Parliament building, wandered up and down a number of narrow, intriguing laneways in Temple Bar, and at last emerged on the quays near O'Connell Bridge. Noticing the Carlisle Building, he went in.

"Mr. Mooney?" repeated the man at the *Irish Independent's* reception desk. "Right through that door and turn left."

With his shirtsleeves rolled up and a green eyeshade on his forehead, Henry Mooney was sitting hunched over a battered desk in a room filled with similarly battered desks. Half a dozen men were busily writing on sheets of foolscap, while an equal number were leaning back in their chairs and staring at the ceiling or talking casually to one another. The air smelled of ink and stale sweat and cigarette smoke.

The moment Henry saw Ned he began rolling down his sleeves. "Your timing is perfect. I was just about to go out and watch the demonstration. Care to join me if I promise you won't be injured this time?"

Ned laughed. "I've forgotten all about that," he lied, well

aware that his "battle wound" had scored points on his behalf with Pádraic Pearse. "What demonstration, Henry?"

"Those new Irish Volunteers are drilling on the quays this afternoon. Could be a story in it, and we can go for a pint afterward." Mooney was already standing up and pulling on his jacket. Ned eagerly fell into step beside him as he headed for the door.

"What brings you to Dublin today?"

Ned was too shy to mention Mary Cosgrave. "Shopping. But it's done now."

Perhaps because he had her on his mind, however, he found his eyes straying to the women they passed. The observant Henry remarked, "You like that one, do you? Look again. She has thick lips and I suspect, though I have no direct proof, thick ankles as well."

Ned was both shocked and delighted. "Do they go together?"

"Not always, but often enough to be noted by a student of female anatomy."

A company of men came marching toward them from George's Quay. They had no uniforms; Sam Browne belts held a variety of coats in place over Sunday suits and weekday work clothes.

Ned was reminded of the Fianna drilling at Saint Enda's. The boys in their neat uniforms were as disciplined as a real army, and trained in marksmanship.

Some of the adult Volunteers were out of step. On their shoulders they carried crudely carved dummy rifles like children playing soldiers.

No one was paying much attention to them. A few street urchins and one scruffy bull terrier trotted in their wake, but otherwise the Dubliners were indifferent. Demonstrations of marching men were all too familiar.

In the front rank was a darkly handsome man of some twenty-nine or thirty years. Although he had a pronounced limp, he moved as if to the beat of an inner drum. Henry Mooney pointed him out to Ned. "That's John MacDermott; Seán, he calls himself. He had infantile paralysis, that's why he drags one leg a bit. He's rumored to be the national organizer for the Irish Republican Brotherhood; travels up and down the country on a bicycle. I must say I'm surprised to see him marching with the Volunteers. Perhaps the IRB's trying to infiltrate this new organization."

"What do you know about the IRB, Henry? No one talks about it very much."

Henry was flattered to show off his knowledge. "For good reason. The Brotherhood is a secret—and secretive—society that was organized by James Stephens and John O'Mahony in the last century. Both were veterans of the failed Rising of 1848. From the beginning its purpose was conspiracy—conspiracy to bring about the establishment of an independent Irish Republic. The IRB receives considerable financial support from America; particularly from an Irish-American group called Clan na Gael. In America, Irish republicans are known as Fenians, after the Fianna."

"But we have Fenians in Clare!"

"You do of course. The name is used on both sides of the Atlantic now. In fact their greatest strength used to be down the country, but with the rise of the labor movement the IRB has become much stronger in Dublin. And Seán MacDermott is one of their most dedicated members."

As if he knew they were talking about him, MacDermott glanced in their direction. For one heartbeat his eyes met Ned's. The challenge they held was like a shout in the blood.

Suddenly Ned longed with all his heart to be marching in the company of grown men, with the golden sunshine pouring over them like a blessing. Summer seemed far too long to wait. He squared his shoulders and lifted his chin. Inside him a drum began to beat.

A young woman carrying a string shopping bag flicked her gaze over him and then stopped on the footpath, staring. After a moment's hesitation she came toward him and laid her hand on his arm.

Ned gave a start. Dragging his thoughts back from brief glory, he looked down to find himself gazing into a familiar face; familiar, yet somehow very changed. At first he could not even think of the name that went with the russet hair, the slanted eyes.

Then, "*Sheila?* Síle Duffy, is it you?"

"It is myself, did you not know me?"

"I did, but . . . I mean . . . you look so . . . different," Ned finished lamely.

When he last saw her in Clare, Dan Duffy's sister had been barefoot and dressed in rags. Two years had wrought a transformation. Her hair no longer resembled raveled rope but was smoothed tight from a center part and then twisted into corkscrew curls that tumbled fetchingly over one shoulder. Her coat was inexpensive but stylish; high-heeled boots peeped from beneath her daringly ankle-length skirt.

Ned was dazzled. "What are you doing in Dublin? I never thought . . . I mean, how did you . . ."

Still laughing, Síle linked her arm with his. He caught a momentary fragrance of white lilac.

"Och, that's a long story, Ned. But if you'll buy me a cup of tea at Bewley's I'll tell you some of it. Then I want to hear about you, which would be ever so much more interesting."

Henry Mooney stepped squarely into their path. "I don't think you want to do that, Ned."

"But I know this young lady. She's the sister of a friend of mine from Clare."

"From Clare, is it?" Henry surveyed Síle with narrowed eyes. "Are you not a long way from home then, missus?"

"What business is it of yours?" She tightened her grip on Ned's arm, pressing her breast against his bicep. Suddenly all his nerve endings were concentrated in his arm.

"It's your business I'm more concerned about. This young man is a friend of mine, a good Catholic boy who has not been exposed to certain aspects of Dublin life. I should not like to see him taken advantage of."

"I'm not taking advantage of him. I just asked him to buy me a cup of tea."

"It's all right, Henry," Ned interjected. "Truly it is. I don't know what you're worried about."

"She knows what I'm worried about," said Henry, keeping

his eyes locked with Síle's. "So you want him to take you to Bewley's. But is the north side not your territory?"

Síle glared at him. "I live on the north side, lots of people do. What difference does that make?"

"Not just the north side. Monto. You live in Mrs. Drumgold's kip in Faithful Place, I believe, with several other young women."

"Where I board and who with is my own concern!" Síle snapped.

As Henry had said, Ned was a good Catholic boy with all the innocence that term implied in the Ireland of 1914, but even so he was beginning to understand. No woman was going to be insulted in Ned Halloran's presence! He did exactly what he thought Mr. Pearse would do. Placing his right hand over Síle's, he said firmly, "We'll go for that tea now, Síle."

But Henry Mooney was not easily outflanked. "I'm ready for a cup myself," he announced, falling into step beside them.

The three made their way to Bewley's Oriental Café in Westmoreland Street. Bewley's specialized in China teas, freshly baked cakes and scones, and an atmosphere that managed to combine the homeyness of the kitchen with the hospitality of the parlor. Although the wood-paneled interior was cozily dark, Dubliners sat for hours reading newspapers or chatting with friends as if they were in their own homes.

Henry pulled out Síle's chair so deftly Ned had no chance to perform the courtesy, then ordered tea and sandwiches for three from the waitress and insisted on paying for them himself. Síle, with equal dexterity, took over the task of pouring the tea from the glazed pot. Ned felt like a child caught between two adults.

As if nothing unpleasant had passed between them, Henry began chatting with the young woman. When he mentioned various events and personalities of the day she was surprisingly knowledgeable. The illiterate peasant in the tumbledown cabin had been replaced by a city girl who now boasted of reading newspapers. Henry complimented her on her "informed conversation." She smiled; he smiled back.

As he watched them Ned became aware of subtle shifts of power from one side to the other, reminding him of points being scored on a playing field. Much social intercourse, he had long since concluded, was based on a degree of hypocrisy. He did not see this realization as a loss of innocence but as an increased understanding of the world.

Staring down into his teacup, he thought longingly of Saint Enda's and Mr. Pearse, who said only what he meant.

Chapter Sixteen

Caitlín, *a chara*,
   Recently I met Dan Duffy's sister in Dublin. Unfortunately, my friend Henry Mooney took an instant dislike to her. After we had tea together in Bewley's he urged me to avoid her in future, which I thought presumptuous of him.

Ned did not report Henry's exact words: "If you want that sort of companionship, let me take you to someone I can vouch for."

   I am old enough to choose my own company, however, and I plan to see Miss Duffy again. A country girl come up to the city must feel rather lost. I know I did when I first came here. So for her brother's sake, God rest him, I shall be her friend.

Ned interrupted his letter writing at that point to attend class. When next he took up his pen he had exciting news to impart.

   Caitlín, you may have an opportunity to meet our Mr. Pearse! Although he has long encouraged Irish nationalism through his writings and speeches, until recently he was not a member of any political organization. But as I told you before, things are changing. He has now joined the Irish Republican Brotherhood. With their help he is going on a lecture tour in America to raise funds for the school. He will be sailing on the *Campania* in February, and his first engagements will be in New York. There will be announcements in the papers.

If you meet him, do not be misled by first impressions. He may seem standoffish, but that is just the way he appears with strangers. He is a different man at home. Did I tell you he takes his meals in the refectory with us? He never minds how much we shout and laugh; he is like one of us then.

After classes when we gather around the fireplace he can be jolly company. Sometimes he recites a rollicking ballad called ''Seamus O'Brien'' with such histrionics that we fall around the place laughing. Just between us, I do not think Mr. Pearse likes adults very much; he says young people are the only ones who make him feel fully alive.

Some days later Ned was called to the headmaster's study to find Pearse poring over a long list of items and checking off various ones with a pencil. In front of him on the desk was an unfinished article on education for the *Irish Review*, the draft of a speech ''To the Boys of Ireland,'' and a cup of tea gone cold. Looking up as the boy entered, Pearse said, ''Thank you for coming, Ned. You are the very person I need. I believe you have had some experience with steamship travel?''

Ned could not help smiling. After a moment, Pearse chuckled, too. ''I realize that sounded absurd. Going down with the *Titanic* constitutes a great deal more than 'some experience.' What I really wanted to discuss with you was, how should I prepare for my journey? For example, is there any sovereign remedy to prevent seasickness?''

Ned sat down and answered Pearse's questions as best he

could. Then the tone of the conversation changed. Pearse confided, "I do not look forward to this voyage. The very thought of drowning is so terrible." He blinked rapidly. "A Christian who believes in the immortality of the soul should not fear death. But I should hate to have it come to me so far from home, with my work yet undone. Tell me, Ned, to what do you credit your survival when the *Titanic* went down? Would you call it divine intervention?"

To the disappointment of his classmates, Ned never talked about the disaster. It hurt too much. But in the book-lined study, encouraged by a man he trusted, he made himself recall that terrible night.

From beyond the window came the shouts of boys on the playing field. For a moment they mimicked the screams of the dying, plunging Ned back into the icy Atlantic. He drew a deep breath and forced himself to be aware of the solidity of the chair beneath him, the hard edge of oak against the backs of his thighs.

The words came slowly. "When it was obvious the ship was going down I leaped from the rail. There was nothing else to do. I couldn't get in a boat. They were all away by that time anyway. I had a life jacket on, but even so when I hit the water I went under. The water was so cold and so dark; I remember how it hissed in my ears. Then I bobbed to the surface. Once I could breathe again I felt—and this is very strange—I felt the most curious *stillness*, as if I were in the eye of a storm. I did nothing, thought nothing. I just floated. All around was pandemonium . . . yet inside of me was total calm."

The older man leaned forward. "That was God's presence," he said with conviction, almost with envy, "assuring you that you were going to live."

Ned did not want to contradict Pearse, but he was bound by truth. "It wasn't like that at all, I'm afraid. On every side I could hear the shrieks of the dying and I was convinced I would die too. I think what I experienced was not . . . not the buoyancy of hope but the certainty of death. It gave me a strange sort of peace."

"Peace," echoed the man. "Indeed. The certainty of death must be a . . . liberating experience. When you know the worst there is nothing left to fear. The idea of death has always broken my heart, destroying as it does the gentle, innocent creatures of this earth, all things bright and green, all things young and happy. But perhaps . . ." Pearse fell silent. The glowing eyes gazed past Ned into some dark space of their own imagining.

Chapter Seventeen

W HEN Ned's letter arrived Kathleen promptly took it to the presbytery. "My brother is full of such excitement," she told Father Paul. "He talks about . . . what did he call it? 'A conspiracy of poets' that's working to improve conditions in Ireland. Now his Mr. Pearse is coming to America on a lecture tour. He'll be speaking right here in New York! I want so much to go and meet him, but Alexander won't take me. He disapproves of the very idea. I can hardly go by myself, a woman without an escort."

In her voice the priest recognized boredom and discontent simmering below the surface. Duty obliged him to say, "It is a wife's place to be obedient to her husband's authority, Kathleen."

" 'A wife's place!' I'm beginning to think my place is to be a stuffed exhibit in a glass bell, one of those trophies Alexander loves to display. Well, I can't live like that, Father. I thought I could, but I can't. It isn't natural."

Looking at her bright eyes and flushed cheeks, he was forced to agree. "No, Kathleen, such a life is not natural. Not for a healthy young woman like you. There is no reason why you should not have interests of your own, and if you want to go to hear this man speak, then I shall escort you myself." As he said the words Paul felt a small thrill of defiance—

defying Alexander Campbell, defying the church, defying all those powers that would crush the natural instincts.

He knew he was flirting with danger; knew, and no longer cared. If Christ wanted him to be celibate, let Christ intervene.

THE lecture Kathleen chose to attend was titled "An Ideal in Education," conveniently scheduled on the same night as one of her husband's Freemasonry meetings. Members of Clan na Gael had arranged for hiring the hall. A large amount of publicity was being generated for Pearse's tour in the columns of the organization's newspaper, the *Gaelic American*, which depicted him as a left-wing Irish nationalist.

Although Father Paul did not subscribe to the *Gaelic American*, his housekeeper did, and made a point of showing him the articles. They disturbed the priest, but he had promised Kathleen he would take her and would not break his word.

On the appointed night he hired a cab and called for Kathleen at her door. A blizzard was threatened; the streets were icy and the air crystalline with frost. As the cab drew up in front of the lecture hall they saw a number of men stationed around the doorway, smoking, talking, coldly inspecting new arrivals from under the brims of their caps. Something about their demeanor made Paul put a protective arm around Kathleen's shoulders. "This may not have been such a good idea," he told her.

She laughed. "Nonsense. I'm with you, amn't I? I feel very safe with you." When she tilted her head back and looked up at him, he was very aware of the confiding way her body nestled into his embrace.

His clerical collar had the usual effect; as they left the cab, the men around the doorway stepped aside respectfully.

The hall was a great barn of a room with bare floors and rows of wooden chairs. In an effort to make it more festive swags of bunting had been draped along the high windowsills and around the edge of the speakers' platform. A crowd of Irish-Americans, well fed and well dressed, were sitting in the audience and chatting amiably among themselves, but around the walls were ranged a number of lean, hard-faced men like those outside; men with nothing of America in their eyes.

John Devoy, the seventy-two-year-old firebrand of Clan na Gael, made an introductory speech in which accents of County Kildare still lingered. It took him a long time to tell his audience that Patrick Henry Pearse was someone who needed no introduction. As Devoy spoke, Pearse sat quietly behind him, arms folded, head down, a man alone in himself. He seemed unaware of the praise being heaped upon him. There was nothing in his appearance to excite interest.

At last Devoy turned and beckoned him forward. "New York City has a population of four million souls, Mr. Pearse," Devoy said proudly, "of which nearly half live on Manhattan Island. Many of them are sympathetic to our cause and are eagerly waiting to hear what you have to say."

Pearse responded with a shy smile. Then he swept his eyes across the audience, cleared his throat nervously, and began to speak.

With his first words he was transformed.

As she listened, Kathleen was enchanted by the Irish in his voice. The land she had left haunted her as never before. In Pearse's speech she heard the cadences of James Clarence Mangan's poetry as read aloud by her father on winter nights, saw the wings of linnets etched against an azure sky, gazed upon reed-fringed lakes enameled with sunset or turned into hammered silver with dawn. Watched the high summer sun transform the thatch of humble cottages into gold.

Ostensibly, Pearse's speech was about his school and his educational theories. But while stressing the need to raise money for Saint Enda's, he placed the school in a larger context. Soon he was describing the Ireland that awaited his pupils: an Ireland they would construct for themselves.

"That man's a real orator," Kathleen whispered to her companion.

"He has a gift for language," the priest agreed, "and he's obviously in love with his subject."

"What's wrong with that? Americans are quick to boast about America, but the Irish in Ireland rarely have a kind word to say about their own country. Such pride was beaten out of us long ago. It's wonderful to hear someone—''

''Ssshhh,'' hissed a man seated behind them.

Kathleen pressed her lips together and folded her hands demurely in her lap. But her eyes were shining.

''Will the young men of Ireland,'' Pearse was saying, ''rise to the opportunity that is given them? The fate of Ireland in our time will very likely be determined by the way in which the Irish volunteer movement develops.

''Remember that the Ulster unionists were the first to introduce the threat of violence into Irish politics. The year 1913 saw the arming of the Ulster Volunteer Force, whose intention is to deny the island of Ireland any hope of self-government. And I say this to you: To the extent they are willing to fight for their beliefs, the unionists may be the best Irishmen of us all!

''The condition on which freedom is given to men is that they are able to make good their claim to it. Before this generation has passed the Irish Volunteers will draw the sword for Ireland. I do not know how nationhood is achieved except by armed men.''

Pearse gazed out over the heads of his listeners as if he could see into some realm beyond the scope of mortal eye. Then he said very softly, so they had to lean forward to hear him, ''Christ's peace is lovely in its coming, beautiful are its feet on the mountains. But it is heralded by terrific messengers; seraphim and cherubim blow trumpets of war before it. We must not flinch when we are passing through that uproar; we must not faint at the sight of blood. Winning through it, we—or those of us who survive—shall come unto great joy. We and our fathers have known the Pax Britannica. To our sons we must bequeath the Peace of the Gael!''

On the last words his voice rose to thunder. When he stopped speaking there was a moment of intense silence. Then a mighty roar filled the hall.

Men leaped to their feet, overturning chairs in their rush to the speaker's platform. Everyone wanted a word with Pearse, or at the least to press his hand.

Within moments the ardent orator was replaced by a diffi-
dent, ill-at-ease man who looked as if he wanted desperately
to escape.

"I must speak to him," Kathleen told Paul as she stood
up.

"I don't think that's such a good . . ."

But she was already edging her way through the crowd and
the priest had no choice but to follow her.

IN the cab on the way home, Kathleen enthused, "Is he not
wonderful? He was so polite to me, and he spoke so highly
of Ned."

"He does seem dedicated," the priest said noncommittally.

"Dedicated. Yes, that's the word. To the school and to
Ireland. And I want to help him."

"Help him raise money for his school, you mean?"

"That wasn't what he was talking about, not really."

"No," Father Paul agreed. "He was talking about raising
money for an armed rebellion. I'm troubled by the fact that
such an otherwise idealistic man is putting his faith in the
gun."

She shook her head. "Not in the gun. In Ireland and her
future; Ned's future and that of all the young people like him.
I tell you, Paul, the Irish have a right to own their own souls!"

"You're too much under the spell of Mr. Pearse's rhetoric," warned the priest. "I urge you not to involve yourself
in these matters, Kathleen."

"Why not? My husband and his Freemasons involve themselves in politics as much as they please. Why should I not
support something I believe in? I've made a few friends in
New York who might be persuaded to donate to a good cause.
It's little enough to be doing for Ned and his future, but I can
do that much, thank God. I thought you would agree with me;
you're Irish too."

"I'm a priest," he reminded her. "I can't condone violence."

"Oh, come, Paul! What were the Crusades but the Church condoning violence?"

"Who told you that?"

"Father Hagerty, our parish priest at home. He was the one who arranged for Ned to go to Mr. Pearse's school."

Paul silently noted her use of the phrase "at home." "Your Father Hagerty expresses an opinion contradictory to church teaching, Kathleen."

"The Church doesn't support his brand of nationalism, either," she replied tartly. "The Irish are urged from the pulpit to be unquestioningly obedient to authority, meaning the Crown as well as Rome. I never questioned it before, but I'm beginning to now."

Paul frowned. "You're beginning to question church teaching?"

"Where it involves itself in politics, yes. In America, Church and state are separate, I've learned that much since I've been here. Ireland's in a very different situation. At home the Church determines every aspect of our lives; we go from cradle to grave as our bishops dictate.

"Is that freedom? Are we not taught that God has given us free will? In Ireland we're not allowed any. I can see that now that I'm away. Plenty of guilt, oh, we're welcome to that, but no freedom."

The priest said, "I'm sure you exaggerate, Kathleen. You're overexcited tonight, otherwise you wouldn't blame the Church for Ireland's ills."

"I'm not; the blame lies at Britain's door. But what have we ever been able to do about it? The tragic thing is that individual priests have been patriots, but Risings have failed in the past when their bishops refused to support them. Some say it was just to protect church property."

"And you believe that?"

"I never thought about it one way or the other until now. Mr. Pearse has started me thinking about a lot of things. . . ." Her voice trailed away. She sat back against the buttoned black leather upholstery of the cab seat and gazed out the window in silence.

Paul watched her out of the corner of his eye. He was annoyed that some turbulent priest back in Ireland had sowed the initial seeds of rebellion in her. Those seeds could bear bitter fruit if men like Patrick Pearse inflamed her passions.

Women had no business involving themselves in politics. The church was right to disapprove. In America over a dozen individual states had by now granted women the right to vote, encouraging them to neglect their proper role as mothers and homemakers. Unsatisfied with this, suffragettes were vociferous in their demands for a female suffrage amendment to the United States Constitution. In Britain as well they were increasingly involved in protests and hunger strikes. At the Derby the year before, a suffragette had even thrown herself in front of the king's horse and been killed.

Surely it was the job of Kathleen's confessor to save her from similar foolhardy passions.

February 25, 1914

CLAIMS THAT ULSTER VOLUNTEER
FORCE NOW HAS 100,000 ARMED MEN

Chapter Eighteen

Wʜɪʟᴇ the headmaster was away in America, his brother Willie functioned as acting headmaster, keeping up everyone's spirits and stalling importunate bank managers. Pádraic Pearse insisted on being sent detailed weekly bulletins of the boys' scholastic progress, so these were added to his duties.

Additional responsibilities fell on the Senior Boys as well, so Ned did not go back into the city until the first Saturday in April. The day was cold, with lowering clouds. It would have been pleasant to stay at Saint Enda's and play chess with Brian Joyce, but Ned was determined to see Mary.

He could not say why she haunted his mind so.

Born and raised around livestock, he was familiar with the mechanics of sex. Since puberty Ned had experienced what he thought of as "rutting dreams." Some were so vivid that he cried out in his sleep, or squirmed beneath the covers seeking relief. Occasionally a particular dream would linger in his memory for days, to be recalled again and again with guilty pleasure.

When he mentioned these dreams in confession, however, the priest reacted as if he were hearing some shocking new sin. But Ned knew he was far from alone. Other boys in his dormitory at Saint Enda's moaned in their sleep, too.

Yet somehow he did not equate the cravings of his body with the longings of his heart.

His Catholic upbringing denied there could be any connection. Purity as represented by the Virgin was the ultimate symbol of virtue. In spite of what Henry Mooney said, Her divine light ennobled all women.

To Ned, Mary Cosgrave represented an ideal just as Mr. Pearse's vision of a free Ireland was an ideal. Both were to be longed for; neither must be contaminated by anything base and vile.

When Ned arrived at Brown Thomas the same commissionaire gave him the same professional smile, but instead of opening the door said, "Sorry, sir. Early closing today, two o'clock."

"You mean the shop's not open?"

"That's right. Come back on Monday."

"But I can't . . ." Just then Ned saw Mary Cosgrave emerge from a side entrance amid a bevy of shop assistants leaving for the day. Thankfully, he hurried toward her.

She was even prettier than he remembered, and smaller. When he called "Miss Cosgrave!" she did not recognize him. She stared blankly at him for a moment, then her face lit with a smile.

"Why, you're Mr. Mooney's friend, aren't you?"

Ned was abashed to realize she had not been thinking of him as much as he had been thinking of her over the winter. "I am Henry Mooney's friend," he replied stiffly. "We met after the Larkin riot."

"Of course! You're the boy who saved my father. How is your poor head now?"

"Fine, thank you. I . . . uh . . . are you going somewhere? May I escort you?"

Mary rewarded him with another smile and put her tiny hand on his arm. "I'm going to meet my friend Eliza Goggins—she works at Switzer's Drapery Shop—so we can have lunch together. It's our weekly treat. Would you care to join us?"

The last thing Ned wanted was to have a third person

around when he finally had the chance to be with Mary. But
there was no graceful way to decline. Soon he was squiring
the two shopgirls to a café nestled among the victuallers,
greengrocers, and poulterers in Chatham Street.

"We often eat here if it's raining," Eliza explained after
they were seated at a small, none-too-clean table. "But when
it's fine we buy white bread and cheese and picnic on the
Green."

"That's ever so much nicer," said Mary, frowning at the
flyspecked menu.

Eliza Goggins was a couple of years older than Mary, a
plain, thin girl with bad posture, a rabbity face, and red-
rimmed eyes. "There's a lot of consumption in her family,"
Mary had confided to Ned while they were waiting for her
outside Switzer's.

"There's consumption in almost every family," he replied.
"They call it tuberculosis now, you know. We read about it
in school. It's caused by a bacillus discovered by a German
physician in 1882."

Ned was mildly disappointed that Mary did not ask him to
tell her more.

During lunch he listened while the two girls chatted. He
had never heard young working women discuss their lives
before.

For his benefit Mary boasted, "Drapery is a highly desirable occupation. Only the most genteel Irish families can apprentice a son or daughter—for a fee, of course—to the better
shops. Eliza and I are lucky. There's hundreds who are
worked to exhaustion in shops not nearly as nice as ours."

"It's better than it used to be, though," Eliza said. She had
the disconcerting habits of twisting her hands together and
fidgeting with her cutlery. "Mary wasn't in employment when
we worked a full six day week, from early morning until long
after the shop closed in the evening. Now thanks to the association we have a weekly half-holiday."

Mary gave a dainty sniff. "You and your association."

"What is that?" asked Ned.

"The Drapers' Assistants' Association," Eliza told him.

She had begun twining her legs together under the table. Ned longed to tell her to sit still; her nervous mannerisms were distracting. "They've done ever so much for us. They're campaigning now for an end to dismissals without cause. I'm a member, and Mary should be, too."

"My father belongs to a union," Mary retorted, "which got him injured in a riot, as Ned here knows very well. If he stayed out of it we would be better off. Employers prefer people who don't make trouble."

Eliza's eyes flashed. "You don't seem to mind sharing the benefits of the association's successes. Because of them you have this afternoon off. And you don't have to live in a dormitory, either."

Ned raised his eyebrows. "A dormitory? What's wrong with that? I live in one at Saint Enda's. It's clean and cheerful and the other lads are good company."

Eliza began folding and refolding her napkin. "Perhaps some dormitories are nicer than others. I wouldn't know about the nice kind. You see, Ned, Dublin drapers provide lodging for their employees so they don't have to pay them a living wage. Brown Thomas stopped last year in response to pressure from the association, that's why Mary can live at home. But a lot of us aren't so lucky.

"I lodge in an old barn of a house off Stephen's Green. Fifty young men and women live there in drafty, curtainless rooms with not a bath in the building, so we have to go out to the public baths. We must keep clean and tidy or we would lose our jobs. Everything we use is taken out of our wages, even soap and shoe polish. The food we are given is the plainest possible—and not very much of that. Fines are levied for unnecessary talking in the rooms, or leaving an article of clothing lying about, or being out at night without a signed docket. Once I was fined tuppence just for losing my copy of the rules."

Ned shook his head in sympathy.

"It's a cold, dreary life and no mistake," Eliza went on. "Although," she dropped her voice to a conspiratorial level—

"there is a depression worn in the floorboards between the men's and women's rooms."

Mary exchanged glances with her, and both girls giggled. Ned was dismayed. Surely Mary did not understand, he told himself. He was thankful she lived at home and was not exposed to the life her friend described. Nothing coarse must ever touch her.

Mr. Pearse was known to have a great devotion to the Virgin Mary. With all the passion of a boy's virgin heart, Ned was developing a similar devotion toward Mary Cosgrave.

After lunch they walked Eliza to her lodgings near Stephen's Green, then he and Mary spent the rest of the afternoon together. They strolled the streets of the city observing other pedestrians, complaining about the deteriorating weather, gazing into shop windows at the spring fashions. Mary seemed to have an endless appetite for shop windows.

"Last year I was terribly extravagant," she confided with a giggle. "Sports costumes were the newest vogue for ladies and I quite lost my heart to a cream corduroy ensemble. I managed to put a few shillings aside for a deposit, and I've been paying it off ever since."

Ned asked in surprise, "You take part in sports?"

"I do not. They're too messy and sweaty. But the color will look grand on me, don't you think?" She pirouetted in front of him, inviting him to imagine her in cream corduroy.

Ned, who had never had such a conversation before, was enchanted by the revelation of her femininity. When she allowed him to escort her all the way home, he walked the considerable distance without his feet ever touching the ground. Once they paused to watch a detachment of cavalry ride by in cross-belted red coats and tall black shakos. For Ned their sabers were a painful reminder of Bloody Sunday, but Mary clasped her hands together and murmured, "Aren't they splendid in their uniforms!"

That night in his bed at Saint Enda's Ned recalled her every word and gesture. On Sunday he awoke to a steady, relentless rain. When he went to Mass he bowed his head in prayer, yet the image in his heart was not that of Christ. A younger,

fresher vision filled him with radiance in spite of the gloom
of the day. He was like someone intoxicated.

When Ned envisioned Mary he first saw her eyes: liquid
eyes, deer's eyes, luminous and vulnerable. And she had a
habit of wrinkling her nose to emphasize certain words, he
remembered that. And the way the hair curled around her
temples as if caressing them. The skin of her throat above her
Limerick lace collar was so soft.

His mind lingered on details of Mary. He thought each
unique. Surely no one else had such a lilting laugh or such
small hands. And of all the women in the world, he had no
doubt, she possessed the loveliest ears, flat against her head
yet curving in a way that tempted his finger to trace the delicate outer flap.

God made Mary, Ned thought with a sense of wonder.
Never had he been so aware of the Creator as in contempla-
tion of His creation. Was this, he asked himself, the real if
unacknowledged reason behind the powerful human impulse
to worship? Shrouded in the mysteries of religion was there
a deeper, simpler truth, a more perfect miracle?

Chapter Nineteen

Father Paul O'Shaughnessy made some discreet inquiries. What he learned did not add to his peace of mind. Among the New York Irish, particularly recent immigrants, there was considerable support for an armed rising against British rule in Ireland. Viewed from a safe distance, the idea seemed both justifiable and romantic.

Not all of the Irish community concurred, however. Exposure to life in America had slowly but surely modified their antipathy toward Britain. If imperialism had been the cause of centuries of tragedy in Ireland, the commercial scope of the British Empire had contributed toward American prosperity. Many second- and third-generation immigrants, beneficiaries of that prosperity, felt only a teary nostalgia for "the auld sod." They could not get excited about winning Ireland's freedom.

John Devoy and his followers in Clan na Gael represented a minority, but it was a passionate minority. About such men there was more than a whiff of danger.

When Kathleen told Paul, "I'm determined to be involved in some way in the wonderful work Mr. Pearse is doing," he urged her to reconsider. But she had the bit in her teeth and would not listen.

She wrote to her brother:

I have met your Mr. Pearse, Ned, and he is everything you said. He spoke in the most complimentary terms of you, but even more exciting was what he had to say about Ireland. I feel—oh my dear, I hardly know how to express this—I feel as if I left home too soon!

I should be there now, as you are, to help with the work that lies ahead. When you write of your friend the countess I am so envious. To think of her marshaling her own little army! She puts me in mind of Saint Joan. I imagine her in shining armor, riding on a massive horse.

In my own small way I too shall help. I plan to invite a number of ladies of my acquaintance to a luncheon to raise funds for Mr. Pearse's cause. Alexander took quite a bit of persuading to allow me to do this, but at last I was successful.

She did not say more. Delicacy forbade giving details of the marital relationship to her brother.

But she did confess to Father Paul, "Alexander is so difficult about anything I want to do on my own. He finally gave permission only when I assured him the money was for Saint Enda's. A gentleman could hardly refuse to allow his wife to benefit her own brother."

"We had this conversation before, Kathleen. The money won't be going to the school, surely you understand that. If you told your husband it would, you lied."

"Yes," she said, and dropped her eyes. She did not sound contrite.

That night Father Paul took a long time to fall asleep. When at last he dropped into an uneasy doze, he found himself standing on the side of a hill overlooking a train track. A figure came walking toward the track from the other side. As it came closer he could tell it was a woman. Reaching the track, she signed the Cross on her bosom and stretched herself out on the rails, then turned her face in his direction.

It was Kathleen Campbell.

In his dream the priest shouted a warning but she did not respond. Cold with sudden terror, he raced down the hill. A train was coming; he could hear it rushing toward them. Still Kathleen did not move. When he reached her she merely smiled up at him with the expression of an innocent child.

He bent and scooped her into his arms. The feel of her was totally convincing. He experienced a rush of throttled desire at the heat and weight of her body. But when he tried to carry her off the tracks, his feet stuck fast to the earth. No matter how hard he tried to break free he could not. With every moment the train was coming closer. At last in desperation he kissed Kathleen hard upon the mouth—wondering at his audacity as he did so—then flung her to safety.

The train was right on top of him. With a sense of awful inevitability he turned to face it . . .

. . . and woke up trembling and sweating in his bed.

The sensation of her lips against his was the clearest thought in his mind.

After Mass the next morning he was unable to eat any breakfast. His housekeeper fussed over him like a hen with one chick. "God love you, Father, try just a bite of hot porridge or a wee taste of egg and sausage. You have to keep your strength up. So many people depend on you."

He gave her a brooding look. "They do, Mrs. Flanagan. I know they do."

He spent several hours in his study, then late in the afternoon sent a message to the Campbell house. "I need to see you on a matter of some urgency," he wrote Kathleen.

He honestly believed as he penned the words that he was referring to her ill-advised fund-raising.

She came to him the next morning after Alexander had gone to work. Mrs. Flanagan ushered her in as always, seated her in the parlor, offered her coffee and freshly baked scones with marmalade. When Paul entered the room a few minutes later he noticed that she had touched neither. Like me, he thought, she has no appetite. Like me.

As soon as Mrs. Flanagan left the room he asked, "Do you know why I sent for you?"

"A matter of some urgency, your note said."

"Yes."

She was gazing at him expectantly. In an effort to focus his thoughts he took a step closer to her chair. When she tilted her head back to look up to him he saw that there were dark shadows under her eyes, and her lips were trembling.

Paul knelt down beside her chair. "About this luncheon of yours."

"Yes."

"I have expressed my misgivings to you before."

"Yes."

As if it had a life of its own divorced from any volition on his part, Paul's hand began stroking Kathleen's dark hair. He said, "Devoy and those like him are planning an armed insurrection. Involving yourself would be madness."

"Yes."

"Surely you cannot condone the willful overthrow of authority!"

"Yes." His hand was cupping the back of her head. She was not hearing his words, only the deep rumble of his voice making her bones resonate like the sounding board of a harp. Her eyes closed.

Insurrection, thought Paul. The overthrow of authority. God help me.

Then she was in his arms.

Neither of them moved. He could smell her scent and hear the clock ticking on the mantel.

As long as I do no more than this, the priest told himself, it is still all right. I am comforting a parishioner.

She had slipped to the floor so that she knelt with him. The top of her head was just below his clerical collar. He had no intention of pressing his lips to her fragrant hair. He never told his arms to tighten so that her breasts were crushed against him.

Mrs. Flanagan's step in the hall outside broke their trance. With a guilty start they pulled away from each other. Kathleen slipped back into her chair; Paul got to his feet and made a futile effort to smooth his clothes with his hand. The housekeeper entered the room carrying a tray with a fresh pot of hot coffee. She set it on the table with her eyes politely averted. Well trained, she knew it was her role to be invisible.

But after she had left the room she paused outside the door. Why had they looked so flustered, the pair of them? Could Mrs. Campbell have been admitting some misbehavior to her priest outside the confessional? A pretty young woman in a wicked city like New York, surely she had temptations. People knew her husband was with White Star and sometimes went away on business.

Mrs. Flanagan wondered if Alderman Claffey's housemaid ever noticed anything suspicious next door. The Claffeys had employed Bridie Lynch after Mrs. Campbell refused her services, and had given her a room at the top of their house. From such a vantage point a young and naturally curious woman like Bridie would have an excellent view of the neighbors.

KATHLEEN left the presbytery in a daze. The unimaginable had happened and she could not yet take it in. Instead of returning home she simply walked and walked, hugging herself. She needed all her strength to hold in the elation that threatened to burst out of her.

At the same time she was appalled by the gravity of her sin. To love a priest! So far they had done nothing more than hold one another, but the very fact that she could think in terms of "so far" meant that she anticipated going farther.

Spring was in the air, New York spring. Kathleen did not know how long she had been walking, nor how far, until she found herself at one of the entrances to Central Park. Ahead were masses of trees clothed in achingly tender leaves, flower-starred meadows, gentle slopes, leafy glens, rocky ravines. Nature in all her abundance, bursting free.

In Ireland, Kathleen would have taken off her shoes and walked on the grass. In Ireland . . .

"It's May Day," she said to herself, astonished that she had forgotten. "Beltane!"

A gray pigeon strutting past her on the sidewalk paused to cock an eye in her direction as if he understood what she was talking about.

At home the young girls would have gone out before sunrise to collect the dew of the first day of May to bathe their faces in. Everyone knew May morning dew had the magical ability to bestow beauty.

"Do you suppose *he* thinks I'm beautiful?" she asked the pigeon. She had to speak to someone, had to acknowledge what was happening. Under the circumstances she could hardly confess to her confessor. Perhaps she could have told her mother, but Theresa Halloran was at the bottom of the Atlantic.

"Does he?" she demanded of the pigeon.

The bird fixed her with an imperious glare, then pointedly began pecking at the sidewalk near her feet. Its eye was circled with bright yellow; its tail was banded with a darker shade of gray. A handsome bird, it was not interested in the vanity of humans, only in their ability to provide corn and crumbs. When the woman failed to take the hint it lost interest and strutted away.

She watched it go. I'm as giddy as some foolish girl, she thought. Imagine talking to a pigeon.

But she was not a girl. She was a married woman with full knowledge of the possible consequences of her actions.

Entering the park, Kathleen walked for a while longer before she realized how tired she was. Then she sat down on a bench, hugging her guilty secret, and watched the passersby. What would they think if they knew? Would they be shocked? That well-dressed woman there with her arm linked through her husband's—it must be her husband, her touch was so proprietary—suppose she knew Kathleen had been locked in the forbidden embrace of a priest?

But perhaps that was not her husband at all. Perhaps he was—she hesitated over the word, even in the privacy of her mind—perhaps he was her lover. And they were going to some discreet little hotel on the other side of the park to spend the afternoon in a room with the blinds drawn . . .

In the third drawer of the mahogany highboy in the bedroom she shared with Alexander was a cheesecloth bag of lavender. Years ago her mother had explained to her, amid many blushes and stammerings, that married women must always keep lavender to tuck among the sheets. "It lessens the smell of certain . . . male discharges," Theresa had confided. Marriage to Alexander Campbell had taught Kathleen the wisdom of her mother's advice.

Now she found herself wondering if Paul's semen would smell so strong, so unpleasant. Or would it be clean and fresh like everything else about him?

Kathleen struggled to check her riotous thoughts. Her emotions were running counter to everything she had been taught. A hundred years of repression by the clergy had made sexual pleasure the ultimate sin. Sex was bad, sex was wrong; its only purpose was the conception of children, and to take any enjoyment from the act was to make oneself lower than the animals. As for desiring a priest . . .

But I do, Kathleen Halloran Campbell admitted to herself as she sat on the wrought iron bench in the warm sunlight. I want him. If I burn in Hell for it, I want Paul O'Shaughnessy.

Chapter Twenty

I<small>N</small> the middle of May, Pádraic Pearse returned from America. On the morning he was expected at Saint Enda's, the Senior Boys took banners and trumpets onto the roof to give the headmaster a festive welcome. The rest of the students lined the drive in a fever of anticipation. Young Denis Larkin was anxious to show the headmaster his plaster cast. He had broken his elbow in a hurling match and was feeling very much the wounded hero.[1]

The headmaster's sisters stationed themselves at the gates so they would be the first to see Pearse when he arrived. A stocky, plain woman, Margaret was a dedicated worrier. "Is there no sign of the motorcar yet?" she kept asking Mary Brigid. "You don't suppose something's happened to him, do you? Can you see the car?" Rising on her tiptoes, she waved her handkerchief back and forth in the air like a tiny white flag.

In addition to her unstable temperament, Mary Brigid was a hypochondriac who wrapped herself in heavy coats even in the warmest weather. "Isn't it hot?" she remarked as she fanned herself with her hand. "Don't you find it dreadfully hot today, Wow-wow?" But she never took off the coat.

On the front steps Mrs. Pearse waited with Willie and the rest of the staff. She too had her handkerchief out, but she was using it to dab at her eyes. From time to time she squeezed her son's arm. "It's glad I am that you didn't go off and leave me too, Little Man," she said. "I need my boys; you and Pat both."

"You have us, Mother; you shall always have us," Willie assured her. "Pat will be here any moment, you'll see."

When at last Count Plunkett's motorcar came down the drive, Ned and his companions gave the traditional three shouts of welcome. Pearse put his head out of the window and looked up at the roof, then responded with a wave that brought on a second round of cheering. Boys tossed their caps in the air and pummeled each other's shoulders.

That evening a weary Pearse reported to the staff of Saint Enda's, "Our mission was a success, I feel. Most audiences were responsive. The thousand pounds I've already sent home should satisfy our more pressing creditors, which means we can reopen next September. And there is the promise of more to come; our American friends plan to arrange dances, stage fund-raisers, that sort of thing."

Privately he confided to Ned, "Not only the school will benefit. We have pledges of aid for the Volunteers as well. Your sister, God be good to her, is one of those who has promised to raise money for us in New York."

"My sister? Kathleen Campbell?"

"Indeed. A fine woman and very devout; she came to my lecture escorted by her priest."

"Bedad," muttered Ned, an expression he had picked up from Thomas MacDonagh.

Pearse shot him a sharp look of reprimand. What the head-master might tolerate from his friends was unacceptable from his students.

Ned was about to become more than a student, however. The very next day Pearse, who had been appointed as organizing director for the Volunteers, entrusted him with carrying dispatches for the corps.

"You will need reliable transportation," Pearse said, "so I am asking Roger Casement to buy you a bicycle from the Volunteers' treasury. The funds are a little depleted at present, but he's going to America soon to raise more. You can ride a bicycle, of course?"

"I can, sir. My father had one."

"Then so shall you."

By Friday a sturdy new machine was delivered to Saint Enda's. Black, with shiny handlebars. After his last class of the afternoon Ned went for a gravel-churning spin up and down the drive and concluded with a circle of the forecourt, no-hands, to the jibes of envious classmates.

That weekend he began making trips farther afield. From Saint Enda's he could reach O'Connell Bridge in forty-five minutes with ease. One of his first calls in the city was to Thomas Clarke, proprietor of a news agency and tobacconist's at 75A Parnell Street. "Tom is one of the hard-liners of the republican movement," Pearse explained before sending Ned to him. "He's a plain man with a rigid code, and a Fenian to the depths of his soul.

"He took part in a dynamiting campaign in England back in the 1880s, offshoot of a failed Irish Rising. It cost him fifteen years in English jails. They starved him and they tortured him, but they could not break him. When he was released he went to the United States, and even became an American citizen, but he never stopped working for the cause of Irish freedom. Eventually he came home to serve on the Supreme Council of the IRB. We have not been able to persuade him to join the executive body of the Volunteers, though.[2] He believes his name would do us more harm than good, and I'm sure he's right."

Pearse's words had excited Ned's curiosity, but whatever he expected it was not the slight, frail man who blinked at him from behind a pair of cheap spectacles. Clarke was in his late fifties, but his sunken cheeks and seedy, drooping mustache made him look a decade older. Life had scraped him to the bone.

"Pádraic Pearse sent me," Ned began, holding out a folded note.

Clarke took the paper without comment and read it while

Ned waited, shifting from one foot to the other. Then the older man slowly removed his spectacles.

The eyes that locked with Ned's were not old and frail, but fierce as an eagle's. "Thank you," Tom Clarke said simply.

He is wearing a mask! Ned thought, delighted with his own perception. A mask of old age and weakness, with the ardent young dynamiter concealed behind it.

Dynamiter. Tom Clarke had been willing to kill people in the name of Ireland. Surely that made him a monster. Yet how could anyone Mr. Pearse admired be a monster? Ned struggled to understand. Was it not possible to love Ireland and want to see her free, without having to resort to violence?

That night he pored over his history books until dawn, tracing the course of one attempt after another to gain justice for Ireland through the British political system. One failure after another.

The system did not work; not for the Irish.

He began to understand how rage and frustration could create a man like Tom Clarke.

"It should not be that way," Ned whispered to himself as the first pale gray light seeped into the room. "But what choice have they given us?"

When he returned to the shop a few days later with another message, Clarke had him wait while he wrote out a reply. A gentle but relentless rain was falling. Ned brushed water from his sleeves and shoulders until he realized he was getting the papers on the counter damp.

"Desperate weather," remarked the shopkeeper.

"It is desperate," the young man agreed. Weather was the universal language.

"And no end to the rain."

"No end at all."

"Still, there are worse places to be. Hotter, drier . . . but just not Ireland."

"I know," said Ned. "I'd rather be here than anywhere. I . . . I had a chance to live in America once, but I turned it down."

Clarke gave him a penetrating look, then asked abruptly, "Do you follow politics?"

"I try to."

"Then you're aware that the Home Rule Bill is in serious difficulties. First there was the suggestion that any Ulster county might, by vote, be allowed to exempt itself from Home Rule for six years. That was bad enough. But just look at today's papers." Clarke drummed the nearest stack with an angry finger. "Now the House of Lords has cobbled together an exclusion amendment for *nine* northern counties *forever*!" John Redmond didn't offer a word of protest, either.

"All the Orangemen had to do to get their own way was threaten violence. There's a lesson for us in that, mark my words. Diplomatic maneuvering is a stalling tactic for the British, but they respond to physical force right smartly. Remember, they built an empire with sword and gun."

Ned said, "That's why it's hard to believe the government of Britain would give in to a relatively small corps like the UVF."

"Not hard at all, when you think of it. Asquith desperately needs the support of the Unionist Party members in Parliament. No one is as vulnerable to intimidation as politicians trying to hold on to power. And Ireland, as always, will have to pay the price. I tell you, lad, if the exclusion amendment's adopted it will amount to the partition of our country."

"Partition?" Ned considered the word. "Two Irelands?"

"That's the idea, and a damned bad one. It would be like cutting off an arm from the body to separate the north from the rest of us. The whole island's no bigger than the American state of Pennsylvania; we can't afford partition either socially or economically. It's madness." Tom Clarke squared his thin shoulders. "Ireland," he vowed fiercely, "shall not be mutilated to please the minority."

His anger and his resolve communicated themselves to Ned. He felt an increased sense of the importance of the messages he was carrying. The recipients were Catholics and Protestants, poets and professional men, academics and the near illiterate, members of the Ascendancy and unemployed labor-

ers. Some, like Sir Roger Casement, had illustrious back-
grounds in the service of Britain.

All had Irish nationalism in common, although it was difficult to separate the varying shades of opinion. They ran the
gamut from simple espousal of the republican ideal to a burning passion for all-out revolution.

As the school year came to a close in mid-June, Ned completed his final term. Aunt Norah wrote to congratulate him.
''Your letters sound so grown-up these days,'' she said. ''All
the books you must have read—your father would be so
proud. Will you be coming back to the farm soon? We do
look forward to taking care of our own dear boy once more.''

The letter was no more than a gentle hint, but Ned sat for
a long time holding it in his hands and staring off into the
distance. Thanks to Lord Inchiquin's kindness, he was
equipped to be much more than a farmer. In the autumn he
might apply for a position on the staff at Saint Enda's, a
teaching apprenticeship that would prepare him for an academic career.

Or—and this was an idea that kept nagging at the edges of
his mind—he might go to work for a newspaper. Henry Mooney made journalism seem a most attractive profession.

The one thing he did not want to do now, if he was being
honest with himself, was go back to the farm.

The weeks he had spent on the farm before he came to
Dublin had taught Ned a bitter lesson. Lost loved ones left
agonizing holes in the landscape. Perhaps if he had never
come away he would have made his peace with grief by now.
But he had missed that chance.

At any rate, the decision did not have to be made immediately. Because his allowance from Lord Inchiquin had
ceased on the last day of school, Frank had begun sending
him some money. Frank Halloran did not have their father's
gift for making the land prosper and was able to spare only
a little. But Ned reckoned it would be sufficient if he had a
roof over his head already.

He wrote his aunt:

Once again I have decided to stay at the school for the summer, helping Mr. MacRory, the chief gardener. In a way he reminds me of Papa. Though he has no formal education, he can quote Rabelais or chant a Gaelic *rann* with equal facility, and has won seven medals for oratory (sometimes he wears them all on the same day!). What might such a man not aspire to in an Ireland that valued him?

Mr. Pearse is involved in matters which will keep him away from Saint Enda's much of the time. At some stage he hopes to go down to Rosmuc in Connemara, where he has a little cottage, for a brief holiday.[3] It will do him a power of good if he knows the school is being well looked after. Perhaps when the new term starts in September I shall come home.

He prudently neglected to mention his position as a courier. To Kathleen, however, he wrote, "I am needed here to do important work for the Volunteers—something I do not want to tell them about at home. Norah would worry. But you understand."

On the last Friday in June, Ned went with the Fianna to a large rally in Bodenstown. The rally was attended by the Irish Volunteers and the labor movement's newly named Irish Citizen Army, led by James Connolly.

Beside the grave of the famous Irish patriot Wolfe Tone, Thomas Clarke spoke of nationalism. Clarke lacked Pádraic Pearse's bardic tongue, but his simple words carried their own weight. As everyone there knew, he had already sacrificed fifteen years of his life for Ireland.

"If we're ever to be granted the dignity of Home Rule on this island," Clarke told his audience, "we must be as prepared to fight for it as the unionists are prepared to fight against it."

Ned applauded wildly. Everyone did, except for a small knot of nondescript men who stood off to one side, listening impassively.

At the conclusion of the meeting Seán MacDermott read

cables of congratulation. One, from John Devoy in America, said, "Best wishes for meeting at the grave of Wolfe Tone, the Protestant apostle of Irish nationalism. The voice from the grave forbids partition, and brands as infamous any man who consents to exclude Ulster for even one day."[4]

The following Monday, Ned was sent to collect a parcel at Eamonn Ceannt's house in the South Circular Road and take it to Clarke. He sped into the city whistling, feeling himself one of the company of heroes. Once he cut in front of a long, gleaming Hupmobile and grinned over his shoulder when the driver gave an angry blast of the horn. "Up the Irish!" Ned called back cheekily.

When he delivered the parcel Clarke offered him a packet of cigarettes. "You should have something more for your trouble than just my thanks."

"I don't smoke, sir."

"Do you not? Good enough. But here, have one of these anyway." From beneath the counter he produced a bowl heaped with fruit. "I buy them from the stalls around the Pillar to give to the children," Clarke explained. "Parents in this neighborhood can't afford to buy fruit for their little ones."

Murmuring thanks, Ned slipped an apple into his pocket. He was just leaving the shop when he saw someone he knew across the street.

"What brings you into the city, Ned?" Síle Duffy asked when his bicycle pulled up alongside her.

"I was doing a message for a friend."

"Oh. And where are you going now?"

"Back to Rathfarnham, I suppose," he replied, dismounting from the machine to walk along the curb with her. "What about you?"

"To Mrs. Drumgold's."

"May I escort you there?"

Her eyes widened. "Och no! . . . I mean . . ." She was horrified at the thought. Going to Mrs. Drumgold's would mark him as a client, someone with cash in hand to pay for services rendered. Ned was no client. Please God, there had to be something in her life other than men who wanted to buy her!

To cover her confusion she fixed her gaze on his bicycle. "That's very nice, so." She pursed her lips as if thinking. "I've never ridden on one. Do you suppose you could carry me on the crossbar?"

Ned was taken aback. The suggestion was incredibly daring. Only once had he seen a young man carrying a girl on his bicycle, and people had turned in the street to stare after them.

"Sitting on the crossbar would be terribly uncomfortable," he told her. "Besides, you'd be in the way of my knees."

"Please?" She looked at him so beguilingly that any argument went out of his head.

"All right, but you sit on the saddle and I'll stand on the pedals." He held the bicycle steady while she seated herself. She was wearing white lilac scent again. For one dizzying moment her skirts were pushed aside and he had a glimpse of her black-stockinged leg almost to the knee. Then he mounted the bicycle in front of her and felt her hands grip his waist. They went spinning down the street with her delighted laughter ringing in his ears.

Ned was in a state of delicious anguish. "Where do you want to go?" he called over his shoulder.

"I don't care. Anywhere. The strand! Let's go look at the sea."

They followed Parnell Street to Summerhill, thence to Fairview. The afternoon was magic. Dublin was gilded by summer; flowers bloomed in the tiny front gardens of every house they passed.

Beyond the railway embankment an empty stretch of grassland gave onto the seafront. They rode as far as the beach, then dismounted and walked the bicycle along the sand. When they came to a deserted spot sheltered from landward sight by dunes topped with coarse grass, Síle said, "Stop here, Ned. This is perfect."

"Have you been here before?"

Instead of answering, she pointed toward the peninsula whose promontory dominated the north side of Dublin Bay.

"Look out there at the Hill of Howth. Isn't it lovely in the sunshine?"

Ned quoted:

On the strand of Howth
Breaks a sounding wave;
A lone sea-gull screams
Above the bay.[5]

Síle was impressed. "Did you make that up just now?"

"I did not. It's from a poem by Pádraic Pearse."

"Do you know many poems?"

"Some. My father could quote reams, and of course we study poetry in school. Both the Irish poets and the English."

She ran her eyes over him, measuring. "It's hard to believe you're still in school. Back home, a man like you would be walking out with his sweetheart."

He felt heat rise in his cheeks.

She saw the flush. "Have you no girl, then?" she asked teasingly. "That's a pity. So tall and strong, and no girl yet." Folding her knees, she sank onto the warm sand and patted the space beside her. "Come sit by me."

Ned laid the bicycle on its side, then reached into his pocket and took out the apple Clarke had given him. "Here, we can share this." He spread his jacket on the sand for her to sit on. They gazed together at the summerblue sea and the soaring gulls. "On the strand of Howth breaks a sounding wave," Síle murmured.

Biting the apple in turns was an act of intimacy. He stared at the bare flesh of the fruit with her teeth marks imprinted on it.

"What are you going to do when you leave school, Ned?"

"I'm not sure yet."

"Really?" She raised one eyebrow.

Ned was intrigued. "How did you do that?"

"Do what?"

"Lift just one eyebrow."

Síle gave a careless shrug. "Oh, I have many talents." She

did not tell him that she had spent hours in front of the mirror perfecting that gesture, holding one eyebrow still with her forefinger while she repeatedly raised the other until its muscles were strong enough to function independently.

She smiled. He smiled.

He was painfully aware of her. He could think of nothing to say; he was almost afraid to breathe.

At last Síle broke the silence. "You don't think . . . badly of me, do you, Ned?" she asked.

"Of course not! Why should I?"

"I was afraid your friend—the one we had tea with that day—might have said something unkind about me."

Against his will, Ned recalled Henry's innuendos. "He didn't say anything unkind."

"Are you certain? I hate it when people lie to me."

Her remark struck Ned as odd. "Do many people lie to you, Síle?"

"All the time," she replied with a sudden hard edge to her voice. Then she threw back her head and pushed at her wind-tousled hair with her hand. "Promise me you won't ever lie to me, Ned," she said earnestly. "Promise. I do so need to have a real friend, someone who will always tell me the truth."

Once again he was taken aback. They hardly knew one another, yet here he was alone with her on the beach and she was asking him for what amounted to a sacred vow. "I try to tell the truth to everyone, Síle. Mr. Pearse sets great store by honesty."

"And do you?"

"I do."

"Oh." A small word, softly whispered. She leaned toward him and laid the tips of her fingers against his cheek. "I'll be honest with you. The first moment I saw you again, down by the quays that day, I liked you. Is that very bold of me?"

"I don't know." Ned stared with unseeing eyes at the sea. He was trying to envision Mary Cosgrave sitting beside him, but the image eluded him. There was only Síle. He could not look at her. Her fingers on his skin felt as if they were made of fire.

She flattened her palm against his cheek and gently turned his head toward her. "Have you ever kissed a girl, Ned? Shall I be your first?" Without waiting for his answer—he could not have shaped coherent words anyway—she laid her lips on his.

The first touch was as light as the brush of a butterfly's wings. He was not certain she was kissing him at all until the pressure intensified.

Her breath smelled of apple. When he hesitantly returned the kiss, her lips parted and began moving against his with tiny, drinking motions. Learning from her, Ned opened his mouth. But when he felt the tip of her tongue he almost drew back.

She sensed his reaction and tightened her arms around him. Her body fitted itself against his with a skillful pliancy, molding to every contour until the tops of her stays dug into his chest. "Hold me, Ned. Yes. Hold me. Ah, just like that!" His innocence excited her. She was still very young, but she had already seen so much; most of it old and cynical and exhausted. Ned was new. Clean and new.

The feel of her in his arms was intoxicating. Ned forgot all about Mary. Only his flesh was conscious. His mind had gone somewhere far away.

A twinge of anxiety brought him back. This was so new, the reality so different from his dreamy imaginings. What did she expect of him? Not . . . not that ultimate act, surely . . . the act his aroused body was clamoring for . . .

She was a woman, she must be treated with delicacy and respect.

Ned moaned with the effort of controlling himself.

In response Síle pressed even closer. His hand found its way to her bosom; fumbled over the lace of her shirtwaist. The garment opened more easily than he had expected and he felt bare flesh.

The first touch of a woman's body was electrifying.

When she did not recoil and push his hand away, he allowed his fingertips to stroke the swell of her upper breast. He dare not go farther. But oh, the magic!

Síle was struggling to conceal her impatience. Did he not know, could he not feel, what was required? The cattle dealer who had first seduced her at Ennis Fair had shown no such restraint. She twisted in Ned's embrace so his hand inadvertently slipped lower.

He was touching her nipple! The next moment he felt her hips move against his agonized erection and the world exploded.

"I didn't mean it to go that far, Ned. Really I didn't. I don't know what came over me."

"No . . . no, it was me. . . . I'm sorry, I don't . . . I mean, I didn't . . ." Ned was mortified, but he could not allow a woman to take the blame for his own lack of control. The sin was his; the contrition must be his also.

They returned in silence to Parnell Street. The sticky wetness in Ned's trousers made him acutely uncomfortable. He pedaled awkwardly while Síle sat behind him, trying to look respectable for his sake.

For a few hours she had been with a young man as other girls might be with their young men. She could even pretend to herself that she was going home to one of those proper houses in Fairview with flowers in the garden, there to eat supper with her family and sleep in a chaste bed, dreaming of Ned Halloran.

The dream evaporated as the smell of the city replaced the clean sea wind. "Let me off anywhere," Síle called to Ned. "I have to collect the papers for Mrs. Drumgold. She likes to have them in the house of an evening."

He went to Tom Clarke's, since that was where he had met her earlier. "You can get the papers here."

"I know."

Ned leaned his bicycle against the wall and escorted her inside.

The man behind the counter nodded at him as coolly as if

they had never met. Had Ned been less dazed, however, he might have noticed the flash of recognition in Clarke's eyes when he saw Síle.

As the young woman selected several newspapers Ned hovered nearby. The hour was growing late, he would be expected back at Saint Enda's, but he could not leave. Not yet. For some reason Síle would not let him accompany her to her lodging house, but he could at least see her safely as far as her street.

Over her shoulder he glimpsed the headline in the *Evening Mail* but it meant nothing to him, not with Síle so close and the feel of her still tingling on his fingers.

There is a light around those two, Clarke thought. He took off his glasses for a moment and polished them vigorously on his sleeve.

During his long years in an English prison he had been asked again and again why he espoused violence. His replies had never satisfied his captors. But as his wistful eyes followed Ned and Síle out into the street, Tom Clarke knew the answer. It was so that young lovers—and old people who had once been young—might live in a free Ireland.

June 28, 1914

ASSASSINATION OF AUSTRIAN ARCHDUKE
FRANZ FERDINAND IN SARAJEVO SHOCKS
WORLD

Chapter Twenty-one

Mrs. Drumgold's brothel was not a flash house, one of the luxurious houses catering to the top of the trade, but in the hierarchy of the Village it was considered upper-middle-class. The madam looked after her girls and usually gave them their fair share of the earnings. Prosperous businessmen and senior civil servants were frequent visitors to Faithful Place.

Unlike the squalid kips where rooms were rented by the half hour, Mrs. Drumgold's girls "lived in" and had their own rooms. There were coal fires, carpets on the floor, and a man had to knock at the front door for admission rather than simply walking in.

Dolly Drumgold was particular about her clients. In her youth, it was rumored, she had been the star attraction in one of the great flash houses.

The eight current inhabitants of her kip were young, attractive, and intelligent enough to carry on a conversation. Several came from respectable families. Sex was a business to them, with special services on offer as required. For the more exotic requests the rate could go as high as fifty pounds. A clever girl who saved her money could secure her future by buying a brothel of her own. One of the more successful Dublin madams had even sent her daughters to a finishing school in England.

Mrs. Drumgold had three unbendable rules. "Let no client leave without paying, do not bring disease into the house, and do not fall in love," Síle had been warned on her first day. She and the other girls kept themselves as clean as they could and submitted to a doctor's examination periodically. But love was another matter. Love could make a girl uncontrollable.

Síle had schooled herself never to use the word *love*, even in the most intimate conversations.

Following her afternoon with Ned, she returned to Mrs. Drumgold's in a mood of euphoria. She wanted to laugh aloud and dance up the stairs; she wanted to throw open the windows and shout "Ned Halloran!" into the street below for the pleasure of hearing his name.

After eighteen months in a brothel, Síle Duffy had seen enough to know that many a romance which blossomed in love and lust withered in guilt and duty. Husbands sought relief with Dolly Drumgold's girls. They complained about wives who did not understand them, wives who understood them too well, wives who lavished all their attention on the children, wives who had turned into replicas of their mothers.

For such men Síle had become expert at simulating the lost rapture of youth, but it was a rapture life had denied her. Until Ned. Until, for a few brief hours, they had been an innocent boy and girl together.

She paced the confines of her room, keeping her eyes averted from the bed with its piled cushions. When she heard the knock on the door summoning her to go below and greet the evening's customers, she took a large drink of brandy from the decanter on the table by the bed. Then she threw back her shoulders. "Party time," she announced to the silent room.

Her breath caught on an unexpected sob.

FOR several days Ned was preoccupied. He wandered along the paths where Robert Emmett had once walked with his sweetheart; he smelled the fecund air of the woods and scuffed the soft earth with his shoe and searched for forget-me-nots amid the ivy, but his thoughts were far away. He had no one with whom he could sort out his confused emotions. By every code of honor he knew, a decent man did not talk about a decent girl to his friends.

He very much wanted to believe that Síle was a decent girl. Did that mean he cared for her? If so, what about Mary Cosgrave? Was something wrong with him that he had feelings for two women that should be reserved for one?

More than ever he regretted the loss of his father. Most Irish men of his acquaintance were singularly devoted to their mothers, yet the deep, quiet steadiness of his father seemed the greater loss now. Patrick Halloran would have listened without judging and advised without preaching, would have puffed on his pipe and quoted a pertinent bit of poetry.

Ned tried not to dwell on such thoughts. His memories had been folded neatly, one by one, smoothed with the hand, and put away; it was the only way he could go on. Some day when they had lost their power to hurt he would take them out again.

Oh, Papa!

On the fifth of July, Ned Halloran joined the Irish Volunteers.

He called first to Tom Clarke to deliver a note from Pearse. The shop brought back memories of Síle. Her scent seemed to linger in the air as he browsed through the stacks of newspapers and periodicals, many of them with a decidedly nationalist slant, then bought one he had not read before and stuffed it into his jacket pocket.

In front of the modest Volunteers' recruitment office in Middle Abbey Street Ned noticed a battered bicycle leaning against a lamppost. He parked his own beside it and went in. Seated behind a table was a man smoking a cigarette while he checked names off a list. As the door opened he looked up.

Ned recognized him at once. How could he forget that challenging glance like a shout in the blood?

"Failte isteach," said Seán MacDermott, rising to his feet and extending his hand across the table. The Irish welcome

seemed a portent, a secret password in a shared language. "Are you here to join the Volunteers?"

"I am," Ned replied, feeling excitement mount in him.

"You understand our aims and purposes?"

"I do."

MacDermott handed Ned a piece of paper. "Then repeat after me, 'I, the undersigned, desire to be enrolled in the Irish Volunteers, founded to secure and maintain the rights and liberties common to all the people of Ireland without distinction of creed, class, or politics.' And sign down there at the bottom."

"Is that all there is to it?"

MacDermott laughed, a flash of white teeth in his darkly handsome face. "What were you expecting, a flourish of trumpets? Would you feel it was more of a ceremony if I asked you to sign in blood?"

Ned laughed too. "I don't need that much ceremony." He repeated the oath and signed at the bottom in black ink.

MacDermott searched for a piece of fresh blotting paper, found none, and instead blew on the paper. Then he tucked it into a drawer.

"Would you care for a cigarette?"

"Uh . . . I don't smoke."

"You're right too. Say, business is slow right now. I'm alone here today but I can close up shop for a little while. Why don't you come along to Kirwan's in Parnell Street—that's my local—and I'll buy you a wee drop.[1] It isn't every day a man joins the army."

As the two men made their way to the public house Ned observed that girls flirted openly with Seán MacDermott. In spite of his limp, there was no denying he was handsome. He had a finely shaped head with glossy black hair, dark eyebrows, and incredibly long lashes. When the girls smiled, he smiled back. He tossed a lighthearted quip to this one, made a date to meet that one later, teased a third until she blushed and gazed rapturously after him as he walked away.

At Kirwan's, MacDermott received a clamorous welcome as he called out, "God bless all here!" After only a few minutes in his company Ned understood why he was so popular. Seán MacDermott brimmed with an irrepressible gaiety. His painful limp made it obvious life had not been easy for him; his cheap suit and twice-turned collar said it was not easy now. Yet being with him made people feel good.

The pub was paneled in dark wood made darker by years of tobacco smoke. The plank floor was carpeted with sawdust, footprinted and furrowed like dirty snow. Wall ornamentation consisted of advertising posters, framed photographs of various unrecognizable men, and in the place of honor over the bar, an ancient pikestaff. At one end of the bar was a gleaming brass scale for weighing grocery items. Like many public houses, Kirwan's sold tea, sugar, meal, and a few other necessities in addition to dispensing drink.

The majority of customers were under thirty. Only three or four elderly men could be seen at the bar, talking with the barman across bowls of boiled eggs and jars of pickled pigs' feet.

From a tiny, high-walled cubicle at the rear came the muffled sound of female voices. Ned had never heard of women being allowed in a pub. He glanced quizzically at MacDermott, who explained, "Those are shawlies in the 'snug' Ned. The grannies can drink because they're beyond sin, and female street traders are such good customers a publican would be a fool to keep them out. You won't see them, though. They stay in their own preserve and smoke their clay pipes and have naught to do with the likes of us."

MacDermott began introducing Ned to his friends. He identified a tall, handsome man with a neatly waxed mustache as Michael O'Rahilly, Director of Arms for the Volunteers.

He was promptly corrected. "I am *The* O'Rahilly, if you please. I use the archaic title that means Chief of the Name."

There was a ripple of good-humored laughter. "And sure won't I be Ard Ri when Ireland has a king again!" someone cried.

A yeasty fragrance filled the air, reminding Ned of his first day in Dublin. When Seán MacDermott asked him what he would drink, he said, "Guinness."

"A pint," MacDermott told the barman.

The stout was "pulled" from a tap and the big glass allowed to sit brimming on the bar until the bubbles stopped rising. Then Ned was handed a beverage so dark as to appear black, with a creamy white collar. "Here's yer parish priest," said the barman.

MacDermott had a pint as well, then laughingly excused himself. "I could stay here all afternoon, but potential Volunteers will be beating down the doors." Ned started to go with him, but MacDermott waved him back. "That's all right, you stay. These are good lads; you'll be serving with most of them."

Ned felt he had truly become a man among men.

After MacDermott had gone, a redheaded man with a face full of freckles confided to Ned, "The real reason our Seán rarely has more than one drink is because he has a swarm of brothers and sisters down the country. Most everything he makes he sends to them. He'll save up enough to stand us all to a shout from time to time, but we don't like to put the pressure on him. Say, though . . . your jar's empty!"

Another pint was pressed into Ned's hand. When the glass was empty he attempted to buy a round for his new friends, but no one would let him. "Your money's no good in Kirwan's on the day you join the Volunteers," The O'Rahilly insisted.

Another pint materialized. While Ned was drinking, The O'Rahilly led the other men in a rousing song of his own composing titled "Thou Art Not Conquered Yet, Dear Land."[2] "They even sing that in the London music halls," a burly tenor told Ned. "He's a great man for the songs, is our Michael."

By the time Ned left the pub his head was buzzing. The afternoon had sped away unnoticed and the summer night had fallen, soft as the petals of a dark flower. The light of the street lamps was too kind to reveal Dublin's squalor. The city looked beautiful.

My city, he thought to himself. My *country*. And I've sworn to defend her.

Unthinking joy burst in him like a skyrocket. The emotion was too big to contain, so he released some of it by breaking into song. He sang the first tune that came into his head, a legacy from his native Clare: a satiric Percy French ditty titled "Shlathery's Mounted Fut." When passersby stared at him he gave them a lopsided grin.

Ned retrieved his bicycle from in front of the Volunteers' office, which by that time was closed. He was about to set off for Rathfarnham when an image of Mary Cosgrave flashed across his mind.

Of course! His sweetheart—that *was* Mary, wasn't it?— must be the first person he told.

When he reached Dorset Street he could smell food cooking, the fragrance drifting out through open windows. The Cosgrave house was one of a row of modest terraced houses fronted with red brick, aggressively respectable. Ned leaned his machine against the front steps and thumped the door with his fist. He could not seem to find the door knocker.

After a considerable wait the door opened halfway and a man peered out. "What is it? Is there trouble?"

"I've come to call on Miss Cosgrave."

The man regarded him owlishly. "And who might you be?"

"Edward Halloran. You remember me, Mr. Cosgrave, I—" His words were interrupted by an embarrassing belch.

The man took half a step out the door to get a better look at him. "I remember. You came to my aid on Bloody Sunday and I'm grateful. But I don't recall you as a drunken lout, Mr. Halloran. In your present condition you can hardly call on my daughter."

"I'm not drunk. I just want to see Mary."

A soft voice inquired from the shadows of the hall, "Who is it, Papa?" Mary peered around her father's shoulder. "Ned! Is that you? What are you doing here?"

Mr. Cosgrave put a barring arm across the doorway. "I won't have you talking to this fellow, Mary."

"What do you mean? Is something wrong?"

"Nothing's wrong," Ned said. "I just came to tell you I

joined the Irish National Volunteer Corps today." He spun
out the full name with pride.

"Oh Ned, is that why you're in this disgraceful state? Did
those . . . those awful *revolutionaries* get you drunk?"

"Of course not, they—"

"They're as bad as the unions, Papa," Mary said to Mr.
Cosgrave. "Taking men away from their homes, giving them
drink, getting them into trouble." Her words seemed to be
part of an angry ongoing conversation between father and
daughter. Then she turned on her young suitor, "Ned, I'm
ashamed of you."

His jaw dropped. "But I'm going to have a uniform! I
thought you liked—"

"Come back to see me when you are yourself again,"
Mary said firmly.

The door slammed.

Ned raised his fist to pound on the wood, thought better of
it, and turned away. Going down the steps, he stumbled.

"Hell. Bloody hell. Dammit it to bloody *hell*!"

The ride back to Rathfarnham was longer than it had ever
been. He neither whistled nor sang.

I always get caught, he thought bitterly. Why me? Why
doesn't this happen to other men?

By the time he reached Saint Enda's he was sober. A driz-
zle of cold rain had begun to fall, emphasizing his bleak
mood. He knew he had made a fool of himself in front of
Mary Cosgrave. When he stepped off his bicycle he aimed a
kick at the front tire. "There," he said. But he felt no better.

Hoping to find Pádraic Pearse, he went first to the dining
room behind Pearse's study. Mary Brigid often practiced there
on the piano or on the harp her older brother had given her.
Pádraic Pearse loved to listen to her play the old Irish airs.

But only Willie was in the dining room. Sitting at the oval
mahogany table, he looked up from a plate smeared with the
last streaks of pudding to say, "Hullo, Ned! You're destroyed
with the damp, take off that jacket and hang it on the back
of a chair. Do you want something to eat?"

"I'm not hungry, thanks. Is the headmaster here?"

"He took the afternoon train to Limerick to make a recruiting speech for the Volunteers. He won't be back until tomorrow."

"That's a coincidence. I wanted to tell him I've joined the Volunteers."

Willie jumped up and clapped Ned on the back. "Good on you, oh, good on you! We'll get the mother to make us a fresh pot of tea and you can tell me all about it."

Warmed by Willie's enthusiasm, Ned's spirits lifted. After Mrs. Pearse brought more tea and a basin of oxtail soup, he related the events of his day. He did not mention Mary, but said offhandedly, "I suppose some might call the Volunteers revolutionaries."

"Nonsense! The desire for independence isn't revolutionary, Ned. It's evolutionary. It's what John Mitchel called 'that holy hatred of foreign dominion.' Once you feel it, there's no going back." Willie's eye fell on the folded newspaper sticking out of Ned's jacket pocket. "You have a copy of *Sinn Féin* there, I see."

"I bought it in Clarke's today."

"The publisher's Arthur Griffith, a good example of political evolution. He trained as a printer and supported Parnell in his last campaign.[3] Later he scraped together all the money he could and began publishing the *United Irishman*. He wrote much of the copy himself so he could explain his ideas for national regeneration.

"Griffith—he's a friend of Pat's, by the way—had spent years developing an elaborate plan that involved mutual cooperation between Irishmen of all classes and faiths. He also advocated compromise and a flexible approach to achieving political aims. He's a moderate sort of man; initially he envisioned working within the British framework and even suggested a dual monarchy.

"But as time passed, Griffith recognized that the British government was never going to do anything for the Irish but take advantage of them. We had no big brother we could trust; we were on our own.

"Griffith's next venture into publishing was a weekly he

called *Sinn Féin*, meaning Ourselves; self-reliance. In the pages of *Sinn Féin* he rejected the right of Britain to rule Ireland and began calling for sovereign independence. See what I mean about evolution? His editorials expressed a deep mistrust of using physical force, however, and insisted that political negotiation was the only way to achieve our freedom.''

"Do you agree with him?''

Willie Pearse sighed. "I wish I could. But negotiation with Britain has never accomplished anything for us. Greed is greed, Ned. You can't talk people out of imperialism when they find it so profitable.

"Anyway, as a result of his writings a political party grew up around Arthur Griffith. Pat was attracted to his ideas about education and attended the inaugural meeting in 1905. He decided not to join, though, because he had too many other things on his plate.

"In 1908, Griffith's party formally adopted the name Sinn Féin. Aside from publishing the newspaper, they haven't done much since. The true believers advocate Griffith's passive resistance, but some of the younger ones feel it's too timid an approach. As a result there's division in the party. You know your history, Ned; the faction fight is nothing new in Ireland. Divide and be conquered, that's always been our problem.''

"Last week the *Irish Times* referred to the Volunteers as Sinn Féiners,'' said Ned. "That made me curious, so I bought the newspaper to help me understand the connection.''

Willie lifted the lid and peered regretfully into the now-empty teapot. "There isn't any connection aside from the fact that both organizations want to see Ireland independent of Britain. The Volunteer Corps is a private army governed by its own Provisional Committee and helped financially by the IRB. Sinn Féin, on the other hand, is a political party like Redmond's Parliamentarians or Carson's Unionists. They fund themselves the way all political parties do, through private donations. But they're certainly not an army. The policy of Sinn Féin is Arthur Griffith's, and he's against any form of militarism.

"The *Times* should know that, Ned, but they mirror the

British attitude. Miscalling the Volunteers is a typical demonstration of British ignorance and arrogance.

"It would be more accurate to describe the Volunteers as
Fenians because of the IRB affiliation. Granted, some members of Sinn Féin have joined the corps. But so have a lot of
Redmondites. And that's another problem. Eamonn Ceannt
and Seán MacDermott were furious about it, but Redmond
insisted on twenty-five of his men being nominated to the
Volunteers' Provisional Committee. Eoin MacNeill and Bulmer Hobson supported him by arguing that the corps is open
to men of any political persuasion. Now Redmond's nominees
form a majority on the council."

"So the *Times* could justifiably call the Volunteers 'Parliamentarians' if they wanted to," Willie Pearse added with a
mischievous chuckle.

Chapter Twenty-two

THE Volunteers had increased their drill schedule and training camps were being opened throughout the country. The corps claimed a nationwide membership in excess of a hundred thousand with more joining every day. A separate women's organization, Cumann na mBan, the Society of Women, had been formed in April and was helping raise funds to equip the Volunteers.[1]

"They are allies, not subordinates," Ned had stressed in his latest letter to his sister. "Madame Markievicz belongs to Cumann na mBan, as you might expect, but so do many women from the middle class. They are dedicated to advancing the cause of liberty and we're dreadfully proud of them."

Kathleen could not help a pang of envy. Allies, not subordinates.

After her first fund-raising luncheon Alexander had announced, "I want no more of those events held in my house, Kate. Do you understand me?"

"But I already have the invitations ordered for another," she protested. "It's for a good cause. My friends think so too, or they wouldn't have given money. And pledged to give more, Alexander. Even Alderman Claffey's wife—"

"I don't care what any other man's wife does. You are *my* wife, and you shall do as I say. That's an end to it."

"I will not be stifled," she whispered to herself in the over-stuffed golden gloom of the parlor. "I will *not*."

Going to their bedroom, she opened the mirrored door of the mahogany wardrobe that faced the bed. Kathleen did not like having a mirror reflecting everything that happened in the bed. If anything, it made her more inhibited than she was. Several times she had asked Alexander to have the piece moved, but it was still there.

At the back of the wardrobe was a row of her shoes, including a pair of kidskin boots. She took these out and from the toe extracted a roll of dollar bills, the most recent pledges. Then she hunted through the wardrobe again until she found a small silk reticule. The purse held a single pasteboard card bearing the name and address of John Devoy, of Clan na Gael.

NED was assigned to Rathfarnham E Company, 4th Battalion, Dublin Brigade—the same company as the Pearse brothers and Con Colbert—and given a dummy wooden rifle. He practiced in front of the mirror, holding the "rifle" at different angles and looking stern.

To his delight, a long march to Howth and back was announced for the twenty-sixth of July. The day was a Sunday. For Ned that meant getting early Mass before hurrying in to the city. The Pearse brothers were not going. "Marching eighteen miles would be a bit too much for Pat," Willie explained. "He looks big and strong but he's not all that fit. I've tried time and again to get him interested in handball but he says he hasn't the time. Which is fair enough, he hasn't.

"As for me, I have to finish the sculpture Mr. Fitzherbert commissioned. He's coming to collect it in the morning and we need the money. Pat and I won't be the only ones not going, though. Seán MacDermott could never walk that far either."

"That's a pity," Ned replied. "He's the very one who would enjoy it the most."

"He would. It's a shame about his leg, but he gets around

well enough on that bicycle of his. There are some who would say he gets around far too well!''

Though Sunday morning dawned without rain, a near gale was blowing. Ned cycled as far as Rathfarnham but was almost blown over, so he left his machine at the tram stop in full confidence it would be waiting for him when he returned, and rode the tram into Dublin. He was glad the orders specified an ''unarmed march,'' and assumed it was because they had such a long way to go. He would have felt silly boarding the tram with a piece of timber crudely carved to resemble a rifle.

The assembly site was a piece of waste ground near the quays. Seán Heuston was already there when Ned arrived. So was Con Colbert, accompanied by a troop of Fianna with a large trek cart.

''What's the cart for?'' Ned asked Heuston.

Seán Heuston was a sturdy young man with a broad forehead and fierce eyebrows above dark, intelligent eyes. His humor ran to sarcasm. ''You're looking at the glorious arsenal of the Dublin Brigade. That cart's loaded with oak batons. Men like The O'Rahilly who have real guns bring them, of course. He has a Mauser pistol he calls 'Peter Painter' that I'd kill for. But no one's selling pistols now.''

''Parliament made it against the law to import arms into this country as soon as the Irish Volunteers were founded,'' Ned reminded him.

''That may be, but just yesterday the *Press* ran a story about the UVF marching through Belfast displaying machine guns. Carson himself claimed credit for bringing the guns in at Larne. You'd think the British would charge him with treason. The leader of the Unionist Party is openly defying the law, yet they treat him like a hero.''

Overhearing them as he passed by, a tall man interjected, ''No effort will be made to halt the gun-running to the north.'' He sounded angry. ''Only we are to be hobbled and crippled.'' His sloping shoulders and long beak of a nose made Ned think of some great, gawky bird. As he walked away he towered head and shoulders over the men around him.

"Do you know him?" Ned asked Heuston.

"He's a mathematics teacher from County Limerick. Name's Eamon de Valera. He's half Irish and half Spanish, but I heard somewhere he was born in America."[2]

The crowd was growing fast, overflowing the rubble-littered waste ground. Bulmer Hobson, wearing binoculars on a thong around his neck, arrived in a motorcar with Thomas MacDonagh and immediately began issuing orders. The two men were in charge of organizing the day's exercise, although MacDonagh was content to let Hobson do the shouting. They were soon joined by Cathal Brugha, who in addition to being an officer in the Volunteers ran a firm manufacturing ecclesiastical candles. This earned him a certain amount of good-natured teasing from the other men.

MacDonagh was electric with excitement. When he saw Ned and Seán Heuston he hurried over to them, bouncing off the balls of his feet as he walked. "I'm glad you could both make it!"

"There's a fine crowd gathered," Ned commented.

"We've eight hundred Volunteers here, more than enough for the job at hand." MacDonagh's eyes were twinkling. "Here, Charley," he called to Cathal Brugha, "since you're organizing a picked squad I recommend these two. They're good men and they know how to take orders."

"Thank you, sir," said Ned.

"You'll thank me more when this day is over. I promise you a tale to tell your grandchildren."

With Bulmer Hobson in the lead and the Fianna bringing up the rear with the trek cart, eight companies of the Dublin Brigade set out to march to Howth. In spite of the threatening weather they were in high spirits.

The column passed unimpeded through the city and its outskirts. People nodded to them as they went by; a few waved and cheered. The Volunteers broke into song. They began with "Native Swords," followed by "Erin Go Bragh" and "Kelly, the Boy from Killane." The martial thunder of "O'Donnell Abu" contrasted dramatically with the lyric tragedy of "Boulavogue."

As Ned sang "A rebel hand set the heather blazing," he felt gloriously alive.

By the time they reached the narrow isthmus of Sutton the wind howling in from the sea was enough to take a man's breath away. Ned wiped his watering eyes and turned up the collar of his jacket.

Famed for its spectacular promontory and historic castle, Howth boasted thirteen hundred inhabitants and a thriving fishing industry. On Howth Head, the Bailey Lighthouse, with its gaslight beacon, had revolutionized the earlier system of oil lamps. Electric trams provided transportation to and from Dublin. In addition to telegraph facilities, the telephone company had recently opened a public call-office.

There were three churches in the town—Catholic, Presbyterian, and Methodist—a coast guard station, and an office of the Royal Irish Constabulary, the police force responsible for the countryside beyond the jurisdiction of the DMP. Like their Dublin counterparts, the rank and file of the constabulary were Irishmen.

Ned wondered what it would be like to live in one of the cottages tucked among the slopes. He imagined himself coming home at the end of the day to find Mary waiting in the parlor, perhaps with a baby in her arms. She would greet him with that sweet smile of hers, while from the kitchen came the aroma of—

"Yer out of step," hissed the man on his right.

The column was marching along the Harbor Road when a gleaming De Dion Bouton roared by. Ned saw Professor MacNeill in the front passenger seat and two women in the back. The touring car had passed before he realized the driver was Michael O'Rahilly.

As the column approached Howth Harbor, Bulmer Hobson called a halt and raised his binoculars. He scanned the sea in the direction of Ireland's Eye, the rocky, deserted islet guarding the harbor mouth. After sweeping the glasses from horizon to horizon he said in a tense voice, "There's no sign of the motorboat. We might as well go on, though. It's almost noon."

Cathal Brugha beckoned to two of the older men in his squad. "You know what to do," he said curtly. They promptly trotted off. The other members of the squad exchanged curious glances, but no one said anything.

When they reached the stone quay fronting the harbor they found The O'Rahilly in civilian clothes already standing there.[3] His automobile, with MacNeill and the two women still inside, was parked a short distance away.

"Right, lads," Brugha said crisply. "We're taking possession of the pier. Look sharp!" While he stationed his squad at intervals along the wooden pier the rest of the column waited at quayside. When everything was ready Brugha conferred in an undertone with The O'Rahilly. The two men took turns looking through the binoculars and consulting their watches.

Within minutes more private cars and motor cabs pulled up and parked nearby. The drivers did not get out, merely sat waiting. Some kept their engines running. Ned noticed spectators gathering on the hillside overlooking the harbor, staring down at the assembled men. A woman waved her parasol; several Volunteers cheerfully waved back.

"What do you think is going on?" Ned asked Seán Heuston out of the side of his mouth.

"Hard to say, we've never had a drill quite like this before. Perhaps we . . . Hullo! Look at that!"

A yacht was beating its way toward Howth through the gale, white sails like flags whipping in the wind.

Cathal Brugha let out a triumphant whoop.

The O'Rahilly shouted, "It's the harbinger of liberty!"

The yacht was riding dangerously low in the heavy swells. Considerable skill was required to maneuver through the narrow harbor mouth and reach the pier without smashing into any of the boats riding at anchor. A small crew, two women among them, began tossing lines to the Volunteers. Within moments the yacht was securely docked.

A tired-looking man in oilskins clambered onto the pier as if his bones ached, and tossed Cathal Brugha a sketchy salute. "Erskine Childers, captain of the *Asgard*, reporting with merchandise from Germany. Bought with American dollars, may I add," he said in a strong British accent.

"You're very welcome," said Brugha. "You and your merchandise both."

"I thought Darrell Figgis was supposed to come meet us in a motorboat if the landing was to go ahead."

"So did we, but he never showed up. You took a chance, coming in anyway."

Childers shrugged. "What should I have done, turn around and go back? I ran enough risk getting here in the first place. My wife and Mary Spring-Rice are with me, you know. Molly wouldn't have it any other way, and Mary played a large part in this."

Ned was listening avidly. He knew of Erskine Childers as the author of a spy novel called *The Riddle of the Sands*, about two yachtsmen discovering a German plan to invade England. The book was a great favorite at Saint Enda's. Sciatica had left Childers with a slight limp but had not prevented him from having a distinguished career in the British army.

Cathal Brugha turned to his men. "Unload this boat as fast as you can—but don't get in one another's way; it's a narrow pier. We need to be out of here as soon as possible."

When the first boxes were brought off the *Asgard* some of the Volunteers on the quay recognized them as rifle cases. With a wild shout they broke ranks and surged onto the pier, shoving Brugha's squad aside. Men were in danger of being pushed into the water as they fought over possession of the prizes: "Sod off, you bugger!" "Fuck off yourself, you cute hoor, this gun's mine!"

Ned made no effort to take one of the rifles without permission, but stood waiting while the officers struggled to regain control of their companies. The most successful was the tall man with spectacles. In a cold, hard voice, Eamon de Valera shamed his men back onto the quay, many still clutching the rifles they had seized.

With the help of the Fianna, who were more disciplined, Brugha's squad unloaded the *Asgard* in less than twenty minutes. Eoin MacNeill was out of the car by this time and stood wordlessly watching as the officers handed out rifles to those Volunteers who did not yet have them.

When Ned received his, he examined it closely. The single-shot rifle had a recessed bolt and manual safety catch. It looked old and neglected; there were flecks of rust on the metal. But at least it was real. He lifted it to his shoulder and sighted along the barrel. "Bang," he whispered.

Bulmer Hobson was asking Erskine Childers, "What was your total cargo?"

"Nine hundred secondhand Mausers. Gewehr 98s. 31 caliber, five-shot magazine."

"And ammunition?"

"Forty-nine thousand rounds. We were so overloaded I had to dump two boxes overboard."

"We don't have enough Volunteers to carry nine hundred rifles," Hobson said. "We were only expecting seven hundred and fifty. The Fianna will have to—"

Thomas MacDonagh interrupted him. "I don't want to be responsible for allowing the Fianna to handle untested rifles. Their mothers would never forgive us if there was an accident."

The O'Rahilly suggested, "Since we'll be transporting the ammunition in the cars, put the extra guns in too. They'll fit somehow; we brought rugs for covering everything anyway."

At the mention of ammunition Seán Heuston asked, "Are we not to be issued cartridges for our rifles, sir?"

"I think not. We're a defensive force only, and we're not under attack," replied Hobson, glancing toward MacNeill as he spoke. "Besides, we've never drilled with live ammunition."

Ned lowered the rifle from his shoulder. Loaded, it could kill another human being. That was its purpose. A cold lump formed in his stomach.

When he looked up his eyes met Thomas MacDonagh's. He was unable to read the expression there.

The column reformed. The Fianna with the trek cart brought up the rear. In case of attack the Volunteers had rifles now.

Rifles without ammunition, of course.

But The O'Rahilly exulted to MacNeill, "Just think, Professor! This afternoon armed Irish men under Irish command are going to march through the streets of Dublin for the first time since 1782."

"It's a good day's work, Michael. Lead the cars on in and warn them not to attract attention. I shouldn't think you and your sisters will have any trouble; you look innocuous enough. I'm going to stay behind and have a bit of lunch in Howth, then take a tram home."

Meanwhile Ned was discovering that his eleven-pound rifle was considerably heavier than a wooden dummy. He had to shift the Mauser several times before he was able to balance it comfortably on his shoulder. But having it made him feel different somehow. Bigger.

As the motorcars sped past carrying their load of arms to prearranged safe houses, someone in the ranks shouted, "Cheers, lads!"

Ned put two fingers to his mouth to salute them with a whistle, but in the process dislodged his rifle. He made a wild lunge to catch it before it hit the ground.

Someone behind him laughed.

The wind was gradually subsiding. At a signal from Bulmer Hobson the column got under way. As they marched from quayside a wildly enthusiastic cheer went up from the onlookers on the slope above. Ned had never been cheered before. It was a heady sensation.

They had not gone very far when a small squad of the Royal Irish Constabulary in their distinctive spiked helmets caught up with them. The column halted while Hobson and MacDonagh spoke briefly with the constables, offering assurances of their peaceable intent. When the Volunteers resumed their march the RIC men accompanied them but made no effort to stop them.

A whisper ran through the ranks. "Dublin doesn't know we're coming. Two of Brugha's lads cut the telegraph wires." Men nudged one another and winked.

When they were halfway to the city Hobson gave the order

to halt. Those who had cigarettes took them out and passed them around, sharing with the RIC men. Several Volunteers produced flasks, but MacDonagh ordered them to be put away unopened.

Ned and Seán Heuston unslung their rifles and sat down together at the side of the road. "Imagine us being able to pull off something like this," Heuston said as he massaged his aching calf muscles. "And right under the noses of the authorities, too. How ever did we manage?"

"We have some powerful friends, Seán. It's interesting, when you think about it. People like Constance Markievicz and Erskine Childers are members of the Ascendancy the same as Edward Carson in Ulster, yet I'm sure they no more think of themselves as traitors than Carson does."

"Did you know anything about this in advance, Ned?"

"Not a whisper. I'm just a foot soldier, no one tells me anything. Ask me again when I get to be an officer."

The column remained halted for half an hour. During that time an inbound tram from Howth went by and Eoin MacNeill got off. "I could see you from the tram," he told Hobson. "Why have you stopped at Raheny? This is no time to lose your nerve."

Bulmer Hobson nodded toward the little band of R.I.C. men standing apart from the Volunteers. "My nerve is fine. They're the ones who suggested we take a rest for the sake of the Fianna, and I thought no purpose would be served in arguing with them."

A muscle tightened in MacNeill's jaw. "All right, but let's go on now. I'll join you for a while and we'll give Tom a turn at command."

The march resumed, this time with Thomas MacDonagh at the head of the column and MacNeill walking with Hobson.

Eoin MacNeill was no soldier. Before they had gone a mile his recent lunch turned to rocks in his stomach. His step faltered and he moved to the side of the road. "Flag down the next motorcar and get a ride into town," MacDonagh advised.

"That's probably a good idea, but are you certain you'll be all right? There'll be no trouble?"

MacDonagh laughed. "Sure, don't we have the Royal Irish Constabulary themselves with us?"

Chapter Twenty-three

PROFESSOR MacNeill was given a ride by a Howth couple on their way into the city to visit Glasnevin Cemetery. The column marched on. By now some were complaining of blistered feet.

Beyond the marshes of Raheny, houses began to line the road on either side. Soon the surrounding fields were thickly dotted with cottages and outbuildings. Women and small children peeped from windows. Dogs ran out to bark. A signpost announced Clontarf.

Ned felt a shudder run up his spine; a presentiment. "Clontarf," he said aloud.

The man to his left glanced toward him. "What?"

"The Battle of Clontarf. Good Friday, 1014. Brian Bóru was killed then."

"A bad Easter for him, but ancient history now," the other said dismissively.

In the lead, Thomas MacDonagh rounded a bend to discover a number of men in the distance. They were deliberately blocking the junction of the Howth and Clontarf roads. He signaled a halt and held a hurried conference with Bulmer Hobson. "Word must have got through to Dublin Castle after all," MacDonagh said. "I thought we'd taken care of that."

Hobson was scowling. "So did I." Raising his binoculars,

he studied the roadblock. "It's a squad of the DMP but they're not alone. There's a detachment of the King's Own Scottish Borderers; there must be a hundred soldiers in addition to the police. Dear God, how did they find out? Well, what's done is done. Fortunately there's another road into the city just over there."

MacDonagh gave the order, and the column prepared to swing right. But immediately men were deployed to block that route also. MacDonagh called for a halt and stood waiting to see what would happen next. He had not long to wait.

A brawny official came striding toward the head of the column. The years had thickened the man's waist without mellowing his disposition. "I am Commissioner W. V. Harrel of the Dublin Metropolitan Police," he announced in a strident voice, "and you will not be allowed to march into Dublin. Furthermore, you are to surrender your weapons at once."

Thomas MacDonagh was a small man, but no one could intimidate him. He faced the police commissioner toe-to-toe. "Let me remind you," he said evenly, "that there is no law to compel us to surrender our personal property. Armed Ulster Volunteers regularly parade through Belfast and no one tries to disarm them."

"I don't care what they do in Belfast," said Harrel. "Dublin is my city, and this sort of thing won't be allowed here. Command your men to stack their rifles."

MacDonagh clamped his jaws shut.

"Disarm them!" the commissioner bawled at his men.

To the surprise of everyone, the policemen refused to obey him. Whether they acted out of sympathy with their fellow Irishmen or because they remembered the condemnation heaped on the DMP after Bloody Sunday, no one knew.

Sputtering with anger, Commissioner Harrel dismissed them on the spot. They fell back a few paces and milled around in disarray. By this time a number of onlookers had appeared, drifting out of nearby houses to stand gawking.

Harrel could not afford to be seen backing down, but since the police had proved unreliable it was left to the soldiers to uphold authority. He held a hurried consultation with the of-

ficer in charge. A command was given; the King's Own
marched forward. The DMP were armed only with batons,
but the British soldiers had modern rifles. When a second
command was given they fixed bayonets.

The Volunteers at the front of the column watched them
apprehensively.

MacDonagh faced about and cried to his men, "Any of
you who have loaded weapons—do not fire, no matter what
the provocation!"

As if this was a signal, the soldiers lunged forward and
tried to wrest the rifles from the foremost Volunteers. They
held on grimly. There was considerable shoving and cursing
and a few blows were struck.

In the midst of all this a motor cab came up the road from
Dublin. The policemen let it pass unchallenged; the cab continued along the length of the column. Suddenly Seán
MacDermott and Tom Clarke leaned out the windows and
shouted, "Hide your weapons! Hurry!"

The Volunteers responded with alacrity. Those not involved
in the scuffle ran to conceal their rifles under hedges and behind walls. When Harrel realized what was happening he
shouted at them to stop, but they paid no attention. By the
time the fracas at the front was under control the rest of the
column had melted away into the surrounding countryside.

Only nineteen rifles were captured, and they were damaged
in the struggle.

Several men had black eyes and multiple bruises. The most
badly injured was a Volunteer who had taken a bayonet thrust
in the shoulder; painful but far from fatal. He was on his feet,
cursing under his breath while one of the policemen stanched
the flow of blood with a borrowed handkerchief.

Harrel decided to make the best of a bad situation by pro-
claiming his defense of the city successful and calling off the
engagement. The policemen departed the scene by tram. But
the officers of the King's Own chose to march their men back
into the city, returning as a victorious army to their barracks
in Phoenix Park.

• • •

NED and Seán Heuston hid their rifles in a shed behind a dilapidated two-room cottage far back from the road. The cottage appeared unoccupied, though for an instant Ned thought he saw a ragged curtain move at a window. No one came out to challenge them, however.

"I think it's safe enough," he told Heuston.

The shed contained a heap of mildewed harness and several sacks of spoiled grain. As soon as they had concealed their guns the two young men hurried out into the fresh air. They trotted across a couple of fields, scrambled over a wall, and found themselves slogging through a manure-mired dairy yard.

"Observe the brave Irish Volunteers on maneuvers," Heuston announced to a dozen curious cows.

Ned raised one filthy boot. "In the uniform of the day!"

They broke into manic laughter and had to stop to catch their breath.

Heuston had a stitch in his side. "What happens now? It's a bit of a damp squib, not marching through the city with our rifles."

"Best leave them where they are for now. But is there any reason we can't go into Dublin anyway?"

"Just ourselves, Ned? Without the column?"

"The column is scattered from here to Bull Island by now. I'm certainly not ready to go back to Rathfarnham; let's get our tea in the city. We can at least show the flag, so to speak."

Heuston grinned. "Right you are."

To avoid meeting any soldiers or policemen the two made their way toward the city across fields and down back roads. But though they struck a brisk pace rumor ran ahead of them. News of the fracas at Clontarf spread like a fire in dry heather, with each retelling enlarging the drama.

"My brother says British soldiers have launched an unprovoked attack on innocent Volunteers."

"Accordin' to me wife's cousin, who saw the whole thing, daycent Irish men wuz battered to the ground."

"It was murder, I tell you! Outright willful murder by them bloody maggots!"

Even people who had been indifferent to the Volunteers were incensed. As the King's Own neared the city, an angry crowd gathered to shout obscenities at them.

In Dublin, Ned and Heuston found themselves caught up in an angry mob. Men, women, and even small children poured into the street as the King's Own passed on their way to their barracks. By now the crowd was hurling rubbish along with insults. The soldiers marched on with impassive faces, but the abuse mounted. A stone was thrown; then another. One of the soldiers was struck on the shoulder with enough force to make him grunt.

When they reached O'Connell Bridge at the bottom of Sackville Street, the King's Own turned right into Bachelor's Walk. By now the mood of the crowd was ugly. Some of the soldiers at the rear faced about and feinted at the civilians with their bayonets. The soldiers chased several of the most obnoxious into shops. A door was slammed; a rifleman drove his bayonet through the wooden panel. "How dare you rabble insult British soldiers!" he cried in outrage.

The DMP had retired to their own depot, so there were no police on hand to quell the crowd. It grew angrier by the minute.

At the corner of Liffey Street opposite the Ha'penny Bridge, a harassed officer finally ordered thirty of the King's Own to form a line with fixed bayonets. Those in front knelt; the others stood behind them with rifles leveled. A barrage of stones and curses fell upon the soldiers.

Ned told his friend, "I think we should—"

His words were interrupted by gunfire.

He heard no order to fire. Afterward he could recall only the sudden, shocking report of a rifle.

Someone screamed and fell.

Glancing toward the soldiers, Ned saw that one of the King's Own was holding a smoking rifle. The man was young and ashen-faced, and looked as frightened as Ned suddenly felt.

The first shot was followed almost instantly by a volley. The soldiers were firing indiscriminately into the crowd. People turned around, tried to run. Rifle fire cut them down like corn in a field. A woman's voice called on God; a man roared in pain for his mother.

Some of the soldiers were shouting too, as if to whip up their courage. A group of them charged the civilians with fixed bayonets. Army boots clattered on cobbles. Screaming rose to an unbearable pitch. To his horror Ned saw a woman not three paces from him skewered on a steel blade. The child who had been clinging to her skirts let out an earsplitting shriek.

Ned lunged forward, grabbed up the toddler as the woman fell, and ran.

July 26, 1914

MASSACRE IN BACHELOR'S WALK

July 28, 1914

AUSTRIA DECLARES WAR ON SERBIA

Chapter Twenty-four

KATHLEEN Campbell was appalled. She read the news-
paper article through, then read it again from the beginning.
By the time she finished her hands were shaking. "Ned. Sweet
Jesus, Ned!"

Alexander was in Boston on business, but she had to share
her anxiety with someone, and at once. She hurried the four
blocks to Saint Xavier's, where she found Father Paul on his
knees in front of the altar. She waited with barely controlled
impatience until he crossed himself, rose, and turned around.

One look at her face told him there was trouble. He hurried
down the aisle toward her. "What is it, what's wrong?"

"Have you seen this?" She waved a folded newspaper.

Kathleen sank into the nearest pew and Paul sat down beside her. In spite of her anxiety he thought she looked very
beautiful. Her dark curls clung to her temples from the summer heat; her muslin shirtwaist was limp with perspiration,
outlining her body.

She handed him the latest edition of the newspaper. The
headlines screamed of Austria's declaration of war on her
neighbor. For months military posturing in Europe had been
escalating, so he was hardly surprised. But before he could
begin to read about the Serbian crisis Kathleen leaned past
him and riffled through the pages. She called his attention to

a column near the back of the paper, almost lost amid date-lines from Britain and France.

He caught the fragrance of lavender rising from her over-heated flesh.

"There," she said, stabbing the article with her finger.

The priest read aloud, " 'Dublin, Ireland. Three civilians were killed outright and at least thirty-five wounded on Sunday when British troops, having failed to impound weapons illegally imported by the Irish Volunteers, opened fire on an angry mob in Bachelor's Walk.' "

"It was Ned," Kathleen said. "They shot Ned!"

"How do you know? There are no names given."

"I can feel it here!" She pressed her hand to her bosom. "And as for those weapons—I've been sending the Volunteers money, Paul! Through John Devoy. I knew they were using it to buy rifles. What if I paid for the gun that got my brother killed?"

He tried to calm her. "You're jumping to conclusions. You have no reason to think Ned was involved in this."

"Yes I do, read on. The Volunteers involved were the Dublin Brigade. Ned's joined the Dublin Brigade; I just received his letter. Oh, Paul, what am I going to do?"

He had no choice but to put his arm around her and press her hot face into his shoulder. "There's nothing you can do. Whatever happened is already over, and besides, it's three thousand miles away. If it will make you feel better, write Ned immediately, or better still, send a cablegram. Surely you can arrange one through the White Star office."

"I feel so helpless."

"Would you like me to go with you to send the cable?"

"Would you?" she asked with heartbreaking eagerness. Then her shoulders slumped. "I can't ask you to do that, you must have a hundred more important things to do."

"No, I don't." And now I'm telling lies, he thought. No, Kathleen, I don't have anything more important to do, just meet the constant demands on my time and energy that each day brings: visit the sick, go over the accounts, answer the correspondence, make out my report for the bishop, teach the confirmation class . . .

THE staff in the White Star office seated Kathleen in a comfortable chair and brought her tea and bonbons while Paul stood in the background, conspicuous in his Roman collar. People were polite to him, but Alexander Campbell's wife received special treatment.

Kathleen sent the cablegram to Saint Enda's, the only address she had for Ned. "While we're here do you want to send one to your other brother? Or the police?" Paul suggested.

"Frank and Aunt Norah would die of heart seizure if they got a cable. They had one before, you know. The *Titanic*. As for the police . . . ah no, this will do. If I don't get a reply from Ned within a day or two I shall cable Mr. Pearse personally."

Kathleen was still upset as Paul escorted her home. Recalling the *Titanic* had increased her anxiety. She linked her hand with Paul's arm and held on tight. On the stoop she paused one step above him, then turned and looked into his eyes. "Would you care to come in? I'll have Della make a pitcher of cold lemonade for us."

"I don't think that's a good idea right now, Kathleen. You're upset; you should go and lie down with a cool cloth on your forehead. You don't need the strain of trying to entertain me."

"It would be no strain. I just don't want to be alone right now." She was flushed and the day was hot: the sultry, pervasive heat of New York in summer. In her overwrought state she might faint, Paul thought.

He meant to say, I must get back to the church. He meant to say a lot of things. Instead he found himself following her into the house and closing the door behind them.

•   •   •   •

WITH a little girl screaming in his arms, Ned fled the bullets. He had no thought but to save the child; the memory of Bloody Sunday was too clear in his mind. It was imperative he get the child someplace safe where she would be looked after until her people came for her.

If they came for her.

The shooting continued behind them.

Glancing down, he observed that she was very thin and far from clean. Her little feet were bare, and her pinafore was ragged. One of the tenement children, probably.

Anger flooded through him.

The Charitable Infirmary in nearby Jervis Street seemed the nearest safe haven. It was likely that other victims would be brought there as well; the child would stand a chance of being united with her mother.

The sound of gunfire on the quays was having a mixed effect on Dubliners. A few bold souls were running down to see, but most were deliberately going the other way. By the time Ned reached Jervis Street the little girl had stopped screaming and was sobbing helplessly.

An elderly Sister of Mercy with a face like crumpled linen met him at the hospital door. "What have we here?"

"The soldiers are firing on people," Ned panted. "I grabbed this child and ran."

"Is she yours?"

"She is not. I don't know her at all. But I saw her mother fall. Bayoneted," he added.

"Merciful hour!" The nun rolled up her eyes. "Here, bring the poor mite in and we'll see what we can do for her. I would say a wash and a cup of milk would be in order. Do you want to wait?"

"I told you, she isn't mine. But I . . . Thank you, I shall wait." He sank gratefully onto a varnished wooden bench in the reception area. He badly needed to catch his breath and collect his scattered thoughts.

Seán Heuston. Where was Seán? He remembered seeing his friend just before the woman dropped her child. He had been standing upright and unharmed, but anything could have happened since then.

I must go back, Ned told himself. But as he stood up another nun came bustling up to him holding a sheaf of papers in one hand. "What's the name of the little girl you brought in?"

"Is she all right?"

"She doesn't appear to be injured, but we haven't got much information from her. Her mother is called Mama and she lives in a house with a 'chimbley.' " Abruptly the woman smiled, revealing the ageless beauty many nuns possessed. "We need a bit more information than that."

"I'm sorry, I can't help. I never saw her before a few minutes ago. Does she not know her own name?"

The nun's smile deepened. "Indeed she does. She insists she is called Precious."

"I'm going back to look for a friend of mine. I'll see what I can find out about her, and—"

"Excuse me a moment." The nun's eyes went past Ned to a dapper, pear-shaped man who had just entered the hospital. He wore a top hat and sported a luxuriant walrus mustache. "Mr. Grantham!" she called. "You're very welcome."

He removed his hat and tucked it under his arm as he came toward her. "Good evening, Sister Concepta. As we were driving in from the Park we discovered there is a riot in progress on the quays. I assume they might bring any injured parties here, and I would appreciate having the details to report." His accent was purest Etonian.

Sister Concepta replied, "This young man was just there; he can tell you more than I. His name is . . ." She glanced quizzically at Ned.

"Ned. Edward Halloran. And it's not just a riot, it's a war."

"Oh, dear, I am sorry to hear that, Mr. Halloran." After a polite pause to express distress the other man extended his hand. "My name is Neville Grantham. I'm employed by the chief secretary's office in Dublin Castle as a liaison officer with His Excellency, the Marquess of Aberdeen."

The Marquess of Aberdeen was Lord Lieutenant of Ireland, the viceroy of a conquered land. King George's surrogate.

The face of the enemy.

Ned ignored the outstretched hand.

Grantham diplomatically turned back to Sister Concepta. "I have a government motorcar and driver outside, and I would be happy to put them at your disposal, Sister. An official vehicle might be the fastest way to transport casualties."

In a voice shaking with anger, Ned cried, "Casualties? People have just been shot down in the street like dogs. *Irish* people!"

"What difference does that make?" asked Grantham. "They're human beings."

Sister Concepta nodded. "Just so, and I thank you for your offer, Mr. Grantham. The chief secretary has been generous with his patronage to us in the past, and we're always grateful." She shot an admonitory glance at Ned.

He realized this was no time to alienate a man who offered help. "I apologize for my rudeness, sir. May I drive down with you? I need to find a friend of mine."

"Of course. Can you leave now?"

"We'll take good care of Precious," Sister Concepta promised Ned. "You call back later and see how she is."

Ned and three nurses fitted easily into the big motorcar with Grantham. Avoiding the congested street, the driver threaded his way through service laneways. During the brief journey Ned told Grantham what little he knew about the shooting, though he neglected to mention that he was a Volunteer.

"Someone's head will roll for this," Grantham predicted. "It's no way to treat people. We would never have had so much trouble in Ireland if we —" He clamped his lips together and said nothing more.

The motorcar purred to a halt on Lower Ormond Quay. By now ambulances were trying to reach the scene, but the milling crowd did not part for them as readily as it did for a car with British flags on the fenders. The DMP were also arriving, too late to do any good. Meanwhile the King's Own were massed on the Ha'penny Bridge, looking, Ned thought, like a herd of cattle alarmed by thunder.

By this time it was after seven. Summer evenings remained light until after ten, so the scene was clearly illumined. The walking wounded were making their way toward home, leaning on one another. Several people were still lying in the street, but none of them was Scán Heuston.

Nor was there any sign of Precious's mother.

Grantham and the others got out of the car. The nurses went to the nearest still bodies while Grantham headed for the bridge, located the officer in charge, and began questioning him.

Ned paced the blood-spattered quayside, romantically called Bachelor's Walk, searching for his friend. He skirted pools of congealing gore. With a sense of unreality he observed a mass of pinkish-gray brain tissue spilling out of the skull of a man who lay facedown across the tram tracks, one arm outstretched as if pleading for mercy.

The man was not Seán Heuston.

Two ambulance attendants brushed Ned aside and lifted the man onto a litter. Ned bent and scooped up the spilled brains and laid them beside the ruined head before it was covered with a blanket. One of the attendants looked at him questioningly.

He had no answer.

Although his car had carried away a load of casualties, Neville Grantham was still questioning witnesses. Policemen were doing the same. By moving unobtrusively from one side of the road to the other Ned managed to avoid speaking to any of the DMP. He waited until Grantham finished talking with one of the army officers, then caught his attention. "I wanted to tell you good-bye, and thank you. I'm going home now, sir," he said politely.

There were dark bags under Grantham's eyes that Ned had not noticed earlier. "Don't judge us all by what happened here today, Edward Halloran. Most of us are just doing our best, given the circumstances as we know them."

The circumstances as we know them. "That's all anyone can do, sir," Ned said aloud.

He called back to the Jervis Street hospital to inquire about Precious. Sister Concepta assured him she was tucked up in a warm bed and fast asleep.

"Has anyone come for her?"

"Not yet. Perhaps tomorrow."

"Let me leave my name, then. I can be reached at Saint Enda's School, if she needs anything."

The ride back to Rathfarnham on the tram took place in daylight, but Ned's soul felt the weight of night.

Chapter Twenty–five

In a land that cherished funerals, the burial of the Bachelor's Walk victims was a major event. Thousands attended. An honor guard of Volunteers accompanied the coffins to the cemetery and fired a volley over the graves. As a sign of respect, men stood with bared heads in a driving rain.

Some of the Dublin shawlies began a wild, mournful keening. The hackle-raising wail of the women was the voice of a conquered people who had felt the heavy hand of their conquerors yet again.

Henry Mooney was among the newspaper reporters at the funeral. He saw Ned with the Volunteers, but waited until the young man was leaving the cemetery before approaching him.

"I was in Bachelor's Walk, Henry," Ned told his friend. "I saw it all."

The newspaperman's eyes lit up. "Would you give me an exclusive interview? The *Independent* would let me run it with a byline, I'm sure."

"I shall, but . . . wait until tomorrow, if you don't mind. I have to go now, I must send a cable to my sister in America to assure her I'm all right."

The next day Henry arrived at Saint Enda's with a fresh notepad and a waistcoat pocket full of sharpened pencils. Mrs. Pearse showed him into the sparsely furnished drawing room, where he found Ned waiting for him. She supplied the men with lemonade and gingersnap biscuits, then left them alone.

"I appreciate this; it's been difficult to get people to talk," the journalist said. "The ones who are willing to tell everything they know are the ones who know nothing."

"What about the official investigation?"

"It's already begun, but in the heel of the hunt it may produce very little. Commissioner Harrel's gone to ground to avoid being questioned. Some claim he was acting on his own. If so, he's not the only person who exceeded his authority that day. The officers of the King's Own have a lot to answer for. Even if the shooting was spontaneous, they should have had better control of their men." Henry dropped his voice. "And there's a rumor it was not spontaneous."

Honesty compelled Ned to say, "I was there and I heard no order to fire."

"That doesn't mean anything. It could have been said under some officer's breath while they were being lined up in the road. Shooting protestors is a very effective way to stop a protest. And start a war," Henry added grimly. "But wonder of wonders, for once the House of Commons is taking our side. Volunteers parading in the streets of Dublin are not, from the Westminster point of view, a threat to the empire. Since the UVF are allowed to parade with arms, the government does not want to be seen as discriminating against the southern Volunteers."

Ned exclaimed, "That was exactly the point Thomas MacDonagh made on the day! But it did him no good with Harrel."

"No amount of reason will sway people who don't want to listen to reason. That peculiar form of deafness has long been a problem in Ireland. Perhaps it's something in the water," Henry added lightly.

Ned was in no mood for levity. "Was Harrel acting on orders from Dublin Castle?"

"If he was—and I honestly don't know—they won't admit it. I've already talked to my contacts there. I was reminded that the Castle has made no effort to quash the Citizen Army or—and this is a direct quote—'any of the other little self-styled militarist groups who like to strut about.' In the current official view, to act against them would be to give them too much importance. I suspect the truth is somewhat different. With the situation in Europe as bad as it is, Britain is looking at the Citizen Army and the Volunteers as ready-made reinforcements.''

With his hands thrust deep in his pockets, Henry went over to the open window and drew a deep breath of fresh air. Summer was drawing to a close. The flowers in the borders Michael MacRory lovingly tended were at their flamboyant best. Sheep were cropping the emerald lawns. No scene could have appeared more peaceful.

He turned back to Ned. ''You never heard me say this, but Dublin Castle has its finger in every unsavory pie in Ireland. They know all the tricks of control and don't hesitate to employ them, up to and including forging police records, that sort of thing. Both the Dublin Metropolitan Police and the Royal Irish Constabulary are under their control, remember. Added to that, for years they've paid informers to monitor the movements of any organization that dares to espouse nationalism.

''The Castle won't try to crush the Volunteers if they think they can use them. I suspect they've already infiltrated the corps with spies. A government bribing people to betray their own kind is reprehensible, yet it's been going on in this country since the time of Queen Elizabeth.''

''Henry Mooney, you're a nationalist through and through!''

''Why do you think I write for the *Independent*? The *Irish Times* wouldn't have me as a feature writer; they have too strong a British bias.''

Ned said, ''War might make a difference. People have always claimed England's difficulty would be Ireland's opportunity.''

''I hope to God that's true, but I fear war can only make things worse for Ireland. Already the bulk of our produce is being shipped to Britain. Thousands of cattle and pigs and tons of corn are going out of here just as they did during the height of the Famine. The excuse now is that the British army needs supplies. But what about the needs of the Irish at home? Are we to subsist on bread and dripping?

"We've seen the politics of domination played out here to the ultimate degree, Ned. Other British colonies are geographically at one remove, but unfortunate Ireland on her doorstep receives the brunt of the bullying. No matter how much they take from us they want more."

"Henry, I never heard you speak so passionately before."

"I never stood in the rain by the graves of slaughtered innocents before, listening to a shriek of grief that's echoed across this land for centuries."

"Is that what you'll say when you write about Bachelor's Walk?"

"I don't know just what I'll say yet. In the heel of the hunt, I may be a bit more restrained. I joked a while ago about being infected by something in the water, but it's not much of a joke. We have been infected, we Irishmen; infected with servility and fear. We cringe before the threat of British disapproval. It's tragic and pathetic and will take generations to overcome. I'm not sure I can throw it off by my next deadline, no matter how much I want to. I envy you, Ned. By nature I'm a peaceful man, but sometimes I wish I had the courage to carry a rifle on my shoulder."

"You would, if you'd listened to Pádraic Pearse as I have."

"Is he really that much of an influence? The consensus in the Castle is that Tom Clarke's the one to watch. Your headmaster is seen as a relatively harmless eccentric, a history-mad schoolteacher who writes poetry. The authorities are compiling a dossier on Pearse, of course, in case there's ever any serious trouble and they want to bring him in. But Clarke's an unreconstructed Fenian; they watch him like hawks watching a hare."

For the first time in days Ned managed a faint smile. "Perhaps they underestimate the power of a conspiracy of poets."

The two men sat in Mrs. Pearse's best armchairs on either side of the white marble fireplace. The red brocade chairs were slightly worn, and the fireplace was cold. There were only a few chairs and a table or two in the room, but the walls were covered with paintings and engravings by Irish artists or of Irish subjects.

When Ned began recounting his memories, Henry took notes, occasionally asking him to repeat a statement or clarify an inconsistency. By the time they were finished Ned felt as if he had lived the twenty-sixth of July all over again. He had omitted certain details, however. He said nothing of the unmanning terror that had raced through him when the shooting began.

Nor did he relate incriminating specifics of the gunrunning at Howth.

Ned trusted Henry, but the journalist's comments about spies and infiltrators had sunk home.

When the interview was over, Henry stood up and stretched his arms toward the high ceiling to relieve the tension in his shoulders. "You've helped make history this morning," he told Ned.

"This morning? I don't understand."

"Nowadays men don't make history; the words printed about them do. Historians of the future will of necessity use today's newspapers for their research."

Ned frowned. "I've read what's been in the papers so far, and a lot of it simply isn't true."

"How will they know, a hundred years from now?"

"That's a cynical remark, Henry."

"Is it? That's why I write for the papers. To put our version of truth on record. I may not carry a rifle, but I can fight in my own way."

Ned gave him a thoughtful look. "And are there not men on the other side doing exactly the same thing? Is not their version of truth as real to them?"

"Pádraic Pearse has taught you to be reflective, I see."

"Oh yes. He encourages us to question and argue. He says he doesn't want us to be blindly indoctrinated by anybody, himself included. The important thing, he tells us over and over again, is to do our own thinking. Which reminds me; may I go into the city with you?''

''I'd be glad of your company,'' Henry replied, ''and we can talk some more on the tram. But why are you going in? Shouldn't think you'd want to see Dublin for a while.''

''Remember the little girl I told you about? I want to find out how she is and if her mother's been found.''

''A woman was among those killed,'' said Henry.

''Bayonetted?''

The journalist shook his head. ''Shot. Besides, we've learned that she was the mother of a serving British soldier; how's that for irony? Precious's mother may be holed up somewhere badly injured, though. She might have no idea what's happened to her child.'' Henry began tucking his pencils into the pocket of his waistcoat. ''There's another possibility, Ned. The mother saw a nicely dressed young man rescue the child and had enough presence of mind to abandon her to him.''

''I can't believe that.''

''You should. Children are frequently abandoned by parents who can't support them anymore. Precious's mother may have seen you as a heaven-sent opportunity to improve her daughter's lot. An act of love, if you look at it that way.''

''I can't take a child, Henry!''

''Would you like to?''

''I have two little sisters myself whom I love very much. Thin and dirty as she was, Precious reminded me of our Eileen. The same fair hair, the same big eyes. But it's out of the question, I'm just starting out myself; I'm not ready for responsibilities like that.'' He hesitated. ''What will happen to her, Henry? If she has been abandoned?''

''She'll be sent to an orphanage, probably the Orphan House For Destitute Females in the North Circular Road.[1] Of course, there's also the Protestant Orphan Society in Molesworth Street, which is better funded, but I'm sure the nuns would never send her there. The society would give her a very strict education in the Protestant faith and eventually put her out to work in a Protestant household.''

"Precious deserves better than an orphanage!" Ned said indignantly. "That's almost as bad as a workhouse."

Henry was amused. "I fail to see what you can do about it."

Ned said nothing more on the subject, but his cleft chin took on the stubborn jut his family knew so well.

The two men took the tram into the city and parted company at Nelson's Pillar. Ned went straight to Jervis Street, where Sister Concepta told him there were still no inquiries for Precious. "We can keep her until the end of the week because she has some congestion in her chest and an inflamed throat. But after that . . ." The nun shrugged regretfully.

Ned found Precious in the children's ward. Her tiny body was almost lost amid the rumpled sheets of an iron hospital bed. She was clean and her hair had been combed, but there was a hectic flush in her cheeks.

He bent over the bed. "Do you know me, little one?"

She put one thumb in her mouth and stared solemnly up at him. Ned tried to guess her age; four, perhaps. She looked younger because she was undersized.

He smiled as encouragingly as he knew how. "Don't be afraid. Everything's all right now."

Precious removed the thumb from her mouth. "Mama?"

Ned's heart turned over. "Your mama isn't here just now." He bent down to stroke the hair back from her feverish forehead.

She reached out and caught his hand with both of hers. "I want my Mama," she said clearly. "Please?"

Her hands were so hot. That was what hurt him most: her tiny hands were so hot.

He left the hospital with tears in his eyes.

His next visit was to Tom Clarke. The old Fenian was able to tell Ned, "All the Volunteers are accounted for. They took a few blows at Clontarf, but no one was killed, thank God."

"How did you and Seán MacDermott happen to arrive when you did?"

"Pure chance. I have a second news agency in Amiens Street and my family lives above the shop. Our rooms afford a fine view of the road. Seán has no family in Dublin, so my wife often invites him to have dinner with us and our three boys on Sunday. We eat early because the children get hungry.

"Before we sat down at table that day, I went into the street and engaged a cab to take us out to Howth afterwards to see how things were going. Then while we were eating Katty happened to glance out the window just as the Howth-bound tram went by.

"When she said the tram was full of armed soldiers we abandoned our meal and ran for the street. Luckily our cab had just pulled up to wait for us. You know the rest. We brought some of the rifles to my place and went back for more, but we didn't find them all by any means.

"The next day a dozen Fianna showed up at Balally with another twenty.[2] Constance Markievicz rents a country cottage there, a sort of personal hideway, so they had come to 'hide the guns away.' They told her they had carried them off in the trek cart hidden under the batons. What about you, Ned? Do you still have your rifle?"

"I'm afraid not. Seán Heuston and I hid ours in a shed a couple of hundred yards from the road."

"Did anyone see you?"

"I can't be sure."

"You'd better collect them then, and quickly. The Citizen Army's searching for any guns that haven't been recovered."

Ned was indignant. "They're stealing our rifles?"

"Rifles have no sense of ownership; they belong to the men who hold them. Connolly's crowd have been drilling with hurley sticks; they're desperate to get their hands on real weapons, even old Mausers that date to the Boer War. So on yer bike, lad," Clarke added in Dublin slang.

Ned took him literally. "I don't have my bike with me; I came in by tram. After what's happened I can't very well go back to Rathfarnham on the tram with two illegal rifles on my lap."

"I'll give you a roll of newspapers and a note for some friends who have a house in Fairview," said Clarke. "Once you have your rifles, wrap them in the papers and take them there—it's not a long walk. Follow the back roads and you won't call any attention to yourself. I can collect the rifles later and hold them for you.''

Ned hesitated. ''Perhaps that's not a good idea. You might be watched.''

The old man's eyes twinkled behind their spectacles. ''If I can't hide a couple more weapons without anyone knowing the better, I'm not the man I used to be. You'll have your rifle. And by the way, the committee has come to a decision about the uniforms. The treasury can't afford to supply them, but we have an official design selected. If you have someone who can make one for you, you'll look a proper soldier.''

A proper soldier. Ned wondered if Precious's mother would have abandoned her child to a uniformed soldier.

Ned was just about to leave the shop when Síle Duffy entered. Seeing him, she threw a startled glance at Clarke. The old man kept his face carefully blank.

''I just came in for something to read,'' Síle said.

Ned observed, ''It's too early for the evening papers.''

''Is it?'' She gave a flustered little laugh. ''I must have lost track of the time.'' She flicked her eyes toward Tom Clarke again.

''You can always come back later,'' the shopkeeper assured her. ''I know what you want; I'll save them for you.''

The two young people left the shop together and stood on the pavement outside, trying to think of things to say to one another.

''What are you doing this afternoon, Síle?''

''Nothing,'' she answered quickly.

''Then would you like to ride the tram out to Clontarf with me? There may be a bit of a walk after.''

She smiled. ''I don't mind a bit of a walk. Sure, amn't I a country girl?''

Ned had dreaded returning to Clontarf alone, though he did not tell that to Síle. If he tried to explain she would laugh at him for being too sensitive, he thought. And perhaps he was.

Long before the geopolitical concept of nationhood was

established, Brian Boru had struggled to make Ireland one nation. He had undertaken the seemingly impossible task of peacefully assimilating the Viking invaders while uniting the contentious native tribes for the common good. And he almost succeeded. He almost made Ireland strong enough to resist any attempt at foreign domination.

Then nine hundred years ago that dream had died with him at the Battle of Clontarf.

To Ned Halloran, Clontarf represented the tragedy of lost possibilities. It was one place he never wanted to be . . . alone.

WITH a roll of newspapers under one arm, Ned fumbled in his pocket for tuppence to pay their tram fare. When several of the male passengers stared at the girl he glared them down. Her features were striking but that was not her fault. Her clothing, though inexpensive, was not vulgar. He resented any man's making assumptions about her which he refused to make himself.

Ned guided her up the stair to the unroofed top section of the tram, where there were fewer passengers. He sat down beside her and watched the sun turn her hair to flame. The white lilac scent she wore filled his nostrils.

They left the tram at the Clontarf stop and strolled down the road. The briars in the ditch on one side looked dusty. It was hard to believe an army had passed this way not long ago.

Ned felt obliged to explain the reason for their journey, so he told Síle about the gunrunning incident and his part in it. Her attitude about the Volunteers proved different from Mary Cosgrave's. "I'm proud of every one of you," she said. "You're actually doing something. Too many people complain about their lot without trying to change it. I did something myself; I know how hard it is."

"What did you do, Síle?"

"You know."

"I do not know, that's why I asked."

She stopped in the road and turned to look at him, searching his face with a strange desperation in her eyes. "I lay down in the hay with a cattle dealer who said he was coming up to Dublin. When he left Clare, I left with him."

Chapter Twenty-six

N ED was ambushed by Síle's honesty. He tried to think of a suitable response but could only stammer, "Why did you tell me that? I . . . I didn't want to know."

"Dublin's like a small town in some ways, Ned. Everyone knows everyone else, or knows someone who does. You would have found out about me eventually. It's best sooner rather than later, that's all. If you're going to hate me I want to know now, I don't want to be afraid it might fall on me when I least expect it."

"I don't hate you, Síle. How could I?"

"We're still friends then, you and me?"

"We are of course."

Some of the tension went out of her face. "I am glad, Ned. But I must tell you; what I did was no mistake. It got me to Dublin and I would do it again, so."

He stared at her aghast, his self-deception in ruins at his feet.

Her mouth twisted. "How else could I get away before I turned into an old woman? You saw my mother. How old do you think she is?"

"I don't know."

"Not twenty years more than me, but she looks like my grandmother. She's worn out; she'll die soon and she's had no life at all. I couldn't settle for that, Ned, like your Volunteers can't settle for Ireland going on the way it is. Sometimes you just have to claw at the world, you know? You have to make things come right or die trying!

"When we got to Dublin I left my cattle dealer and set out on my own, but I soon realized there was no future in being on the streets. If anything, my life was worse than it had been in Clare. So I went to Mrs. Drumgold and asked her to take me in. At first she refused. She said I was too common, but I convinced her I could learn. And I have, Ned. I have."

Ned had gazed at her wordlessly throughout this recital, but now he reached out and took her hand. Holding it tightly, he set off down the road again. Síle's hand felt the same as before, but everything else had changed.

Irish people were reticent to divulge anything of a personal nature. Yet Síle had entrusted Ned with a shocking revelation and obviously thought he would be man enough to understand. Would he? Could he?

He chewed on his lip and kept his eyes on the road ahead of them.

Síle walked beside him, astonished with herself. What devil had compelled her to be honest with this man when she lied so glibly to others? She desired Ned's good opinion more than anything, and now . . . his silence was telling her more than words ever could.

He did hate her. He was just too polite to say so.

So be it, Síle told herself, gritting her teeth. Life was hard, and the only way to get through it was to face things square. Even a girl who worked in a kip could have principles. Perhaps such a girl needed them more than most.

When they came to the next bend in the road Ned said, "This is where we were stopped by the soldiers and the DMP. We hid our rifles behind that cottage back there." He pointed toward a small house some distance from the road. "I'll go, you stop here. In case anyone's watching there's no need for you to be implicated."

"Do you think I'm afraid of that?" she asked scornfully.

It was his turn to search her face. "I don't think you're

afraid of anything. You're very brave. It must have taken great courage to tell me what you did.''

Something twisted inside her. ''Let's collect those rifles.''

They left the road together and made their way toward the cottage. When they were halfway there Ned realized Síle's shoulders were shaking. He put one hand on her arm and turned her toward him. She felt wooden beneath his touch. Her face was impassive, but her eyes were glittering with tears.

''Why are you crying?''

''I'm not crying. I never cry,'' she said as her eyes brimmed over.

''You are. What have I done to hurt you?''

''Nothing. How could you possibly hurt me? I won't let any man do that. Is your rifle in that old shed I see over there?''

He nodded, relieved that she had changed the subject. He had no idea how one dealt with a woman's tears.

When they reached the shed, Ned cast a nervous glance toward the cottage. This time no curtain moved. He ducked into the small timber outbuilding with Síle close behind him. He and Seán had buried their weapons in a hastily scooped-out shallow pit in the earth floor, then piled sacks of musty grain on top. Nothing appeared to have been disturbed.

''Phew! The smell in here reminds me of the country,'' Síle said, wrinkling her nose.

''I think the country smells a lot better than the city,'' Ned retorted. ''But give me a hand here and we'll be outside again soon.''

She helped Ned drag the sacks away, then knelt with him to scrape aside the earth.

The pit was empty.

Ned sat back on his heels, aghast.

''Where are the rifles, Ned?''

''I knew someone was watching us that day, I knew it! We've been betrayed. The Citizen Army must have got them.''

''Are you not both on the same side?''

"We're both on the side of Ireland, but we're separate armies with different leaders. Connolly's supporters want a socialist country for the sake of the working class; the Volunteers want a free Ireland for everybody's sake. And even within the Volunteers there's a difference of opinion as to how to achieve it."

She was shaking her head. "Can't you work together?"

"You haven't studied Irish history or you would know we've always been too tribal for that. Each group has its own philosophy and insists on its own individuality."

"Like the unionists in Ulster," the girl said.

Ned looked at her in surprise. He had not expected such an astute observation from—

No! He slammed the door on his thoughts. This was no common whore, this was his friend. His friend gazing at him with the tracks of salt tears on her cheeks . . . unthinkingly he reached out and put an arm around her. The shed was dark and private, and he had just had a shock. He did not want to talk politics. He wanted the feel of another human being close to him, the warmth and comfort two people could offer one another.

Síle relaxed against him. When she lifted her face to his he kissed her as naturally as breathing.

This time he parted his lips first and caressed hers with his tongue. She tasted sweet except for a trace of salt where one of the tears had reached her mouth. That salty tang was an added spice, making the kiss sweeter.

Síle knew what Ned must think of her now. She was ruined in his eyes; any respect he had for her was destroyed. From now on he would see her as other men did and use her in the same way if she let him. The very thought made her flinch inside, yet she did not flinch away from him.

What's done is done, she thought ruefully. She might as well go the rest of the way and extract what pleasure she could. Her profession gave her no physical pleasure. She regarded her clients with a remote scorn, as she would regard pigs rooting in a trough. But Ned's touch was different, perhaps because the relationship had not begun as a business transaction. The first time they kissed she had allowed her feelings to rise to the surface. They could not be driven back now. She would have this much, Síle resolved, if she never had anything else!

Her arms tightened around Ned so fiercely the embrace took his breath away.

There need be no pretense of innocence now. Ned did not have to control himself as he would have done with someone like Mary Cosgrave. With a sense of relief he gave himself over to passion, a passion Síle met and amplified. She pressed her body against his until he was afraid he would have another premature ejaculation, but she eased away in time. Her hands slid to his trousers and skillfully unbuttoned them.

The touch of her fingers on his springing erection was maddening.

"Not here," Ned said hoarsely. "I will not make love to you in a filthy shed."

Síle was touched that he did not use any of the common names for the act they were about to perform. *Make love*. She would cherish the phrase even if it was meaningless, even if she did not dare use the word *love* herself. "Then where shall we go, Ned?"

"Let's look in the cottage. If no one's there . . ."

They rearranged their clothes and hurried to the cottage with a combination of stealth and desperation. The door facing onto the yard was not fastened; people in rural Ireland never fastened their doors. Ned pushed it open and peered in.

There was no fire on the kitchen hearth.

"It's all right," he said over his shoulder. He went inside, then turned to face her. *"Failte isteach."*

The cottage appeared deserted. A layer of dust covered its few remaining bits of furniture, and the air was stale. But when Ned went to the window where he had seen the curtain move on Sunday, he noticed that the dust on the deep sill had been disturbed.

Across from the fireplace was an old settle, a wooden bench meant to double as a bed. When Síle lifted the seat the customary straw mattress and flour-sack sheeting were not stored inside, but there was a tattered shawl hanging on a peg on the back of the door.

"There may be a bed inside," Ned suggested, indicating the other room.

"If there is, it's likely damp. This will do us." As Síle folded the shawl to pad the bench she thought briefly of her comfortable room at Mrs. Drumgold's, with all the appurtenances for making love save love itself.

Then she put everything out of her mind but Ned.

She let him undress her and smiled at the dawning wonder in his face. When he knelt before her and unbuckled her shoes, she lifted her petticoat so he could take down her stockings. Delay had restored a measure of self-control; he was able to savor his first view of a naked woman. "How beautiful you are."

Síle had heard those same words many times before, but never believed them. Until now. "Touch me," she whispered. "Touch me wherever you like."

With reverent fingers he traced the curve of her breasts. Holding his breath, he stroked the tight red curls of pubic hair. In the dim light filtering through the tattered curtains Síle read his eyes and knew he could not wait any longer. She lay back on the settle and opened her arms.

"Now, Ned. Now."

He tried to ease his weight onto her gently. But as her thighs parted she cupped his buttocks and pulled him hard against her pelvis. His penis plunged into a hot, moist haven that squeezed him like a hand. Ned gasped with shock at a pleasure so intense it bordered on pain. Then his body took over with a joyous pounding lust. There was no room in his mind for thought, only for waves of sensation. A great sweetness welled up into his throat even as the heat and pressure built in his groin. Síle matched her rhythm to his, two bodies moving as one.

The climax, when it came, shuddered through them both together.

He lay panting on top of her, believing all passion spent. When she moved under him he realized his mistake.

This time she allowed him to be gentle.

Slowly, softly, he stroked her with warm hands. When she responded with a little moan, molding herself to his touch, he ignored his own body's need and lingered over the caress. He wanted to learn what gave her pleasure. Woman was a new territory, wondrous and strange, and he was an explorer on a voyage of discovery.

No man had ever been so gentle, so tender, with Síle Duffy. Ned's tenderness seduced her in a totally new way.

Time stopped in the cottage.

She gave him everything he wanted, leading him step by step until he was ready to run ahead of her. His healthy passion was a delight. So many of her clients brought flaccid organs and flagging desire and expected her to restore both. Ned was as hard as an oak tree and as tireless as the wind.

But at last they burned all moisture dry and lay helpless in each other's arms. Ned whispered, "Thank you."

She replied with something she had never said to any man. "Thank you." Then she was content to lie still, listening to the deepening rhythm of his breathing.

Ned stirred, sat up. "I'd best be taking you back."

"I suppose so. Will we walk?"

"There's no need now. We'll ride the tram."

"It's glad I am to hear it. I don't know that I could walk." He said quickly, "Did I hurt you?"

"You didn't hurt me. Far from it."

"Are you sure?" Ned asked as he fumbled for his clothes. "Will you ever want to see me again?"

Instead of replying, she reached for him.

Hidden within the veil of her hair, Síle sucked him with a slow hot mouth. He reacted like one of Galvani's frogs, spasming uncontrollably. When at last he could speak, he said, "Who taught you to do that?"

She did not answer, merely looked at him slantwise. And smiled.

        •   •   •

A week after the gunrunning at Howth, six hundred rifles with ammunition were brought ashore at Kilcoole in County Wicklow and distributed to the Dublin Brigade.[1]

August 3, 1914

GERMANY DECLARES WAR ON FRANCE

August 4, 1914

BRITAIN DECLARES WAR ON GERMANY

Chapter Twenty-seven

KNEELING on the unpadded bench in the confessional, the man bowed his head over his folded hands. "Bless me Father for I have sinned." Too late he realized he had rattled off the words by rote.

They had a new meaning now.

"How long since your last confession?" asked the disembodied voice on the other side of the grille.

"Monday."

"What sins have you committed since?"

He paused, gathering his courage. "I have been with a woman, Father."

Silence on the other side of the grille. Then a surprised whisper, "You?"

"Yes."

When the priest spoke again his voice was deliberately uninflected, yet one could sense the distaste beneath the words. "Did you commit a sexual act or acts?"

"I did, Father." The penitent's head sank lower over his folded hands.

"What acts?"

He hesitated. How could he describe the closeness, the warmth, the unexpected feeling of completeness? Any words he used would make it sound . . . dirty. Sinful because the church insisted it was a sin.

"I kissed her, Father."

The voice bore on relentlessly, a dog worrying a bone to extract every fragment of marrow. "Was your mouth open or closed?"

FATHER Paul O'Shaughnessy emerged from the confessional a shaken man. He stood outside on the church steps trying to regain some composure. Father Bertolucci had known who he was, of course, even though he had made a point of traveling across Manhattan. Most priests in the diocese recognized one another even with the grille between them. But none admitted it; the anonymity of the confessional was sacred.

There was something else he had not admitted to Father Bertolucci. That was not the first time he had kissed Kathleen Campbell, and in spite of being adjured to go and sin no more, it might not be the last. Nor, he feared, would it always stop with kissing.

Feared.

Hoped.

Dear God, where were they going?

FOLLOWING the Bachelor's Walk incident, Volunteer support increased dramatically. Men flocked to join the Irish corps while ignoring recruiters for the British army. They saw Britain's involvement with mainland Europe as another expression of imperialism, of no relevance to them. Ireland had suffered enough because of imperialism.

On the day Britain entered the war, the British-owned Cunard liner *Lusitania* sneaked out of New York Harbor at one in the morning, heading for home. She was flying the American flag. Her electric lights were disconnected and her portholes were covered by blankets.

The war in Europe expanded hour by hour. Nations were

settling old grudges and seizing new territory. The first shots
had been fired in a conflict between the German kaiser and
his cousin, the Russian czar. No sooner had Britain promised
to uphold Belgian neutrality and defend the coasts of France
than Germany invaded Belgium. Austria declared war on Russia; Germany and Austria threatened to attack Italy unless it
renounced neutrality; the emperor of Japan declared war on
Germany.

Britain was not yet invaded, but the possibility was growing. As her threshold on the Atlantic, Ireland was strategically
important. In Dublin a number of "suspicious individuals"
were arrested, bewildered foreign born waiters and elderly
shopkeepers who had dutifully registered as aliens and were
now considered to be spies. Members of the army reserve
were called up. Many of them were laborers from the building
trades whose families came down to the North Wall to cheer
as they boarded the troopships.

RUNNING against the tide, the pages of *Sinn Féin* began to
protest British recruitment. Passionate editorials argued the
injustice of having Irishmen involve themselves in wars they
had not started, and fight for land not theirs. People who had
never paid much attention to the paper before began to buy
and read it, and discuss it among themselves.

AT first people believed the war would be over by Christmas.
Then reports from the front line began to shake that optimism.
Horrific battles were being fought. There had been a blood-
bath at Mons, and small Belgium was being overrun. British
hospitals throughout the United Kingdom would soon be
flooded with the mutilated and dying. The contagion of war
was spreading; digging in.

WHEN Ned called in to Tom Clarke's news agency, the two
men discussed the situation. Leaning his elbows on the

counter, Clarke said, "I know a lot about war, lad, and make no mistake, Ireland's at war against England. Always has been; still is. It's not just about flags flying and marching off to glory, either. It's about men being dragged out of their homes in the middle of the night to be tortured. It's about perjured evidence and falsified police records. I could tell you a lot of things that would shake your faith in British justice."

"Are you saying you were innocent of the charges against you?"

Clarke smiled bleakly. "Oh no, I was guilty enough. But I know men who will go to their graves with convictions against them for things they never did."

"Does it have to be that way? What makes men hate each other so much?"

Clarke adjusted his spectacles with his forefinger. "In a war you don't necessarily hate the poor bastard on the other side. You don't even know him, though you may have a lot in common. You just go on fighting because fighting has come to be the way you live. The way your father and his father before him lived, maybe. You don't think about the morality of it, right and wrong, good and evil. You don't think at all; you don't dare. It might unman you."

EARLY in September, Pádraic Pearse spent the day in the Dublin offices of the Gaelic League. Ned mowed lawns at Saint Enda's. Sweaty and itchy, he returned to the house at twilight just in time to see Pearse arriving. The headmaster, usually a man of abnormal energy, looked exhausted. The skin around his eyes was slack; when he spoke his voice was as hoarse as if he had been lecturing for hours. "Would you be kind enough to join Willie and me in the dining room in half an hour?" he asked Ned. "There is something I want to tell you privately."

Ned ran to the dining room with his hair still damp from the comb. The Pearse brothers were already sitting on either side of the table. Mrs. Pearse lit a fire in the fireplace and then lingered in the doorway until her elder son made shooing gestures with his hands. "Go on now, Mother, and fetch us a pot of tea. We're in dire need of some."

Willie added, "And perhaps some sandwiches if there is any cold chicken left?" His tone was casual, but he kept watchful eyes fixed on his brother.

When she was out of earshot, Pádraic Pearse said, "Ned, I must ask you not to speak of this conversation to anyone. I shall explain everything to Mother later, in my own way.

"Firstly, you should know that for some time the IRB has had an advisory committee consisting of Joe Plunkett, Eamonn Ceannt, and myself drawing up plans for a proposed insurrection.[1] We all three belong to both the Brotherhood and the Volunteer Corps, and in addition military strategy is one of Joe's enthusiasms.

"In July I was co-opted onto the Supreme Council of the IRB.[2] Between them the members represent all shades of nationalist philosophy. Today I attended a very long council meeting at which the plans for insurrection were thoroughly discussed. We may have another meeting in a few days and invite a few interested parties outside the Brotherhood."[3] Pearse closed his eyes and wearily massaged the bridge of his nose.

Willie interjected, "I presume Seán MacDermott was on one side and Arthur Griffith on the other when it came to discussing the use of physical force?"

"At first there was some . . . ah, heated discussion," his brother admitted. "But eventually we reached a consensus. With Britain distracted by the European war our opportunity has come at last, so the IRB has now officially agreed on an armed insurrection.[4] If we are successful this will be the last Rising after so many failed attempts.

"Ned, this is why the Volunteers are so important. They will become Ireland's army of independence."

Ned's heart gave a violent thud.

"We have voted to accept any assistance Germany may offer us," Pearse went on, speaking in a grave, measured voice. "As James Connolly has written, 'Over the centuries

Britain, not Germany, has been our only enemy among the nations of the world.' "

In a hoarse whisper, Willie asked, "When?"

"No specific date is set, but the Rising will take place under any one of three conditions. First, if Britain attempts to force conscription on Ireland. Secondly, if German troops land here. Or if the European war draws to a close and Ireland still is denied Home Rule. At least one of these is, we are convinced, inevitable."

The three men sat looking at one another in the quiet room.

A Rising—to set Ireland free.

THAT night Ned lay sleepless in his bed and stared at the ceiling. Pearse had taught him to think, and now he could not stop thinking.

What was proposed was glorious in theory, but the reality could be very different. Armed insurrection meant killing or being killed.

What could possibly justify such an act to a Christian conscience?

Something Pearse had once said came back to him: "The church has always taught that its men and women are soldiers for Christ and should be willing to die for their faith. What is the difference between that, and being ready to die as Robert Emmet did in the cause of freedom?"

Alone in the dark, Ned struggled to answer the question to his own satisfaction.

Questions stripped away the platitudes and undermined the verities that provided a sheltered, nursery existence for people who did not want to think. Questions were the obligation of the intellect. Pádraic Pearse said that, too.

Sometime before dawn, Ned slept.

THE following week Ned had his new Volunteer uniform. He could not afford a professional tailor, but had bought gray-green serge from which Margaret Pearse sewed a single-

breasted tunic and matching trousers, cut like breeches.[5] In
lieu of high-topped riding boots, cloth puttees in the same
heathery green would wrap snugly around his legs from ankle
to knee. In addition he bought a Sam Browne belt, a flat-
topped military hat with a smart brim, brass buttons embossed
with a harp, and one of the bronze Volunteer badges Eoin
MacNeill had designed. These purchases left Ned with empty
pockets, but he did not care.

He donned the uniform for Mrs. Pearse's inspection. By
now she knew about the plans for insurrection. Pádraic had
assured his mother that no violence was intended, merely a
show of armed force like that which had been so successful
in the north in influencing British policy. But there was a
lurking anxiety at the back of her eyes as she surveyed Ned
in his new gear. "It's a wee bit tight across the shoulders,"
she pronounced. "Take off that tunic and I'll ease the back
seam."

Mama would have done the same, thought Ned. Mama had
never been happy with any garment until she made her own
adjustments.

"But how do I *look*?" he insisted.

Mrs. Pearse forced a smile. "Splendid, lad. Just splendid."

Mama would have said "Splendid," too.

Ned wore his new uniform for the first time when the Volunteers went on training maneuvers in the Dublin mountains.
The Fianna, who had drilled many times in the same area,
served as their guides. The discipline and dependability of
"Madame's army" were invaluable. "And a little child shall
lead them," Thomas MacDonagh joked as they marched
along.

Ned remarked, "When I was in the Fianna I thought I was
a man, but now I see I was only a child. Yet I still don't feel
like a grown-up man, not completely. How soon does that
happen?"

"You never get there, bedad. It's the great lesson of maturity. The longing and impatience of boyhood give way to
the longing and discontent of manhood, and the future you
anticipate is still just around the corner. Yet no matter how

far you run or how fast, you never quite turn that corner.''
MacDonagh gave Ned an affectionate dig in the ribs with his
elbow. "Don't you know we're all boys at heart?"

Ned's duties as a courier were multiplying. The war seemed
to make everything more urgent. While pedaling his bicycle
at top speed along South King Street one afternoon, he almost
ran into a couple outside McDowell's Oyster Bar.

"Whoa there!" cried Joe Plunkett as he put a protective
arm around the slender young woman beside him. "Oh, it's
you, Ned."

"I apologize, I was in such a hurry . . ."

"All is forgiven friends," Plunkett replied. His voice was
very hoarse. "But no matter how much of a hurry you're in,
do stop a moment and meet Miss Gifford. Grace, this is one
of Pádraic Pearse's star pupils, Ned Halloran."

As Ned and Grace Gifford shook hands, he observed that
she had a short upper lip and a round, pretty chin. Smartly
dressed in a fitted dove-gray jacket and narrow skirt, her
broad-brimmed hat set at a becoming angle, she held her own
against the drama of Joe Plunkett's mulberry-colored cape.

"Miss Gifford's an artist," Plunkett explained. "She's just
done some illustrations for the *Irish Review.* Since it sells for
sixpence and we can't afford to pay our contributors, I took
her to lunch as a way of saying thank-you. It turns out her
sister is married to our friend Tom MacDonagh, though I
didn't realize that when I bought her drawings."

The trio chatted for a few moments while traffic flowed
around them. Plunkett was obviously impressed with Miss
Gifford. "Her paintings will hang in a gallery someday," he
predicted.

Ned replied, "And we'll all go to see them and say, 'I knew
her when.' "

Before Plunkett could agree he bent over with a fit of
coughing. When he straightened up again his eyes met Ned's.
"Promise me you will," he said, "if I can't be there."

"Of course you'll be there! Don't talk rubbish."

But as Ned rode away he found himself pondering the brevity of life. With great nations going to war, any future was uncertain.

Ned's last message of the day was for Seán MacDermott, who lived in a boardinghouse in the North Circular Road.[6] He looked forward to seeing MacDermott. His love of fun and laughter could be counted upon to lift any dark mood. In addition, he and Ned shared a dependence on the bicycle, and he often asked, jokingly, after the health of Ned's machine.

"Is your push-bike feeling well today?" he inquired.

"Well enough. Bit of the collywobbles in the steering column, though."

"Take it around to the back and let me look at it." In a lean-to shed behind the house, MacDermott tinkered with the bicycle for a while, then pronounced it cured. "You need to put a bit of grease there every so often. Men like us who have to rely on their machines must keep them working."

"You travel farther on yours than I ever do on mine," Ned replied.

"Ah, well, that's my job. Ever since '08 I've been on the road at thirty shillings a week, organizing desperadoes."

When he threw back his head and laughed, Ned laughed, too. "That's us, desperadoes!"

A shadow stirred in MacDermott's eyes. "It's better than being a part-time barman in a poor village in Leitrim,[7] or cleaning Dublin trams for starvation wages. For an Irishman with a bad leg there aren't a lot of jobs on offer. The Brotherhood's been good to me, almost like family. A fellow needs a family, Ned; everyone does."

SINCE he was already in the North Circular Road, when Ned left MacDermott he went to the Orphan House for Destitute Females. The place reeked of carbolic and bewilderment and loneliness. A matron who rustled with starch assured him that no one there was called "Precious."

Almost too late, Ned remembered the name the nuns had given the child. "What about Ursula Jervis? Is she here?"

"Are you a relative?"

"Just a friend."

She looked as if she did not believe him; orphans had no friends. But she directed him to an antechamber to wait. The room was equipped with hard benches and curtainless windows. The only decoration was a lurid picture of the Sacred Heart, spouting blood. Ned paced the bare floor and listened to the echo of his footsteps. Eventually the matron half dragged a child to the doorway. "Stop being stubborn, Ursula," she hissed.

The name of a medieval saint was too pretentious for the tiny girl who stood staring at Ned.

"Precious!"

Pulling away from the matron, she ran to him, and he folded her into his arms. She hugged his neck with all her small strength.

"Are you going to take me home?"

"Do you remember where you live?"

Precious began to tremble. "Can't remember." She was on the verge of tears.

"It's all right, little one," he assured her. "Don't worry, everything will be fine."

They allowed Ned half an hour with her in that bare and cheerless room. He entertained her with stories about the boyhood of Cuchulain in which he played all the parts, and he combed her hair with his pocket comb.

When the matron returned to take Precious away the child clung to his hand and cried.

"I'll be back soon, I promise," he told her.

The matron looked unconvinced.

INSTEAD of taking the most straightforward way back to Rathfarnham, Ned followed the route by which Mary Cosgrave would return home from Brown Thomas. Vague plans, little more than daydreams, had begun swirling through his head.

When he saw her walking toward him he had a strong sense

of inevitability. "Miss Cosgrave!" he called. "May I escort you home?"

She stopped on the footpath and folded her arms. "Are you sober now?"

He could not tell if she was teasing. "I am sober, I haven't had a drink since you last saw me."

"In that case you may escort me," she replied like a queen conferring a favor on a courtier. Then she gave Ned one of her lovely smiles and he knew he was forgiven.

They made their way toward the Cosgrave house slowly, with many pauses. When Mary admired some roses in a garden Ned hopped over the low brick wall to pick them for her, daring thorns and the householder's wrath. Farther on he leaned his machine against a lamppost so he could adjust the chain, and she waited beside him, chatting idly about her friend Eliza and her work at the shop and her mother's migraine headaches.

They had almost reached Mary's house before the war in Europe entered the conversation. The latest recruiting poster for the British army was prominently displayed in the window of a corner shop. "Join the Fight on Behalf of Small Nations!" it trumpeted. "Free Belgium and Serbia from the Hun!"

Mary said, "Just think of those brave soldiers going off to fight for the oppressed. Aren't they wonderful? I'm sure my brothers in England will enlist."

"Perhaps they'll have better luck over there, though I doubt it."

"What do you mean?"

"The British authorities are doing everything they can to persuade Irishmen to enlist, but it's a different matter once your name is signed on the line. It's the same old discrimination, Mary. Our lads are being sent straight to the front lines, where the bullets will find them first. It's almost impossible for a Catholic to get a commission. All the cadets in the officer training corps at Trinity are Protestants, of course.

"Irish regiments are permitted to march only under the Union Jack—although Carson's been given special privileges for his Ulster Volunteers. They're enrolled as a separate unit with their own colors and their choice of officers.''

"I'm sure the government knows what's best," Mary said complacently. "And when my brothers join up I shall be very proud of them.''

"I thought you disapproved of the military.''

"I disapprove of grown men strutting around like little boys, criticizing the king and wanting to throw out the government. That's just playacting, Ned. But a man who is willing to lay down his life for his country is a hero.''

"Our country has not declared war against Germany," he reminded her.

"England has. It's the same thing.''

He did not want to argue with her. Their reestablished friendship was too important to him. But as he pedaled home in the twilight he was thinking, It isn't the same. It isn't the same at all.

As he turned in at the gate of Saint Enda's, Ned was pondering his own military future. The IRB was planning a Rising, but Ireland's independence was still a dream. For the present her fate was inextricably linked to Britain's.

Of all the major European powers, only Britain depended upon a volunteer army. Lord Kitchener, Secretary of State for War, had undertaken a vigorous recruiting campaign. From Irish pulpits and sporting fields alike voices urged men to join the British army. Many Irish farm lads, bored with cattle and pigs and plowing, bored with local girls and bottled coffee essence and limited horizons, enlisted because it gave them the opportunity of Going Somewhere Else. They neither knew nor cared who they would have to fight, nor what the issues were.

On the ninth of September, the British prime minister visited the Mansion House in Dublin to make a formal appeal to Dublin men to "take the king's shilling" and sign up. He made it plain that he was asking for recruits in return for Home Rule, the "free gift of a free people.''

Asquith's offer did not fall on deaf ears. Times were hard and prices were high. For men out of work any wages were

better than none, and the British War Department was a reliable paymaster. Their wives could not be blamed for encouraging them. The dependents' allowance granted to the
families of soldiers away at the front would give many of
them the first real income they had ever known.

The Irish National Volunteer Corps, on the other hand, was
unpaid. Each man must support himself. Frank was doing his
best to help, but it had been a bad year on the farm. "It rains
eight days out of seven and the fields are drowned," Norah
had recently written, cataloging woes. "And that ungrateful
Janey Devlin has run off with a tinker. The wet weather has
made my arthritis worse and we need to find someone else to
help in the house but cannot afford to pay her. It is the will
of God, Ned, but sometimes it's hard to accept so many troubles in one lifetime."

Money. If Ned was to stay in Dublin he had to make his
own living. Personal independence had a price. He could not
in good conscience continue to take a share of the Halloran
farm income when he was not helping on the farm. Work as
a groundsman at Saint Enda's provided him with bed and
board but put no money in his pocket.

Becoming an apprentice teacher was not the answer, either.
The staff had been reduced recently due to the loss of Mary
Brigid, whose behavior had become increasingly erratic until
at last it had been decided that in everyone's interest she
should live away from the school. But Ned did not have the
skills to replace her. Besides, the Pearse family was valiantly
struggling to keep Saint Enda's afloat. Even the small stipend
due an apprentice teacher was a burden, one Ned would not
place upon them.

He must find a different source of income. That night he
lay on his bed and stared up at the crucifix on the wall above
the iron headboard. Christ gazed back from an upside-down
face.

Did you ever worry about money? You were fed and sheltered by people who often didn't have enough for themselves,
and in the end You paid with Your blood.

Shuddering, Ned turned over and buried his face in his pillow. But sleep was a long time coming.

The next day he called at the *Independent* to invite Henry Mooney to lunch.

"Have you seen this?" Henry asked angrily, fumbling in a stack of papers and pulling out a yellow sheet with the Dublin Castle emblem at the top. "Of course not, how could you? This notice was issued on the fifteenth of August and delivered to every newspaper in the country, but we weren't allowed to publish it. The Castle says press censorship is to be enforced 'for the duration of the war.' "

Ned scanned the announcement. "How will this affect you?"

"Fortunately I, ah, knew about it in advance, so I've proceeded accordingly and tamed my rhetoric a little. We shall all have to clear every article we write from now on. And republican papers like *Sinn Féin* and *Irish Freedom* may be closed down altogether if they keep on urging Irishmen not to enlist in the British army. Since war has been declared that amounts to sedition."

Ned ran his thumb along the cleft in his chin. "I suppose it does," he said thoughtfully, "if we accept that we are British subjects. On the other hand, if we refuse to acknowledge British sovereignty why should we fight in their army?"

"Did Patrick Pearse teach you to think like that?"

"Pádraic Pearse taught me to think," Ned corrected. "The rest is up to me. Come on, I'll buy you lunch to cheer you up, provided it's a cheap lunch."

"I'm a newspaperman. That's the only sort of lunch we eat."

Over pints of stout and hot meat pies in the Grand Central Bar on D'Olier Street, Ned began working his way around to the subject of a job. "Remember what you said about newspapers making history? That remark stuck in my mind, Henry. I'm constantly surprised at how many people outside the Gaelic League know nothing about Irish history."

Henry's eyes smoldered in their deep sockets. "The reason is obvious. Interest in it has been actively discouraged. 'Forget,' we are told. 'Don't be haunted by your history,' we are urged. And by whom? There lies the answer.

"Those who encourage the Irish to forget their history are the very ones who made it a nightmare, Ned. They urge amnesia on us so we'll be ripe for the plucking again. Look at this censorship business. What is that but an attempt to control history?"

"That's a bleak view."

"I have bleak days." Henry stared down into his pint.

Ned waited while the silence lengthened. At last he said, "Do you think . . . I mean, could I be a newspaperman?"

His friend looked up. "It's as good a job as any other, I suppose. And you're ideally qualified; you're curious and articulate and have no extra mouths to feed. Mind you, since your family doesn't own a newspaper you would have to start at the bottom and work your way up. It's damned hard work. I began as a 'printer's devil,' doing the odd jobs no one else would do. I had to collect the used lead type—slugs, we call them—for remelting, and after the first day my hands were so black no amount of soap would clean them." His glum expression melted into a chuckle. "That's how to get printer's ink in your veins."

"I'm used to dirty hands; I was raised on a farm. How do I apply for a job?"

"I'll be happy to give you an introduction at the *Independent*. From there you're on your own, though."

"I'm in your debt, Henry."

"Not at all. But if you'd like to show your gratitude, how about a little inside information? Something that would make a good story—provided I can get it past the censors?"

"I don't have any information," Ned replied as he probed the greasy golden crust of his steak-and-kidney pie with the tip of his knife. A cloud of fragrant steam emerged.

"Are you sure? It seems to me you're ideally placed to know a lot. For example, there's a rumor that James Connolly and the IRB jointly considered seizing the Mansion House to keep Asquith from appearing there. Could you confirm that?

Or give me any details about that recent top secret meeting of the IRB Supreme Council?''

Ned speared a gobbet of meat with his fork. ''You're talking to the wrong man. I'm just an assistant groundsman at Saint Enda's.''

''Come on, you can't cod me. You're in it head-neck-and-heels.''

Putting down his fork, Ned met the journalist's eyes and held them. His gaze was dead level; his green eyes fathomless. ''I'm telling you the truth when I say I'm not a member of the IRB and I have no plans to join. But even if I did know anything, it would not be for sale. Not at any price.''

Henry surveyed his young friend with new respect. The boy was gone; a man sat before him. A man who carried a dangerous tension in every line of his body.

''I think you mean that, Ned.''

''I assure you I do.''

The journalist smiled to himself as if his companion had just passed some obscure test. ''Yours is a refreshing attitude in a city awash with informers. I won't ask you again to divulge anything you'd rather not. And I'm glad you're my friend. I wouldn't like to see those eyes of yours looking at me down a rifle barrel.''

Chapter Twenty-eight

SEPTEMBER in New York was hotter than August had been. The city simmered beneath an oppressive blanket of humidity. Men worked in their shirtsleeves in defiance of office regulations. Women in the home loosened their stays or left them off altogether. Dogs lay panting in the shade of fire hydrants, too fatigued to rummage through overflowing garbage cans. War in Europe seemed a world away; New Yorkers were preoccupied with the more immediate fight against the heat.

A succession of headaches kept Kathleen in her bedroom with the shades drawn and a cloth soaked in eau de cologne across her forehead. But nothing really helped. "Back home in Ireland we used to long for a hot climate," she told Della when the housemaid brought her a glass of iced tea. "We did not know when we were well off."

"Folks never does," Della Thornberry replied. A stout, plain woman in her middle years, she had coarse hands but a silky voice. "When I was single I wanted to get married. When me and Jake got married I wanted to have babies. When my babies came and cried all night with the colic I wished I was single."

In spite of her headache Kathleen laughed. "You didn't mean that, not really."

"Oh, yes'm, I did!" Della said quickly. "Still do, to be honest. When I think of that worthless man of mine lying up in the bed till all hours, wantin' me to fetch this and do that . . . I tell you, Missus Campbell, a man's nothin' but a child with a bigger appetite."

"Is Jake ill?"

"No'm, he ain't ill. Not unless laziness is a sickness. If it is, I'd say he's close to dying tomorrow."

Kathleen gingerly turned her head on the pillow. She could just make out Della's bulk silhouetted in the doorway. "What would you do if you weren't married, Della?"

"Me? Why, I'd go home so fast I'd just be a streak in the air."

"Where's home? I always thought you were a New Yorker."

"Not me, missus. I was born in the New Jersey pine barrens. My folks worked for a chicken farmer there. When I was a young'un I hated it 'cause it was so lonely, but now I'm sorry we left. It's the only place where my skin fits me."

The only place where my skin fits me. After Della left the room her words continued to echo through Kathleen's aching head.

When Alexander came to bed that night, Kathleen pulled back even before he touched her.

"What's the matter, Kate?"

"I have a headache."

"Still? You had a headache last night."

"It's the heat. I cannot bear the heat."

"You had a chance to go to Saratoga Springs with Mrs. Claffey and you refused," he reminded her. "You could have spent the whole summer in the mountains."

"Mercedes Claffey doesn't like me."

"That's not true."

"Well, then, I don't like her!"

"Now you're being ridiculous. She's a charming woman who even came to that ill-advised luncheon of yours and gave you money for Ned's school."

"She looks down on me, Alexander."

"Why on earth would she do that?" He was making an effort to keep his temper.

"Because I'm a foreigner."

"But her own husband is Irish, Kate."

"His grandparents were Irish, that's all. He was born here and so was his wife. They grew up on American food and they speak American English and they know different songs and they say 'Excuse me' instead of 'Sorry' and to them an anniversary means a wedding anniversary and not the commemoration of a death as it does at home and . . ." She was running on and she could not help it; words were spilling out of her mouth without any thought behind them. They were just words; a torrent of unreasoning protest. "And their gods are not my gods!" she heard herself crying.

Alexander sat upright in bed. "Is that what this is all about? Religion? Great thunder, Kate! When I married you I thought you had some sense, at least you didn't mouth papist dogma and rattle your beads at me. But now you're raving about your gods like some ignorant peasant who's never come out of the bog!"

"I don't mean gods in the religious sense, I mean . . . Oh, Alexander, this isn't my place, can't you understand? I thought it was, I wanted it to be. But it isn't. I want to go home. I want to go home!" Her voice spiraled upward and she sat up as if to follow it.

His thread of patience finally snapped. "You're not going anywhere!" He caught her by the shoulders and threw her back onto her pillows. When she tried to break free of his grasp a delicious heat rose in him. For once she was showing some spirit in bed. The reason did not matter. It was unbearably exciting to feel her struggle, pitting her puny strength against his.

Her shoulders were narrow beneath the silky skin; the bones in her arms were fragile. He could break them if he wanted. The knowledge filled him with exultation. Her smallness made him feel larger, her vulnerability gave him a thrilling sense of power. She was helplessly his in spite of all she could do, and in that moment he loved her as never before.

He pounded her into the bed with his strength and his maleness, hurting her until she fought back and then hurting her again, just to show how much he loved her.

Kathleen realized she was being raped and her resistance was only making it worse. But she had to fight back. She was an individual in her own right; he exceeded his authority in violating her just because he could.

The struggle became a war, became rage and fury.

WHEN Della arrived for work the next morning the house was very quiet. That in itself was unusual. No matter how bad the headaches, Kathleen was usually up with the dawn. She had never developed the habit of other women in her social circle of staying abed until ten at the earliest.

Knocking softly on the closed bedroom door, Della heard a female voice mumble a response. She eased the door open and peered inside. A solitary figure lay on the bed amid chaotically disarranged bedclothes. The maid discreetly withdrew and went to the kitchen. There she found a half-empty cup of cold coffee on the table. But Alexander Campbell had gone.

Della made a fresh pot of coffee and carried a tray in to Kathleen. "I see you're still hurtin'," she commented. "The mister's gone to work already, so you'll have the house to yourself. I'll be as quiet as a fly on sugar."

Kathleen groaned and tentatively extended her legs. Then she groaned again. "Della."

"Yes'm?"

"Don't go."

"No'm." Della waited patiently but Kathleen said nothing else.

Her whole body ached. Worse—her soul felt degraded.

Last night her sense of sexuality, so newly awakened, had received a nasty shock. Her husband's behavior had disgusted her even more than it had frightened her. Was that what men really were?

Alexander's courtesy had been his initial attraction. With him she had once felt as safe as with her father. But Papa would never have assaulted Mama. Kathleen could not imagine such a thing. If all men were like Alexander, how could women remain sane? And to think she was bound to him for life!

She licked cracked lips. "Della, I need you to take a message for me. Bring me some notepaper, will you?"

"You can't write no letter with a headache, missus."

"Don't tell me what I can do!" Kathleen snapped. "Just bring the paper."

Della was startled. On more than one occasion she had remarked that her mistress was "as sweet as any angel." But it was no angel who abruptly threw back the covers and glared from the bed. It was a flushed, angry woman whose torn nightdress revealed massive bruises on her arms and bosom. In one or two places the skin was broken and oozing blood.

"Sweet jumping Jesus!" Della gasped.

Wincing, Kathleen pulled up her nightdress. "It isn't as bad as it looks. I've been hurt worse falling out of a tree as a child. There is yellow salve in Mr. Campbell's dressing room, I think, and a bottle of witch hazel and some cotton wool. Fetch them when you bring the notepaper."

They tended to her injuries together. Then Kathleen insisted upon dressing, although Della protested, "You should spend the day in bed, missus."

"Nonsense. I'll feel better if I get up. Did you bring that notepaper? Good. Put it on the dressing table. But keep those shades down, will you?" She scribbled a few words on the paper, folded it into an envelope, and handed the envelope to Della. "Take this to Father Paul at Saint Xavier's. And hurry."

BRIDIE Lynch had always resented the fact that young Mrs. Campbell would not employ her. "Married above her station, that one," Bridie said. "Gives herself airs, and her as Irish as meself." After the Claffeys hired her as housemaid Bridie took pleasure in gossiping about the Campbells with her friends. Little happened next door that she did not notice.

That September morning she was sweeping the Claffeys' front stoop when she saw Della Thornberry leave the Campbell house. The big woman hurried past and turned the corner almost at the run. A short time later Bridie was lowering the shades in the east-facing windows against the encroaching heat when she observed Della returning, accompanied by a priest. The two entered the Campbell house together. Della soon came out again with her marketing basket on her arm and was gone all morning.

The priest did not leave until noon.

M RS. Flanagan was worried about Father Paul. When he returned from visiting Kathleen Campbell that September morning he was not himself at all. In the days that followed he was uncharacteristically short-tempered and sometimes snapped at the other priests in the house. He was often absent without any explanation. His appetite fell off alarmingly. She knew there were nights when he never went to bed but knelt for long hours in prayer or paced the floor in his room until sunrise.

Mrs. Flanagan's late husband had been a heavy drinker who chased anything in skirts. Since his death she had served as housekeeper to the priests of Saint Xavier's, which she described to friends as "Heaven after years of purgatory." Her other two charges were in their sixties, like herself. One was devoted to studying the writings of Saint Augustine, and the other to golf. Paul O'Shaughnessy, however, was young and undeniably handsome. For such a man clerical robes might not be enough protection. There were always women who were tempted by forbidden fruit.

Daughters of Eve could put a godly man's soul in jeopardy. Mrs. Flanagan knew.

In warm weather Abruzzio's Ice Cream Parlor was a favorite gathering place for young housemaids on their afternoons off. Mrs. Flanagan never visited Abruzzio's. To her mind there was something risqué, almost sinful, about sodas and phosphates and particularly that newfangled creation from the 1904 World's Fair, the ice cream cone. She suspected they were an attempt on the part of greedy capitalists to lure honest folk away from home-cooked food. And she was absolutely certain that the maids who congregated at Abruzzio's spent their time gossiping. Mrs. Flanagan prided herself on not being a gossip. She could have told many a story if she chose, but a priest's housekeeper held a position of trust.

Her marketing sometimes led her past Abruzzio's, however. On a hot September afternoon a whiff of vanilla as intense as unrequited love poured out through the open door. Glancing through the window, Mrs. Flanagan noticed Bridie Lynch sitting alone at one of the tiny wrought iron tables.

On impulse she went in.

Bridie Lynch was surprised to see Mrs. Flanagan, but was flattered when the woman asked to join her. A priest's housekeeper had considerable status in the hierarchy of domestics. Over dishes of ice cream—Mrs. Flanagan eschewed the more exotic chocolate and strawberry and ordered plain vanilla—the two discussed furniture polishes and the relative merits of broom and carpet sweeper.

When Bridie was sufficiently bored to be off guard, Mrs. Flanagan asked casually, "Do you see much of the Campbells next door?"

"Hunh. Them. Herself goes one way and himself the other. You'd need an eye on either side of your head to watch the pair of them."

"Is Mr. Campbell often away, then?"

Bridie laughed. "Not often enough for his wife, I'd say. But you'd know that better than meself."

"What do you mean?"

"You 'do' for Father Paul, don't you? Him that's been alone with her in her house every afternoon this week. With the shades down," Bridie added with happy malice.

Mrs. Flanagan pushed away the empty ice cream dish. Suddenly there was a bad taste in her mouth. "Every afternoon? Alone?"

"The housemaid only works until three. There's just the

two of them to do for, you see. The Alexanders don't have
any children.''

"Father Paul is a priest, and priests are supposed to visit
the sick,'' Mrs. Flanagan said. "Mrs. Campbell's ill.''

"Don't you believe it. If she was, my mistress would be
running over there making a fuss over her and feeding her
calves' foot jelly. And there would be a doctor called; that
sort of people are great ones for doctoring. No, Mrs. Campbell
is as healthy as meself. She should be; she's getting plenty of
exercise. Her housemaid washes bedsheets every morning.
Every single morning!'' Bridie Lynch gave Mrs. Flanagan a
lewd wink that shocked the older woman to the depths of her
soul.

The housekeeper returned to the presbytery deeply troubled. Father Paul would not be the first priest to carry on an
indiscreet relationship.

Kathleen Campbell was a beautiful woman with discon-
tented eyes, and Mrs. Flanagan was in a position of trust.

She could not speak to the bishop, that would be disloyal
to Father Paul. It was Mrs. Campbell who had to be dealt
with, somehow.

Mrs. Flanagan tightened her lips and prepared to do battle.
She had always been devoted to "her priests.'' For them she
would fight tigers.

September 18, 1914

HOME RULE BILL RECEIVES
ROYAL ASSENT

Chapter Twenty-nine

Ned's new job was not glamorous, but at the end of each week he received a pay packet. With a sense of satisfaction he wrote Frank not to send him any more money: "I can get by on what I can earn for myself." The boast contained a degree of bravado, as he was making very little. But he was putting his trust in his abilities and the future.

His next letter was to Kathleen:

I'm employed as a copyboy, which means they have the legs run off me most of the time. I carry copy from the editorial offices to the printing plant in Middle Abbey Street. It's just across O'Connell Bridge, but I make dozens of trips a day. However, if I prove myself I can work my way up to apprentice reporter before too long. And I have my evenings free for the Volunteers.

My friend Henry Mooney tells me that the American papers carry little news about Ireland, and what there is comes through British channels. So you may not even know that the Home Rule Act is at last on the statute books. But don't rejoice for us. At the same time—and using the European war as a justification—Parliament passed a Suspensory Act postponing Home Rule indefinitely.[1] So the Unionists have had their way after all.

Yet John Redmond of the Irish Parliamentary Party
went into veritable ecstasies, announcing that Ireland had
got "a great charter of freedom." Freedom! The Home
Rule Act is no more than a useless scrap of paper now.
I personally do not think we will ever see it go into
effect, with or without the exclusion amendment.

On the 20th of September Redmond spoke at a Volunteer rally in County Wicklow. Henry was assigned to
report on the speech for the paper, and because it was a
Sunday I was free to go down with him.

It was a soft day; you could catch the air in both hands
and squeeze it. But in spite of the damp a big crowd
turned up at a place called Woodenbridge. There were
banners and flowers on the speakers' platform and even
a band playing. Some of the Volunteers brought their
wives and sweethearts for an outing in the country.

What we got was a blatant recruiting speech for the
British army. Redmond claimed that Britain had kept
faith with Ireland (in what manner, I wonder?) so now
we must keep faith with her. We must enlist to fight and
die on her behalf. His exact words were, "The Empire
is engulfed in the most serious war in history. It is a war
for the defense of the sacred rights and liberties of small
nations."

What about *this* small nation, Caitlín? When did Britain ever do anything but trample on *our* sacred rights
and liberties?

Redmond said the Volunteers must "account for your-
selves wherever the firing line extends, in defense of
right, of freedom, and religion in this war."

But what about *Irish* rights, freedom, and religion,
Caitlín? All three have repeatedly been denied us in the
long sad history of our relationship with Britain. Does
Redmond not see the irony? But no; he urges us to rush
out and join the army to serve wherever they send us.
Rather than allowing us to defend this island, he has
consigned the Irish to Flanders as British cannon fodder.
In return he assures us a grateful Britain will reward Ire-

land with the implementation of Home Rule.[2] Someday. (When pigs fly, as Henry said to me under his breath.)

It would be hopelessly naive to believe this, no matter what promises Prime Minister Asquith has made. Individually, the people of England are as decent and honorable as any other. They cherish their reputation for fair play. But their government does not reflect the national character, at least in its dealings with Ireland. Anything to do with Ireland provokes British politicians into the worst excesses of imperialism. I doubt if one Englishman in a hundred has any idea what perfidy and duplicity have been visited upon this small island in his name.

Redmond urges us to lay down our lives on behalf of a foreign power whose policy toward Ireland has been one of unremitting contempt—the guilty hatred of the conqueror for the conquered. England justifies her behavior by depicting the Irish as ignorant, impoverished barbarians. We are ignorant because educating ourselves was, until recent times, against English law. We are impoverished because the natural resources of this island have been thoroughly looted. As for being barbarians, it was Ireland which kept the lamp of literacy alight when the Dark Ages descended on the rest of Europe— England included.

While going through the archives of the *Independent* I accidentally found a quote from the *London Times* during the Famine years. Only sixty years ago that paper positively exulted, "They are going! They are going! The Irish are going with a vengeance. Soon a Celt will be as rare in Ireland as a Red Indian on the shores of Manhattan. Law has ridden through Ireland; it has been taught with bayonets, and interpreted with ruin. Townships leveled with the ground, straggling columns of exiles, workhouses multiplied and still crowded, express the determination of the legislature to rescue Ireland from its slovenly old barbarism, and to plant there the institutions of this more civilized land."[3]

That was how Britain looked upon us then; how the

British government still looks upon us. Nothing's changed. Yet they expect us to be willing cannon fodder for them. Think of the Irish Brigade they sent to die in the Boer War. In spite of all the fancy slogans, those men were sacrificed just to help the empire seize more territory. The same thing was done in South Africa as had once been done to Ireland.

Oh, Caitlín, we *must* have our independence. Ireland must be free of imperialism once and for all.

He showed Henry the letter before he sent it. The journalist's comment was, "Jesus, Mary, and Joseph! It's good writing but those are strong words, Ned. You better hope that letter doesn't fall into the wrong hands."

"Are you implying the post isn't safe?"

"I'm just saying be careful."

"John Redmond wasn't careful in his speech."

"He doesn't have to worry. He was promoting imperial policy."

Ned shook his head. "I'll never understand why."

"You're still young; everything is black and white for you. Age and experience will knock that out of you and eventually you'll see there are only shades of gray. In the meantime let me tell you something. John Redmond believes as firmly in the rightness of his point of view as you do in yours.

"I know Redmond's very anglicized, yet consider how many Irish people have adopted the manners and customs of England. Just listen to yourself; thanks to your education you're now speaking with an accent that owes almost as much to London as to Clare.

"Don't scowl at me like that, Ned, I'm not saying it's wrong. I'm saying it was inevitable.

"For centuries we had it hammered into us that everything English was better than anything Irish. When their own self-esteem was destroyed some people began imitating their conquerors. Don't be too hasty to condemn Redmond and men like him; they're the product of history. But they're still Irish for all of that. Remember, John Redmond was one of Charles

Parnell's strongest supporters when the church turned against him over the Kitty O'Shea affair. I'm convinced he believes he's doing what's best for Ireland now."

"Surely you don't agree with him, Henry!"

"You're right, I don't. But I'm not going to launch an attack against the leader of the Parliamentary Party in the pages of the *Independent*."

"You're letting the imposition of censorship intimidate you," Ned accused.

Henry looked hurt. "I prefer to think of it as being prudent. Let me give you some information you may not know. According to my sources, the Castle's compiling dossiers on every member of the IRB in Ireland. And I suspect they're not the only ones being watched. We all have to be careful these days."

Ned set his jaw at a stubborn angle—and sent the letter.

"INDEPENDENCE!" Kathleen exclaimed when she read what he had written. The word was like a knife in her heart. She crumpled the letter into a ball of paper and threw it as hard as she could.

NOW that he had his own income, Ned set about creating his own life. The school year was starting again, but his days as a pupil were over; it was time to leave Saint Enda's for the larger world. When he told Henry he was looking for a place to live in the city, the journalist said, "You're welcome to share my digs at number sixteen if you like. I have only the one room, but it's quite large. There's plenty of space for two beds, and we can bring in another wardrobe for you."

"I don't have that many clothes. Mostly I need space for my books. But are you sure Mrs. Kearney won't object to me moving in?"

"Louise? She'll be delighted to have another bachelor with tidy habits. You are tidy, I trust?"

"Mr. Pearse insisted on it."

"Good. I warn you, Louise may raise the rent a wee bit, but you'll still be paying less than anywhere else because we'll split it. And as an added inducement there's a grand big bathtub on the third floor."

"Done!" said Ned.

Living in Dublin was exciting. At first he did not miss the deep silences of rural Rathfarnham or the pleasures of lying abed in the early morning with the windows open, listening to the dawn chorus of thrush and lark and blackbird. The myriad voices of a living city were a novel sensation. Besides, the Orphan House for Destitute Females in the North Circular Road was not so far away.

Ned visited Precious as often as he could. Usually this meant early mornings before he went to work. Foregoing breakfast, he would hurry to the orphanage and be waiting when the doors were unlocked. The matron always looked surprised to see him, but Precious was not surprised. After his second or third dawn visit she expected him and would be waiting to run into his arms: "NedNedNedNed!" When he lifted her up and swung her around her small face lit with joy.

Precious.

She was but one of his commitments. In order to keep carrying messages for Pearse and the Volunteers, Ned had to have access to swift communication. The newspaper had telephones, but they were not for the use of a lowly copyboy. Fortunately a public call box had been set up outside Gills' Confectioners in Middle Gardiner Street. From this box, Ned rang each morning to a similar call box in Rathfarnham, where, at a preappointed time, one of the Saint Enda's Fianna was waiting. Sometimes he made a second phone call to Larkfield, the Plunkett estate on the Kimmage Road. Count Plunkett had been one of the first private citizens in Ireland to have a telephone installed in his home.

Evenings after work would find him on his bicycle, whistling Irish tunes as he rode a circuit through Dublin and its environs. He sometimes thought wistfully of lazy mornings spent listening to the dawn chorus.

When he received his second pay packet—the first having gone toward his rent and to put a few pennies into a jam jar, for savings—he called upon Mary Cosgrave. It was Sunday afternoon, golden with autumn. Ned wore his best clothes and the most sober expression he could manage. To his relief her father did not refer to their previous encounter, but kept him company in the parlor until Mary came down.

She was dressed in a dainty blue frock that complimented her rosy cheeks. Ned had scrubbed himself raw in the big claw-footed tub on the third floor and liberally applied Henry's bay rum lotion, but he felt grubby by comparison.

"Where are we going?" she asked as she pirouetted for his inspection. "The cinema?"

Ned hesitated. Now that he was supporting himself he had less pocket money than when he was a student at Saint Enda's. In Clare it was traditional to take a girl "walking out," which cost no money at all. In fact, it had a romantic connotation. A couple might be "walking out" for years without making any public announcement, but everyone understood they were almost betrothed.

Mary Cosgrave was a Dublin girl, however, and entertaining a girl in Dublin could be expensive. The Antient Concert Rooms in Great Brunswick Street presented the sort of performances popular with fashionable society, and the rebuilt Theatre Royal had even presented Wagnerian opera. There were other theaters, including the Abbey and the Gaiety, music halls, and a number of cinemas. The motion picture had been introduced to Ireland only a dozen years before, but already Dublin was becoming a city of picture palaces.

Even two cinema tickets were more than Ned could afford at the moment, however. "How about a stroll?" he suggested. "It's a fine afternoon, it would be a great pity to stay inside."

"We went for a walk the last time we were together. I hoped we might do something different today."

He swallowed hard. "We can go to the cinema if that's what you want."

Mary rewarded him with a radiant smile. As they started out the door she said unexpectedly, "We must collect Eliza and bring her with us. She loves the cinema. You won't mind, will you?''

''Of course not,'' he lied.

And there must be refreshments after the cinema, Mary airily informed Ned. ''I want Eliza to see how generous you are with me.''

He forced a gallant smile. ''Whatever I have is yours.''

Ned sat between two girls in the O'Connell Street Picture House and tried to concentrate on the jerky black-and-white figures flickering on the screen while Mary and Eliza leaned across him to talk to each other. He was uncomfortably aware of their bodies.

Flesh. Soft and yielding flesh. Welcoming thighs; enveloping heat. Sweet intense agony of . . .

Inept policeman chasing equally inept bank robbers. Guns exploding with great discharges of smoke, men taking pratfalls, motorcars careering down American streets while doors fell off. Ned made himself laugh when the rest of the audience laughed.

Afterward they lingered over hot chocolate and fairy cakes in Robert Roberts in Grafton Street. While Ned mentally counted the coins he had left, Eliza brought up the subject of her own poverty. ''Switzer's has declared a twenty percent pay reduction for its clerks,'' she moaned. ''They're blaming the war, saying trade has fallen off because prices are going up.''

Ned turned toward her. ''Is that true?''

''It is true, but people still have to buy clothes and dishes, don't they? I think management is taking advantage of us and I'm going to ask the Drapers' Assistants' Association to do something.''

''Like what?''

''Call out a strike. It's worked for the other trade unions, why not for us?''

Mary was horrified. ''You can't be serious! What if the other shops got involved? We could all be fired. I don't have any argument with Brown Thomas, and I don't see why my job should be put at risk.''

"Well, perhaps not a strike. But at least we could have the Association write Switzer's an angry letter. What do you think, Ned?"

"I think it's a good idea. You should support your friend, Mary. There's strength in unity."

Eliza turned to Ned. "Exactly. Have you heard James Connolly speak?"

"Not yet."

"Oh but you must! He says what you just did. And he's a grand bull of a man; when he's talking you feel he could do anything." A sudden intensity focused her as if a burning-glass had been turned upon her personality. Her drab little face lit with enthusiasm.

"Connolly's nothing but a socialist," Mary said petulantly. "My mother says socialists want to take the money away from everyone who has any. I think that's stupid. Where would the jobs come from if there were no rich people anymore? We would all be dreadfully poor then, and no one would have any nice things."

Ned couldn't help laughing. "I don't think you've quite grasped the principles of socialism, Mary."

"I don't care. It's tiresome."

To Ned's surprise, Eliza said, "That's the trouble with you, Mary Cosgrave. You aren't interested in ideas, only in things."

Mary was helping herself to Ned's uneaten cake. "Nice things are important. Take clothes for instance. When I'm well turned out I feel better. You like pretty clothes yourself, Eliza Goggins, don't pretend with me."

The permanently red tip of Eliza's nose twitched. "I do, of course, but there are larger issues. I think—"

"Oh, we know what you think. You want us to march about waving trade union placards and looking as dowdy as suffragettes. Sometimes you can be a dreadful bore, Eliza. Don't you think so, Ned?" She flashed him a coquettish smile.

But Ned was looking at Eliza. Plain, unappealing Eliza—coming to life before his eyes with the burgeoning of a new faith.

Chapter Thirty

THE Woodenbridge speech had far-reaching consequences. The next meeting of the Volunteers' governing board was on the night of September 24, and a violent argument broke out almost at once. The IRB men on the board were furious that, without prior consultation, Redmond had pledged the Irish National Volunteers to support Britain's war. Seán Mac-Dermott cried, "Asquith dangled Home Rule in front of him as a bribe to buy the Volunteers with and he was fool enough to take it! Have we not learned the hard way that we can't trust Parliament?"

Even Eoin MacNeill thought Redmond had made a bad mistake. "Home Rule is a check the British will continually postdate," he said.

By the end of the meeting there was an irreconcilable split between the Redmondites and the republicans. Bulmer Hobson took Redmond's side; Tom Clarke announced he would never speak to Hobson again.[1] "How much did the British pay you?" he asked Hobson savagely.

Most of the original members of the committee signed a statement to the effect that they no longer considered Redmond's nominees as part of the governing body. As a result, two separate branches of the Volunteers developed. Those who agreed with Redmond chose to call themselves the Na-

tional Volunteer Corps, and set up their own executive committee.

Meanwhile, the more militant republicans assumed the title
Irish Volunteers, and set up headquarters at number 2, Dawson Street.[2] Eoin MacNeill continued to serve as President and
Chief of Staff, chairing meetings of the Provisional Committee and overseeing policy. MacNeill was not a revolutionary;
his goal was to build the Volunteers into a force capable of
defending Ireland.

But there was another layer of leadership now. The IRB
men on the Provisional Committee were quietly making their
own plans.

THROUGH his increasing circle of contacts, Ned was aware
of the power struggles taking place within the nationalist
movement. The split in the Volunteers was but one example.
The romantic Erin of Yeats and Synge and Lady Gregory was
a far cry from Connolly's vision of a modern socialist state.
Sinn Féin as conceived by Arthur Griffith did not subscribe
to the physical force doctrine of the Fenians. Even as the
nationalists planned to disentangle Ireland from England, Irish
men conspired against one another in hopes of shaping the
fledgling nation to their particular dream.

Meanwhile, Carson's Unionist Party sought to enlarge Protestant privilege through the political arena, Redmondites put
their faith in Home Rule and in remaining part of the empire,
and the plain people of Ireland struggled from day to day to
keep food on the table and a roof over their heads.

From a seething cauldron of passion and frustration and
hope, something was bound to be born.

AUTUMN passed into winter. For days at a time the sky was
overcast, sea and cloud melding on the horizon into icy gray.
Rain swept across Ireland, dragging cold mud on the hem of
her skirts.

The weather meant agony for Joe Plunkett, yet he valiantly

attended meetings of both the Irish Volunteers and the IRB and was frequently seen around the city. One bitter November night Ned happened to glimpse him crossing Prince's Street swathed in a greatcoat and bent double against the wind. His body was wracked with coughing.

Ned hurriedly caught up with him and urged him into the lobby of the Hotel Metropole. "You shouldn't be walking on a night like this. Where's your motorcar?"

In the light of the electric chandeliers Plunkett's face was livid, but he smiled and slapped at the pockets of his coat as if searching for something. "Motorcar? I must have misplaced it. You know how easy it is to forget where you leave those things."

"Sit down and let me bring you a hot whiskey from the bar. Then I'll get a cab for you."

Plunkett waved one ring-laden hand. "Not yet, Ned, please. I'll go home in a while and let them fuss over me. In the meantime, stop with me for a few minutes, can you? And I wouldn't say no to that hot whiskey. Here, wait a minute." He took out a pigskin wallet and selected a banknote. "Order one for yourself and let me pay for both of them. That way I won't have to drink alone."

"I couldn't let you—"

"I insist."

They took their whiskey to a dim corner of the lobby and sat across from each other at a small table. At first Plunkett scarcely seemed able to lift his glass. But as the warmth and the whiskey seeped into him, he straightened up and insisted on ordering another round. With the second drink a little color began to creep into his cheeks. He caught Ned watching him.

"Don't look so worried, Ned. I'm all right, truly I am. My little walk was just an impulse. Bit of fresh air to clear the head."

"You shouldn't be out in this weather."

"I do a lot of things I shouldn't. If I give in to the illness, it's won."

Emboldened by the whiskey, Ned asked, "Your illness . . . is it very serious?"

"It's glandular tuberculosis of the throat. That's always serious. If you mean am I going to die—I am. We all are, you know; someday. But right now I stay busy living. This evening, for example, I enjoyed a play at the new Irish Theatre in Hardwicke Street. I helped Edward Martyn found that theater, so I go to every performance I can. And I love exploring the beauties of the Irish countryside, no matter what the weather. You can live outside yourself and your infirmities if you put your mind to it, Ned. If you have enough faith. Faith supports you when nothing else will."

Plunkett paused, coughed apologetically, and went on. "Drier climates are better for me, but I always come back here because I'm not happy anywhere else. Life inflicts so many blows that we're obliged in the interests of natural justice to extract all the happiness we can. So I live my life with a passion." A smile played around his lips. "Have you a sweetheart?"

Caught off guard, Ned stared down into his glass.

"I'm sorry, forgive me. Sometimes I speak without thinking."

"It's all right. I asked you a personal question too. And I do have a sweetheart. Sort of," Ned amended. Mary was everything a sweetheart should be, pretty and proper and pure. But . . .

Joseph Mary Plunkett was a sophisticated man from a background of money and privilege. He had traveled extensively and spoke several languages. Would he understand about Síle?

"I asked that question," Plunkett was saying, "because I want to read you something. Poetry is a conversation you have with yourself in the secret places of your soul. Much of what I write is never intended for anyone else, but this one is. I'm thinking of giving it as a Christmas present and I would appreciate your opinion—if you have a sweetheart yourself, if you know what those feelings are like for a man."

He took out a small copybook with a tooled leather binding, hunted through it for a few moments, then began to read. His hoarse voice was little more than a whisper, but curiously compelling.

> *The day I knew you loved me we had lain*
> *Deep in Coill Doraca down by Gleann na Scath*
> *Unknown to each other till suddenly I saw*
> *You in the shadow, knew oppressive pain*
> *Stopping my heart, and there you did remain*
> *In dreadful beauty fair without a flaw,*
> *Blinding the eyes that yet could not withdraw*
> *Till wild between us drove the wind and rain.*
> *Breathless we reached the brugh before the west*
> *Burst in full fury—then with lightning stroke*
> *The tempest in my heart roared up and broke*
> *Its barriers, and I swore I would not rest*
> *Till that mad heart was worthy of your breast*
> *Or dead for you—and then this love awoke.[3]*

"I live my life with a passion," Joe Plunkett had said. The passion leaped from the poem.

Ned was overwhelmed.

That was how one should feel love: as a tempest in the heart! Anything less was unworthy.

In December the newspapers *Sinn Féin* and *Irish Freedom* were officially suppressed. A few days later soldiers raided the offices of the *Irish Worker,* the socialist newspaper founded by Jim Larkin, and destroyed its machinery, but James Connolly was soon running a private printing press in Liberty Hall. A new socialist paper titled the *Workers' Republic* appeared. The masthead bore a quotation from the French journalist and revolutionary Desmoulins: "The great only appear great because we are on our knees; let us arise."[4]

The publishing operation was protected by armed members of the Citizen Army—including Constance Markievicz, a recent recruit. Even women were being allowed to join the organization, to the outrage of many Dubliners.

"Nothing frightens Madame," laughed Thomas Mac-Donagh when he heard. "Bedad, I pity the policeman who challenges her!"

By the end of 1914 the British army stood at 720,000 men. In spite of Dublin Castle censorship, however, it was obvious to the Irish that the war was not going well. Britain and her allies had badly underestimated Germany.

On New Year's Day a German submarine sank H. M. S. *Formidable* in the North Sea.

A drill was planned for the Dublin Brigade on the following Sunday. When Seán Heuston met Ned there, he greeted him with a single word: "Conscription."

Ned drew a sharp breath. "Are you serious?"

"Everyone's talking about it. They say it could come within weeks now."

"Rumor isn't good enough. You forget I work for a newspaper. We'll be the first to know if conscription is introduced; until then it's nothing but speculation."

"You sound like a reporter," Seán said.

Ned shrugged. But he was increasingly certain of the future he wanted. He enjoyed everything about the newspaper business, from the clattering banks of modern Linotype machines to the morning coats and striped trousers some of the older journalists still wore.[5] When he had the time, he loved to linger in the printing plant and watch the presses running. The sound was hypnotic, the smell of ink intoxicating. The thunder of the machines drowned out all thought, leaving only an impression of massive power.

The newspaper staff, Dublin men for the most part, shared a bawdy, earthy humor that was truly Irish but which had not been allowed at Saint Enda's. The younger reporters competed vigorously to see who could invent the most original profanities.

Ned began adding colorful new phrases to his vocabulary.

The *Independent* was at the heart of a broad information network. The events of the day were its lifeblood. Items of Irish interest predominated, but international news was also covered. In January the Mexican Pancho Villa signed a treaty with the United States, ending a bitter border war, and Alexander Graham Bell successfully placed a telephone call between New York and San Francisco, setting a new distance record.

Ned was intrigued by the latter item. "Rural Ireland has no electricity," he said to Henry, "yet someday I might actually hear my sister's voice all the way across the Atlantic Ocean."

His friend replied, "It's called progress, lad. A mixed blessing, I suspect. We live in an age when the small print in newspapers destroys your vision, but at least you can buy good reading spectacles."

A Russian army of 80,000 men was marching on West Prussia. A new weapon called tear gas was used for the first time against them.

And in the Irish Sea, three British merchant ships were sunk by German submarines.

In February the Marquess of Aberdeen left Ireland and a new lord lieutenant, Sir Ivor Churchill Guest, Baron Wimborne, moved into the Viceregal Lodge. The Dublin social set, which had languished under the drab Aberdeens, was excited by the prospect of a younger, more energetic viceroy.

In February also, America's President Wilson protested the policy of British-owned ships such as the *Lusitania* flying U.S. flags in order to dupe the Germans. "America's neutrality is not to be used as camouflage," he stressed.

Lord Kitchener's office announced that total United Kingdom casualties had reached 104,000. Germany proclaimed a sea blockade of the British Isles intended to destroy the United Kingdom's economy. A Norwegian ship was the first target, torpedoed off Folkestone.

The war had taken to the high seas with a vengeance. The implications for an island nation were obvious. Ireland was now on the front lines.

The British army raised its recruiting efforts to fever pitch.

The pages of *Sinn Féin* responded with increasingly strident antirecruitment editorials.

On a hoarding on Parnell Street was a British recruitment poster emblazoned with the slogan "Remember Belgium!"

Across it someone had painted, in bold red letters, "Remember Bachelor's Walk!"

IN March, Pádraic Pearse issued instructions that every Volunteer company was to provide itself with an Irish flag.[6] The
customary flag with its gold harp surmounted by a crown was
to be replaced by one displaying a plain gold harp on a green
background. No crown.

ON those evenings when Ned was not involved with the Irish
Volunteers and Henry was not going back to the paper to file
copy for the early edition, they often went down to the pub
for a pint together. Ned considered these hours as akin to a
class in journalism. "Here's how I plan to write about the
troopships arriving with the wounded," Henry would say.
"For this article I want to focus on the hospitals, how they're
coping with the casualties flooding in, how the doctors feel
when they see all these broken young Irish men . . ."
    Ned listened eagerly. The craft of writing took on sculptural
dimensions in his mind. There were some basic rules to follow, but there was also a tantalizing, elusive magic that could
not be described but was instantly recognizable on the page.
The books he loved had furnished his mind with a treasury
of words. As he listened to Henry he found himself shaping
descriptive words into paragraphs and columns in his mind.
    Someday he might see them in print. The idea was seduc-
tive.
    While Ned learned the newspaper trade, the republican
movement was fully occupying Pádraic Pearse. He employed
a former pupil, Desmond Ryan, a member of the IRB, to help
with the mounting volume of correspondence.[7] Ned felt a
pang of envy, but as he told Henry, "If I were Mr. Pearse's
secretary I would have no time to work for the paper, and I
think I've already got printer's ink in my veins."
    Busy as he was, he never missed a drill with the Dublin
Brigade. Few of its members had enlisted in the British army,

at least so far. But they were all conscious of the missing faces.

No one said anything about them. There was no point. Each man had his own reasons; that was understood. Life forced choices.

Thomas MacDonagh never missed a drill, either, until March. When he appeared at the next one he announced joyously, "It's a daughter! We're calling her Barbara."

His friends crowded around to warm themselves by the heat of his happiness. "Good man yerself," they cried, pummeling his shoulders.

War and death and babies being born. Ned tried to stretch the horizons of his mind to encompass them all in one world vision. It was the babies, he decided, who made the rest of it bearable, who redeemed the horror adults could perpetrate. A child like Precious or the MacDonaghs' new daughter was created by the same species that manufactured guns and submarines—but with one added element: the Divine spark, an immortal soul.

Like a transatlantic telephone conversation, the family he would have someday took on a distant but certain reality.

His daydreams were of Mary. Mary as wife, mother, Madonna. He envisioned her and a bevy of laughing children in a cottage on Howth with a view of the sea.

In spite of himself, at night he thought of Síle. *The tempest in my heart.*

What spare time he could find during the week he spent with Precious. She needed him the most.

The spreading conflagration in Europe was extinguishing innocence. The elaborate facade of nineteenth-century social mores was crumbling. Young men about to fight and perhaps die might dream of marrying nice girls after the war, but in the meantime they wanted something more immediately life-affirming.

Business at Mrs. Drumgold's had quadrupled since the outbreak of the war. It was impossible for Síle to slip away in the afternoon or evening, but in the early mornings she could leave the house for a few hours while everyone else was asleep.

After visiting Precious one morning, Ned accidentally met Síle in Tom Clarke's. He did not ask why she was there; he only knew there was a certain inevitability about it. He and Clarke had just concluded an exchange of messages when she entered. Tom Clarke gave a polite cough and excused himself to the rear of the shop, leaving the two young people alone.

"I'm on my way to work now," Ned told Síle regretfully. "I'm a copyboy at—"

"The *Irish Independent*. I know."

"You do? How? Did Mr. Clarke tell you?"

Instead of answering, Síle turned to gaze out the window at the street. "Everything's happening very fast now. Do you feel it too, Ned?"

"The war, you mean?"

"Life. It's running by like water poured out of a jug."

"Indeed. It seems like only a few days ago I was a schoolboy. Now one lad I knew at Saint Enda's is working as Mr. Pearse's secretary, and another friend, Seán Heuston, has just been promoted to leader of D Company, First Battalion of the Irish Volunteers. And I'm at the *Independent*. We're all doing men's jobs."

"Not all of us," said Síle softly.

"I'm sorry, I didn't mean . . . but actually some women are doing the work of men these days. Take Constance Markievicz . . . You know who she is?"

Síle raised one eyebrow. "I know who she is."

"Madame's a crack shot and as good a soldier as any man. I'm not sure I approve; she's a wife and mother, after all. Yet . . . it suits her, somehow. Mr. Pearse says we should use our talents to become the best of whatever we can be."

Síle looked dubious. "That's all very well for a countess, but not for an ordinary Irish woman. No matter what talents we have we're supposed to live the lives our mothers lived— or be disgraced forever, like me.

"We must be virgins until we marry. Fetch and carry and obey the husband, never mind if he drinks and beats us. Pro-

duce at least one son for the priesthood. Then that's us done.
Nothing left but to get old and die. If we don't marry, we're
expected to stay home and take care of our parents until
they're dead and we're too old to live. Done and finished
again.''

'' 'Thou shalt not' is half the law of Ireland, and 'Thou
must' the other half,'' Ned quoted. ''And each of these is a
tyrant.''[8]

''Who said that?''

''Mr. Pearse again.''

''I think I like your Mr. Pearse.''

Ned enjoyed talking to Síle. He saw her frankness as an
expression of intellectual freedom. Most women were as cir-
cumspect as their men. The Irish relished conversation as an
art form, but it was often style without substance, a way of
protecting the secret inner self.

Síle was different. Talking with her was almost as pleasurable, in a different way, as making love to her. One seemed
part of the other; it was all Síle.

''I have to go to work or I'll be late, but can I see you
again?'' he asked hopefully.

''You can meet me here at about this time most mornings.
I come for the papers.''

Only later did Ned wonder if that was the only reason Síle
visited Tom Clarke's shop. There were news agents much
closer to Mrs. Drumgold's house in Faithful Place.

A new element was somehow fitted into his morning. Up
at dawn while Henry still lay snoring, throw on his clothes in
the unheated room, splash his face with water from the pitcher
on the washstand, a hasty shave, a swift bicycle ride to the
orphanage, half an hour with Precious, another hurried ride to
75A Parnell Street, where Síle was waiting for him.

They had neither time nor opportunity for anything but talking.

To his surprise, Ned found himself telling Síle about the
Titanic. He had never been able to tell Mary. The only time
he mentioned it she had put her hands over her ears and cried,
''Oh, don't talk about that, it's too terrible!''

Mary was delicate, she must be protected, so he never mentioned the subject again.

But Síle listened.

He told her about Precious, too, and his sister in America and his family back in Clare. He spoke at length of Mr. Pearse and Saint Enda's and the things that mattered to him. She told him of her own life, with neither self-pity nor apology.

They talked as if they could never get enough of conversation. When the weather allowed, they strolled around Rutland Square, past the Rotunda Lying-In Hospital, with its peripheral buildings and park. Since the onset of war the Union Jack was prominently displayed in the area, as blatant in its message as the recruiting posters. But Ned was, for a while, able to ignore them.

I'm walking out with Síle Duffy, he thought to himself.

It was ridiculous, of course. A decent Irish man did not walk out with a girl like Síle Duffy.

He had to keep his life compartmentalized: Síle in one section, Mary in another, and no cross-referencing. His two jobs were equally separate. A copyboy saw the news of the day before it ever reached the streets, but he was ordered not to divulge what he knew ahead of the next edition. It was still more imperative that he tell no one about messages he was relaying. As preparations for the Rising gained momentum, an air of almost total secrecy prevailed. "Everything must be on a 'need to know' basis," Tom Clarke told Ned.

Early in April, Ned was summoned to Larkfield. A maid-servant led him into a drawing room where he was soon joined by Joe Plunkett, who looked as pale and delicate as ever. He was shivering in spite of a cheerful fire in the fireplace.

Within moments another maid entered carrying a decanter and two glasses on a silver tray. When she had gone Plunkett went to a writing desk between two of the tall windows, unlocked a drawer, and took out a sheaf of documents. Putting these into a manila envelope, he sealed it and gave it to Ned.

"Take this to Tom for me, will you? It seems I'm off to Germany to help Roger Casement."

Ned put down his glass. "Casement's in Germany? I didn't know."

"No reason why you should until now. I've arranged a code with my sister Gerry so I can send messages through her to Seán or Pat. But if anything happens I want you to be available as a backup conduit for information. Do you agree?"

Ned nodded.

Plunkett said, "For a long time Casement has insisted that Germany's goodwill could be a great asset to Ireland."[9]

Ned felt a sudden, inexplicable chill, as if he knew what was coming next. The mention of Germany was innocent enough; Ireland had always enjoyed amicable relations with Germany. But with the outbreak of war Germany had taken on the sinister image of imperialist aggressor, and Ireland had seen far too much imperial aggression.

We should not trust Germany, Ned thought with the prescience that occasionally troubled him. A strange vista opened in his imagination, a road stretching through the years into dark and deadly territory.

But who was he to disagree with Roger Casement?

He bit his lip and kept silent as Plunkett continued, "Although he's treasurer for the Volunteers, Sir Roger's not a member of the IRB. But he believes so strongly in this German idea of his that last year he went to America to persuade Clan na Gael to petition the kaiser.

"I'm not convinced that John Devoy thought it was a good idea, but when a man of Casement's stature offered to help the cause he could hardly refuse. Sir Roger's international reputation for courage and integrity is above question.

"In the autumn Casement personally took the petition to Berlin. His mission had several purposes. The first was to secure an official statement of support for Irish independence from the German government. Second, he wanted to organize Irish-born prisoners of war—and there are quite a few of them among the British soldiers in German prison camps—into a brigade to fight for Irish freedom. The third purpose, of course, was to procure more arms for us."

Ned let out a low whistle.

"It's an extremely dangerous undertaking for a former British consul," Plunkett went on, "and I confess I have misgivings. Other nations will always put their own national interest first; we should know that by now. Ireland has to learn to stand alone; that's the essence of independence.

"However, Casement's been given permission to organize an Irish Brigade in the prison camps. The understanding is that if Germany wins her war, she will send them to us at her own expense as a gift for the Irish people, to help with our struggle for independence.

"The Germans want to consult with a member of the IRB before any final arrangements are made. Since there's a war on between Britain and Germany, we can hardly cable Berlin from Dublin. It means a personal trip, and I'm the obvious man to go. I speak several languages, and my health gives me a perfect excuse for leaving the country. My family will tell people I've gone to Jersey for a while. Word will filter back to Dublin Castle, and in case they're watching me, they'll think I'm safely out of the way and forget about me.

"As a precaution I'm going to destroy all photographs of myself before I leave, and once out of Ireland I shall start growing a mustache. I plan to assume a false identity and travel by way of Spain and Italy."[10] Suddenly he gave Ned an astonishingly boyish wink. "I always did have a taste for cloak-and-dagger."

Ned smiled back. Like Tom Clarke, Joe Plunkett wore a mask. He was deeply devout and known for having a particular devotion to Saint John of the Cross.[11] Of the three poets, he was the most otherworldly, the most mystical. Yet beneath his frail exterior was an individual of reckless courage and steely resolve.

Before they parted Plunkett gave Ned notes to deliver to several members of the IRB. The last thing he said was, "I'm only sorry I shan't be in Ireland for Easter. It's my favorite time of year. The promise of the Resurrection."

• • •

HENRY Mooney never questioned Ned about his activities outside of the newspaper. But on several occasions Ned caught his friend watching him through narrowed eyes. Eventually he challenged, "What is it, Henry? Why are you looking at me that way?"

"I was just thinking what a deep one you are. You once told me you're not in the IRB and I believe you. But you certainly work hand and glove with them, don't you?"

"What makes you think so?"

"I have my sources."

"Well, whatever you think you know, forget it."

"In your case I do, Ned," Henry replied. "We're friends, and more than that, we're on the same side. I hope you know you can trust me."

What was that Henry had once said? Ned asked himself later. *In a city awash with informers . . .*

Who could one trust?

Chapter Thirty-one

Alexander Campbell was not a stupid man. The third time he heard his wife mention the priest in the same day he asked sharply, "When did you become so religious, Kate?"

"I've always been a devout Catholic; you knew that when you married me."

"Not so devout that you'd refuse to marry a Protestant once you were in America. And not so devout that you went to Mass every morning—until recently. Now it's Father Paul says this, and Father Paul thinks that, and Father Paul needs you at Saint Xavier's to arrange flowers and decant incense."

Kathleen laughed. "Oh, Alexander, one doesn't decant incense!" But her laughter was forced and her eyes were wary.

He came to her in the afternoons while Alexander was at work. After the first week he did not visit her every day. Her bruises had faded by then, and neither of them could maintain the pretense that he was ministering to an injured parishioner.

Once or twice a week Della would meet him at the door, let him in, and serve afternoon coffee and cake to the pair of them in unconscious imitation of Mrs. Flanagan at the presbytery. Then she would put on her battered straw hat, wish them good-day, and leave. Once or twice a week—through the autumn, the winter, the spring.

HE sat beside her on the couch and held her. Held her; stroked her hair. Kissed her eyelids.

"In the beginning I truly believed I loved Alexander," Kathleen said. "But what did I know? I'd never been with a man. And he wasn't just any man; he was new and different and . . . and American. He was electric lights and Fifth Avenue and strawberries out of season. I thought I loved him."

"I know," he whispered into her hair. "I know."

Paul O'Shaughnessy did not want to hate any man, but he hated Alexander Campbell for brutalizing this woman.

The ordeal she had undergone placed an added constraint upon him. As her priest he would be violating his vows if he touched her carnally; as a man he would be adding to the physical insult she already had suffered. Or so he thought. Until the day she caught his hand and gently laid it upon the swell of her breast.

Autumn into winter, winter into spring.

When Father Paul returned to the presbytery from his afternoons with Kathleen, Mrs. Flanagan always knew where he had been. He was not a man who could mask his feelings. His Irish-blue eyes were brimming with pain and guilt, yet there was a strange sort of radiance about him, too—the look of a man who has briefly touched magic.

Magic had no part in Mrs. Flanagan's theology.

She tried everything she could think of to save him. She larded her conversation with constant veiled references to the dangers of temptation and brazen hussies, until eventually he lost his temper. "Mrs. Flanagan, you are worse than a fire-and-brimstone revivalist. I assure you I am perfectly aware of the evils of this world—I hear about them in the confessional every day. If you don't mind, I would prefer not to be reminded of them in my own house."

Kathleen Campbell had ceased visiting the presbytery. Whenever Mrs. Flanagan saw her at Mass, she tried to catch the young woman's eye and give her a hard look. A creature of any sensitivity would have understood and been chastened.

But it would take more than a housekeeper's disapproval to discourage Kathleen.

Discouraging gossip was just as difficult. Among the domestics of the neighborhood, Bridie's spiteful tongue had done its work. They all knew. It was obvious his visits were timed to coincide with the maid's departure and to have him out of the house before Alexander Campbell returned home at the end of the day. Parlormaids claimed they "could set the hall clock by Father Paul passing."

But as the months went by, newer, fresher scandal caught their attention. This was New York; there was no shortage of delicious gossip provided by its most respectable citizens. The priest's relationship became old news, accepted if not condoned—except by Mrs. Flanagan.

She was angry that Mr. Campbell seemed to be ignoring the situation. Why did he not take his young wife in hand; that would solve the problem. Surely he knew.

Or did he?

WITH the outbreak of war in Europe, the pace of Alexander Campbell's life had grown hectic. Although President Wilson was determined to maintain American neutrality, any threat to shipping on the world's oceans had to be taken with the utmost seriousness. There were urgent meetings almost daily in the White Star offices.

Meanwhile, other shipping companies were doing what they could to protect their vessels. Alexander Campbell was assigned to serve as liaison between White Star and the British-owned Cunard Company. The two firms were great rivals, but war made them allies against the menace of German submarines. Charles Sumner, Cunard's New York manager, began inviting Alexander out to his Long Island home for long weekend discussions.

The Freemasons were not idle, either. As war convulsed Europe, the interests of the international brotherhood were unavoidably involved. American Masons were called upon to write letters, send cables, transfer funds, and organize protective structures for colleagues abroad. A member well placed in the shipping industry was endlessly useful.

Alexander Campbell was rarely home in the spring of 1915.

May 8, 1915

CUNARD LINER *LUSITANIA* TORPEDOED
OFF IRISH COAST

Chapter Thirty-two

PAUL told Kathleen, "The priesthood was my mother's vocation, not mine. I was the youngest, her gift to God. She thought she was doing me a favor. How could she have known about you? How could either of us have known about you?"

"What are we going to do, Paul?"

"I don't know. I honest-to-God do not know. I never expected this."

Kathleen gestured toward the newspaper lying on the table. The headlines shrieked of the *Lusitania* tragedy. Fourteen hundred people were reported dead. Among them were 128 American citizens, including the fabulously wealthy Alfred Vanderbilt. "Vanderbilt didn't expect what happened to him, either," she commented. "He probably sailed through life thinking he was in control, then all at once . . ."

"Yes. All at once."

ALTHOUGH Alexander suspected his wife was infatuated with Father Paul, he did not think she was unfaithful. From his own experience he knew she was not a sensual woman. And, of course, she was Catholic, and the Catholics looked upon their priests as saints rather than men.

Masons were encouraged to confide in one another to tighten the bonds of brotherhood, so Alexander mentioned the situation to the Grand Master of his lodge, including a delicate reference to Kathleen's disinterest in sex. "Under the circumstances I would see that as a virtue," the man replied. "Your wife is suffering a variant of papist idolatry, Sandy. If you don't make an issue of it, she's not likely to allow the relationship to go any farther. It's just the pastime of a bored woman. They all have them, I assure you, and many are much worse."

Alexander was reassured. As long as Kathleen did not betray him physically, the marriage was not threatened. When he had the time he would give her more of what she so obviously needed: a strong husband who would tolerate no foolishness. Then there would be babies to keep her busy and she would forget about priests and piety.

He was unprepared for the shock he received one Sunday afternoon in May. He was returning home from Long Island, and had just stepped out of a cab in front of his house when an elderly woman in a black dress and bonnet confronted him on the sidewalk.

"Are you Mr. Campbell?"

"I am, madam. How may I help you?"

"I'm not one to gossip, but . . ."

"Neither am I," he said shortly. "If that's all, I hope you will excuse me?" He lifted his hat and started to pass by her, but she took a step sideways and stationed herself in front of him again.

"You must listen to me." Her eyes were darting from side to side as if she was afraid of being overheard. "There's something you should know. Not to help me, but someone else."

"Tell me then if you must, but make it quick. My wife is expecting me."

"Is she?" Mrs. Flanagan peered up into his face. "Is she indeed?"

"What do you mean by that?"

Mrs. Flanagan clenched her fists against the sides of her skirt. Never in her life had she done anything like this. She had no way of predicting how this stern, rather intimidating man would react when she said, "Your wife is breaking God's law."

Alexander stared at her. "What?"

It was hard to shape the words. Fear and anger combined to make her lips tremble. "Thou shalt not commit adultery. Your wife is."

"What?" he repeated numbly.

"Committing adultery. With a priest. I'm his housekeeper and I know. You have to stop her. She's endangering his immortal soul!"

A small dead boy from the *Lusitania* was found washed up on a beach in southern Ireland. He was still wearing his blue Little Lord Fauntleroy suit when members of the Royal Irish Constabulary photographed the body. The *Independent* obtained a copy of the picture, but to protect public sensibilities decided not to print it.

The staff of the paper gathered around the editor's desk to stare down at the grainy photograph.

"Those bastards. Those bloody bastards!" A reporter slammed his fist against the nearest wall. Another was weeping.

Ned took one look and turned away.

The *Lusitania* disaster had brought back terrible memories, but the pitiful little corpse made them worse. Lying on the sand with its head pillowed on one arm, it could have been any child fast asleep.

It could have been Precious.

After work Ned called in at Gill's Confectioners, the sweets shop in Middle Gardiner Street not far from Mrs. Kearney's.

As always, the fragrance wafting from the ground-floor windows of number 33 made his mouth water. He lost himself amid tall glass jars brimming with bulls' eyes, anise seed balls, jellybabies, and licorice allsorts. For a time he was tempted by blocks of sticky Yellow Man, but eventually chose a dozen chocolate mice—for Precious.

The following Sunday, Mary Cosgrave allowed Ned to escort her to Saint Saviour's in Dominick Street. He was aware of the importance of the gesture. Attending Mass with her formalized their relationship; made them a couple.

Kneeling beside her, he was more conscious of her beauty than of the fine marble altar and justly famed reredos. In this setting it was easy to imagine Mary in a virginal white dress, with wax orange blossoms holding her veil. The Nuptial Mass, the beaming relatives, the proper conclusion to a proper courtship.

With a demure gesture she removed her little kidskin gloves before saying the rosary. Ned was enchanted. When the rosary was concluded he reached out shyly and put his hand over hers.

She peeped at him sidewise from beneath her eyelashes.

Abashed, he took his hand away. But she smiled. All was forgiven.

He could feel his heart hammering.

Mary, Mary. Hail Mary, full of grace.

Emerging from the church after Mass, they were greeted by a cloudless May sky, a burning blue as intoxicating as liquor. Massgoers stopped on the steps to chat with the priest. When it was Ned's turn, the priest shook his hand like a benediction.

"What shall we do now?" he asked Mary as they went down the steps together.

"I'm hungry," she confessed with a giggle. "Fasting before Mass always makes me ravenous. I sat through the entire sermon thinking of food instead of God."

He loved her for her human frailty. "There aren't many places open on Sunday, I'm afraid."

"I know the perfect one—the XL Café and Restaurant in Grafton Street. They serve a lovely lunch. It's a bit of a walk, but very nice."

As Ned had learned, Mary's definition of *nice* was synonymous with *expensive*. By the time they reached the XL Café he was famished, but he prudently limited his meal to a cup of oxtail soup.

Mary ordered soup, Dublin Bay prawns with a side salad and potato cakes, and rice pudding with almond biscuits. She ate heartily, then complained about the damage she had done to her tiny, tightly-corseted waist.

Ned assured her, "There's no cause for worry."

"But are my arms not too plump?"

"They're perfect. Just perfect."

"Are you sure? Sometimes I look in the mirror and think they're just a bit too full . . . just here . . ." She pushed up her sleeve and extended a rounded white arm for his inspection. He pronounced it exquisite. Smiling, she ate another biscuit.

When the young couple left the restaurant they found themselves caught up in a river of people. Dubliners of every social class were making their way to Stephen's Green for the traditional Sunday stroll and free music, so Ned and Mary joined them. The day took on a festive air.

At the entrance to the park an imposing stone archway had been erected in memory of the men of the Royal Dublin Fusiliers who had fallen in the Boer War.

Beyond the arch, neatly raked gravel paths bordered a meandering lake. Sunlight streamed through a canopy of leaves; the air was fragrant with flowers. Children laughed and played and fed the ducks. Adults sauntered across the grass or sat on wooden benches and chatted with friends and strangers. Lovely, leisurely Sunday.

On a little humpbacked bridge Mary paused to admire a flotilla of swans with their cygnets, while Ned leaned his elbows on the stone parapet and admired her profile in the leaf-dappled light. He gave a sigh of contentment. Sunday with Mary.

"What are you thinking about?" she asked. "Me?"

He smiled at her. "Mary dear."

She smiled back and linked her arm through his. They strolled on together.

In the octagonal bandstand across the Green a British army band was striking up—minus the customary Germanic *oom-pah-pah* of the tuba. The triumphal strains of "Hail, Britannia, Britannia Rules the Waves" soon thundered through the park.

Mary tugged at Ned's arm. "Let's go over there. I do so love a band."

But he was listening to a different music. In his memory the Volunteers were singing "For God and Ireland" on their way to Howth.

"That isn't my army," he said abruptly. He turned his back on the bandstand.

Mary tightened her grip on his arm. "Where are you going? I want to listen to them."

He turned to face her. "I don't. I told you, that isn't my army."

"It will be as soon as you enlist."

"I shan't."

"But you must! It's your duty."

"My duty? Is it my duty to kill men I don't hate on behalf of a government I have every reason to hate?"

She stared at him blankly.

"Once again Britain is asking Irish men to serve as cannon fodder. And for what? So another commemorative arch can be erected in Stephen's Green?"

She put her hands on her hips and looked at him as if he were a naughty child. "I'm ashamed of you, Ned Halloran. My brothers are already in the army. Where's your patriotism?"

"I'm more patriotic than you know."

"I don't believe it. If you were, you would enlist so I can be proud of you." She pouted prettily.

For once the effect was lost on Ned. "Can you not be proud of me anyway?" They were close to a quarrel, but he could not give in to her on this; it was central to who he was. "I'm already a soldier, Mary; a member of the Irish Volunteers."

"Redmond's National Volunteers are the real soldiers," she insisted. "He's going to have them all enlist, I read it in the *Times*. That other lot are nothing but rascals and rebels, like the people who read *Sinn Féin*. How can you associate with them?"

"Because contrary to what you may think, they are fine men. They have pledged their lives to make Ireland free."

"Free! I don't know what you mean. I'm perfectly free now."

"Are you content to be a second-class citizen in the land where you were born?"

Her eyes flashed. "I'm not a second-class anything, Ned Halloran! I will not stand here and be insulted by a man who's afraid to fight for his country."

Though a muscle twitched in his jaw, he struggled to keep his voice calm. "My country is Ireland, and I'm defending her the best way I know how. Please listen to me, dearest, and try to understand."

She clapped her hands over her ears. "Don't call me dearest! If you won't join the army you're a coward, you're a dreadful coward and I don't want anything to do with you!" She whirled and ran from him.

Ned started to follow her.

Stopped.

Stood motionless.

At that moment he saw a fork in the road of his life as clearly as he saw the graveled path in front of him. He could obey the impulse to run after Mary and make up with her. It would mean giving in, because she would not accept anything less, but afterward they could go on as before. Sundays with Mary. A white dress and a veil. A cottage on Howth and a baby in her arms.

Or he could take the other road. He could go on without her.

On a knife edge, the future balanced.

Ned stood alone in the sunshine. And all at once, in the quietness of his soul, he knew.

Something tore inside him.

His eyes followed Mary's diminishing figure with aching regret. They came from the same land, the same race, even the same faith. Yet there was a gulf between them he could not bridge.

He could never make her understand what he felt. His dreams threatened hers. Mary would always cling to the status quo, fiercely protective of what she saw as security. In that respect she was closer to the Ulster Unionists than she was to Ned Halloran.

Had he loved Mary with his whole heart it might have been enough to overcome their differences, allowing him to accept her loving, unthinking tyranny. "Anything for a quiet life," many an Irish husband said over his pint in his favorite pub.

But that was the trouble. Ned's heart was already fragmented. Too large a part of it was committed to Ireland.

In New York, Alexander Campbell paid a call on a man he was certain he could trust.

"I have a problem," he said. "I expect your help."

When he had explained the situation he was told, "I cannot do this myself, Sandy, or allow it to be traced to me in any way. But I can give you the name of someone who knows someone who . . ."

"Yes," said Alexander. "Yes."

Every Tuesday morning, Father Paul O'Shaughnessy made his pastoral calls in the area north of Saint Xavier's. The neighborhood was less affluent than the rest of the parish but still respectable. He had no reason to be on his guard as he walked past the entrance to a narrow alleyway—until a trio of roughly dressed men leaped out at him.

They grabbed his shoulders and shoved him into the alley. "What do you want?" he protested. "I have no mon—"

One of them hit him in the mouth. "Shaddup, ya idol-worshippin' bastid."

The priest's astonishment lasted only an instant. Then something ancient and savage rose up in him, something he had never suspected. With a shout of rage he crashed a fist into the man's jaw.

The next moment he was staggering backward with badly bruised knuckles. Before he could recover the other two threw him to the ground amid the trash cans. One can was knocked

over; the metal lid rolled with a clatter down the paved alleyway.

Paul was strong, but these were men who earned their living through hard labor. They set to work beating him with
practiced expertise. The only sounds in the alley were hoarse
grunts and the thuds of fists hitting flesh. Paul fought back
with grim determination only to be knocked flat again.

He drew up his knees and then lashed out with both feet,
catching one man in the groin. There was a howl of agony.

The next thing he knew he was being stomped.

He heard bone crunch as a sheet of white-hot pain tore
through him. He lurched up, and for a moment almost succeeded in throwing them off.

Then someone hit him over the head with a bottle.

Blessed oblivion enfolded him.

When Paul came to he was disoriented and violently nau-
seated. Every breath was agony. He lay helpless until a
butcher's assistant making a delivery found him and summoned aid. But before it arrived, the darkness swallowed him
again.

THE bishop, a stout, asthmatic man with a big pale face like
a looming moon, visited him in the hospital. "You're lucky
to be alive," he wheezed. "Concussion, broken ribs, a bruised
kidney—who did this to you, Father Paul?"

"I didn't get a good look at them. But they were dressed
like dockworkers. I suppose they meant to rob me."

"Do you have any explanation for this?" The bishop held
out a crumpled piece of paper. "The police found it pinned
to your clothes."

"Keep your fucking papist hands off the wives of decent
men," someone had printed in thick black letters.

Chapter Thirty-three

ON the sixteenth of May, Henry Mooney left the *Independent* offices for a private meeting with one of his contacts. In past months his articles had become more moderate. Instead of criticizing Dublin Castle he was adopting a more conciliatory tone, which Ned attributed to the imposition of censorship. At the same time Henry was exploring and explaining the nationalist movement, sculpting every sentence with the precision of a poet.

When one of the other reporters called "Copyboy!" that morning, Ned dutifully trotted over to collect the story. He already had a sheaf of copy in an oilskin pouch ready to be carried to the printing plant, but he automatically flicked his eyes over the latest typewritten page. Then he gasped. "Seán MacDermott's been arrested!"[1]

Several men glanced up. "What's that you say?"

"He made an antirecruiting speech in County Galway. The British claim it was 'calculated to endanger the Realm,' so they're going to bring him back to Dublin tonight and put him in Arbour Hill."

"That's the military detention barracks," one of the reporters pointed out. "So at least they're acknowledging that the Volunteers are legitimate soldiers."

Ned asked, "What will happen to MacDermott?"

"He'll be tried and back in his cell by dinner tomorrow."

The thought of lame, brave, merry Seán MacDermott locked in a prison cell made Ned wince. "Is that a foregone conclusion?"

The man rolled an eye at Ned. "It's British justice, lad. MacDermott's Irish, that's his real crime. He'll go to prison right enough."

Ned struggled with his conscience, then for the first time broke the rule of confidentiality. As soon as he could get away he sped to 75A Parnell Street.

When Tom Clarke heard the news his lips tightened over his teeth. "Bloody bastards. Since Seán doesn't have any family in Dublin I'll send my wife to visit him as soon as he's been sentenced. They'll let her in, I expect."

"I'd be glad to go," Ned offered. "He's my friend, too."

"Best not. You don't want your name on a subversives list in the Castle, do you? I've already warned Katty—not that anyone could stop her from doing something once she's set herself to it."

"What's she done now?"

Clarke's eyes twinkled. "The little darlin' is so angry about seeing the Union Jack all over the city that she's bought a lot of green, white, and orange ribbons and made up badges like the ones Clan na Gael wear in America."[2] He reached under the counter and held up a sample. "She's offering them at a penny apiece. Yesterday I sold a hundred out of this shop alone."

Ned bought one of the badges and pinned it to his jacket.

At Seán MacDermott's trial, testimony was offered by people who had heard his speech in Tuam. Two reporters for the local newspaper had been present and had written down his words. Both agreed that his most inflammatory statement was "Irish patriotism is condemned as a crime. We are told that the only honorable patriotism is that which sends Irishmen to die in an English war. Is this not obscene?"

Their testimony was not admitted.

He was convicted as a result of evidence given by a member of the Royal Irish Constabulary.[3] The man claimed to have made a "mental note" of everything MacDermott said in Tuam. Though he could quote nothing, he assured the court it was highly seditious. The sentence was six months in prison, subsequently reduced to four.[4]

The authorities were arresting hundreds of suspected nationalists and charging them with everything from making inflammatory statements to immoral behavior in a public place. Even an unsubstantiated accusation could be enough to put a man behind bars, thus giving him a police record that might be used against him later.

"They'd love to get me," Tom Clarke told Ned, "but I don't give them the slightest excuse these days. I'm not making any more public speeches, and I never leave my shops or the house unattended. I wouldn't put it past the police to plant something incriminating."

For every Union Jack flying in Dublin, Kathleen Clarke made a tricolor Irish badge. Even Dublin Castle dared not arrest a woman for sewing ribbons. Her little badges began to appear openly on the streets. Some men wore them on their lapels; some women pinned them to their hats.

The majority, however, remained indifferent to the urge for independence. Like Mary Cosgrave, they wanted things to stay as they were. They had grown up under British government and British law; whatever education they had received had been heavily influenced by the British educational system, even if their teachers were Irish Catholic. Censored newspapers assured them daily of the glory and ultimate triumph of the empire.

Besides, "The divvil ye know is better than the divvil ye don't know," as the shawlies said.

When Prime Minister Asquith dissolved his Liberal Cabinet on the nineteenth of May and formed a new Coalition Ministry, the plain people of Ireland saw little relevance to themselves.[5] Only one item excited any strong reaction.

Sir Edward Carson was named Attorney General and given a seat in the new cabinet.

The foremost enemy of Home Rule, a man who had openly defied the imperial law against gunrunning and marched heav-

ily armed men through the streets of Belfast, had been rewarded with one of the most influential positions the empire
could offer.

The implications were clear. A number of people who had
supported John Redmond's Parliamentarians promptly joined
the Sinn Féin Party instead. But it was no longer the patient,
non-violent Sinn Féin of Arthur Griffith. This was a party
increasingly committed to the doctrine of physical force.

To Ned's surprise, Síle had become his confidante. After the
first time they made love, time and circumstance had combined to keep them from physical intimacy again. Sex was
something she did elsewhere. Ned tried not to think about
that.

But they could meet. And talk. They could talk on a personal level available only to people who have shared their
bodies.

When he called on Tom Clarke he left messages for her,
and sometimes she left messages for him. They met when they
could, and he found himself telling her things he had never
told anyone.

She never criticized, never judged, simply listened with a
gift for attentiveness that equaled his own. Confidential information was sacrosanct, but Ned could share his personal
fears with Síle without feeling unmanly. Her own honesty was
liberating.

"There was a time after the *Titanic* when I felt invulnerable," he told her. "I had survived, you know? It was like a
gift from God. But after Bloody Sunday that wore off. Now
sometimes I lie awake at night and wonder what I would do
in a real battle. Would I be brave? Or would I turn and run?"

"No one knows what they'll do until the moment comes,
Ned. We are one sort of person in our heads, and somebody
else in real life. I don't think you would run, though. You
couldn't live with yourself if you did that."

"Some people think men are cowards if they don't enlist
in the British army."

Síle gave a hard, scornful laugh. "Some people think a lot of goddam foolishness."

MEMBERSHIP in Redmond's National Volunteers was declining sharply. A combination of enlistment in the British army and general demoralization was taking its toll. For some a deep resentment of Britain was translating into a pro-German attitude. The tragedy of the *Lusitania* was not forgotten, but centuries of tragedy caused by British imperialism weighed heavier.

Francis Sheehy-Skeffington was arrested for campaigning against military recruitment.[6] He went on a hunger strike and was released after nine days. Even the most callous judge could see no harm in the gentle pacifist, but he had a police "jacket" now, an incriminating file that would follow him the rest of his life. Dublin Castle fully appreciated the value of such files.

Meanwhile, the Irish Volunteers were gaining in strength. Coordination of resources became imperative. Although the constitution of the IRB did not provide for a Military Council,[7] the executives quietly created one around the three Volunteers who had been working on the insurrection plans.

Because he was not a member of the Brotherhood, Eoin MacNeill was neither informed nor included.

Initially the Military Council was composed of Pádraic Pearse and Eamonn Ceannt, with a place held for Joe Plunkett when he returned from Germany.[8] They were in almost daily consultation with Tom Clarke, and through him with Seán MacDermott in Arbour Hill, both of whom were on the executive committee of the IRB. Clarke also relayed messages to Clan na Gael, in the States, using Irish stewards on Atlantic liners.[9]

WHEN Plunkett returned to Ireland in June he was ill and spitting blood.

His sister Geraldine sent for Ned. "We need you to give

his report to the others," she explained, "because Joe isn't able for much talking right now."

"Will he be all right?"

"If he's good and stays in bed as the doctor wants. You know Joe, though; it's hard to keep him down. Ask his friends not to call until I send word, will you? He simply must rest."

After spending an hour with Plunkett, Ned went straight to Saint Enda's. Pádraic Pearse was in his study, updating student records. His first question to Ned was about Plunkett's health.

"His family's worried about him, but Joe assures me he'll be on his feet again soon."

"How does he look?"

"Desperately pale and thin. Both he and Sir Roger fell ill in Germany.[10] Joe says the situation there has grown very confused. Sir Roger feels that Clan na Gael gave his venture only halfhearted support and ultimately turned against him, which made the German Foreign Office suspicious. The officials are courteous enough on the surface, but there is all sorts of skullduggery going on behind the scenes. It sounds like an Erskine Childers spy novel. Joe says Sir Roger's become morbidly depressed."

"I now think this German venture may be a serious mistake," Pearse said. "After the *Lusitania* was torpedoed I was ill for days.[11] What sort of people are we dealing with? The Germans destroyed hundreds of innocent lives simply to intimidate and terrify. They're no better than Oliver Cromwell. For the sake of Ireland, we must set a better example."

Pearse was staring down at his folded hands. "We must always be sure of the moral rectitude of our acts, Ned," he went on. "There is absolutely no justification for wanton butchery, no matter how many men claim otherwise. And given human nature, there are always some who will.

"Remember this: any good cause can be subverted for a wicked purpose. The more noble the cause, the more ignoble will be its subverters."

"I shall remember, sir," Ned promised.

Pearse drew a slow, deep breath, then looked up. "Have you anything more to report?"

"Joe says Sir Roger's had almost no luck forming an Irish brigade in the prison camps. Perhaps fifty men out of all he's spoken to have shown any interest. Now John Devoy's asking him to abandon the idea altogether."

"It's just as well," said Pearse. "How could we trust men who have taken an oath to fight in the British army, then are willing to break it to fight against the British? This whole business . . ." He clucked his tongue in disapproval. "Sir Roger did succeed in persuading the German chancellor to issue an official statement of support for Irish independence. That's something, I suppose. But the *Lusitania* has destroyed my faith in German honor."

"Where does that leave Sir Roger?"

"That's a good question, Ned. He is claiming one other success. The weapons Childers brought us are of wretched quality, as you know. The Mausers are obsolete; Tom Clarke tells me they were made for the Prussian forces of 1870. And the ammunition that came with them consists of explosive bullets. Such bullets are against all rules of civilized warfare; I won't allow them to be given to our men. We desperately need more weapons, and Sir Roger has obtained a promise of them from the Germans. Perhaps by September."

"When did you learn about that?"

"Joe Plunkett sent us the message while he was in Berlin. You'll be amused by the story, Ned. Apparently Joe issued two dispatches about the weapons, but only one got through. He wrote it in code on the flyleaf of Leland's *Italian Folk Tales*, then sent the book through the German Foreign Office to his sister. The code took the form of a mock dedication in Latin."

"Very Joe Plunkett," Ned remarked.

For the first time, Pearse's somber face lit with a smile. "Very."

As Ned pedaled back to the city, he found himself thinking in the way Pádraic Pearse had taught him to do. Looking at both sides of the issue, trying to be intellectually honest.

According to Plunkett, Roger Casement believed Eoin MacNeill was in charge of the Irish Volunteers. MacNeill believed so himself. Yet the truth was, the IRB men were really running the show. Mr. Pearse spoke of moral rectitude while a deliberate deception was being practiced on Eoin MacNeill. Through the Brotherhood a tangled network now stretched from the shores of America to the battlefields of Europe. The network was concealed beneath the surface of the larger war.

Across Europe strangers were hastening to slaughter one another, hastening to join the brotherhood of the dead.

The dead who lay in rotting heaps on the battlefield, embracing their enemies.

The dead who lay in neat rows in cemeteries, all enmity forgotten.

Was that what waited in store for Ireland?

Any good cause can be subverted for a wicked purpose.

Aᴛ the next drill of the Dublin Brigade there were a number of new men. MacDonagh pointed them out to Ned. "Quite an increase in the ranks, eh? The IRB ordered all its members to join us. I'd pit our army against any now."

"I never thought of you as a violent person."

"I'm not. Tom Clarke's the only real warrior amongst us. The leaders of the Irish Volunteers are mostly like myself, poets and professors. Thinkers, not fighters."

Ned rubbed his chin. "Yet what I see advancing toward us, step by step, is another war right here on Irish soil. Does it have to be that way?"

MacDonagh's cheerful expression faded. "I would give anything short of my immortal soul to have it otherwise, Ned," he said soberly. "But we've been taught by England herself. She seized our land with sword and gun and has never respected anything else.

"Time and again the gullible Irish have undertaken political negotiations with the British government in good faith, only to be deceived. The perpetual postponement of Home Rule is just the latest example. Even the most law-abiding people will resort to arms when they lose all faith in the political system. It's as simple as that. And as terrible.''

He reached into the pocket of his tunic and handed Ned a folded piece of paper. ''Do you remember when my daughter was born, my little Barbara? I've just finished writing this poem for her.''

Ned's eyes ran down the neatly penned stanzas. Some he murmured aloud:

> *You come in the day of destiny,*
> *Barbara, born to the air of Mars;*
> *The greater glory you shall see,*
> *And the greater peace, beyond these wars.*
>
> *For the old flags wave again, like trees:*
> *The forest will come with the timid things*
> *That are stronger than the dynasties,*
> *As your curls are stronger than iron rings.*
>
> *Be one with Nature, with that which begins,*
> *One with the fruitful power of God:*
> *A virtue clean among our sins,*
> *'Mid the stones of our ruin a flowering rod.*[12]

Ned folded the paper and handed it back to MacDonagh. ''I'm not sure I understand.''

''What we're doing is for the children, don't you see? To give them a better future than any Irish person has had in eight hundred years.''

''But is it not arrogant,'' Ned argued, ''to assume that one small group of men knows what's best for the entire country?''

''A small group always makes decisions for the majority,'' MacDonagh pointed out. ''They're called the government. All we're asking is the freedom to choose our own government and pass our own laws for the benefit of our own children.''

On his next visit to Precious, Ned hugged the little girl so hard she fought free of his embrace. "Don't *do* that!" she admonished. "You crush me."

"No one will ever crush you," he told her passionately.

THOUGH Paul O'Shaughnessy had been badly injured, he refused to press charges. In this, his bishop concurred. "You could only do damage by making this disgraceful business public," he told the priest after Paul left the hospital. "I am assuming the accusation is a lie?"

Paul hesitated. "I have never slept with the woman in question, Your Excellency."

The bishop fixed him with a hard blue stare. "Is that so. Is . . . that . . . so. Suppose I asked if you've ever touched her. Carnally, that is. What would you say then?"

"Are you asking?"

The stare was unwavering. "No. Father Paul, in my considered opinion, I think it might be best if you took a sabbatical. There comes a time in a priest's life when he may need to take a long look at himself and his vocation in order to renew his commitment. Usually that happens somewhat later, in midlife, but in your case, a sabbatical now is very much called for."

"I don't think—"

"Perhaps you don't, but I do. A complete change of scene would be best. Distance. Mmm, yes. Considerable distance." The bishop spoke like a man thinking out loud. "Do I recall that you have family living in Ireland?"

"Several cousins, though I've never seen them."

"Then I think it advisable that you visit them as soon as you are fit to travel. A sea voyage and, mmm, a year's sabbatical will do you immense good."

Paul tried to argue, but it was no use. The vows he had taken gave the church absolute authority over his life.

His fellow priests took over his duties while Paul was recuperating in the presbytery, and Mrs. Flanagan fussed over her patient like a hen with one chick. He felt smothered.

He also felt as if he was being watched.

At first it was no more than a vague disquiet caused by glimpsing disreputable-looking strangers loitering outside the house. But when he started going for short walks to build up his strength, he noticed that at least one of the men always kept him in sight.

When he mentioned it to Mrs. Flanagan she said, ''You're imagining things, Father. You took a fearful crack on the head, you know. In my day we would have treated it with brown paper and vinegar, but these modern doctors . . .'' She snorted contemptuously.

When Paul asked her to carry a message to Mrs. Alexander Campbell, she refused. ''Now Father, you don't want to be bothering yourself with that. Leave her be.''

''I won't have you dictating to me, Mrs. Flanagan.''

''It's not me that's dictating. The bishop himself told me you were not to get in touch with that woman. It's for your own sake, Father. You'll thank me some day.''

Although he waited hopefully, Kathleen did not come to the presbytery to inquire about him. He could not imagine what she might have been told.

Youth and strength were on his side, and his injuries healed fast. Soon he felt strong enough to walk the four blocks to her house. But the first time he made the attempt, two burly strangers fell into step behind him. When he crossed the street, they crossed too. When he speeded up and changed direction, they followed him.

At last he turned back, afraid of what he might be leading to Kathleen.

That same evening the bishop paid him a call. ''God works in providential ways,'' he told Paul as soon as Mrs. Flanagan had served them a glass of whiskey apiece and left the room. ''You remember our conversation about a sabbatical in Ireland?''

''I do, Your Excellency, and I wanted to talk with you about that. It really would be most inconven—''

''On the contrary, it is highly opportune. Don't you read the obituaries? A man known as Jeremiah O'Donovan Rossa died in this city on the twenty-ninth of June. He was an old

Fenian, a hero to certain elements in the Irish community.
John Devoy has been in touch with me about shipping the
body back to Ireland for burial. Devoy's requested a priest to
accompany the widow and the remains, and your doctors assure me you're up to the voyage if you take it easy. So pack
your bags, Father. You sail on Thursday.''

Chapter Thirty-four

PAUL accepted the bishop's arrangements fatalistically. In them was a circularity that appealed to his Celtic soul. He had warned Kathleen against consorting with Devoy and the Irish nationalists. Now for his sins he was being sent to Ireland, out of the reach of temptation.

In a strange way he was relieved. God was taking the problem out of his hands. But he could not leave America for a year without seeing her one more time.

During the summer a gardener came to the presbytery every Monday to tend the flower beds and the tiny patch of lawn. The man kept a stained gardening smock and wide-brimmed straw hat on a peg inside the back door. A battered wheelbarrow and various tools were in the carriage house at the rear of the property.

On Tuesday, Paul waited until Mrs. Flanagan had gone out to do the shopping before he changed into his oldest shirt and trousers. He did not put on the Roman collar. Instead he donned the smock, pulled the hat down over his eyes, put the tools into the wheelbarrow, and wheeled them around to the front of the house. Instead of his normal walk he adopted an old man's slouch.

A surly-looking stranger was leaning against a lamppost across the street, watching the front door of the house. He

paid no attention to the departing gardener as Paul pushed his
barrow up the street and around the corner. Once out of sight
the disguised priest parked the barrow and, straightening up,
set off at a brisk walk.

When he reached the Stewart house Kathleen answered the
door herself. She went white when she saw him. "D-Della
isn't here, it's her day off."

"I'm not here to call on your maid. May I come in?"

For a moment he feared she would refuse him. Then she
swung the door wide and stepped aside. "If you wish."

This time there was no offer of refreshments in the parlor.
She seated herself on a chair across from him, her spine more
rigid than corseting demanded.

"I've wanted to come to you," he began, "but it's been
impossible."

"For weeks, Paul? There's another priest serving Mass at
Saint Xavier's, and no word from you."

"Please don't judge me until you know the facts."

She kept her eyes downcast so he could not read the expression there. "I know you were attacked by hooligans and
sent to the hospital. I called there to see you and was told no
visitors were allowed. When I told Alexander where I'd been,
he was furious with me. He said he knew about us and forbade
me to go anywhere near the hospital, Paul. He intimated that
he was responsible for what had happened to you.

"I do think he might be capable of it, but I have no proof.
He might simply have heard about the attack and decided to
take credit for it to frighten me. I wouldn't put it past him."
But she did not look frightened. She raised her chin; the stubborn Halloran cleft was clearly visible. Her eyes met his.
"When I heard you'd been discharged, I went to the presbytery anyway. I couldn't help myself, I had to. But Mrs.
Flanagan told me you wouldn't see visitors. I thought you
wanted nothing more to do with me."

"That's not true," Paul protested. "I would never have
treated you that way, breaking off without a word."

"I didn't think so. But Alexander said . . ."

Her beautiful eyes were filled with more distress than he

could bear. "Perhaps it's for the best, Kathleen," he said gently. "It could only end in tears, and I would not hurt you for the world, I hope you know that. Nor do I want to break my vows. You must understand that about me, too. I meant them when I took them, I can't throw all that away."

"I never asked you to," she said in a whisper.

"No, in all fairness you didn't. Now, well, we've been given a breathing space. A chance to be apart from one another and let our emotions settle so we can think more clearly."

He told her then about the sabbatical.

Kathleen sat with her hands folded in her lap; her eyes fixed on his. When he finished she said, "So that's it? You're just going to sail off to Ireland and leave me here?"

"You make it sound as if I'm abandoning you and I'm not, I never would. But I must go. What else can I do, Kathleen!"

"Stay here. For me; for us."

"And what about Alexander?"

"People get divorces in America."

"You know divorce is prohibited to Catholics."

"Marriage is prohibited to priests," she countered. "But if it were not for Alexander, would you marry me?"

"Now you're suggesting I leave the priesthood."

"I'm not suggesting anything. I'm simply asking. If you know the answer already, and it's no, then there's no need for you to go away. We can say good-bye here and now and I promise I shan't trouble you further. I'll go to a different church; you won't even have to see me at Mass. If that's what you want. Is it? *Is it?*"

To Paul's relief, he and O'Donovan Rossa were not booked on a White Star liner. Instead they would travel on one of the smaller Cunard ships, the *Laconia*. The war had caused an inevitable disruption of sailing schedules as the large Atlantic liners were being returned to their home ports for refitting. Some would become troopships or hospital ships, others would transport armaments.

The *Laconia* left New York at night with minimal lights showing, as secretive about her departure as anything so large could be. The old Fenian's widow and his daughter Eileen stayed in their cabin, but Paul was on deck. He had hoped for a daylight view of the great city as seen from the harbor. The dazzle of its lights against the night sky was achingly beautiful, however, like a constellation from which he was being expelled against his will.

The man next to him at the rail remarked, "Gorgeous, isn't it? Makes one proud to be an American."

"Yes," said Paul.

"Wish Tillie—that's my wife—could see this. But she's in our cabin throwing up. Happens every voyage. But there you are, there's no other way to get to London. Been going every summer for twenty years, we have. No point in breaking the habit now just because there's a war on, eh?"

"No point at all," Paul agreed politely. He wanted to be left alone to concentrate on the sensation of leaving America. Physically leaving America. But the other man, almost invisible in the darkness, was lamentably talkative.

"Was the *Laconia* your first choice? 'Twasn't ours. Personally, we like the big ones better. Less sensation of being at sea, if you know what I mean. Folks like us, we only sail because there's no other way to get across the Big Pond. You ever see the *Mauretania*? It's a floating luxury hotel. You'd hardly know all that cold water was out there if you didn't go on deck, and lots don't. Be damned glad when this idiotic war's over and the big liners come back."

Watching the lights of New York slip away to stern, Paul was mildly amused at a man who wanted to pretend he was not on a ship at all.

A ship. On the ocean. With the night wind blowing, smelling of salt and emptiness.

A ship transfixed between worlds, between America and Ireland.

As Paul was transfixed between the priesthood and Kathleen.

What do you want? she had asked.

God help me, he thought. I don't know. He leaned forward and put his head on the rail.

His loquacious companion said, "No sea legs yet? It'll be hell for three days, then you should be right as rain—unless you're like my Tillie. I never get sick, got an iron belly. But I hate the Atlantic. Damn, I hate the Atlantic," he repeated as the *Laconia* began to roll with the ocean swells.

That night, as he lay in his cabin fighting to keep down his dinner, Paul agreed.

Sunrise dawned on a relatively calm sea. Paul felt better—until all passengers were called on deck for lifeboat drill. Those who neglected to appear wearing their life jackets were sent back for them. The ship's officers were crisp and businesslike. "We're beyond United States territorial waters now," they announced, "which means we're fair game for German U-boats. We don't want to alarm you, but it's best to be prepared."

At these words every passenger on the *Laconia* cast an apprehensive glance at the sea beyond the rail.

Anything could lurk beneath that gently heaving surface.

The only one on board who doesn't need to worry is old O'Donovan Rossa, Paul thought with grim amusement.

PÁDRAIC Pearse had been traveling around Ireland giving speech after speech. The subject was Irish independence, the subtext antirecruitment: "Do not fight for a foreign power when we need you for Ireland." Sometimes his words were greeted enthusiastically, though in garrison towns like Limerick he was heckled and jeered by the families of British army men. Ned worried that Pearse would be arrested.

Henry reassured him. "Dublin Castle still isn't overly concerned about Mr. Pearse. They can have him arrested any time they like, but he's a negligible threat compared to men like Tom Clarke and Seán MacDermott. Or James Connolly, for that matter. Connolly's spread a banner across the front of Liberty Hall that says, "We serve neither King nor Kaiser, but Ireland.""

"For Mr. Pearse's sake," Ned replied, "I hope the Castle keeps on underestimating him."

"Don't worry. I shan't tell them any different."

When Pearse summoned Ned to meet him at Eamonn Ceannt's house in July, the strain of his efforts was showing in his face, but his spirits were high. "You know about O'Donovan Rossa's death, of course?"

"I do," Ned replied. "We covered it in the *Independent*, though it wasn't as big a news item as the war—or the parties the new viceroy's giving."

"Well, here is something I promise will become very big news: Clan na Gael is sending Rossa's body home for burial with full military honors."

"Are you serious?"

"I am. We shall lay him to rest in Glasnevin Cemetery on the first of August, the Celtic festival of Lughnasa. We hope to have a lying-in-state for him, then a procession through the city to the cemetery. The Irish Volunteers, the Irish Citizen Army, the Fianna, and members of the Irish Republican Brotherhood will attend the ceremony."

Ned recognized the plan for what it was: the most audacious propaganda exercise the republicans had yet undertaken.

"Tom Clarke has asked me to deliver the funeral oration," Pearse subsequently told him, "so I'm going down to Connemara to work on it. Willie and Des Ryan will accompany me. I have some other writings I need to finish while I'm there, too." He paused, then added, "I may never have the chance again."

Tom Clarke and Thomas MacDonagh were organizing the funeral. Ned's assignment was the daily delivery of updated instructions to the numerous people involved. This meant giving up, for a time, his mornings with Precious and Síle.

Síle was understanding when he explained to her, but Precious was less sanguine. "Ned-Ned, why can't you come see me for just a little while?"

"I will soon, Precious, but not for the next few days. I have more to do than there are hours to do it in."

"I don't have anything to do," the child responded dolefully.

"Of course you do! You have toys to play with. I know, I've bought them for you. And you have friends . . ."

"Don't have friends," she interrupted. "The other children don't like me very much."

Ned was astonished. How could anyone fail to love her? "Why do they not like you?"

"They say I talk fancy. But I don't: I'm just learning lots of words so I can sound like you!" she finished triumphantly.

Ned stared at her in wonderment, suddenly understanding. This tiny mite, this abandoned scrap of humanity, was intelligent, with a hungry mind like his own.

He felt a burgeoning sense of pride in Precious. The future would *have* to be better . . . for her sake.

As the date set for the Rossa funeral approached, Ned was on his bicycle at first light every day, dashing about the city and its outskirts. He only finished in time to race in to work, sweaty and disheveled.

"What are you up to?" Henry asked him—but only once.

Ned shrugged. "Working all the hours God sends, same as always."

That same evening he noticed a member of the DMP standing across the street, openly watching Clarke's shop.

Clarke laughed it off. "Dublin Castle has someone out there every day now. Mostly what they get is rain down the backs of their necks. A lad yesterday took a bad chill, so I fetched him in here and gave him a drop of hot whiskey before he went back to his post."

"Does it not make you nervous, being watched?"

"It doesn't take a feather out of me, Ned. After so many years of British surveillance I'd take it as an insult if they stopped. They'd be saying 'You're too old, Clarke; we don't think you're dangerous anymore.' "

Ned gave him a note from Thomas MacDonagh. Clarke read swiftly, scribbled something at the bottom, then tucked the single sheet between the pages of the latest edition of the

Freeman's Journal and handed the newspaper to Ned. "Take this back to him, will you?"

"How do you like working with Professor MacDonagh?"

"I'm glad of the chance to get to know him better. I don't have a lot in common with bookish people, but he strikes me as a decent fellow, straight and clear in thought and action.[1] When the time comes . . ." Clarke left the thought hanging in the air. "Now run along," he said briskly. "Why are you still standing there?"

"I just wanted to ask if you'd heard anything from Connemara."

"You miss Pat, don't you?"

"I suppose I do."

"He has work to do, same as the rest of us. And what he does, no one else can. Before he left he asked my advice about how far to go with his speech, and my instructions to him were, 'Make it as hot as hell, throw discretion to the winds.' "[2] Fiery young eyes flashed in Tom Clarke's old face. "Did you know the IRB's persuaded James Connolly to write an article about O'Donovan Rossa? It's to be in the program we'll hand out at Glasnevin."

"That's grand news. Does it mean Connolly's finally committed to the IRB?"

"Not yet. He has his own plans for revolution; he wants to create a socialist state for the workers. He's converted part of Liberty Hall into a munitions factory, and he's making bombs and bayonets for the Citizen Army. There's no holding him; he's even recruiting women. He's made Constance Markievicz a company commander. We'd like to have Connolly himself on our Military Council, but at first he even refused to write that article for us. He said, 'Why are you fellows blethering on about dead Fenians? What you need is some live ones for a change.' "

Ned burst into laughter.

"So they sent him to me and we had a pleasant little talk," Clarke went on blandly. "Good man, James Connolly. Tough, no pretense about him—and an excellent mind. In the finish-up he agreed to write the article. He's calling it 'Why the Citizen Army Honours Rossa.' ''

"I would like to have been a fly on the wall for that 'pleasant little talk' of yours," said Ned. "I look forward to reading what he wrote."

"You'll have your program on the day and Connolly will sign it for you personally; I'll see to it. By the way, my Katty will be at the funeral too, though I'll be too busy to spend any time with her. What say we have her bring along that friend of yours? They can keep each other company."

Ned felt his cheeks flame. He was a grown man, yet to his embarrassment he still blushed like a schoolboy over certain subjects. "Do you mean Síle Duffy?"

"I do of course."

"Does your wife know her well enough?"

Clarke began rearranging the tobacco tins behind the counter. "Well enough."

Ned was surprised. He had met Tom Clarke's wife on several occasions and would not have taken her for the sort of person who would befriend a prostitute.

Yet had he not done so himself?

Sometimes, he thought, the labels we put on people simply don't fit.

THE next night Ned was home early for once. He thought of going to see Precious, but the activity of recent days was catching up with him. More than anything else he just wanted to go to bed. No sooner had he crawled under the covers, however, than he heard Henry's voice on the stair, talking in low tones to someone else.

Henry entered the room and fumbled beside the door to turn up the gaslight.

When Neville Grantham came through the doorway Ned sat up with a start.

"What are you doing here?" he and the Englishman asked each other simultaneously.

Henry drawled, "I don't think I need to introduce you two.

Ned, you once mentioned meeting Neville. If I recall your exact words, he seemed 'a decent sort.' "

The Englishman was peering intently at the young man sitting bolt upright on the bed. "Jervis Street Infirmary, was it not?"

Ned nodded. "And then Bachelor's Walk. A year ago this month."

Grantham's frown changed to a smile. "Dublin really is a small town. I never expected to meet you under these circumstances, but it's a pleasure to see you again."

Ned replied coldly, "May I ask why an employee of the Castle is calling on this house?"

Grantham and Henry exchanged glances. Then Henry gestured toward his own neatly made bed. "Please take a seat there, Neville, it's more comfortable than either of the chairs. This might be a long night."

"YOU must accept," Neville Grantham told Ned, "that I love my country. But love does not necessarily confer blind loyalty. I am quite aware that we have made—are making—mistakes in our policy toward Ireland."

Ned had hastily dressed and was now sitting in one of the room's two straight-backed chairs. "That's no explanation," he told the Englishman. "I repeat: Dublin Castle has no business here."

Henry started to say something, but Grantham held up his hand. "Let me elaborate. I realize the average Irish person sees the Castle as a 'sink of jobbery and corruption.' When Arthur Norway was put in charge of the Post Office there was outrage because a man who was both Protestant and a Mason had been given preference over well-qualified Irish Catholics. The newspapers claimed it was a conspiracy."

"Conspiracy is not unknown in the Castle," Henry remarked dryly from his seat in the other chair.

"Occasionally we even conspire against ourselves," Grantham conceded. "My being here is rather a case in point. You see, Ned, the senior civil servants and army officers solidly support British policy toward Ireland. In the current war situation the possibility of invasion is never far from their minds. Every effort is being made to provide the United Kingdom with adequate reserves for the military. Any action counter to that objective is considered treasonous.

"However, a few of us believe the government is blind to reality. We English have always liked to think we're in Ireland 'for Ireland's own good.' But the Irish are not by nature a subservient race. We should have recognized that long ago and made concessions to their dignity. If we had granted *and enforced* Home Rule thirty years ago, a unified Ireland might stand with us today as a loyal member of the kingdom.

"Unfortunately, Parliament continues to withhold Home Rule for the sake of political expediency. This is losing us a lot of Irish sympathy. Meanwhile, there is considerable support for an Irish republic coming from abroad—it isn't just the Sinn Féiners and their army anymore."

Grantham did not notice the sudden flicker of contempt in Ned's face. He went on, "Other nations think Ireland's aspirations are not unreasonable. Given the state of war between our countries, Germany's sympathy toward Ireland creates a particularly dangerous situation.

"When Baron Wimborne was named as viceroy I was hopeful at first. The post is mostly ceremonial; the chief secretary runs the Irish government and the under-secretary implements his policies. There we touch on part of the problem: a certain indecisiveness as to what policy to adopt in relation to the nationalists.

"A diplomatic and well-informed viceroy could be most helpful in the current climate. Sadly, that description doesn't fit Wimborne, who is a crude young man with no sensitivity. If he were a horse in the hunting field we would call him a 'thruster': one who wants to take the bit in his teeth. He's absolutely bombarding the Castle with unasked-for advice. As for the chief secretary, when Alexander Birrell was first appointed he took quite an interest in Ireland. But since his wife died he directs Castle operations from his London office and hardly ever comes here. He's out of touch; he's no longer 'the man on the ground.'

"The man on the ground now is the new under-secretary, Sir Matthew Nathan, who is a most intelligent fellow but hasn't had enough time to get a feel for the situation. Because his background is German Jewish, he doesn't have the confidence of the other senior civil servants.[3] He's aware of their attitude, and the result is he won't be guided by anyone but Birrell. So here I am in a Dublin lodging house, conspiring against my superiors in hopes of getting my own views across. If they knew I was talking to a reporter without authorization . . ." Grantham gave a nervous laugh and shifted his weight on the bed. A bedspring creaked protest.

Henry told Ned, "When I happened to meet Neville at some Castle function, I recalled what you had said about him. And you were right, he is a decent sort. He's genuinely concerned about Ireland and the Irish. I persuaded him to become one of my contacts by arguing that since everyone reads the newspapers, he can have some influence that way. As you've no doubt already realized, Ned, I'm trying to encourage the government to accept the legitimacy of the nationalist movement."

A muscle tightened in Ned's jaw. "Then I think you should explain to them that the Irish Volunteers and Sinn Féin are not the same. The *Sinn Féin* newspaper has been very vocal in condemning British recruitment, so since we share that conviction I suppose the political party and the Irish Volunteers are linked in the minds of people who don't bother to understand. But how can such people presume to govern Ireland?"

In the light from the overhead fixture Neville Grantham's face had deep pouches under the eyes. "I'm afraid I didn't fully realize that myself," he said apologetically. "A basic lack of understanding is part of the problem, Ned. That's why I'm willing to work with Henry. His writing helps clarify issues without being confrontational.

"For example, Dublin Castle has been monitoring preparations for the Rossa funeral. Henry's articles have made them aware of the love Dubliners have for the man. He's a folk hero and any interference with his funeral just might cause a riot, so the under-secretary has decided to keep hands off. He's even granted permission for the body to lie in state in City Hall. A Fenian on the threshold of Dublin Castle; you can't ask for fairer than that.''

WHEN the Englishman had gone, Ned asked Henry, ''What did you tell him about me?''

''Nothing. I don't discuss my friends with him, nor he with me.''

''You didn't mention that I was in the Volunteers?''

''I told you, Ned, I didn't mention you at all. He didn't even know we knew each other until tonight.''

''Do you trust him?''

''He's given me good information in the past.''

''What if Neville Grantham's really an informant for the Castle?''

''I'm careful about what I tell him. From me he hears nationalist philosophy, not strategy plans.''

''Do you know any?''

Henry chuckled. ''If I do, I certainly didn't learn them from you. You've the best-sealed lip of anyone I know.''

But in spite of Grantham's assurances Ned was nervous about the upcoming funeral. He knew what the Englishman did not—that Pádraic Pearse was writing a graveside oration intended to set the fires of freedom ablaze.

Chapter Thirty-five

Aт the end of July, Jeremiah O'Donovan Rossa came home to Ireland. The embalmed remains were taken to the Pro-Cathedral for the first night and laid before the high altar. The next day Ned Halloran was assigned to be one of the Volunteers serving as guard of honor while the body lay in state in City Hall.[1] He arrived to find the open coffin already in place on trestles. At the head stood a priest with his eyes downcast in prayer.

When Father Paul looked up, he found a ruggedly masculine version of Kathleen Campbell's face gazing at him across the body of the dead Fenian.

Like a ghost, she had followed him three thousand miles, only to materialize in the form of a tall young man.

It was not quite her face; the cheekbones and jaw were broader, and the eyes, though the same shape, were sea-green rather than sky-blue. But he knew that cleft chin, that vulnerable mouth.

An invisible hand squeezed Paul's heart so hard he caught his breath.

Then he noticed the Volunteer uniform and realized he must be looking at Ned Halloran.

As the honor guard took their places, Brian Joyce, one of Ned's former classmates from Saint Enda's, muttered out of the side of his mouth, "That priest's staring at you, Ned. What have you done now?"

"I haven't had time to commit even a venial sin in weeks."

Brian snickered. The priest turned his eyes on him and the young man sobered at once. "Sorry, Father."

THE honor guard stood tall and straight, eyes fixed on distant glory. Within the casket, the well-embalmed Jeremiah O'Donovan Rossa lay with his eyes closed on eternity.

AUGUST 1. Lughnasa, the ancient Celtic feast of the sun. The weather was typically Irish, with bands of rain clouds chasing one another across the sky between intervals of glorious sunshine.

A great crowd accompanied O'Donovan Rossa's horse-drawn hearse to Glasnevin Cemetery. Father Paul O'Shaughnessy walked with the other clergy in the procession. In his clerical garments he looked as much a native as any of them. For the first time since his arrival in Ireland, a peculiar feeling of being at home crept over him.

He did not have the same feeling in the house of the Dublin cousins with whom he was staying. An elderly couple whose children had long since emigrated, Des and Ina Cahill lived in a working-class cottage in Ringsend. The redbrick walls of their house were crumbled and eroded by generations of weather, and the roof slumped in the middle like a sway-backed horse.

Paul had been astonished to discover that husband and wife had not spoken to one another for fifteen years.

Ina called her husband "that man," when she had to mention him at all. For his part, Des referred to his wife with a toss of his head like a nervous tic. Yet they seemed comfort-

able enough with their relationship. Over the years the pair
had grown to look remarkably alike, the major difference being Ina's ubiquitous shawl. Though they never spoke directly,
when one began a sentence the other could finish it with no
break in continuity.

In this fashion Paul was informed that O'Donovan Rossa
was "a great man for the jest, sure he was," according to
Des. "Them Brits never took the smile off his face, even
when they had him in prison . . ."

". . . and was torturin' the poor divvil night and day, day
and night," Ina had finished for her husband. "Och, was he
not after laughin' aloud and singin' Irish songs in his cell with
the blood runnin' off him?"

Now, as Paul paced steadily along in the funeral cortege,
he recalled the gaunt, proud face in the open coffin in City
Hall, and the way Dubliners had filed by, fingering rosaries
and weeping as if O'Donovan Rossa had belonged to each
one of them. As perhaps he had.

To his surprise, Paul O'Shaughnessy was beginning to feel
Irish.

His eyes sought and found Ned Halloran, marching with
the honor guard. In Paul's pocket was a card carrying Ned's
address that Kathleen had given him at the close of their last
painful meeting. "Please see my brother," she had urged.
"Do that much for me; assure me that he's all right."

No. He must not think of Kathleen. To meet with Ned and
look into that face—it was too painful. Best to make a clean
and total break, like a form of surgery. Cut Kathleen out of
his life.

Against his will his eyes sought Ned again.

He tore his gaze away and concentrated on his surroundings.

There were a number of military contingents in the procession. Following a banner reading "Citizen Army" was a tall,
lean woman wearing the insignia of a company commander
on her dark green uniform.[2] Her slouch hat was turned up at
one side and bore a jaunty feathered cockade. The company
she led marched in perfect step. The Citizen Army included

other women as well, Paul observed to his surprise. Straight, proud, Irish women.

Kathleen, he thought. Kathleen. You would want to be here.

AT the gates of Glasnevin Cemetery a company of Dublin Metropolitan Police were waiting. They watched the crowds pouring through the gates but made no effort to stop them, though several policemen had notebooks in their hands and appeared to be taking names.

A boy in a kilt and tunic asked Paul, "Are you with the corpse, Father?"

The question made him smile. "I accompanied O'Donovan Rossa from America, yes."

The boy handed Paul a pasteboard ticket and a pamphlet. "This is your pass to the graveside, Father—it's just through the gates. This is the literary program; it will tell you about the nationalist movement."

Paul's smile deepened. "I've already heard quite a lot about the nationalist movement."

But he leafed idly through the program until his attention was caught by the words: "Slavery is a thing of the soul. Before a nation can be reduced to slavery its soul must have been cowed, intimidated or corrupted by the oppressor." The author of the words was James Connolly.[3]

The scene around the graveside more nearly resembled a festival than a funeral. Many people were wearing tricolor ribbon badges. More ribbons cordoned off the select area around the grave, which was fast filling up with men in military uniforms and civilians in their Sunday best.

As the coffin was carried forward the honor guard took their positions. Paul could not help looking at Ned Halloran. Then he noticed a young woman in the crowd beside an older one; she too kept her eyes fixed on Ned.

She's quite striking, thought Paul. But not as beautiful as my Kathleen.

My Kathleen.

The priest dug his fingernails into the palms of his hands like the nails in Christ's hands upon the cross.

WHEN the coffin had been lowered into the earth Pádraic Pearse stepped forward to deliver the funeral oration. He wore the insignia of Rathfarnham E Company, Dublin Brigade, Irish Volunteers, on his uniform. From his tunic pocket he took out his speech, then removed his hat and tucked it in the crook of his elbow before he began to speak.[4]

"It has seemed right," he said in his measured cadence, "before we turn away from this place in which we have laid the mortal remains of O'Donovan Rossa, that one amongst us should, in the name of all, speak the praise of that valiant man, and endeavor to formulate the thought and the hope that are in us as we stand around his grave."

SÍLE Duffy moved away from Tom Clarke's wife a few steps until Ned could see her. He gave her an almost imperceptible wink, then his eyes widened in astonishment.

She was holding a tiny girl by the hand.

"I propose to you then, that here by the grave of this unrepentant Fenian we renew our baptismal vows; that here by the grave of this unconquered and unconquerable man we ask of God, each one for himself, such unshakable purpose, such high and gallant courage, such unbreakable strength of soul as belonged to O'Donovan Rossa."

As Pearse spoke his eyes flashed; his usually stolid figure was alight with animation.

"We stand at Rossa's grave, not in sadness, but rather in exaltation of spirit. Splendid and holy causes are served by men who are themselves splendid and holy. O'Donovan Rossa was splendid in the proud manhood of him, splendid in the heroic grace of him, splendid in the Gaelic strength and clarity and truth of him. And all that splendor and pride and strength was compatible with a humility and a simplicity of devotion to Ireland.''

PAUL O'Shaughnessy, who had Pearse speak once before, was struck by the passion of his delivery on this occasion. The orator was laying a spell upon the crowd. No program rustled, no one coughed. It hardly seemed they breathed.

"THIS is a place of peace, sacred to the dead, where men should speak with all charity and all restraint. But I hold it a Christian thing, as O'Donovan Rossa held it, to hate evil, to hate untruth, to hate oppression, and hating them, to strive to overthrow them.

"Our foes are strong, and wise, and wary; but they cannot undo the miracles of God, Who ripens in the hearts of young men the seeds sown by the young men of a former generation. Rulers and defenders of realms had need to be wary if they would guard against such processes.

"Life springs from death, and from the graves of patriot men spring live nations. The defenders of this realm have worked well in secret and in the open. They think they have pacified Ireland. They think that they have purchased half of us, and intimidated the other half.''

Pearse paused to draw a deep breath. Then his voice became a trumpet of defiance, blasting the summer air. Ned Halloran felt a chill run up his spine.

"They think that they have provided against everything; but the fools, the fools, the fools! They have left us our Fenian dead, and while Ireland holds these graves, Ireland unfree shall never be at peace!''

Chapter Thirty-six

In the thundering silence that followed, the only sound was a military command. Rifles were lifted; aimed at the sky. A volley of honor was fired over the grave.

Pádraic Pearse donned his hat and put the folded speech back in his tunic pocket.

People slowly wandered away, still silent, dreaming Pearse's dream; seeing the Ireland he envisioned, Gaelic and free. If he had asked them, they would at that moment have taken up weapons and swept away Britain and all her devices.

Henry Mooney had come to cover the funeral for the *Independent*. He also left deeply moved. How could the Castle underestimate this man? he asked himself. They do so at their peril.

He would not say that, however, in the article he wrote.

As soon as the formalities were over and the honor guard dismissed, Ned plunged into the crowd in search of Síle. At first he could not find her—there were too many people, and few of them were leaving. Everyone present had somebody buried in Glasnevin. Single individuals and family groups still carrying Pearse's words within them like a brimming chalice were seeking the graves of their dear ones.

At last Ned saw Síle and Tom Clarke's wife standing under a somber Irish yew, talking together. His eyes had not deceived him; Precious, half hidden by the long black dress Síle wore, was clinging to her hand.

He strode toward them.

Precious gave a squeal of delight when she saw Ned. Tearing free from Síle, she ran to him. Her laughter as he swept her into his arms rang among the tombstones.

Kathleen Clarke greeted him with a compliment about the fit of his uniform. She had a long oval face and wore her graying hair parted in the middle and drawn softly back. Her clothing was dark and sober—except for the brilliant tricolor badge pinned defiantly to her shoulder.

After chatting for a few moments she went off in search of her husband, and Ned turned to Síle. "What's Precious doing here?"

"I knew you hadn't had a chance to see her lately, so I went to the orphanage and collected her this morning before I met Mrs. Clarke."

"How on earth did you get them to give her to you?"

Síle smiled. "I told them I was your fiancée and we wanted to give the child an outing. You should have seen the look on the matron's face! I'm sure she's counting the days until she gets one of her charges permanently off her hands."

In her sober clothing she might have been any respectable woman. Only her mischievous eyes betrayed her.

Fiancée. How dare she? Ned clenched his teeth. Imagine some common little whore claiming . . . but she wasn't . . . she was . . .

Precious stirred in his arms, twisted around and reached out. "Miss Síle! Now you hold me."

"How did you win her so fast?" Ned wanted to know. "She's a shy girl."

Síle lifted the child from his arms and cuddled her, looking down into her upturned face. "Och, you're not shy, are you?"

"I'm not shy," the child replied. "I'm precious."

Ned and Síle laughed together.

All around them were families paying their respect to the

dead, murmuring prayers, communing with loved ones. Ned and Síle strolled through the cemetery with Precious between them, holding their hands. Ancient yew trees cast pools of funereal shade. The adults paused from time to time to read an inscription on a gravestone, but the child was drawn to images. A marble lamb on a small pedestal caught her attention. "Is a lamb buried here?"

Síle said, "A lot of lambs are buried here, Precious."

"Why?"

"Because they died."

Precious turned to Ned. "Will I die?"

He looked stricken. "Not for a long, long time."

"But I will die?" the child persisted.

Síle met his eyes. "Tell her the truth, Ned. You must always tell children the truth."

"When they're old enough, when they can understand. But not now. Why destroy her innocence?"

"You'll destroy her innocence if you lie to her." She bent to the child. "You will die, Precious; we all will. But none of us knows when."

"And we'll be buried in the ground?"

"We'll go to Jesus," Ned interjected.

Precious gave him a wide-eyed look. "How?"

"He'll come for us."

"Like you came for me when the bad men were shooting? But you left me then. Will Jesus leave us, too?"

Ned had the despairing feeling of someone digging himself deeper into a hole of his own making. "Jesus never leaves us. He is with us always."

"Where?" Precious gazed around at the people walking among the graves. "Which one is Jesus?"

"You can't see him."

"Why? Is he dead like the lamb? I want to understand!"

Síle bit her lip to keep from laughing. "I warned you," she told Ned. Crouching down so her eyes were level with the child's, she said, "Jesus was a very good man who died. His body was put into the ground to sleep. But no one ever completely dies. The part of Jesus we call his spirit lives on."

"Spirit?"

"You have one living inside of you this very minute. It's what makes you Precious."

The little girl looked down at her body. "I don't see it."

"You can't see the wind, either," Síle pointed out. "But it's very real."

"Will my spirit keep living when my body goes to sleep in the ground?"

"It will, I promise."

A smile spread across the small face. "Then that's all right, so!" In another moment she danced away on twinkling feet, pursuing a passing butterfly.

Ned was gazing at Síle as if he had never seen her before. In truth, he felt that he had not; not seen the real Síle, the one inside. The spirit.

THEY spent the rest of the day with Precious. Síle suggested they buy her a meal before returning her to the orphanage. "Look at her, Ned, she's very small for her age. This child wants feeding up."

"What do you know about mothering?"

"Whores know a lot about mothering," she replied with the frankness that always startled him. "That's what many men come to us for, though they would never admit it."

"How can you say things like that, Síle?"

"I've helped bathe the newborn and helped bury the dead; I've seen too much of reality to pretend it doesn't exist."

Not far from the front gates of Glasnevin stood a small restaurant advertising "Tea and Wholesome Cookery." Mary Cosgrave would have scorned the modest facade and grease-stained menu, but Precious was aglow with excitement. "Are we really going to eat here, Ned-Ned?" she asked as he tucked a napkin beneath her chin. "I never ate in a restaurant before. What's on that plate over there? Can I have some?"

"May I have some," Ned corrected gently.

She regarded him solemnly, then repeated, "May I have some?"

"All you want, pet."

The adults watched with amusement as she devoured a portion of roast chicken with bacon, two glasses of milk, and three slices of soda bread with butter. "You're going to explode," teased Síle.

A man at the next table overheard and clapped his hands together. "Boom!"

Fear leaped in the little girl's eyes.

Before she could begin to cry Ned pulled her onto his lap and held her close.

Síle asked anxiously, "What's wrong?"

"Loud noises. Bachelor's Walk."

Síle moved her chair closer to add the circle of her own arms to the wall of protection around Precious, and eventually the child's trembling stopped. "I'm not scared," she insisted.

When it was time to take her back to the orphanage the little girl clung to them. "I want to go home with you, Ned-Ned."

"I can't take you there, sweetheart. I live in a boarding-house for men."

The child turned to Síle. "Then you take me, Miss Síle."

"I'm afraid I don't have a home, at least not a real one."

Precious considered this gravely. Then she said as if the matter was decided, "You shall come and stay with me then. I have a bed anyway."

Síle turned her head away so Ned would not see the glitter of tears in her eyes.

When Precious had been handed over to the matron at the orphanage, Ned told Síle, "I shall take you home now."

"Och, not at all, I can see myself back."

"I cannot allow—"

"Please, Ned. I don't want you to see me there."

He turned toward her. "You said you don't avoid reality. Are you ashamed of what you do?"

She would not look at him. "How could I be otherwise?"

"Then why not give it up? You're still young, you could go back home and make a new start."

"Go home? To Clare?" Her laugh was bitter. "Oh, they

would give me a big welcome, would they not. The girl who ran off with the cattle dealer. Even the dogs in the road know about me back home. In the country gossip outlives the grave. There's no new start to be made there, Ned, not for me.''

"Stay in Dublin then. But leave that house."

"And do what? How would I keep myself?"

"Surely you could find honest work. At least you can read and write."

"I went to the National School for a while." Her lip curled at the memory. "Went barefoot and ragged, with a cold potato in my pocket for my dinner."

"Could you not apply as a shop assistant?"

"And who would I use for references, Mrs. Dolly Drumgold of Faithful Place?"

"What about Tom Clarke? Or is he . . ." Ned hesitated, but he had to ask. "Is he a client?"

To his relief, Síle threw back her head and laughed. "Tom Clarke? You must be joking! If every man was as devoted a husband as Tom Clarke there would be no unhappy wives in this country—and a lot less business for girls like me."

"Then how did you come to know one another?"

"Sometimes I despair of you, Ned me lad. You're as thick as a plank. Do you think only men can be patriots? I come from a Fenian family that goes back generations. The British took everything from them but their longing for freedom. I didn't come away from Clare with my parents' blessing, but I brought their politics with me.

"This city is divided between the rich and the poor, and the poor are Irish. In Clare I had never seen any rich people, I didn't even know what rich was, or how much better life could be. But now I know. I see it every day. I have my nose rubbed in it.

"You ask how I know Tom Clarke? The aristocracy may go to the flash houses, but the middle-level British civil servants and the 'Castle Catholics' come to us. You'd be surprised what men will tell a whore.

"Whenever I hear something useful, I take it to Tom Clarke.''

Chapter Thirty-seven

THE defiance of Pádraic Pearse's graveside oration attracted the attention of the authorities to him at last. For once they were decisive; reprisal was swift. The government launched an examination of his personal finances. In mid-August, the solicitor handling the estate from which Pearse rented the Hermitage received a letter from the Castle warning him of his tenant's "dangerous position."[1] He promptly submitted a demand to Saint Enda's for the immediate payment of six months' rent.

Pádraic Pearse could not meet the demand. But the loss of Saint Enda's would not only break his heart, it would also damage the cause. Through Tom Clarke, he turned in desperation to America for help. Three hundred pounds was sent in time to pay the rent, and the school was safe—for a while.

IN September twelve hundred Irish Volunteers, Ned among them, marched openly through Dublin carrying Howth rifles. The weapons were old but the symbol was potent. That same month the members of Cumann na mBan staged their first parade in their new uniforms. The Fianna were drilling like veterans all around the city. Another corps, the Hibernian Rifles, was formed as an armed breakaway group from the Ancient Order of Hibernians.[2] Meanwhile, a new round of strikes and lockouts on the docks was resulting in increased membership for Connolly's Citizen Army.

No serious attempt was made to restrict any of them.

Neville Grantham told Henry, "One of the reasons the Castle's keeping hands off is because of John Redmond. He insists that interference with the militants would only excite more support for them. Conversely, a few of the senior civil servants agree with the viceroy that we should be taking punitive action 'as a preventive measure.' Birrell's more or less leaving it up to Nathan, and Nathan blows hot and cold; he's just not sure of himself. There's no solid policy, I'm afraid."

That same month Seán MacDermott was released from prison, and he and Thomas Clarke were sworn in as members of the Military Council.[3]

NEWS from the front continued to excite the Irish imagination. Since the Boer War, telegraphy, field telephones, and handheld cameras were giving battle an immediacy previous wars had lacked. Generals had learned the value of propaganda.

THERE was great excitement at Saint Enda's. Between gales of laughter, one of the Fianna told Ned over the telephone, "A British film company paid to use the school as a locale for some 'war' scenes for a historical film. I guess the headmaster forgot to tell his mother. When Mrs. Pearse looked out the window yesterday she saw a company of redcoats come marching up the avenue and the poor woman almost collapsed. She screamed, 'Oh God, they're coming to shoot Pat!' "

Ned remarked, "Fair play to Mr. Pearse for finding a way to make money from the British army."

• • • •

A letter arrived for Ned from New York. Mrs. Kearney gave it to him when he returned home from work, wet through with September rain. "Female handwriting," she commented with no inflection at all.

"A very good friend of mine has gone to Ireland," Kathleen had written. "His name is Father Paul O'Shaughnessy and I believe he is staying with cousins in Dublin. He will be there for some months, so I have asked him to call on you. Please write me when he does, and let me know how he is."

Ned was puzzled by the letter. His sister had not mentioned the priest to him before. But as the weeks passed and no Father O'Shaughnessy appeared, he forgot about him. More pressing matters occupied his mind.

James Connolly was growing increasingly belligerent. The Citizen Army, like the Irish Volunteers, was using the *Fianna Handbook* as its training manual because it was the best source available.[4] The handbook gave detailed directions for various simulated battle situations.

In October, Connolly and Constance Markievicz led members of the Citizen Army and the Fianna on a mock attack of Dublin Castle.

"According to one of my clients, the government was scared witless," Síle told Ned afterward. "The night was hopelessly foggy, and they had no warning. Men and even women came at the Castle from every direction, shouting. The civil servants who were still working inside thought it was a serious attack. Some of them even ran for their lives, leaving doors unlocked behind them. The army *could* have captured the Castle if they meant to!"

The farce reminded Ned of a jerky black-and-white cinema image of cops and robbers, and he laughed. But he hated hearing Síle refer so casually to her "clients."

Pádraic Pearse was not amused by the attack on the Castle: "James Connolly is a loose cannon. If we do not forestall him, he may launch his own revolution on behalf of the workers and end up staging a riot that will destroy any hope of a successful Rising."

Chapter Thirty-eight

N ED looked down at the tearsheet a reporter had just handed him. "Cunard won't take British bookings? What does that mean?"

"They've issued notice that they won't accept as passengers any British subjects who are fit and eligible for service in the army."[1]

"Does that include Irishmen?"

"It will." Henry Mooney looked up from the telephone on his desk. "I've just had word that four hundred emigrants headed for the United States have been refused boarding at Queenstown."

As December dawned the newspapers reported ever more appalling scenes from the battle front. Rumors abounded that Lord Kitchener might be sacked as war secretary. As morale continued to fall, British army recruitment declined further. So did membership in Redmond's National Volunteers. Men continued to join the Irish Volunteers, however, particularly in the country.

Dublin, the 'foreign' city, remained more susceptible to British influence. But even there support for the Irish Volunteers increased substantially.

On the twentieth of December, a single-sentence communiqué from the War Office in London announced that the al-

lies were retreating from the disaster of Gallipoli.[2] Stark black
headlines in the Irish newspapers cast a pall over preparations
for Christmas. Families with menfolk in the British army were
appalled to read the casualty figures: 25,000 dead in the Dar-
danelles, 76,000 wounded, 13,000 missing, and 96,000 seriously ill.

To M and Katty Clarke went to her family home in Limerick
for Christmas, taking Katty's brother Edward Daly and Seán
MacDermott with them.[3] As it happened they traveled down
on the same train as Henry Mooney, who confessed to Ned
before he left, "Even the most rebellious son has to give in
to his mother once in a while."

"Will you go home to Clare for Christmas?" Pádraic
Pearse asked Ned when they met at Volunteer Headquarters
the next day.

"They've urged me to come, but I have dear friends in
Dublin whom I don't want to leave this Christmas. With all
that's going on, it just doesn't seem a good time to be away."

Pearse gave him a strangely sad smile. "I understand. Why
do you not come to us at Saint Enda's for Christmas dinner
and bring your friends with you? I should like all our boys
to regard Saint Enda's as home from home."

Ned was torn. He had asked the orphanage if he might have
Precious for Christmas Day, and permission had been granted.
There was no reason why he could not bring her to Saint
Enda's. Being welcomed into the loving bosom of the Pearse
family would be a wonderful treat for the little girl.

To be honest with himself, Ned wanted to spend Christmas
with Síle, too. But how could he possibly introduce Síle Duffy
to Pádraic Pearse?

Best not to say anything to her about Christmas, then. An
Irish solution for an Irish problem: pretend it does not exist.

His life had become divided into so many parts. There were
moments when he was tired and overextended and wished
with all his heart for one glorious resolution that would bring

everything together, make everything whole and simple and easy.

On Christmas Eve, Father Paul O'Shaughnessy attended Mass and then walked back alone to the cheerless little house in Ringsend. Sometimes he tilted his head and looked up at the stars. Was the same configuration over New York? he wondered.

Christmas for Des and Ina Cahill brought no truce. They still did not speak to one another, a situation whose difficulties were compounded by the fact that Des was ill. He was running a high temperature and eating hardly anything. Ina nursed him conscientiously but offered no word of comfort, though she plumped the solitary pillow and sat on the edge of the bed, offering him spoonfuls of chicken broth.

"Should I go for a doctor?" Paul asked.

Ina looked up. "It's only a cold."

Gazing down at the old man's pasty, bewhiskered face, Paul was dubious. "I would be happy to pay."

Des growled, "Waste of money. Doctors just make you worse." He turned his face away from the proffered spoon.

In the distance the Christmas bells rang out over Dublin.

In the house on Oakley Road in Rathmines a Christmas tree had been set up in the parlor. Thomas MacDonagh carefully tied candles to the branches after little Donagh and baby Barbara were asleep.

"Do make certain they won't tip over," his wife, Muriel, urged as she knelt on the floor, wrapping the last present. "So many fires are started that way."

Tom smiled indulgently at his pretty wife. "I'm very careful."

"Are you? I used to think so, but now . . . I didn't like it, Tom, when you let Seán MacDermott swear you in to the IRB in September.[4] You're in enough danger already with the Volunteers."

"I'm director of training for the country and I command the Second Battalion of the Dublin Brigade. That's all. Both of those positions are honors, Muriel; neither of them is dangerous."

"But why do you have to do them?"

"I thought you understood."

She gave him the patient, loving look women have been giving their menfolk for millennia. "I do understand, Tom; more than you know. You love me and the children very much, but that's never been quite enough. You've always yearned for something... beyond, somewhere. It's as if you're listening to music I could never quite hear. I hoped writing poetry might satisfy you, but I was wrong. You're the sort of man who needs a cause to which he can devote his whole soul, and you've found it in the Irish Volunteers.[5] How can a mere woman compete with that?"

Abandoning the tree, Thomas MacDonagh knelt on the floor beside his wife and gathered her into his arms.

JOSEPH Mary Plunkett kept one drawer of his desk locked at all times. The success of the mock attack on Dublin Castle had not been lost on him. When he returned from the United States in November after having spent two months there working with Clan na Gael on preparations for the Rising, he had promptly begun drawing up outlines for the occupation of Dublin's public buildings.[6]

He was poring over his notes on Christmas Eve when a knock at the door summoned him back to reality. "Joe?" called a feminine voice. "Are you going to Mass with us?"

With a start, he thrust his notebooks back in the drawer and turned the key.

When he opened the door Grace Gifford was standing in the hall chatting with his sisters, Geraldine and Philomena, and his younger brothers, George and Jack. Grace was swathed in a heavy coat and a fur scarf; she smelled of fresh air. The sight of her brought a smile to his face. Grace Gifford was light and life.

When she saw how pale he was, she said, "It's very cold out, Joe. Perhaps it would be best if you stay in tonight?"

"Not at all. I feel fine." He was already reaching for his coat. His throat ached and every breath hurt, but he had no intention of missing Mass.

The summons to God was the overriding imperative; his earliest, deepest love.

SÍLE Duffy's evening lasted very late. The house was ablaze with lights and shrill gaiety. Men who had no place else to go on Christmas Eve—or no place they wanted to go—were more in need of solace on this night than any other. Mrs. Drumgold's reception room reeked of cigar smoke and whiskey, and there was a constant flow of men up and down the stairs. As the night progressed, the customers became soddenly, determinedly drunk.

A man in full evening dress was sprawled at the foot of the stairs, weeping like a baby. Another was leaning against the mantelpiece in the parlor and vomiting into the coal fire in the grate. From one of the bedrooms came squeals of laughter.

Síle accompanied her most recent client to the front door, bade him good-bye, and turned wearily to survey the crowd in the reception room. None of her regulars remained, thank God. And tomorrow the house would be closed; even the brothels observed Christmas Day. Perhaps she could slip upstairs for a few moments and—

"Copper Clare!" Mrs. Drumgold called.

At the sound of her 'house name,' Síle stiffened. "I'm here."

"This nice gentleman has just been asking if we had any redheads in residence." The madam gestured toward a doleful-looking man who stood beside her, nervously twisting his hands. "Would you care to make his acquaintance, my dear? He's come to Dublin from Brussels on business, and Christmas is a bad time to be alone."

"A bad time to be alone," Síle echoed. Then she pasted a smile on her face and held out her hand to the Belgian.

On Christmas morning Mrs. Kearney intercepted Ned as he was leaving his room. "Before Mr. Mooney caught the train for Limerick yesterday he asked me to give you this present," she said, holding out a small parcel wrapped in brown paper and tied with string.

Ned opened the package carefully so the wrappings could be saved. Inside he found the copy of *The Golden Joy* that Henry had purchased on Bloody Sunday. He turned to the page Thomas MacDonagh had signed and smiled down at the familiar handwriting. "A treasure," he murmured to himself.

Tucking the book into his pocket, he set out for the Orphan House for Destitute Females. Precious, freshly scrubbed and with a rather bedraggled pink ribbon in her hair, was waiting for him.

"Where are we going, Ned-Ned?"

"Would you like to go to the country?"

The little girl slipped her hand into his. "Will Miss Síle be there?"

"I'm afraid not, pet."

"Can we bring her with us?"

Ned hesitated. "I imagine she has her own plans."

Precious sighed. "Everybody has plans. Everybody but me. When I'm big, will I have plans?"

"I expect you will. There are things you may want beyond mere subsistence, so you'll need to make plans for them."

"Sub . . . sistence? What does that mean, Ned-Ned?"

"What do you think it means?"

The little girl wrinkled her forehead in a laughable imitation of a frown. "I s'pose . . . it's what you eat and what you wear?"

Ned shook his head. "You continue to astonish me."

"I know what astonish means! It's surprise!"

Ned was grinning. "It is indeed."

But as they boarded the Rathfarnham tram, his good mood

was replaced by a sense of guilt. Síle *should* be with them. He had betrayed her by being afraid of what other people might think.

Coward, he thought. Coward, coward!

In Rathfarnham, Ned engaged the one horse-drawn cab he found waiting at the tram station. "Saint Enda's, please," he told the driver.

The man nodded and tipped his cap to Precious, then handed her aboard as if she were a great lady. His horse had a sprig of holly tucked into the headband of its bridle.

Precious was silent as they turned in at the front gates of the school and proceeded up the drive, but when she saw the house she gasped. "Is this where you live?"

"This is where I went to school."

Her eyes were enormous. "I'm almost old enough to go to school. Can I come here . . . I mean, may I come here?"

Ned hugged her. "You'll attend a school very like this, I hope. If all goes well."

He felt her small body press against the book in his pocket.

When Mrs. Pearse opened the front door to them, Precious peered past her. She seemed afraid to go in. Then she saw the painting of the joyous child above the fireplace and gave a cry of delight. "Look, Ned-Ned! It's me!"

January 6, 1916

HOUSE OF COMMONS VOTES FOR CONSCRIPTION

Chapter Thirty-nine

In the offices of the *Independent* men exchanged glances as the news was relayed to them over the telephone. Once the bill received royal assent it would become the law of the land. One reporter asked the question the others were thinking: "Is Ireland included in the conscription order?"

"Not yet," said their editor, putting down the telephone receiver, "but we bloody well will be. This war began as a European family squabble but it's gone beyond that now; the empire's taking a beating. No man will have the luxury of being allowed to volunteer. We'll all be dragged in by the scruff of the neck if necessary."

That day Ned performed his duties perfunctorily. He had the strange sensation that the earth was shifting under him, and he wondered what Pádraic Pearse was feeling.

Away from the seductive influence of Saint Enda's, Ned realized that Pearse's vision of resurrecting the noble Gael was a romantic dream. In the newspaper business, Ned was constantly confronted with reality.

Some of the Irish were every bit as stupid or as feckless as the English claimed. Others simply did whatever they must in order to survive, even if it meant breaking the law.

And some of the most flawed individuals were also truly great men and women.

No, Ireland's children were not perfect and never would be. But they were human. They deserved to be accorded human dignity. Perhaps they deserved it more than people who had the perceived advantages of wealth and social position, yet treated those at their mercy with the utmost contempt.

For centuries Ireland had paid, in blood, the price of a place in the sun.

The time had come to collect.

ONE of the most ardent enemies of conscription was James Connolly, who had been holding anticonscription rallies for months. He wanted to see Irish manpower put to another use, that of socialist revolution. In the *Workers' Republic* he wrote, "Are we not waiting too long? The time for Ireland's battle is NOW, the place for Ireland's battle is HERE."[1]

On the night of January 18, Tom Clarke told Ned, "A date's been tentatively fixed for the Rising. The Supreme Council's chosen Easter Sunday, the twenty-third of April.[2] In light of this the Military Council think it's imperative we meet with James Connolly to discuss our plans before he goes any further with his own."[3]

The next day Ned went to Liberty Hall.

The hall was a handsomely proportioned building on Beresford Place, facing the quays. It possessed two full storeys and a basement, and once had housed prosperous commercial firms. Changing tenantry had brought about a decline, however. As home for Dublin's labor movement, the hall was decidedly shabby.

Until recently anyone—aside from the police—could enter Union Headquarters whenever they pleased. But times had changed. Now there was a guard at the ground floor entrance. He stopped Ned and asked his business just as Constance Markievicz arrived.

She was wearing a complete Citizen Army uniform, but had covered the trousers with a skirt to avoid shocking the good people of Dublin.[4] "It's all right," she assured the sentry. "I know this man. His name's Ned Halloran and he's a Volunteer."

"I'm here to see James Connolly, Madame."

"You'll find him up on the first floor; anyone there can point him out to you. When you've finished, come back to me if you have time."

Ned was pleased by the invitation. "I'll make time, Madame." He knew her friends called her "Con," but such familiarity was beyond him. Not with a countess!

The dilapidated printing press in the basement was propped up on bricks and made a fearful clatter that reverberated through the building.⁵ Ned was glad to escape to the first-floor offices, although they were not much quieter. Dingy corridors opened into small, equally dingy cubicles crowded with a jumble of boxes, cartons, paper stock, and makeshift filing cabinets. A youth in shirtsleeves directed him toward a bull of a man who was giving a coworker a blistering tongue-lashing. Ned waited until the tirade stopped, then politely cleared his throat.

James Connolly whirled around. "And what the hell do you want?"

It was Ned's first face-to-face meeting with the labor leader. Short and stocky, bandy-legged, with unkempt eyebrows and a thick mustache, he was very much one of the working class he championed. When Ned introduced himself, Connolly's handshake crushed his fingers. "You're one of Pearse's lads, are you?"

"I was, sir; a student at Saint Enda's. I'm a Volunteer now."

Glowering, Connolly turned Ned's hand over. "No blisters on your palm. You elitists have life too bloody soft."

Ned had never been dismissed as an elitist before. The assumption startled him.

"I met Pearse last September in the Gaelic League offices," Connolly remarked, "when it looked like the IRB was going to put together an insurrection and employ the Volunteers. But nothing's come of it. That's what happens when you have a lot of idealists sitting around philosophizing. Since then I've talked with Pearse several times—and with Eoin MacNeill, too—but it's a waste of energy. They're too cautious to be revolutionaries; it's up to the Citizen Army now. Everything's always up to the working man. We carry the whole world on our backs and don't get a blind bit of thanks.''

As he spoke Connolly simultaneously watched the work going on around him and added a column of figures on the back of an envelope.

He's like Mr. Pearse, Ned thought; busy every moment. ''We're not as idle as you think, sir. In fact, that's why I'm here. The Military Council would like you to come meet with them so they can inform you of their plans.''

Connolly raised his bushy eyebrows. ''The Military Council?''

''Will you meet them, sir? Now?''

''Bloody hell, can't you see we're busy here? Who the hell do they think they are?''

''Pádraic Pearse, Joseph Plunkett, Seán MacDermott, Eamonn Ceannt,'' Ned replied literally. ''And Thomas Clarke, of course.''

Connolly fixed him with a hard stare. The silence lengthened. Then, ''All right. I'll spare an hour, no more. Where do we go?''

''There's a motor cab waiting in the service alley behind the hall.''[6]

Connolly raised his eyebrows still farther. ''Is there indeed? They were that sure of me, were they?''

''Not at all, Mr. Connolly. If you don't come out in the next thirty minutes the cab will drive away without you.''

''And you, are you coming with me?''

Don't be seen leaving with him, Tom Clarke had said.

''I'm afraid I have to go back to my own work, sir.''

''But it's all right to take me away from mine, is it?'' Connolly gave an angry snort as he turned on his heel and left the room.

He then disappeared as completely as if the earth had swallowed him.[7]

•   •   •

H<small>IS</small> assignment completed, Ned went in search of Constance Markievicz. He found her in a small room in the basement where she was packing grenades into straw-filled boxes.[8] Other boxes were plainly marked "Gelignite." The thundering printing press made the whole area vibrate.

Ned felt his scrotum tighten. "Are those things safe?"

"Of course not, that's the whole point." She wiped her hands and turned toward him. "Are you hungry? Since it's almost two o'clock I assume you're here instead of eating your dinner. I always bring a bag of cakes for the sentries, and I may even have brought a couple of sandwiches for myself. Shall we go upstairs and see?"

Ned was glad to leave the basement, but he remained acutely conscious of the potential explosive power beneath them.

He wondered what Mama would say if she could see the company he was keeping. "It's hard to think of you as a countess, Madame," he confessed as he lifted a slice of bread and found cheese and pickle. Ned was fond of cheese and pickle himself.

She laughed an easy, full-throated laugh, throwing back her head like a man. "Sometimes it is for me, too. A title was never my ambition."

"What did you want, then?"

She stopped chewing to consider the question. "Simply to be the person I needed to be. Looking back, I suppose I was a disappointment to my parents. You see, they were so very *English.* From the first they assumed I'd marry a wealthy man of my own class, have a fine home, and raise more little aristocrats in the same mold. I don't think they ever considered any other possibility. Surely they didn't expect me to become an Irish revolutionary. But for me, being Irish was not a condition of birth but an option. It was something I chose of my own free will."

"Forgive me for asking, Madame, but why?"

"Ah. How to answer that? Let me just say . . . magic came into my life.

"I have pictures of my sister and myself as young girls in white lace and elegant poses.[9] We had such complexions! The young men clustered around us like bees to the lilacs. Eva was considered one of the greatest beauties in Ireland, and I wasn't so bad myself. I was presented to Queen Victoria and went to London 'for the season.' But then in 1894 a man called Willie Yeats came to visit my family at Lissadell. He spoke of fairies, and magic, and old Irish legends, and though I was a grown woman I was enchanted. Not by Willie—by Ireland.

"Marriage didn't interest me. Being some man's adjunct looked like a trap, and I had no intention of falling into a trap. I ignored the plans Mother had made for my life and set off for Paris to study art instead. Women in our set didn't do that—but I did. I lived, ah, how I lived! I even"—she smiled reminiscently—"had a photograph taken of myself smoking and wearing knickerbockers that showed my legs below the knee. People at home were scandalized, but I enjoyed every minute.

"Then when I was thirty and a confirmed spinster I finally fell in love. It was as much a shock to me as to everyone else. Casimir Markievicz was huge and gorgeous and good at everything he did. But he wasn't an Anglo-Irish Protestant. He was Polish, a second son living on an allowance, and his title was only a courtesy inherited from an obscure ancestor. Worse still, he was Roman Catholic. *And* years younger than myself. *And* had already been married and had children.

"If I had wed a Hottentot my family could hardly have been more dismayed," Madame concluded airily.

Obviously what her family thought was of little importance. Ned was enthralled. The freedom she had taken for herself was one most Irish women did not dare dream about. There were rumors that she had allowed her husband to sunbathe in the nude at her country cottage before he went off to the Balkans as a war correspondent. Subsequently, a visiting French journalist had written of her Rathmines home, Surrey House: "The salon of Madame Markievicz is not a salon, it's a military HQ."[10] Any militant friend who needed a bed was welcome, and several of the Fianna were always in residence.

Ned entertained a delicious daydream of being invited there himself as he drank the last of his tea and finished his sandwich.

Dining with Madame.

WALKING back across Butt Bridge—which Dubliners more descriptively called the Swivel Bridge[11]—Ned was hardly aware of the bustling boat traffic beneath him. As a navigable tidal river, the Liffey had brought Dublin into being more than a thousand years earlier and remained its commercial gateway to Europe. Without the river the city's economic base would collapse. Dublin Port provided thousands of jobs.

Usually Ned found the river's commercial activity fascinating. What cargo was that ship bringing from what exotic port? Where were those laden barges going? What sort of lives were lived by the men who owned them? He could stand on the quays for hours if he had the time, spinning romances in his head.

On this afternoon, however, his thoughts about the river were different. He was trying to shape abstractions into words which he might, someday, write down.

Someday.

He envisioned the Liffey's dark current as Now, separating Past and Future. One must cross over that darkness to get from one to the other. They would all have to cross. But what were they leaving?

As surely as Gaelic Ireland had seduced Pádraic Pearse, it had captivated Constance Markievicz. And how many others?

He paused in the middle of the bridge to stare down into the water.

Perhaps Ireland had never been what they imagined. Perhaps the looted, impoverished land the emigrants fled was all there was of *Cathleen ni Houlihan,* and her ancient splendor was only the landscape of the heart.

Did that make her less real—or more?

THE next day was Friday. The *Workers' Republic* was published, as usual, bearing Saturday's date. Connolly customarily wrote his editorials a week ahead. The editorial of the twenty-second was defiantly critical of the republican movement for its perceived lack of revolutionary will. It condemned the non-labor patriot for believing that "patriotism needs no foundation to rest upon other than the brainstorms of its poets, orators, journalists, and leaders."[12]

On the surface everything seemed normal at Liberty Hall. But an astute observer would have noticed increased activity, with more members of the Citizen Army arriving every hour.

Late Friday afternoon Constance Markievicz sent a message to Ned. The note was handed to him by a small boy in a tweed cap as Ned was leaving the Carlisle Building. "Must talk to you," was all it said. "Hurry. Con."

When Ned reached Liberty Hall one of the first people he saw there was Mary Cosgrave's friend, Eliza Goggins. With a preoccupied expression on her face, she was just leaving the building. Ned nodded to her but she gave no sign of recognition.

Con Markievicz met him just inside the door. This time there was a Browning automatic pistol in her belt. "Where is Jim?" she demanded without preamble.

"Is he not here?"

"Of course he's not here; surely you know that. You were the last person to see him yesterday. What happened between you?"

Ned kept his voice steady. "I delivered a confidential message to him and then had a sandwich with you and went back to the *Independent*. Where Mr. Connolly went I cannot say."

Her gray-blue eyes flashed fire. "Can't? Or won't?"

"Please don't ask me to lie, Madame."

"Pádraic Pearse has a long reach," she observed wryly. "No, I won't ask you to lie. But tell me this, was he kidnapped? Or arrested?"

Ned did not answer.

In an urgent voice she said, "You must understand. We've already telephoned his family in Belfast but they know nothing.[13] This is very serious. We had an agreement among us— Jim, his second-in-command Michael Mallin, and myself— that if any one of us was arrested, the other two would act immediately.[14] I am determined to start the revolution myself, *today,* if anything's happened to James Connolly!"

This was the very thing Pearse had feared. There was no time to ask anyone else's advice, Ned would have to handle it himself. All right, he thought. All right.

He chose each word with utmost care. "Madame, I can assure you Mr. Connolly was not arrested. I can also assure you he is safe."

A little of the tension went out of her face. "And you don't lie."

"I do not lie."

She drew a deep breath. "All right, then, I believe you— though hundreds might not. Michael Mallin is convinced the IRB's behind it and has gone to deliver an ultimatum to them. We're on the brink of an explosion, so I urge you to get word to whoever is with Jim, wherever he is, that unless he returns to us soon there will be dire consequences!"

Chapter Forty

NED was afraid Madame Markievicz might never speak to him again. He felt the loss keenly. In the peculiar way of people who appreciate something most after it is gone, he realized that her singular personality carried a message for him. Pádraic Pearse admired her, this woman whose reputation shocked the establishment.

If Pearse approved of Markievicz, might he not approve of Síle Duffy?

But it was too late to go back and take Síle to Saint Enda's for Christmas.

ON Sunday afternoon Ned made a telephone call to Larkfield and waited impatiently while a maid summoned Joe Plunkett to the phone. In the background he could hear a clamor as if a party was in progress.

"Is there any news of Mr. Connolly?" Ned asked when Plunkett came on the line.

"I understand he showed up very late last night at Surrey House and told Con Markievicz he'd 'been through hell.' But he wouldn't tell her anything else."

"Is he all right?"

"Of course he is. Superb, in fact. A good man with a fine

mind, James Connolly. We're delighted that he's seen where our common interest lies and is throwing in his lot with the Brotherhood. The Citizen Army and the Volunteers will be working together from now on."

Ned digested this news with a sense of relief. If the Citizen Army and the Volunteers were going to be allies, surely Madame Markievicz would forgive him for the small part he had played. She was far too bighearted to hold a grudge. He hoped.

Suddenly a blast of laughter came through the telephone receiver. "What's going on over there?" he asked Plunkett.

"Can you hear them? That's just the lads skylarking about."

"What lads?"

"Since the war began quite a few Irish men are coming home from England to join the Volunteers. We're putting up as many as we can here. Larkfield's turned into a garrison. We've made the old mill on the estate into a barracks for them, but they're in and out of the house all the time. And you'll enjoy this: they've begun calling themselves 'Pearse's Own.' "[1]

"How does your family feel about seeing their home turned into a military camp?"

Plunkett laughed. "The girls enjoy it tremendously, and Father's hired one of the lads, Michael Collins, as his bookkeeper. Mick is a West Cork man who was employed in London as a civil servant. Father gives him a pound a week and his lunch." Plunkett interrupted himself with a fit of coughing.

James Connolly might be all right, but Ned had serious doubts about Joe Plunkett's health. Since the trip to America it had been going downhill.

The day was bitterly cold. When Ned stepped out of the call box the wind hit him like a fist to the face. I hope Joe doesn't go out in this, he thought.

He was not surprised to find Tom Clarke in a good mood. "Well done," he said as Ned entered the news agency. "Have you heard anything?"

"I just talked to Joe Plunkett. He told me Connolly's with us at last."

"We're going to make real progress now, and not a moment too soon. The Rising's coming, Ned. *Our* Rising." In an ebullient mood, Clarke leaned his elbows on the counter. "My mother was from Tipperary and my father was a Fermanagh man, but the aftermath of the Famine drove them out long before I was born. I didn't see Ireland until I was ten years old—the year of the 1867 Rising, that was.² The air was full of talk about the Fenians then. For a time, just a very short time, there was hope in Ireland. I remember. I remember how my parents lit up with it like a flame."

That flame has never been extinguished, Ned thought as he watched Tom Clarke. "Has Miss Duffy been in today?"

Clarke's eyes glinted mischievously. "Strange thing about the two of you; I'd swear you know what each other's thinking. She was in here not ten minutes ago asking about you.

"My Katty and me are like that. Let me yearn to be out in my garden, and even if I don't say a word, she knows somehow. See that jam jar on the shelf behind me? It's empty now, but when the first daffodils bloom she'll cut some for me so I'll have flowers in here."

Ned was impatient with the digression. "Do you know where Síle went?"

"Back to the house, I expect."

Back to Mrs. Drumgold's, though Clarke was too tactful to use the name.

"If I had any courage . . ."

Clarke gave Ned a sharp look. "What's that you say?"

"Nothing. I'll see you tomorrow."

He knew where the house was. In his rounds he had learned every street and laneway in Dublin, but had assiduously avoided Faithful Place. Until now.

Returning to his room, Ned shaved and dressed in his best clothes. He was glad Henry was not there to ask embarrassing questions; his friend had not returned after Mass that morning. Ned fumbled under the mattress until he found a jam jar of his own, the one containing his savings. Then he put the entire amount into his pocket and set off for the brothel.

At the corner opposite Faithful Place he noticed the latest recruiting poster.[3] Plastered on a wall was a large, brilliantly colored picture of two women and a small child standing in an open window, gazing out at the landscape. Uniformed soldiers were marching away through that landscape. The women were clasping each other and wearing exalted expressions. The slogan on the poster read "Women of Britain say GO!"

Ned gave a wry smile. It must be getting harder to find men who would volunteer to die in France and Belgium.

When he reached Mrs. Drumgold's house, the hardest part was knocking on the door. After a considerable wait it opened and a heavily made-up woman with frizzed hair looked out at him. "Can I help you?"

"I'm here to call upon Miss Síle Duffy."

"To call upon?" she mimicked. "Miss Síle Duffy?"

"If you please."

The woman flashed a professional style and held the door a little wider. Ned caught a glimpse of a carpeted staircase ascending into gloom. "I think you mean Copper Clare. She's one of our best girls, though. Are you sure you can afford her services?"

In all their conversations, Síle had never mentioned her professional name. Ned was taken aback, but he swiftly recovered. Once employed, courage was gathering momentum. In his most formal Saint Enda's style he said, "I am able to pay for her time if that is what you require, but I do not seek her 'services.' I have come to ask her to have dinner with me in a respectable restaurant."

"Respectable?" The woman's eyes widened. "Aren't you the funny one? Clare!" she shouted over her shoulder. "Someone here for you! Step inside, young man, and wait in the parlor. You want to buy a drink while you wait? We have wine or whiskey."

Feeling decidedly uncomfortable, Ned took a seat on a brocaded couch facing a large gilt-framed mirror. There were two young women in the room, neither of them Síle. They darted amused glances at him and giggled behind their hands.

Within a few moments Síle herself appeared, dressed in a skimpy frock with too much bosom exposed. When she saw Ned the color drained from her face.

He stood up politely. "I came to ask if you would have dinner with me."

"If he pays me for your time before you leave this house," said the madam in a no-nonsense voice, "he can take you wherever he likes."

Síle was struggling for words. Ned took a step toward her and held out his hand. "Please. Just do it."

She turned and fled from the parlor.

Ned sat back down on the couch. Mrs. Drumgold folded her arms across her chest and stood looking at him, bemused.

After what seemed an interminable wait, Síle reentered the room. This time she was wearing a plain hobble skirt with a ruffled shirtwaist and carrying a coat over her arm. Her face glowed from recent scrubbing.

Mrs. Drumgold went to stand in front of the door with her hand out. Ned held Síle's coat while she put it on, then paid the madam the amount demanded. When she stepped aside he put his hand under Síle's elbow and ushered her through the door as a gentleman should.

But he could not resist saying over his shoulder, "Don't worry. I'll have her back at a 'respectable' hour."

When they were safely on the street Síle burst into laughter. "You're mad, you know that? Barking mad!"

"Copper Clare?"

"After my hair color and my birthplace. When a girl enters a house the first thing she loses is her identity."

"You haven't lost your identity. You're my friend Síle Duffy and we're walking out together."

He took her to the Gresham Hotel for dinner. If he was going to be public about his affection, he reasoned, he might as well go the whole way. Then perhaps he would not be afraid anymore.

She hesitated at the broad front steps leading to the hotel lobby. "There might be men in there who know me, Ned. Are you sure you want to be seen with me?"

"Take my arm."

The headwaiter in the Gresham's handsomely furnished dining room gestured toward a table snowy with linen. "Will that do, sir?"

Ned turned to Síle. "Will it?"

She squeezed his arm. "I think it's just grand."

As they followed the headwaiter Ned noticed several men looking at Síle. From their expressions he could not tell if any of them recognized her or if they were simply admiring her.

She walked like a queen.

When they were seated Ned ordered for both of them. The prices alarmed him, but on Mr. Pearse's advice he had been saving since he first went to work at the *Independent*. In addition, Kathleen always sent him money for his birthday and Christmas. Without Mary to spend it on, the amount in the jam jar had grown. If this night cost his last ha'penny he would not complain. It was worth it for the way Síle looked sitting across the table from him.

Basking in her happy smile, Ned indulged in a moment of self-congratulation. I'm doing this well, he thought. I'm really doing this well.

Then over Síle's shoulder he saw Henry Mooney enter the dining room with another man and two well-dressed young women.

Ned fought back an urge to dive under the table, but it was too late. Henry saw him, sketched a salute, and made some smiling remark to his companions. All four came over to the table. Henry did not see Síle's face until he stood beside her and she looked up at him.

There could be no doubt about recognition now; it leaped between them like a hostile spark. But before Henry could say anything Ned was on his feet. His eyes locked with the journalist's. "Allow me to present Miss Síle Duffy," he said. "My fiancée."

WHEN a leisurely dinner was finally concluded, Ned walked Síle back to Faithful Place. Through their linked arms he could feel her shaking with laughter.

"What's so funny?"

"I wouldn't have missed that for anything! There was your friend introducing his friend, and you being so polite and formal, and the three of you chatting away about sport and politics. And me and Tess Trilby and The Diamond looking as if we dined on feathers and shat pearls."

"Tess Trilby and The Diamond?"

"Introduced to you as Miss This and Miss That, or somesuch. They're whores, same as me. Did you not know?" She was laughing so hard she pulled her arm away from his and leaned against a lamppost, hands pressed to her stomach.

"But they looked like . . . I mean . . ."

"Like ladies? They should. They're very expensive, they work in a flash house. Gentlemen escort them to the best places to show them off to other gentlemen."

Ned's jaw muscles clenched. "Is that what gentlemen do with you? Take you to places like the Gresham?"

"Och, Ned, I'm not in a flash house. No man's ever taken me to a fancy restaurant or much of anyplace, except you. It put a real flea in their ears, seeing me there. I'll be the talk of the Village tomorrow. Imagine me being introduced as someone's fiancée in the Gresham Hotel!"

Ned was struggling to keep his temper. "I did not say it as a joke."

Síle stopped laughing. Her eyes searched his face in the light of the street lamps. "Then why?"

"Mr. Pearse taught me to say what I mean and mean what I say. Unless I've lost my temper entirely, I do. Does that not tell you anything?"

When she spoke, her voice was almost a whisper. "I'm afraid to believe what it tells me."

Ned gathered her into his arms and pressed her cheek against his shoulder. "Don't be afraid, Síle Duffy. Don't you ever be afraid. I'm afraid enough for both of us."

Returning her to Mrs. Drumgold was out of the question now. Nor could Ned take Síle to Middle Gardiner Street. Louise Kearney was a highly respectable widow woman; no female visitors were allowed in the rooms of her gentlemen lodgers. As he held her in his arms, his mind was racing.

His impetuosity had presented him with an enormous problem. But had he been so impetuous, really? Had he not been giving expression to something that had been growing inside him for a long time? Perhaps that is what all ideas were: seeds that grew in the dark until it was time to burst in the light.

"I don't have enough money to support a wife yet, Síle," he said, burying his nose in her fragrant hair. The smell of white lilac. "But I shall. I'm ambitious. I'm going to work hard and make a name for myself."

"Are you asking me to wait for you?"

"I'm asking you to be my intended wife."

She was very still in his arms.

He said, "That means leaving Mrs. Drumgold and all she represents."

"Where would I go?"

"What about the Clarkes? They have a house on Richmond Avenue now, with a garden for Tom. I could take you there tonight if you're willing. It's where they took Seán MacDermott when he was released from prison."

"A proper house in Fairview? With a garden?"

"Indeed."

Her body was shaking again. This time she was crying.

Within the hour Síle Duffy was in Tom Clarke's parlor. She was sitting on the edge of her chair while Ned stood beside her and held her hand as tightly as he dared.

"I'm not sure about this," she was saying. "I have money saved, hidden in my room. And my clothes—I can't just abandon everything I worked so hard for."

"Don't worry," Tom said. "I'll send someone to collect your belongings in the morning. Just tell me what you want and where it is."

"I don't want to cause you any trouble. Mrs. Drumgold has some dangerous men working for her."

Behind his spectacles, Clarke's eyes gleamed. "So do I, Little Girl." It was the first time Ned had heard Clarke call Síle by a nickname, but after tonight he thought nothing would surprise him anymore.

Katty Clarke served tea all around, with a stiff dose of whiskey in the men's cups. "There's no question of you going back," she told Síle firmly. "We'll put you on the couch tonight, then tomorrow I'll ask around and see if we can find you another place. Someplace nice. You would be welcome to stay here indefinitely, but every nationalist household in Dublin has become a hostel lately. We're packed chock-a-block as it is—not to mention having two cats, a dog, and a dozen canaries."[4]

"I can pay my way out of my savings," Síle offered.

Tom Clarke shook his head. "You can earn your keep by helping the cause. There's going to be plenty of work to do, don't you worry. Some men think women are fragile flowers that have to be kept out of harm's way, but—"

"Women," his wife interrupted, "are the backbone of nationalism. As you know, Cumann na mBan split when the Volunteers split, and the majority went with Redmond. I daresay they're sorry now! But it meant that those of us in Central Branch who kept the faith, like me and Eamonn Ceannt's wife, have ten times more to do. The men simply could not get along without us. I myself have all sorts of assignments, some of them top secret."

Clarke winked at Ned. "Indispensable," he said solemnly. It was a long word for Tom Clarke.

By the time Ned wearily bade Síle good night and headed back toward Middle Gardiner Street, the first pale streaks of dawn were showing over the Irish Sea.

When he entered the room he shared with Henry Mooney, the journalist woke up. He sat up in bed and started to say something.

Ned reached for the gaslight and turned it up to high. "What?"

Once again Henry found himself regarded by cold green eyes he would not have liked to see looking down a rifle barrel at him. "Were you serious tonight?"

"Dead serious."

"You know what you're doing?"

"I'm planning to marry an exceptional woman. I suspect they aren't that easy to find."

Henry read those eyes a moment longer, then held out his hand. "You're right, they aren't. Let me be the first to wish you, sincerely, the greatest happiness. If there's anything I can ever do for either of you, I will."

January 27, 1916

BRITISH LABOUR PARTY VOTES
OVERWHELMINGLY AGAINST CONSCRIPTION

January 27, 1916

MILITARY SERVICE BILL RECEIVES
ROYAL ASSENT. CONSCRIPTION BECOMES LAW.

Chapter Forty-one

JAMES Connolly was back. He told no one aside from his wife where he had been. "I've been walking in the country," was his standard answer to everyone but Con Markievicz. To her he confided, "I've been through hell," but gave no details. He simply resumed managing the union, printing a newspaper, and leading his militia with his usual dynamism.

In an editorial on the fifth of February, Connolly wrote, "Deep in the heart of Ireland has sunk the sense of the degradation wrought upon its people, so deep and humiliating that no agency less powerful than the red tide of war on Irish soil will ever enable the Irish race to recover its self-respect."[1]

It was observed, however, that he was no longer condemning the republicans for their inaction.

OTHER writers were making their voices heard. The *Daily Express* published the Manifesto of the Irish Volunteers on its front page.[2] Even the avowed pacifist Francis Sheehy-Skeffington wrote a strongly nationalistic article for the *Century*.[3]

• • •

BEYOND the shores of Ireland the world and the war went
on. On the seventh of February, the *Independent* reported that
Germany had accepted full responsibility for the loss of lives
on the *Lusitania* and had agreed that the United States had
the right to claim indemnity.[4]

Food shortages in Berlin were causing riots.

In London the government announced that 400,000 women
would be recruited to till the fields in the absence of their
menfolk. A royal proclamation banned the importation of paper and tobacco, and there was an appeal against the use of
motorcars and motorcycles for pleasure.

NED'S latest letter from Kathleen said:

> You have not written in many weeks and I am worried
> about you. Is everything all right? I try to follow news
> from home as best I can. A young Irishwoman called
> Nora Connolly was in New York in December and John
> Devoy introduced us.[5] I like her very much. She is only
> nineteen, your age. Her family lived here for years while
> her father was learning about American trade unions and
> "breathing the air of freedom" as Nora puts it. They are
> back in Ireland now, where her father is the leader of a
> working-class militia called the Citizen Army. Have you
> ever heard of them?
>
>   Nora says there are women in the Citizen Army who
> drill right along with the men. She tells me it is not like
> that with Cumann na mBan because the Volunteers only
> allow women to do things like cooking meals and rolling
> bandages.
>
>   I promised her I would help raise money for the Cit-
> izen Army, but realistically I do not know how much I
> can do. Alexander is not as generous with me as he used
> to be. He has fired my housemaid, Della, who was a good
> friend to me, and hired another woman whom I do not
> like. I feel as if I am being watched all the time.
>
>   By the way, have you heard anything from my friend,

Father O'Shaughnessy? Please do let me have news of
him.

    Your loving sister,
    Caitlín

Ned was disturbed by the letter. Obviously there were problems in his sister's marriage; problems severe enough to make
her hand shake when she penned ''I feel as if I am being
watched all the time.''

He resolved to find Kathleen's priest and question him.

Ned had become almost as good as Henry at sniffing out
information. Within a day of receiving the letter he discovered
that a Father O'Shaughnessy had accompanied O'Donovan
Rossa's body to Ireland and was remaining in the country for
a year on sabbatical. His address was a cottage in Ringsend.

By the time Ned left work that February afternoon it was
already dark. As he cycled along the quays, yellow lights
danced like malign spirits on the oily surface of the Liffey.

When Ned reached Ringsend he called in to the Yacht Pub
and a toothless barman gave him directions to the Cahill
house. ''This ain't Dessie's local, but I know the place sure.
Go up the road to the first right but don't take that. Go on to
the T-junction and then go left and right again. It's the second
door down from where the public watering trough used to be.
Ye can't miss it.''

He might have, except there was a crowd gathering outside
the house. As Ned was leaning his bicycle against the wall a
priest came out to invite them inside. In the light from the
open doorway Ned recognized him. ''Father, weren't you at
City Hall with O'Donovan Rossa?''

The priest turned toward Ned. His eyes widened. ''You
were there, too. I remember.''

''I was there, Father. I'm—''

''Ned Halloran.'' The priest exhaled slowly. ''You couldn't
be anyone else. Please come inside for a few minutes, will
you? I apologize for this, but my cousin died and we're about
to take the body to the church for tomorrow's funeral. You
and I can talk afterwards.''

Ned whipped off his tweed cap and arranged his features in a suitable expression of reverence, then followed Paul into the dingy little house. He understood the Removal of the Remains as an American might not.

Des Cahill, in his open coffin, occupied a table in the center of the room. Ned and the priest had to edge their way through a crowd of relatives, friends, neighbors, and the ubiquitous strangers drawn to any death in Ireland.

Paul said, "Excuse me please," in his confident American voice.

Ned shyly murmured, "Sorry."

The air was stifling. Paul knelt and prayed silently beside the coffin while an elderly woman Ned assumed to be the widow stood to one side, fingering her rosary. Ned made his way over to her and whispered, "Sorry for your trouble." Other women were patting her solicitously, and an ancient shawlie kept rocking back and forth and wailing in Irish, *Ochóne, ochóne!*

The priest signed the cross and stood up. The coffin was closed, the lid screwed in place. Four men hoisted it onto their shoulders and set off with the rest of the procession forming behind them. The widow paused to take her heavy shawl from the peg and sweep it across her shoulders.

"I never did like that man," she said.

Then she followed the corpse out the door.

After the Removal Ned and Father Paul went to Dessie's local, a pub called Peter North's.[6] The publican had attended the Removal. As Mrs. Cahill was heading for home he had given her a sugar bag clinking with coins. "We collected from Dessie's mates to help you in your time of trouble."

At the funeral the next day the publican would be standing right beside the family. Such customs were the same, city or country. Afterward he would shepherd Dessie's pub mates back to his establishment to give the deceased a properly wet send-off. The postfuneral "sympathizing" would include a tearful and lofty tribute to the dead man and conclude with a boisterous singsong in the small hours.

On the evening of Dessie's Removal, Peter North's was crowded with dockworkers. The spittoons were overflowing.

Ned and Paul managed to find a relatively quiet corner, and Ned ordered ale for both of them.

"I should have looked you up sooner," Paul apologized. "Kathleen did give me your address."

"You might not have found me anyway, I'm rarely at home these days."

"Ah, yes, the Volunteers."

"Among other things." Ned did not intend to divulge any information about himself to this stranger.

Paul was equally unwilling to discuss personal matters.

They circled each other conversationally in the same way that two dogs meeting in the street circle one another.

"Judging from her letters, my sister thinks highly of you."

"I hold Mrs. Campbell in the highest regard."

"Do you see much of her?"

"Until I came to Ireland I did. I was her parish priest."

Ned rubbed the cleft in his chin with his thumb. He was going to have to give something to get something, it appeared. "Her last letter to me indicated she was having some problems."

"With her husband?" The response came too fast; the anxiety that leaped in the priest's eyes gave too much away.

"Has she been having trouble with her husband, Father? As her priest, I assume you would know."

Paul retired behind his professional mask. "You know I can't repeat anything revealed to me in the confessional."

"What about outside the confessional? I've met Alexander Campbell; he isn't the man I would have wanted for her."

"No."

"He seems coarse-fibered under that smooth surface."

"Yes."

By now Ned was certain something was very wrong. He determined to force the priest out of his reticence. "She says she's being watched. She makes it sound quite sinister"— Ned chose the word deliberately—"and I'm worried about her safety."

Paul stared at him for a long moment, then closed his eyes. "Oh, God."

Ned caught the priest's wrist in an iron grasp. "You do know about her trouble, whatever it is! I think you'd best tell me."

"There isn't anything you can do about it, not with her in New York."

"When you were in New York did you do anything about it?" Ned replied harshly. The priest winced, but Ned did not care. "Tell me this: is Alexander abusive? It might surprise you to know, Father, that Ireland has a long reach. I have certain connections in America. If Campbell's done anything to hurt my sister I'll see that he regrets it."

Looking at those green eyes, Paul did not have a doubt in the world.

Actually, Ned had no idea if anyone in the IRB could or would help him. But if his sister was in danger he would do whatever he must.

Paul stood up. "Do you want a whiskey? I think I need one." He thrust his hand into his pocket and drew out his wallet. "It's my shout."

Ned smiled. At least the priest was learning Dublin slang.

The whiskey was strong and good. Paul took a deep drink and shuddered as the liquid burned down his throat. Ned waited for the Irish "water of life" to work its magic, then leaned toward Paul and said, "Please talk to me now, Father. I'm her brother; you can trust me."

To his surprise, Paul found himself relaxing. There was something about the young man that encouraged confidence—or perhaps it was just the whiskey. "I did try to help your sister, Ned. Her husband had some thugs beat me up."

Ned was shocked. "He had a priest *assaulted*? Why?"

Paul chose to answer the first question but not the second. "I can't prove he was responsible, but I'm relatively certain. That's the reason I'm here, you see. My bishop felt it would be a good idea to send me away for a while for my own safety."

"And leave Kathleen unprotected?"

"My being there just made things worse, I'm afraid."

"Why?" Even as Ned repeated the question, a suspicion was dawning. "You . . . and my sister?"

"We're not lovers," Paul said quickly. "I give you my word it hasn't gone that far. But I love her. And I think she loves me."

Never in his life had Ned read such misery in another man's face.

THE next day Ned spoke to Tom Clarke. It was no good taking the problem to Pádraic Pearse; Pearse would only have sent him to Clarke anyway.

Ned had never asked the old Fenian anything about the IRB's American connections; Clarke told people what they needed to know and nothing more. But now Ned had to ask, which meant giving some sort of explanation.

"My sister's husband is abusing her," he told Clarke. "Rather badly, I am told. Is there someone in New York who could . . ."

"Threaten him for you? The Brotherhood doesn't go in for bullyboy tactics, Ned; it was formed to put an end to that very sort of thing. Why doesn't she go to the police?"

"The police here aren't interested in domestic squabbles, and I doubt if the New York police are any different. But you just said the Fenians were organized to resist the bullying of the weak by the strong. My sister's been good to the cause, Tom. She's raised money for Saint Enda's and the Volunteers both. Now she's being bullied—and worse. Her priest told me she was . . . intimately assaulted . . . in a way no man should treat his wife." Ned hated to reveal something so personal, but he was desperate.

Tom Clarke's lips tightened. "Leave it with me. I'll do what I can. Give me her name and address."

"Will you be contacting New York soon?"

"Today, as it happens. I'm writing an urgent letter to be entrusted to a reliable steward on one of the steamship lines. Now that a date's been fixed for the Rising the Military Council has to be sure of sufficient weapons. Pat's lost all faith in the promises the Germans made to Roger Casement. He's been urging John Devoy and Clan na Gael to help us get arms immediately and I'm about to add my plea to his.[7] I can certainly mention your sister at the same time. Perhaps a few of our lads in New York might have a quiet word with your brother-in-law—just to let him know his actions are being watched. Put a bit of a fright on him."

"I'm very grateful, Tom."

The other man shrugged his narrow shoulders. "Don't be grateful for anything until it's actually done."

On the second of March the British Military Service Act came into force in England, Scotland, and Wales.[8] Conscription in Ireland was expected any day.

Emerging from his house that very morning, Alexander Campbell drew a deep breath and looked around with his usual air of self-satisfaction. The crisp March air smelled of coal dust and automobile exhaust, but he liked the smell. The city was awake and busy, like himself.

As he started down the steps two men approached him. They were very large but neatly dressed; not street toughs. He nodded and was about to pass them by when one called his name.

"Yes?"

"Your wife is Kathleen Halloran?"

"My wife is Kathleen Campbell, and I do not discuss her with strangers on the street."

"It's thoughtful of you to be so considerate," replied the younger of the two men. "You always treat your wife like a lady, do you?"

Alexander's face reddened with anger. "How dare you!"

The man caught him by the lapels of his overcoat. "How dare you," he said in a low voice that positively vibrated with menace, "mistreat a woman."

"You don't know what you're—"

"We know all we need to know," said the second man, thrusting his face forward belligerently. The smashed nose and the set of the jaw were those of a prizefighter. "And all you need to know, mister, is that your wife's not alone in the world, sure she's not. She has friends. Friends who will be watching you from now on."

The other man added, "Anything you do to her will be done to you. Double." Suddenly he grinned, a suggestive leer that chilled Alexander to the bone. "*Anything* you do to her."

The prizefighter laughed.

Badly shaken, Alexander stumbled back into his house and slammed the door behind him.

On March fourth, twenty-three hundred delegates attended the annual Irish Race Convention at the Hotel Astor in New York.[9] The Ancient Order of Hibernians and every other active Irish-American organization took part. The convention concluded with the establishment of a new organization to be known as the Friends of Irish Freedom.

The story was covered in the *Gaelic American*. Kathleen bought the newspaper secretly, but did not get a chance to read it until the next morning when Alexander left for work. As soon as she heard him go out the door she hurried to her room and took the folded paper from the bottom of the wardrobe. Then she sat down on her brocaded slipper-chair and began to read.

According to the article, the purpose of the Friends was to encourage and assist the national independence of Ireland. John Devoy had said an appeal must be made to the international powers once the European war ended. Ireland should have a seat at the peace conference, which would be the best forum for putting forward its case, but to be included they would have to be announced belligerents. "Therefore," Devoy had told the new group, "we urge Irish patriots to establish a national government and take up military posts—now."

"Merciful Hour," Kathleen breathed. "It's the Rising at last." She was exhilarated and terrified. Freedom for Ireland!

But if there was any fighting, Ned and the Volunteers would surely be involved. God protect him; let it be anyone but Ned!

The article mentioned a new Victory Fund to be used solely for the purpose of winning Irish independence. Kathleen went to the wardrobe to see if any money remained in her private purse. Just as she reached for it she heard the front door slam.

She straightened up. A few moments later Alexander stood in the doorway.

Kathleen held the newspaper behind her back, but he was not interested in newspapers. He looked like a man who had just received a bad shock.

"Are you all right?"

He was staring at her most peculiarly.

"I said, 'Are you all right?' Speak to me, Alexander."

His mouth worked but no sound came out. After a few moments he turned and left the room. She heard him say something to the new housemaid and go out again. Returning to her newspaper, Kathleen put her husband's odd behavior out of her mind. She was more worried about her brother.

Oh, Ned, for God's sake don't do anything rash!

Chapter Forty-two

THOUGH he had been suffering from one cold after another since Christmas, Joe Plunkett was busy drawing up his most recent set of military strategies. Ned found him lying on a couch with a coverlet across his legs and a mountain of pillows at his back. There were papers spread all over the coverlet. He glanced up as Ned entered the room. "I'll be through with these in a minute and then you can take them to Pat. Where is he?"

"He's been at Volunteer Headquarters all day, trying to prepare for the Rising without making Bulmer Hobson suspicious. Fortunately, Hobson doesn't check through the files very often."

"What would happen if he did?"

"He'd go straight to Eoin MacNeill, of course, and then we would have a problem. We need to keep MacNeill in the dark until the last minute so he doesn't overturn our plans. He's still dead set against taking any form of initiative. James Connolly was wrong to worry about us; it's MacNeill and the overly cautious men like him who would waste the best chance we'll ever have."

Plunkett wrote a few last words, then handed Ned the papers. "Here, fold these and put them under your shirt. And may they warm your heart."

Ned grinned.

"I have some heartwarming news myself," Plunkett told him, turning to punch up his pillows. "We're keeping quiet about it for now, but in December Miss Gifford consented to marry me. You might as well know since we'll invite you to the wedding."

"Joe, that's just splendid. Congratulations, she's a lovely girl."

Plunkett beamed. "She is, isn't she? When she was studying art with William Orpen, he painted a portrait of her. It's called *Young Ireland*.

"She's Protestant and I'm Catholic, and her family has some reservations about the marriage. But Grace is studying Catholicism and hopes to convert in time for the wedding. And I'm determined to be healthier by then, even if it means going abroad for an operation."

"I couldn't be happier for you. When's the wedding?"

"We were planning to marry at Easter, but now with the Rising scheduled, I'm not certain. Soon, though. We're promised to one another, and I would never break a promise to Grace."

At Volunteer Headquarters in Dawson Street, Pádraic Pearse was in animated conversation with Seán MacDermott. There was no sign of Bulmer Hobson.

Both men looked up as Ned entered. "How's Joe?"

"He's resting today but says he'll be out and about again by tomorrow. He's planning to go to Switzerland for an operation on his throat."[1]

"That could be most opportune," said MacDermott.

"What do you mean?"

"We've had a positive response from Clan na Gael about supplying us with arms.[2] At first they were going to send them through a South American port but that fell through, so now they've applied direct to the Germans. John Devoy's raised additional funds to pay for the weapons. The plan is for three German trawlers to land at least twenty thousand rifles and

ammunition in Tralee Bay in time for the Rising. We can have
Joe make the final arrangements with Berlin as soon as he
gets to Switzerland. The government here won't know a thing.

"Once we have those weapons we're on our way. We have
a chance, a damned good chance, of pulling this off. The odds
against us are long but they're far from hopeless.[3] Thanks to
the war there are only about six thousand soldiers in the country right now, plus some ten thousand policemen. We have at
least eighteen thousand Irish Volunteers ready to take to the
field tomorrow. If we can arm all of them, we can make a
real fight of it."

Pearse added, "The longer we last, the more the Irish people will get behind us. They are beaten down now; they need
something to pull them out of their lethargy. The Rising will
do that."

"You really think we can win?" Ned asked eagerly.

Pearse gazed at him with those visionary's eyes. "We *will*
win. One way or another, we will win."

Mrs. Clarke had arranged for Síle to board with a republican family who lived in the same neighborhood. When Ned
called on her that evening he found her brimming with excitement. She did not know the particulars, but she knew the
revolution was coming. She could feel it like some great
sleeping beast beneath their feet, stirring with the arrival of
spring.

"I'm taking first aid classes at Liberty Hall, Ned! Dr. Kathleen Lynn's teaching them; she's the medical officer for the
Citizen Army. I'm learning how to treat battle wounds so I
can help the Volunteers."

Ned told her, "If the British government responds to us the
way they did to the threat of force from the Ulster Volunteers,
an accommodation might be reached without a shot being
fired."

"Will there be no fighting, then?"

He would not meet her eyes. "It's hard to say."

A little of the light went out of her face, as if she had caught him being dishonest with her.

Ned longed to share everything with Síle, but he could not be specific about what he knew. Secrecy was imposed by the IRB for a good reason. Risings in the past had been betrayed by as little as an accidental slip of the tongue.

NED wrote to his Aunt Norah: "We are very busy in Dublin these days, but I want you to know that I would come home for a visit if I could. My heart is with you and Frank and the girls. Kiss them for me."

He dare not tell her good-bye.

Increasingly his dreams were of Clare, of the limestone-studded Burren and the high sky and the Atlantic light. The curve of the hills; the white lace of the whitethorn blooming in May. The cuckoo's cry. Thinking of them sent a pain as sharp as a lance through his soul.

James Connolly had said, "Ireland as distinct from her people is nothing to me." Forced to consider the possibility of his own mortality, Ned realized it was the land he loved, the formidable and formative topography of Clare. The doors of possibility the *Titanic* had opened revealed vistas not half as appealing as home.

But he would never go home again. Even if they won, even if Ireland was free. To go back to Clare would mean giving up Síle, who could not go home.

"Sometime," Ned remarked to Henry one morning as they were preparing to go to work, "I should like to write about what things cost."

"Too bloody much," his friend growled as he adjusted his suspenders. "And now there's talk of raising the price of the pint."

ON Saint Patrick's Day, the Irish Volunteers assembled in College Green for a display of military maneuvers that lasted almost two hours, considerably interfering with traffic around the former Irish Parliament building.[4] The Castle sent police-men down, but though they paced back and forth and slapped their batons against the palms of their hands, they did not interfere with the march.

"They can't decide whether they want to beat us or join us," Ned remarked to Seán Heuston.

Eoin MacNeill proudly reviewed the troops. He did not know that many of them were carrying rounds of live am-munition.

ON the twenty-first of March the fortnightly *céili* was held at Saint Enda's.[5] As this was also the traditional Saint Enda's Day celebration, the Hermitage was thrown open and every-one who had any connection with the school was welcome. Willie Pearse hand-lettered hundreds of invitations. When Thomas MacDonagh received his, he laughed to his wife, "I see Pat's been sternly organizing the merrymaking again."

Although the twenty-first was a Tuesday, classes at Saint Enda's were canceled for the day. That same morning there was news of an affray at Tullamore. Members of the Royal Irish Constabulary had attempted to disarm the local Irish Volunteers and shots had been exchanged. A constable had been wounded, though not seriously.

Pádraic Pearse expressed the concern everyone felt. "The unionists are going to demand suppression of all republican activities now," he warned his brother.

Willie replied with a nervous laugh, "Good job they don't know about this one, then."

By two o'clock a crowd that included a number of Vol-unteers had filled the school gymnasium. Eamonn Ceannt played the pipes; Mary Brigid, who had returned for the oc-casion, performed on the piano. Students sang traditional airs and demonstrated Irish dancing. The music drifted out toward the dreaming Dublin mountains.

Ned and Thomas MacDonagh were sitting together at one side of the gymnasium. Indicating the singers, Ned remarked,

"How young they look! Their eyes are as clear as their voices."

MacDonagh replied, "Pat's killing himself by inches to assure a better future for these boys."

"I'm sure they appreciate him as much as I did."

"Not necessarily. A small percentage of boys always resent any attempt to civilize them. There are lads in this hall tonight having a high old time who will write their parents tomorrow and tell them the headmaster is a monster of the first order." MacDonagh shook his head. "I know from experience. No one is more lied about than a teacher of young boys."

"I think I'd rather be a newspaperman," said Ned.

At the end of the afternoon the headmaster made a speech. In the few past weeks his manner had become more solemn than ever, with a grave, underlying gentleness. "Scoil Eanna has been an accomplished fact for eight years," he told his audience. "I hope it will continue for eighty more, but as far as I am concerned my work here is done. So in a sense, this is my farewell.

"As I have often stressed, Man is not primarily a member of a State, but a human individuality. Just so, this school is not a thing of bricks and mortar made by the State, but the creation of dedicated human beings.

"As I look around today I see fine young men who have reached their maturity here, young men who are prepared to become efficient soldiers in battles both spiritual and temporal for the sake of Ireland. No headmaster could ask for greater joy than the knowledge that he has had some small part in shaping such men. You are our gift to the future. The happiness we have endeavored to give you during your years at Scoil Eanna is our gift to you."

He nodded to Mary Brigid, who brought her fingers down on the piano keys in a rousing rendition of "Bold Robert Emmet." Everyone joined in. As they swung into the refrain, Thomas MacDonagh's bright baritone rang strongly in Ned's ear: "My crime was my love of the land I was born in. A hero I've lived and a hero I'll die."

When the formalities were concluded the guests wandered

through the school, admiring the projects the boys had on display. Mrs. Pearse and her daughters began setting up tables for refreshments. Almost unnoticed, at the end of the afternoon Pádraic Pearse slipped away to the school chapel off the study hall.

On impulse Ned followed him.

When Ned opened the door he saw Pearse kneeling with his head bowed, halfway to the front of the chapel. The draft from the open door caught his attention and he turned around. At that moment a cold, greenish-purple twilight fell across his face from one of the stained-glass windows.

He looked drowned.

Catastrophe . . . the great ship upended in the cold sea, the lights blinking out, and the people in the dark water, screaming . . .

Suddenly Ned was frightened for him. Frightened for all of them, for Pearse and Plunkett and McDonagh, for the poets who misread war for glory.

Never mind the sun shining outside; the storm was rushing toward them. Instead of trumpets and banners there would be the thunder of guns and the lightning of sabers.

Ned stood rooted by the door, unable to move. Pearse realized something was wrong. "Are you ill, Ned?"

"I'm not ill. I was just worried about you, sir."

"How kind you are. But there is no need to worry; I know what I'm doing."

"Are you certain? It's not too late to call everything off."

To Ned's surprise, Pearse laughed. "Prudence is the only vice, Ned.[6] When we were children Mother arranged for us to take proper horse-riding lessons. I rather enjoyed them until the day we started jumping hurdles. 'Throw your heart over the fence and follow it,' our instructor told us, 'and you'll be all right.'

"I was expected to set the example, so while Willie and the girls applauded I cantered down toward the first jump. Then at the last moment I lost my nerve and tried to stop. The pony promptly pitched me off. I was hurt; I had to miss school for a week. But I learned my lesson."

They walked together to the refectory, where Mrs. Pearse was serving the guests what she called "a light collation": platters of cold sliced chicken, Dublin Bay prawns, hot pork pies, chutney sandwiches with the crusts cut off, apple tarts, fruitcake, tea with cream. Thomas MacDonagh had piled his plate with chocolate biscuits. Ned opted for two pork pies and an apple tart; Pádraic Pearse nibbled part of a sandwich.

Liquor was not served at Saint Enda's. Those men who had brought flasks slipped outside for a discreet drink.

The headmaster seemed calm, even relaxed. But whenever Ned glanced at Pearse he recalled the greenish light on his face; the drowned look.

INSTEAD of going to see Precious before he went to work the next morning, Ned cycled to Ringsend and called on Father Paul. He met the priest just as he was coming out the door. "I'm expected at Kilmainham," Paul explained.

"Sorry?"

"Kilmainham Jail. Don't look so appalled, Ned, I'm not being arrested. I've applied to the bishop for something to do, and he's sending me to work with the prison chaplain."

"Seems to me he could have found you something more pleasant."

Paul shrugged. "I don't mind."

"You haven't seen Kilmainham."

Walking his bicycle, Ned accompanied the priest to the tram stop. Along the way he brought up the reason for his visit. "What do you know about adoptions, Father?"

"They're not my line of expertise, but I'll tell you what I can. Why do you ask?"

"There's a little girl here in Dublin who's had a rather terrible start in life. She's in an orphanage now, but I'd like to see her go to a good home. A safe home," he said, stressing the word safe. "Dublin may not be safe for a while."

"What are you trying to tell me?"

Ned ignored the question. "Is it possible to send children to America for adoption?"

"I'm sure it is, though I don't know just how to go about it. Do you want me to find out for you?"

"Please. And as quickly as you can."

Paul stopped walking and turned to face Ned. "I think you'd better tell me what's wrong."

"There's nothing you need to know except that the child's name is Ursula Jervis and she's at the Orphan House for Destitute Females in the North Circular Road. If anything should happen to me, I want you to do what you can for her. Take her back to America with you when you go."

"Is she your child?"

Ned did not answer.

Paul drew a deep breath. "I'm not certain I'm going back to America. It might be better if I stayed here."

Abruptly Ned recalled Síle's words: "Sometimes you just have to claw at the world. You have to make things come right or die trying!"

He told Paul, "If you really care for Kathleen, you'll go back to her. Don't leave her to Alexander Campbell. Go back and fight for her yourself."

"But I'm a priest."

Ned lost his temper. "You were a man before you were a priest, Goddamn it!"

Paul thrust his fists deep into his pockets. "I'm afraid you don't understand. I'm doing the best I can; I simply don't have any choice."

On April 3, Pádraic Pearse, as organizing director, issued orders for extensive maneuvers and a parade of the Irish Volunteers to be held in Dublin on Easter Sunday.

Chapter Forty-three

Seán MacDermott unrolled a calendar and spread it out on Eamonn Ceannt's dining table. "Joe's arranged with the Germans for the weapons to reach the Irish coast by Thursday the twentieth.[1] But I see something we should have noticed before. There's a full moon at Easter, which means no secret night landing. The arms will have to be landed openly and not one hour sooner than is absolutely necessary, or the British could learn what's happening and seize them. That means landing them Saturday the twenty-second at dawn, which will just give us time to get them to the distribution points. The instructions to the Germans have to be changed immediately."

"But Joe is in hospital now," Pearse protested, "or on his way home. We cannot ask him to do any more so soon after his surgery. And we cannot contact Berlin from Dublin while Britain's at war with Germany."

MacDermott said, "John Devoy could contact the Germans from America and authorize changing the arrangements. He's supplying the money, after all. But we can't cable Devoy from Ireland because the British are probably monitoring outgoing messages. We need to send someone to him in person; someone we can trust absolutely."

"How about one of Joe Plunkett's sisters?" suggested Tom Clarke.

Within the hour Ned Halloran was on his way to Larkfield with an urgent message and a steamship ticket for Philomena Plunkett. She was to board the next liner for America, enabling her to reach Devoy by the fourteenth of April.[2] "Tell him that the arms must be landed no earlier than Holy Saturday," Ned stressed. "Make him understand how crucial that is."

JOE Plunkett returned from Switzerland more ill than ever. The operation on his throat for tuberculosis did not seem to have done any good in spite of his high hopes. He insisted on meeting with the Military Council, then allowed his family to send him to Miss Quinn's Private Nursing Home in Mountjoy Square.[3]

Ned went to visit him.

"We've just co-opted Thomas MacDonagh onto the Military Council,"[4] Plunkett announced, "which is why I can be spared for a little while. We'll let him do some of the work until I'm up again." His eyes were glittering with fever.

THE tranquillity of Lent was interrupted by the discovery of a coded document purporting to be from Dublin Castle and setting forth detailed plans for the military occupation of Dublin.[5]

People were shocked.

When the document first appeared, Dublin Castle tried to enforce censorship. That soon failed; the story broke in the papers and the authorities rushed into print themselves to proclaim the document a blatant forgery, an "absolute fabrication from beginning to end."

They had good reason to be alarmed. Almost every phrase was inflammatory. Perched on the corner of his desk, Henry Mooney read aloud to his colleagues at the *Independent*: "We have learned from a reliable source that the military authorities plan to take severe punitive action against the Irish Volunteers, the Citizen Army, Sinn Féin, the Gaelic League, and the National Volunteers, among others. Nationalist centers are to be occupied by British troops and wholesale arrests and deportations are anticipated. Premises to be occupied include 2 Dawson Street, Liberty Hall, 6 Harcourt Street, 25 Rutland Square . . .''

Men were looking at one another and shaking their heads.

Henry went on reading: "We understand that even private homes are not to be exempt. According to the document which has come into our possession, the Archbishop's Palace in Drumcondra is to be searched and put under armed guard. Similar treatment is planned for the homes of Count George Plunkett, Professor Eoin MacNeill, Countess Constance Markievicz, Michael George O'Rahilly, Saint Enda's School in Rathfarnham . . .'' Henry paused, looked up, grinned. "See additional listings on page three, with maps.''

"How dare they drag the Archbishop of Dublin into this!'' a reporter exclaimed. "Walsh is sympathetic to the nationalist cause, but that's no reason to treat him like a pariah. This will turn people against the government if anything will.''

Someone else said, "Don't be too sure. The well-off want things to stay as they are, while all the poor feel is apathy. Still, I have no doubt a lot of questions are being asked this morning. Maybe it will do some good, stir things up.''

Henry caught Ned's eye. "The power of the press,'' he said smugly.

The document's authenticity was hotly debated. It proved to have a curious pedigree. The document had first come to light when it was brought to the attention of the Provisional Committee of the Irish Volunteers, including Eoin MacNeill, by Joe Plunkett.[6] Thomas MacDonagh asserted that the document had been given to the Volunteers by friends in the Castle and decoded by Plunkett himself. Alderman Tom Kelly had read it aloud to an alarmed Dublin Corporation. Patrick J. Little, editor of *New Ireland,* had attempted to print it but been censored by the Castle, only to see the major dailies subsequently carry the story in bold type.

Major-General Lovick Friend, currently commanding the British forces in Ireland, was known to be taking precautionary measures against anticipated "Sinn Féin trouble." Yet Dublin Castle officially denied that any document describing plans for military occupation of the city had ever existed.

Because of the document, however, Eoin MacNeill issued an executive order to the Volunteers to be ready to defend themselves and their weapons.[7] It was tantamount to a call to arms.

Volunteers and the Citizen Army alike thronged shops such as Lawlor's in Foynes Street to buy bandoliers, Sam Browne belts, haversacks, canteens, swords, bayonets. Mysterious parcels were delivered to hotels in the sidecars of motorcycles. A steady stream of dispatch carriers set out for Volunteer posts throughout the country.

Yet in spite of the uproar caused by the so-called Castle Document, official Dublin continued to function as normal.

"The Castle's adopting a very Irish attitude," Henry commented wryly. "When there's a problem, look the other way."

Ned went to Larkfield to collect some maps for Seán MacDermott and discovered that Joe Plunkett had returned from the nursing home. Plunkett's throat was heavily bandaged and his voice no more than a whisper, but he greeted Ned with shining eyes. "The Castle Document has really set them on their ears!" he crowed.

Ned suddenly remembered that there was a small, hand-operated printing press at Larkfield,[8] one the count sometimes used in connection with his business. "Are you sure that document's genuine?"

Plunkett laughed; a thin, nervy laugh, almost on the edge of hysteria. In that moment Ned realized how ill he really was. "Grace was with me when I decoded it. Plus we have a signed statement from a telegraphist at Dublin Castle to the effect that it's genuine, abstracted from their own files. Sometimes you have to fight them with their own weapons," he added with a dramatic flourish of his hand, like a fencer going for touch.

CHIEF Secretary Birrell and Major-General Friend were spending the Easter holidays in London. Under-secretary Nathan reported things were peaceful enough in Dublin. He wrote, "Though the Irish Volunteer element has been active of late, I do not believe that its leaders mean insurrection or that the Volunteers have sufficient arms if the leaders do mean it."

ON Palm Saturday, the Dublin branch of Cumann na mBan held a *céili* in Grocers' Hall.[9] It was organized at the request of Seán MacDermott to serve as cover so that Volunteer officers from distant counties could meet with the Military Council. Republican strongholds such as Cork and Clare were anxious to know just what the latest plans were.

Síle Duffy went to the *céili*—but not to dance. Instead she flirted outrageously with the policemen on the street outside to distract them.

When Ned arrived he saw Síle standing on the corner laughing with a member of the DMP. He understood at once what she was doing, but that did not make it any less painful. All my life, he thought, I shall feel this whenever I see her with another man.

Everything had a price.

She pretended not to notice him as he brushed past her, but the sound of her laughter followed him into the hall.

Just inside, Kathleen Clarke and another woman were standing on either side of Seán MacDermott to discourage people from stopping to chat with him. Every girl who attended the dance seemed to want to speak to him, but he was watching for other faces; men to be sent upstairs.

MacDermott nodded to Ned. "Enjoy yourself."

"What about you?"

"I shall leave soon," said MacDermott, glancing toward the stairs at the back of the hall.

Music played and the respectable middle-class ladies of Cumann na mBan danced with their husbands and sweethearts, while in a sparsely furnished room overhead tense men spoke in low tones of the Rising. Ned helped himself to a glass of punch and wandered around for a few minutes, trying to get up nerve to ask one of the women to dance. Then he noticed a commotion at the door and went over.

Con Colbert had just arrived, obviously unhappy. "It isn't right to hold a *céili* during Lent," he was protesting to Tom Clarke's wife.

"Oh go on, Con, don't be so squeamish," she teased. "A boy your age should dance when he can; for all you know you might be dancing at the end of a rope one of these days."[10]

No sooner had she spoken the words than she went white and clapped her hand to her mouth, but it was too late.

Ned patted her shoulder. "That's all right, I know you didn't mean it and so does Con. We're all under a strain."

On Palm Sunday, James Connolly flew the green flag of Ireland, with its golden harp unsullied by a crown, over Liberty Hall.[11]

That same night Bulmer Hobson, speaking at a Cumann na mBan concert, guardedly warned the Volunteers against precipitate action.[12] He insisted that Ireland's hopes for freedom depended not upon militancy, but upon the peace conference after the European war.

"Another bloody conference, another bloody wait," a man in the audience muttered to his wife. "Another bloody chance for Ireland to be put on the long finger while the rest of the world goes on without us."

On Tuesday the eighteenth of April, the Military Council called a special meeting for that night. Ned was entrusted with notifying everybody. As soon as he finished his shift at the *Independent* he was on his bicycle. His last stop was at Larkfield, where Joe Plunkett took one look at his perspiring face and offered, "Would you like to ride back with me? My father's driver will take us and we can put your push-bike in the boot of the car."

Ned gave him a weary grin. "I should appreciate that very much."

As they drove, Plunkett asked, "Did anyone tell you what this meeting is about?"

"It's none of my business."

"Oh, I think it is. Why don't you come in with me?"

"Are you sure? I wasn't asked."

"I'm asking you, Ned. Let's just say I have a sense of the dramatic."

The meeting was being held in a house in Henry Street belonging to Jenny Wyse Power, a friend of Con Markievicz.[13] As the motorcar purred to a halt in front of the house Ned observed a score of Volunteers stationed up and down the street. They were trying to be unobtrusive, but he recognized both Seán Heuston and Brian Joyce.

Plunkett knocked once, three times, once again. The door opened a crack and he whispered a password. A woman in a blue dress opened the door and showed them to an upstairs room.

Six men were seated around a table. Pádraic Pearse looked up when Ned entered. "Joe invited me," Ned said quickly.

"I'm glad he did; I should have done so myself. It's appropriate that one of the Saint Enda's boys be a witness tonight."

"A witness to what, sir?"

Pearse handed him a single sheet of paper.

THE PROCLAMATION OF
POBLACHT NA N-EMEANN
THE PROVISIONAL GOVERNMENT
OF THE
IRISH REPUBLIC
TO THE PEOPLE OF IRELAND

Irishmen and Irishwomen:

In the name of God and of the dead generations from which she receives her old tradition of nationhood, Ireland, through us, summons her children to her flag and strikes for her freedom. Having organised and trained her manhood through her secret revolutionary organisation the Irish Republican Brotherhood, and through her open military organisations, the Irish Volunteers and the Irish Citizen Army, having patiently perfected her discipline, having resolutely waited for the right moment to reveal itself, she now seizes that moment, and supported by her exiled children in America and by gallant allies in Europe, but relying in the first on her own strength, she strikes in full confidence of victory.

We declare the right of the people of Ireland to the ownership of Ireland, and to the unfettered control of Irish destinies, to be sovereign and indefeasible. The long usurpation of that right by a foreign people and government has not extinguished the right, nor can it ever be extinguished except by the destruction of the Irish people. In every generation the Irish people have asserted their right to national freedom and sovereignty: six times during the past three hundred years they have asserted it in arms. Standing on that fundamental right and again asserting it in arms in the face of the world, we hereby proclaim the Irish Republic as a Sovereign Independent State, and pledge our lives and the lives of our comrades-in-arms to the cause of its freedom, of its welfare, and of its exaltation among the nations.

The Irish Republic is entitled to, and hereby claims, the allegiance of every Irishman and Irishwoman. The Republic guarantees religious and civil liberty, equal rights and equal opportunities to all its citizens, and declares its resolve to pursue the happiness and prosperity of the whole nation and of all its parts, cherishing all the children of the nation equally, and oblivious of the differences carefully fostered by an alien government, which have divided a minority from the majority in the past.

Until our arms have brought the opportune moment for the establishment of a permanent National Government, representative of the whole people of Ireland and elected by suffrages of all her men and women, the Provisional Government, hereby constituted, will administer the civil and military affairs of the Republic in trust for the people.

We place the cause of the Irish Republic under the protection of the Most High God, whose blessing we invoke upon our arms, and we pray that no one who serves that cause will dishonour it by cowardice, inhumanity, or rapine. In this supreme hour the Irish nation must, by its valour and discipline and by the readiness of its children to sacrifice themselves for the common good, prove itself worthy of the august destiny to which it is called.

"This is magnificent," Ned said when he finished reading. It was hard to speak around the lump in his throat.

"This is freedom," said Seán MacDermott. He produced a pen and a bottle of ink. "Pat drafted the original document and the rest of us suggested a few small changes. All that remains is to sign our names." He spread the document on a table and held out the pen to Tom Clarke.

For once the old Fenian was flustered. "I can't . . . It's too great an honor . . . Someone else . . ."

Thomas MacDonagh raised his voice. "You're our senior member. You sign first; no man will precede you."

Hand trembling with emotion, Tom Clarke took the pen.

One by one they signed. Thomas J. Clarke. Seán Mac Diarmada. Thomas MacDonagh. P. H. Pearse. Eamonn Ceannt. James Connolly. Joseph Plunkett.

Ned felt as if he had been present on the fourth of July when the American Declaration of Independence was signed, or in Paris for the storming of the Bastille.

We declare the right of the people of Ireland to the ownership of Ireland.

For the rest of his life he had only to close his eyes to see the seven names signed on the paper. Burning there, like words written in flame.

Chapter Forty-four

J OE Plunkett drove to Eoin MacNeill's house on Lower Hatch Street to inform him of the document and ask him to agree to add his name to those of the signatories.[1] He soon returned to report glumly, "MacNeill won't promise to sign any document he hasn't studied thoroughly. He said if I'd bring it back to him he'd look at it overnight, but otherwise, forget it."

Tom Clarke cried, "We can't let him read the Proclamation, not yet! It tells too much. He'd try to stop us sure."

"Perhaps we could modify it," Eamonn Ceannt suggested.

James Connolly thundered, "Under no circumstances! If we back down now, we return to where we've always been. Cringing!"

The others agreed. They would go ahead and form a national government without MacNeill.

So Tom Clarke, as first signatory of the Proclamation, became President of the Provisional Government of Ireland. Pádraic Pearse, who was better equipped to be president, was appointed Commander-in-Chief. James Connolly was named Commandant-General of the Dublin District. The other signatories would comprise the Provisional Government, together with various prominent citizens known to be sympathetic to the nationalist cause.

• • •

As Ned left work the next evening he saw Seán MacDermott talking to two pretty girls just outside the Carlisle Building. The weather was warm and misty, the smell from the river drifted up to them. When Seán caught Ned's eye he said to the girls, "I've promised to buy a drink for my friend there because it's his birthday. Run along now and let us lads celebrate."

They protested and offered to join in the celebration, but MacDermott was an old hand at clever banter. He soon sent them on their way laughing.

Ned told him, "You've made a mistake; it isn't my birthday."

"Let's have a drink anyway."

"At Kirwan's?"

"I think not. We need someplace less likely to be watched."

Ned left his bicycle in the alley behind the *Independent* offices and followed MacDermott to a tiny pub wedged between two ramshackle warehouses on the quays. The place was empty except for a bored barman and a pair of extremely drunk dockers playing a game of darts. MacDermott motioned to a dingy, high-backed booth where they could not be seen from the doorway. "We probably won't have long. It's the end of the shift and this place will fill up soon. Here—take these." Reaching under his coat, he drew out a brown envelope. "These are for Pat's signature as commander-in-chief; you'll probably find him at Volunteer Headquarters. I'd take them to him myself, but we better not be seen meeting for the next few days. Tell him these are the final plans and for God's sake don't let Hobson see them."

The two men shared a quick drink and then Ned hurried to Dawson Street. He kept glancing around, wondering who was watching him, how much they knew. Every policeman or soldier he saw made him sweat.

At the same time the excitement was exhilarating.

At Volunteer Headquarters, Pádraic Pearse was talking with

Bulmer Hobson. Ned busied himself until the conversation was over and Hobson left the office for a few minutes, then he asked to speak to Pearse privately.

They went into a back room and closed the door. "Wait while I have a look at these." Affixing his pince-nez, Pearse read through the pages carefully, occasionally making some half-muttered comment.

When he finished he signed his name at the bottom, then told Ned, "Here, you read these now and memorize the information. Next week you will need to know where everyone is at all times."

Dublin was at the heart of a complex logistical plan. The orders Pearse had just signed meant that urgent dispatches would be sent to Cork, Tipperary, Limerick, and points west, where brigade and battalion organization had already been intensified. As soon as the German weapons were landed on the southwest coast on Saturday they would be rushed to distribution points to arm the provincial Irish Volunteers, currently numbered at around thirteen thousand.[2] Cork Volunteers would then link up with the Kerry Brigade, which would be in close communication with companies from Limerick, Clare, and Galway. Military camps at the Curragh and Athlone were to be contained, while Irish Volunteers from Belfast were in charge of encircling the British garrison at Enniskillen. Keeping British reinforcements from getting into Dublin was crucial.

Meanwhile, the Easter Sunday maneuvers meant that the entire Dublin Brigade would be assembled in the city with their weapons. According to Joe Plunkett's plan they would then be joined by the Citizen Army, and the combined force would seize and fortify strategic points throughout Dublin. The First Battalion, under the command of Kathleen Clarke's brother, Edward Daly, was to occupy the Four Courts. From there they could cover the northwest approaches to the city center.

Thomas MacDonagh's Second Battalion, with Major John MacBride, husband of the celebrated beauty Maud Gonne, as second-in-command, would guard the southern approaches from a garrison in Jacob's Biscuit Factory. The garrison would include Michael O'Hanrahan, who was appointed Quartermaster-General. "That lot will have access to all the sweet biscuits they want," Ned remarked with a chuckle. "Who did Professor MacDonagh have to bribe?"

Pádraic Pearse smiled. "He simply asked. Thomas thinks ahead."

Eamon de Valera and the Third Battalion would make Boland's Mills and Bakery, strategically located near both the railway and the main road leading from Kingstown Harbor to Dublin, their command post.³ Their mission was to block any British reinforcements landing from England.

Eamonn Ceannt was appointed Director of Communications. His Fourth Battalion, with Cathal Brugha as second-in-command, would seize the warehouse known as the South Dublin Union and from there control Kingsbridge Station and the southwest approaches.

An additional rural battalion under the command of Thomas Ashe was to operate in north County Dublin and County Meath.⁴ The Fianna would serve as dispatch carriers and stretcher bearers throughout the area of operations. Cumann na mBan had persuaded the Volunteers to allow them to take an active part in the Rising, if only as nurses and cooks.

With a mixed company of Volunteers and Citizen Army, James Connolly would occupy the General Post Office and oversee the establishment of the headquarters of the Provisional Government. The choice of the G.P.O. was partly practical, due to its central location, and partly symbolic. The imposing classical structure looked like the capitol building of a noble nation.

Joseph Mary Plunkett was named Chief of Staff. Although The O'Rahilly had steadfastly refused to join the IRB because he disapproved of secret organizations,⁵ he was assigned as Pearse's aide-de-camp. Con Colbert was chosen as Pearse's bodyguard and Ned Halloran as his personal courier.

"I certainly don't need a bodyguard," Pearse remarked, sounding annoyed, "but I shall need my own courier, so you will be with me in headquarters."

Headquarters staff, thought Ned. Me.

• • •

EARLY next morning Ned called on Tom Clarke. The date
was the twentieth of April, Maundy Thursday in the church
calendar.

"I've been waiting for you," Clarke said as soon as Ned
entered the shop. "Have you something for me?"

Ned handed him a sealed envelope. "Is Mrs. Clarke mind-
ing your Amiens Street shop?" he asked, to make conversation.

"I've sent Katty to Limerick with some dispatches.[6] She's
taking the children with her to leave them with her mother,
then she will come back on the mail train."

"You don't want your children in Dublin?"

"Of course not."

"Is it going to be bad, do you think?"

"Figure it out for yourself, Ned. We're going to have three
thousand armed troops in the city, counting the Dublin Brigade and the Citizen Army and a small squad of Hibernian
Rifles. That doesn't take into account how many British soldiers and policemen we may have to contend with. So for the
next few weeks I want my children with their grandmother.
Just in case."

When Ned left the news agency he hurried to the orphanage. He would be late for work, but that no longer mattered.

Holding Precious in his arms, he told the little girl as gently
as he could, "You may not see me for a while, but you're
not to fret. I'm counting on you to be good."

"You won't forget me?" she asked anxiously.

"I'll be thinking of you almost every minute."

"I'll be thinking of you, too," she promised. Her breath
was soft upon his cheek. "Where are you going, Ned-Ned?"

"To do something for you and children like you."

"For orphans?"

"For everybody."

She drew back and looked at him. "Something good?"

"I hope so."

As he left the orphanage he almost stopped to have a word

with the matron. Then he changed his mind. He could not ask her to send Precious out of the city without telling her about the Rising, and he could not betray that trust.

Why did everything have to be so hard?

Outside on the street he stopped and looked back at the orphanage. Its curtainless windows stared at him like blank, soulless eyes.

"God take care of them," Ned whispered under his breath. "All the little lambs."

He arrived at work very late and was taken to task for his repeated tardiness. Copyboys were at the bottom of the pecking order. Several hours were added to his shift to make up for the time he had missed. It was after ten o'clock at night when Ned finally left the newspaper office, but he decided he had best report to Volunteer Headquarters anyway.

As he turned his bicycle into Dawson Street, he saw Seán Heuston walking toward him. He wheeled over and stopped to talk with his friend.

Heuston met him with a conspiratorial wink. "I have my orders. How about you?"

"I have mine, too. Where are you assigned, Seán?"

"I'm company leader for D Company, First Battalion. Most of the battalion's going to the Four Courts, but we'll be seeing action at the Mendicity Institute on the south quays.[7] Our job is to delay any troops approaching the Four Courts from that direction."[8]

"Seeing action. It's all really about to happen, isn't it?"

"It is. Are you scared?"

"Not a bit of it!" Ned hesitated. "Well, perhaps a little. More anxious than scared."

"Me too."

"Do you think anyone will be killed?"

Heuston pushed back the tweed cap he was wearing—none of them were appearing on the streets in military uniform this week—and scratched his head. "I can't believe the British will let us seize the city without fighting back."

"James Connolly says a capitalist government will never destroy capitalist property."[9]

Heuston snorted. "I don't have Connolly's faith. I think they'll fight like hell. I'm surprised we're not garrisoning Trinity College, though. It's certainly in a strategic position."

"The officer training corps for the British army is in there, Seán. We'd have a hard time getting any of our men inside without heavy losses. Besides, Mr. Pearse won't hear of an assault on the college. He's a headmaster himself, remember. Which reminds me—do you know if he's still at Volunteer Headquarters?"

"He was earlier, but he's gone back to Saint Enda's now. If you want to see him you'd best go out there."

The weather was cold, the hour late. For a moment Ned thought wistfully of going home and having a good sleep, but he remounted his bicycle and headed for Saint Enda's instead. He could ask Mrs. Pearse for a bed and return to the city early in the morning with any messages Pearse needed him to carry.

Riding alone through the night, he imagined Seán Heuston and a company of Volunteers at the Mendicity Institute. He knew the place as he now knew most of Dublin. One of the oldest charitable institutions in the city, it was a former Ascendancy mansion transformed into a warren of shabby chambers where the city's destitute elderly were given subsistence fare by an overworked, underfunded staff.

The institute smelled the way the orphanage smelled, of poverty and pathos.

As he neared Rathfarnham, Ned was trying to compose a picture with words that would capture—

A bicycle tire blew and the machine wobbled violently sideways. A moment later he was lying in a ditch, suffering a banged head and a skinned knee. When he examined the bicycle by the light of the nearly full moon, he found the front wheel badly out of alignment.

"Everything happens to me," Ned informed the night.

He recalled seeing a sign for bicycle repair on a shopfront in Rathfarnham, so he walked the damaged bike into the village. If he could possibly get someone to repair the machine tonight he must; he would need it tomorrow.

A man who lived over the shop eventually responded to

his knock and came down. He wanted an exorbitant price to fix the bicycle, but Ned was in no position to argue. He waited impatiently for an interminable time while the stars wheeled in the Irish sky.

It was close to two in the morning when he finally reached Saint Enda's. As he was propping his bicycle against the side wall he was astonished to see a motorcar pulling up to the front steps. Several men got out. Ned recognized Eoin MacNeill and Bulmer Hobson, both looking very grim, and a third man whom he did not know.

MacNeill strode up the steps and pounded the door with an angry fist.[10] For a few moments nothing happened, then lights went on upstairs. Soon Pádraic Pearse, in his dressing gown, opened the door.

"We have to talk to you," MacNeill said curtly, brushing past him.

Before Ned could make his presence known, the men entered the building and the door closed behind them.

A light went on in the headmaster's study.

Uncertain what to do, Ned drifted toward the nearest study window. Pearse liked to keep his windows slightly open at the top so there would always be fresh air in the room no matter how cold the season. Ned could hear the voices distinctly.

Eoin MacNeill was doing the talking. He was in a towering rage. "Damn it, Pádraic! We have to have this out right now. In Dawson Street today Bulmer overheard a bit of conversation he obviously wasn't meant to hear. Orders have been issued which can only have one interpretation. You're planning an insurrection on Easter Sunday without my knowledge and in direct contravention of my policy!"

"To which orders do you refer?" Pearse asked calmly.

"Railway seizures, blowing up bridges, cutting off Dublin from the rest of the country—what in God's name are you thinking of!"

Crouching beneath the window, shivering from cold and exhaustion, Ned knew the answer before he heard Pearse speak.

"I am thinking of Ireland."

"Ireland!"

"The Ireland you love as well as I do. You are right, Eoin. A Rising is scheduled."

"And was the Castle Document just a ruse to get me on your side, to urge me toward this madness? If so, I bitterly resent the deception. I resent all the deceptions. I see now that your crowd has kept things from me for months. You knew I would never agree to this, yet you let me think we were in agreement while all the time—"

"We are in agreement," Pearse interrupted. "You want independence for Ireland as much as I do."

Bulmer Hobson interjected, "But not this way, not now! We aren't ready. I thought we would wait and consolidate our position and then after the next war—"

"What next war?" Pearse's voice was suddenly sharp. "Haven't the British told us this is the war to end all wars?"

"Oh there'll be another one, you know that. The European countries will always fight over territory. We can wait until we're stronger and the situation is more to our advantage."

"So you want us to put Ireland's freedom on the long finger yet again," Pearse replied bitterly. "We have the perfect opportunity now but you haven't the nerve."

"It isn't a question of nerve," Hobson began, but Mac-Neill's voice overrode him. "You deceived me!"

Pearse somehow remained calm. "You were deceived, but it was necessary. You are by nature too cautious when what is required is audacity. James Connolly understands this much better than you do.

"Leaders in Ireland have nearly always failed their people at the crucial moment.[11] We are determined that will not happen this time. We are determined that this shall be the last, the successful, Rising, and so we have kept it from you, knowing that you would try to interfere.

"We are only a few days away from success, Eoin. To attempt to stop all the forces that have been brought into play would lead to disaster."

"Going through with it will lead to disaster!" MacNeill

shouted at him. ''I can't be responsible for putting half-armed men into the field to be slaughtered. Before God, I'll do everything in my power to stop you; everything except ring up Dublin Castle myself!''[12]

Chapter Forty-five

MACNEILL and his companions stormed out of the building. In their excitement they did not notice the young man half-hidden in the darkness. As they got into their car, Ned heard MacNeill say, "I'm going to cancel all orders for Volunteer activity over the weekend. We'll put a stop to this here and now."

The car door slammed. Tires squealed on gravel. They were gone.

Badly shaken, Ned made his way to the door and knocked. Pearse opened to him almost at once, looking surprised to see him. "Come in! You are very welcome. Forgive my informality, but I just had visitors who did not give me time to put on my clothes."

"I know, I heard them from outside your window," Ned admitted as he followed Pearse into the study. "I think Professor MacNeill means to do what he says, sir."

"So do I. We cannot let that happen. We've gone too far and it is almost within our grasp now. What was it Seán MacDermott said to me last year? 'If we can hold Dublin for one week, we'll hold Ireland forever.' We have to have that week."

"Professor MacNeill will stop you."

"Not if we are persuasive enough. He caught me unawares

tonight; I had no time to prepare. I shall go to him later today with Seán and Thomas and explain that no matter what we do, there's no holding James Connolly. That is certainly true. If we also tell Eoin about the shipment of German arms he will realize there can be no turning back.

"In his heart he wants what we all want, I'm convinced of that. He knew we were headed toward this from the beginning, but he would not admit it to himself because it frightened him. No one admires Eoin MacNeill more than I do, but he simply does not have those particular qualities needed to be a leader of revolutionaries." Pearse gave a faint smile. "Perhaps that is to his credit."

He noticed Ned was shivering. "Here, you should be in bed. There is plenty of room upstairs. Mary Brigid's not here and the students have gone home for Easter, but Des Ryan and Con Colbert are with us. I believe your old dormitory is unoccupied, however. Go up and get a night's sleep; you will need it."

Ned left Pádraic Pearse sitting at his desk, writing.

Tired as he was, Ned could not sleep. He tossed and turned on the familiar bed in Saint Brendan's dormitory, then lay on his back with his arms folded beneath his head and stared unseeingly toward the crucifix on the wall. He felt as if he stood on the edge of a cliff—the Cliffs of Moher in Clare, perhaps, with the Atlantic thundering below. He was cut loose from reality, adrift in space and time. Scenes flickered through his head like scenes in a play as his imagination strove to create the days to come.

In the morning he rode into the city with Pádraic Pearse in an unfamiliar Ford motorcar. Con Colbert drove. As he was helping Ned put his bicycle into the boot, Colbert explained, "I'm supposed to be Mr. Pearse's bodyguard but he insists he won't have one. I don't think he wants a driver, either, but I have to justify my existence somehow, so I borrowed this from a friend of mine. I felt our commander-in-chief should travel in style like the British officers. We only have it until Sunday, though.''

Ned was impressed. ''Do you think you could teach me to drive?''

''I can of course; we'll do it after the Rising.''

Pearse and Ned sat in the back. With a great clash of gears, the Ford lurched off down the lane.

''How long have you been driving?'' Ned wondered.

Colbert glanced over his shoulder with a jaunty grin. ''A week. A whole week tomorrow.''

The car narrowly avoiding hitting one of the gates, swerved onto the main road, and headed for Dublin.

By the time Ned was left in Gardiner Street the morning sun was high in the sky. Good Friday. Before he did anything else he wanted to change clothes and go to church for the Stations of the Cross. He was already so late for work another hour would hardly make a difference. After the Rising it could all be sorted out.

He slipped upstairs as quietly as he could. When he reached the room he shared with Henry he opened the door without knocking—just in time to hear Neville Grantham say ''. . . for the rebellion.''

Ned's heart leaped like a salmon. ''What rebellion?''

Startled, both men turned toward him. Grantham said, ''You weren't supposed to hear that.''

''Then why were you telling a journalist?''

''Because I gave my word as an Etonian that I would inform Henry if we heard anything definite about a rebellion.''

In spite of the gravity of the moment, Ned was amused. ''Not a vow before God, but your word as an Etonian.''

Grantham looked hurt.

''And I gave my word,'' said Henry, ''that whatever he told me would be held in strictest confidence. I'm asking you to honor that, Ned.''

''Why? I didn't give any such pledge.''

''I'm asking you for it now in the name of our friendship. Being a newspaperman means protecting one's sources. What

Neville's been telling me could get him in very serious trouble.''

Ned was exhausted after his troubled night. His eyes were grainy, his head an echoing cavern. At Saint Enda's the precept of honor had been rigorously drilled into the students, and his honor was being called upon now. ''All right, I give you my word I won't say anything. But don't you think you owe me an explanation? You can't leave me with just the wee bit I heard; that's worse than not knowing anything.''

''Very well,'' said Grantham, ''but you never heard this from me. Since February, His Majesty's government has been intercepting and decoding all essential messages passing between the United States, Germany, and Ireland.[1] For reasons I can only speculate about, the Castle hasn't been told. But the viceroy's been taking a keen interest.

''I just learned that on Tuesday the viceroy was informed that a German trawler called the *Aud* is known to be on its way to Ireland, loaded with weapons for the Irish rebels.[2] She's expected to make landfall today, and she'll meet with a rough reception.''

''But today's Good Friday!'' Ned cried in horror. ''I have to warn—''

''You can't tell anyone,'' Grantham interrupted. ''You gave your word.''

Chapter Forty-six

NED saw Henry staring at him, then watched the light of understanding dawn in the journalist's eyes. "Neville, you can't hold Ned to that promise. You don't know what you're asking."

"I don't know anything!" the Englishman snapped. "We none of us know more than bits and pieces, unfortunately. Something's going on, though, something very serious. I don't even know why I came here to tell you, except I should like to think we've become friends, and I have a terrible feeling the situation's about to explode."

Both men looked at Ned.

"Is it?" Henry asked him quietly.

Ned was teetering on the brink of that cliff now. One tiny loss of balance could send him tumbling over, dragging so many friends with him.

If the British knew about the German arms and forestalled them, the provincial Volunteers would have insufficient weapons. MacNeill would be proved right; the corps would be half-armed at best. The Rising might be doomed. Weighed against that possibility even his own honor was expendable.

Ned faced Grantham squarely. "You said it yourself, we none of us know more than bits and pieces. The only thing

I'm sure of is that it's Good Friday and I'm going to do my devotions. So, if you gentlemen will excuse me . . .''

THE horror of it was, he could not find anyone.

His bicycle wheel had been badly mended, but he rode as fast as he dared to the North Circular Road, only to learn that Seán MacDermott had driven off with Pádraic Pearse and Thomas MacDonagh. To make matters worse, Tom Clarke was not in either of his shops and Mrs. Clarke could not, or would not, say where he might be found. Secrecy was clamping down hard.

As for Eamonn Ceannt, his wife reported he had left home early that morning and she did not know where he had gone. She did not know when he would return. She did not know anything, period.

In desperation, Ned went to MacNeill's house on Hatch Street. There was no motorcar parked in front. The curtains were closed. He shouted and banged on the front door and finally kicked it in desperation, but all he could rouse were echoes. No one was home.

Ned sat on the curb for a few minutes with his head in his hands. Then he got back on his bicycle.

At Volunteer Headquarters he found Bulmer Hobson removing papers from boxes and file drawers.[1] He glanced up as Ned entered. "Halloran! You're just in time to help me destroy these records. Fetch a metal wastepaper basket and we'll start burning them. I'd hate to have them fall into the wrong hands." Before Hobson could put action to word, however, a messenger arrived and handed him a folded sheet of letter paper.[2] He scanned its contents at a glance, shook his head, read it again.

"Wait a minute," he told Ned. He read the note a third time, then crumpled it up and threw it on the floor. "Why the hell can't that man make up his mind!" Hobson strode from the room.

Ned retrieved the note and spread it smooth. "Take no further action at present. MacNeill." Dated the same day, it was written on the letterhead of Woodtown Park, a country house belonging to MacNeill's brother.[3]

Obviously, thought Ned, MacNeill had gone to spend the holiday there and Pearse and the others had found him after all and convinced him to hold off. But what would that mean to the overall plan? How did things stand? What should he do?

His eye fell on a paper that had blown off the desk, and he stooped to pick it up.

It was a notice intended for officers, reading, "You will report at Temporary Headquarters, Beresford Place, on Sunday next at 4 p.m. You will provide yourself with a bicycle, a street map of Dublin City, a road map of the Dublin District, and a field message book. You will carry full arms and ammunition, field equipment including overcoat, and rations for eight hours."[4]

Ned took it as a sign. Beresford Place: Liberty Hall. He ran out into Dawson Street and remounted his bicycle.

The armed sentry at the door of Liberty Hall was Eliza Goggins. This time she called his name. "Ned Halloran! It is you, is it not?"

As with the Irish Volunteers, many of Connolly's militia lacked official uniforms. Eliza Goggins was one of the lucky ones. She was still thin, but the dark green tunic gave her a new dignity. She stood proudly erect; she did not fidget.

At her hip she wore a Luger Parabellum pistol.[5]

With an effort Ned tore his eyes away from the weapon. "Miss Goggins, how kind of you to remember me."

"Oh, I couldn't forget you."

"I need to see Mr. Connolly, is he here?"

"He's gone out for a while, but he'll be back. Do you want to wait?"

"I'll wait, I have to talk to him." Ned was still disturbed by Eliza's pistol. He felt there was something vaguely obscene about a woman, aside from Constance Markievicz, carrying a weapon. "That's a fine pistol," he commented.

"Mr. Connolly gave it to me because I couldn't afford to buy one. I know how to use it, too. Madame taught me."

"Madame! Is she here?"

"She's off somewhere with the Fianna. There's a lot of activity today," Eliza added unnecessarily. "I think something's about to happen." Her eyes were sparkling with excitement, bringing a flush of beauty to her plain little face.

"I take it you don't know the plans?"

"I'll be told what I need to know when the time comes," she replied like a good soldier.

All of them waiting. All of them poised on the brink of that cliff.

Ned sat down on a bench near the door and fought to keep awake. The afternoon was passing; time was the enemy now. He did not know what to do except wait for Connolly. He could not think past that point.

Once he went over and tried to start a conversation with Eliza Goggins but she discouraged him. Casual chat was not properly military.

Activity swirled around him, but no one else had time for conversation, either. Men and women were constantly entering and leaving the hall, many of them carrying weapons.

At last James Connolly came striding through the doorway. Ned hurried to intercept him. "I have to speak to you right away, sir, on a matter of the utmost urgency."

"The last time you spoke to me here on a matter of urgency—"

"I know, and I apologize. But please?"

Connolly read the desperation in his eyes. "All right, what is it?"

He listened with growing alarm. When Ned told him there was only one German trawler instead of the expected three, he struck his forehead with the heel of his hand in frustration. "If what you say is true, Halloran, the British know all about those weapons by now! They may even have captured them."

"I'm afraid it is true. I have no reason to doubt my source; he took a fearful risk in telling me."

"Shite!" Connolly spat out the vulgarity as if it burned his mouth.

"Furthermore," Ned went on, "Mr. Pearse told Professor

MacNeill the German arms were coming to persuade him to let the Rising go ahead.''

"You're certain of that too, I suppose?"

Ned related the scene with Bulmer Hobson at Volunteer Headquarters.

Connolly pounded his fist against the nearest wall. "What a blasted cock-up! We'd better have a meeting of the Military Council right away. I'll send a motor cab to collect them and bring them here, that's the quickest. Do you think Pearse will be back at Saint Enda's by now?"

"I imagine he will."

"Well, you've done your duty for today, Halloran. I'll take it from here. Why don't you get some supper for yourself?"

"I don't think I could swallow a bite," Ned said truthfully. While he was waiting for Connolly he had become aware of a pounding headache.

"Go anyway. Nothing will be happening for a while."

As he left the building Ned paused to repeat Connolly's words to Eliza Goggins. "Nothing will be happening for a while."

"When it does, I'm ready," she assured him.

GOOD Friday was almost over and he had not yet been to church.

He wondered if Mr. Pearse had.

By the time Ned returned to Gardiner Place and tumbled into bed his head hurt so badly he could hardly bear to blink his eyes. Henry was not home yet, for which Ned was thankful. His head hurt dreadfully and he did not want to talk. He just wanted to sleep for days and days.

HE came swimming up through layers of fuzziness to find someone shaking his shoulder none too gently.

"Ned. Ned! Wake up, will you? What the hell's going on?"

"How should I know? I'm asleep."

"You're awake now. Talk to me."

"What time is it? What *day* is it?"

"Saturday, middle of the afternoon. You seemed so exhausted I let you sleep this morning, but you can't sleep any longer. Open your eyes, Ned!"

The room swam into focus. Henry was bending over him. One look at the man's face made Ned sit bolt upright. "What's happened?"

"I was hoping you could tell me. Late yesterday Seán MacDermott and some other men took over Volunteer Headquarters. Bulmer Hobson's nowhere to be found.[6] Rumors are running wild. I just spoke to Neville Grantham, who says Dublin Castle's finally been told about the German trawler. They're furious that the Admiralty informed the viceroy but didn't tell them."

"What about the ship, Henry?"

"When the *Aud* arrived twenty-nine English warships were waiting for her, I'm afraid.[7] The German commander scuttled his vessel off Queenstown. She's taken the weapons to the bottom, but her officers and crew were captured."

Ned stared at him aghast.

"Apparently there was another ship," Henry went on, "a German U-boat that put three men ashore on Banna Strand in Tralee Bay. A British intelligence officer has already called on the *Independent* to tell us we can't publish anything about the *Aud*, and all we can say about the three men on Banna Strand is that one of them has been arrested. No names. But between you and me, he's Sir Roger Casement."

"Sir Roger?" Ned was totally, terribly, awake. "Oh God, Henry, what's happening?"

"That's what I was hoping you could tell me."

"I don't know anything at this stage, except I'd best find Mr. Pearse."

Henry said, "It *is* Pearse, isn't it? Pearse is leading a Rising."

"Not just him. It's Seán MacDermott and Tom Clarke and—"

The journalist abruptly put his hand over Ned's mouth.

"Don't tell me any more. I was wrong to ask you."

"But I thought—"

"Never mind what you thought. I have ethics, too. Go find Pearse and warn him."

THE bicycle looked worse than Ned remembered. It was actually dangerous to ride, but that could hardly matter now. He raced through the streets, taking fearful risks with the cobblestones.

When he reached Volunteer Headquarters there was no sign of Pearse, but Seán MacDermott was there. For once the laughter had gone out of him. His handsome face was grim as he affirmed, "It was Casement, all right. God alone knows what he was doing there. Maybe he was just trying to get home for the Rising.

"Anyway, last night we had an emergency conference and decided Eoin MacNeill had to be informed, so Pat and Thomas MacDonagh went to tell him. We hoped MacNeill would agree that fast action is imperative now, but the news about the *Aud* had the opposite effect on him. He's definitely decided to cancel the Easter Sunday maneuvers, and he won't change his mind this time.[8] He's sent out orders countermanding Pearse's orders, he's putting notices in the newspapers, and he's even sent The O'Rahilly down to Limerick to cancel arrangements there."

Over. It was over, then, Ned thought with sudden anguish. Snatched away at the last moment, all those months and years of work, the dreams of centuries . . .

MacDermott was saying, "Of course, this has given the Castle the excuse they've been looking for. Everyone's in jeopardy—Volunteers, Citizen Army, the lot. God knows what dossiers they've compiled to use against us. If we *don't* act fast we'll all be arrested and everything really will be lost."

Ned's breath caught in his throat. "Do you mean—go ahead anyway?"

"I don't see that we have any choice. We can stack the

cards in our favor, though. Easter Monday is the big race meet at Fairyhouse. Most of the Dublin garrison will be out there, miles from anywhere, especially since they think any danger is past. Postponing the Rising for a day would give us an almost unguarded city. Joe and Thomas are in agreement with me.''

''Have you spoken to Mr. Pearse yet?''

''Not yet; he went back to Saint Enda's last night. Are you going out there?''

''I'm on my bike!''

''Good. We can hold a strategy meeting at Liberty Hall first thing in the morning. The only person I'm worried about notifying is Eamonn; he's been scouting around the city trying to get his communications network set up, and I don't know where he is. I've sent Cathal Brugha to look for him.''

''I'm sorry I can't help you. Mr. Pearse says I'm supposed to know where everyone is this week.''

At last the tension went out of MacDermott's face and he laughed. ''This is a revolution, Ned! You'll be lucky to know where you are yourself.''

''I'll just stay close to Mr. Pearse, then. But before I go, would you take a look at my bicycle? I had an accident the other day and it wasn't mended properly. A bicycle will get me to Saint Enda's faster than the Rathfarnham tram, but I don't want to wind up in a ditch again.''

MacDermott followed Ned out into the street and crouched down beside his machine, muttering good-naturedly, ''The things I do for Ireland.''

As he rode through the city, Ned glanced wistfully at the public call boxes he passed. How much simpler it would be if he could telephone. But artificial forms of communication were suspect now. He recalled a line from one of Pádraic Pearse's lectures: ''The words of the bards come down the centuries to us, warm with living breath.''

That was all one could trust: the message warm with living breath.

As Ned pedaled up the drive of Saint Enda's, Pádraic Pearse came out of the house to meet him. "I saw you from my window. Come into my study and we'll talk privately. I don't want to alarm the women."

He listened gravely while Ned explained what he knew of the situation, concluding with, "Seán MacDermott wants to have a meeting on Sunday morning in Liberty Hall."

"Willie and I will be there. In fact, I think we should leave Saint Enda's tonight, just in case someone is sent to arrest us. You wait here, Ned; I'll get Willie and we'll go in to Dublin together. He and I can spend the night at a safe house, and it will give me a chance to talk to Connolly and one or two others before the meeting."[9]

Ned sat on the edge of his chair in Pearse's study for a while, then got up and paced the floor. As he looked out the big windows he could see the full glory of Irish Eastertide in bloom.

It's so beautiful, he thought, and it's our country. Why can't they simply let us have it? We've never invaded anyone else's country. All we ask is to hold ours in peace. Is that too much?

Chapter Forty-seven

Easter Sunday. Ned went to Mass and took Communion, then ate a hearty breakfast at his boardinghouse before going to Liberty Hall. He suspected he would need the energy.

Once again Eliza Goggins was on sentry duty, together with several armed men who eyed each new arrival with suspicion. "There's a big meeting in Mr. Connolly's office," she told Ned. "Have you seen the papers? The *Sunday Independent* is carrying an order signed by Eoin MacNeill and calling off the maneuvers today."

"I know."

"What does it mean? I don't understand."

Ned gave Eliza a wry smile. "Here's your brother. I don't understand, either."

Eventually the meeting broke up and people began leaving the building. As Eamonn Ceannt headed for the door Ned heard him say, "If we last a month the British will come to terms." James Connolly called after him, "If we win we'll all be great fellows. If we lose we'll be the greatest scoundrels in history."[1]

Pádraic Pearse and Con Markievicz stopped to hold an earnest conversation with Seán MacDermott, but Thomas MacDonagh noticed Ned and came over to him.

Ned greeted him with, "Where's Joe Plunkett?"

"He's ill, I'm afraid. Michael Collins brought him to the Hotel Metropole to be closer to the G.P.O.,[2] but we're letting him sleep for now. We'll tell him about this later on today."

"Was there a decision in the meeting?"

"Not at first. We're all determined the Rising go forward, but there was a difference of opinion as to timing. Seán suggested we postpone it until Monday, while Pat and I both felt we needed more time to reorganize.[3]

"But Tom Clarke said it would be too confusing to make changes at this late date. He argued that if the Rising went ahead as planned the Volunteers would assume MacNeill's countermand was a Castle hoax and ignore it. Of course Connolly simply wants the revolution to begin, the sooner the better. Last month would have suited him just fine.

"I think we reached the best possible compromise under the circumstances. Pat will issue orders supporting MacNeill's countermand. That should lull the Castle into thinking the danger's over and staying their hand, at least for a few days. So Easter Sunday maneuvers are officially canceled."

Ned was puzzled. "You call that a compromise?"

MacDonagh's eyes danced. "There'll be a second set of orders. The Rising begins noon Monday instead."

"Yes!" Ned punched the air with his fist. He could feel a bubble rising in him, filling him with radiance.

PÁDRAIC Pearse was going to prepare the new orders and wait long enough to see them printed and sent out. James Connolly anticipated little difficulty in notifying the Citizen Army, as they were Dubliners anyway. But the wide-flung Volunteers were a different story.

Members of Cumann na mBan were to carry the orders to the Volunteers in the rest of the country.[4] Con Markievicz had argued that women were best for the job because they were less likely to be suspected, and the men—with the exception of Pádraic Pearse—agreed. James Connolly volunteered his daughter, Nora, to inform the Irish Volunteers in Belfast.

Once the dispatch carriers were on their way Pearse intended to go home. "Willie and I want to have Easter dinner at Saint Enda's," he told Ned. "I believe it's safe enough now for one more night, and we need to say a proper farewell to Mother. Would you like to come with us?"

"I would surely!"

But first he had to see Síle.

He sped to the Fairview house. Hearing his familiar whistle, she came out to meet him. In spite of Ned's tension he noticed how the sunlight burnished her hair. "Do you know what's happened?" she asked as he parked his bicycle. "I've been reading the papers. I can't believe it's canceled."

Ned fought back his desire to tell her everything. "There won't be any maneuvers today, Síle. Mr. Pearse is preparing new orders to that effect right now. Then he's going back to Saint Enda's and I'm going with him."

"Oh." Her eyes told her disappointment.

He understood what she was feeling and opened his arms. She folded herself into his embrace like a bird settling into its nest. They stood holding each other, letting their bodies do the talking.

At last Síle spoke. "There's no one in the house; they've all gone home to be with their families. Except for me."

Her hair smelled of white lilac. "You are with your family," Ned told her.

THEY lay together on her bed, floating in opalescent light. April glowed through the lace curtains on the window. A quiet Easter in Dublin.

Sunday with Síle.

She kept her room spotlessly clean. The sheets were soft from countless boilings and smelled of sun and wind from hanging on the clothesline. Síle's counterpane was blue. Her pillowcase was embroidered. Everything was fresh and wholesome—even the vase of daffodils on the windowsill.

Ned ran his palm over the curves of her naked body, memorizing the texture of her skin. He wanted to know all of Síle, not just her sex but the wings of her shoulder blades and the taut column of her throat. He loved the soft little roll of fat below her waist. He could take hold of it with his two hands and pull her tight against him. He loved the seashell shape of her ears and her fox-colored hair. Her eyelids with their tiny blue veins, closing in pleasure when he kissed them. The dimples in her buttocks.

The glisten of his semen drying on her thighs.

"You flooded me," she said with a lazy laugh. "I'm overflowing."

"Is there room for more?"

"There's always room for more." She reached for him.

Suddenly Ned was suffocating with desire. He wanted to take her again, slow and tender, then urgent and intense, loving her for hours, making it last forever. In Síle's arms he could forget the world beyond. Let the revolution start without him.

Time. There is never enough time!

Leaving her was the hardest thing he had ever done. But Pádraic Pearse was waiting.

Síle walked out with him to his bicycle. "When will I see you again?"

He could not tell her the whole truth, but he would not lie to her. "I don't know; it may be several days. In the meantime, take care of yourself and . . . do something for me?"

"I will of course."

"Keep an eye on Precious, will you?"

Síle caught him by the arm and made him face her. "What's wrong, Ned?"

"Just look after Precious. There is a man, a priest, called Father Paul O'Shaughnessy; he's assisting the chaplain at Kilmainham. If anything should happen to me, get to him and tell him. He's to take Precious to my sister in America."

Her eyes were wide with alarm. "What are you trying to tell me?"

"Just promise me, Síle."

"I won't promise you any such thing. Precious is ours, don't you know that? If anything happened to you I would take her and keep her myself, I would . . . Oh Ned, tell me!"

WITH the students gone home for the holidays, Saint Enda's was strangely quiet. Mary Brigid came back for Easter Sunday, but her mother warned everyone to say nothing about the Rising in her hearing. "There is no point in upsetting the child," Mrs. Pearse said. "We don't know how she may take it."

Family and guests gathered around the mahogany table in the dining room, pretending to eat the Sunday dinner Mrs. Pearse had lovingly prepared. So much food, so little appetite. Only Mary Brigid ate with enthusiasm, taking second helpings. Ned mashed his peas into his potatoes and hid the debris with bread.

They spoke of the fine weather and the summer to come. They spoke of the autumn and the next school term.

When dinner was over Mary Brigid gave an impromptu concert on her harp. Con Colbert took her home before returning the borrowed Ford to its owners. Afterward he went for a stroll through the grounds of Saint Enda's with Des Ryan and Ned. "I really hated returning that motorcar," Colbert confessed to them. "But I had given my word."

The echo of the harp seemed to linger on the twilight air. In the fireplace of his cottage on the grounds, Michael MacRory was burning turf, and the fragrance gave Ned an aching nostalgia. "Will it ever be like this again?"

Des Ryan shook his head. "Not for us, I suspect."

"Just think," mused Con Colbert. "This morning the Volunteers woke up expecting a big march today. What a surprise they had when they read the papers."

Ned said, "Some of them may already have gone away for the holidays because they think everything's canceled. We've dispatched the new orders, but I don't know if they'll reach the men in time."

"Do we stand a chance of winning if they don't?"

Ned was watching the last glow of light fade in the western sky. He turned slowly to face his friends. "I think not."

"Do *they* know?" Ryan inclined his head toward the house.

"I'm sure they do. Patrick Henry Pearse—the headmaster has the same name as a hero of the American Revolution, did you know that? The American Patrick Henry said 'Give me liberty or give me death.' That's how our Mr. Pearse feels, too."

They were Saint Enda's boys, encouraged to debate. For the sake of the old custom Ryan argued, "Mr. Pearse has that right, but does he also have the right to sacrifice other men?"

"We are none of us being forced. We're Volunteers, remember? That's how it should be; that's what makes conscription so awful. If we decide to put our lives at risk in the name of freedom, that is our choice."

Con Colbert joined the debate. "But we'll also be committing treason. What do you say about that?"

Ned was ready for him. At some point he had stopped questioning. In the words of Pearse's boyhood riding instructor, he had "thrown his heart over the fence" and was prepared to follow wherever it led. He told Colbert, "The definition of *treason* in the Oxford English Dictionary is 'violation by subject of allegiance to sovereign or State.'[5] Ireland can't be considered disloyal to England because it has never been loyal to England. Edward Carson and his Unionists don't speak for the majority in this country, not by a long chalk. *We* haven't sworn allegiance to King George or his Great Britain. We're Irish. Our allegiance is to Ireland." He set his jaw at the stubborn angle his family knew so well. "If we fail at least we'll have tried."

Des Ryan shouted, "Right you are!"

Con Colbert put two fingers in his mouth and gave an ear-splitting whistle.

They rambled on until they came to the playing field where they had enjoyed so many hurling matches. They took imaginary swings with invisible hurling sticks, and Ned made a spectacular run down the field with the other two after him.

Eventually a chill breeze sent them back to the house.

Night was falling.

Ned was awake before dawn on Monday morning. He knelt on the bare floor of Saint Brendan's dormitory checking off his kit against the Volunteer equipment leaflet: Uniform or clothes of neutral color, nothing white or shiny.[6] *Uniform; I have that.* Strong comfortable boots or heavy shoes. Overcoat.

Rifle with sling and cleaning outfit. *One of the old Mausers from Howth, though not my original weapon.* Ammunition with bandolier or ammunition pouches. Bayonet with scabbard. *Bought from Lawlor's, almost the last one they had left. Charged me too much for it.* Strong knife.

Haversack with water bottle, mess tin, knife, fork, spoon, cup, one dry stick for starting a fire. Knapsack containing spare shirt, pair of socks, towel, soap, comb, scissors, needle, thread, safety pins.

In tunic pocket: clasp knife, notebook and pencil, matches in a tin box, bootlaces, strong cord, a candle, colored handkerchiefs.

Maps. *Lots of maps.*

His heart was thundering as he dressed. His fingers were so cold he had to warm them in his armpits before he could fasten the buttons.

When he came down the stairs he could hear a murmur of voices from the dining room. Margaret Pearse sounded upset; Willie was trying to soothe her. Plates clattered. Someone dropped a cup.

"Do you want some breakfast, Ned?" Mrs. Pearse asked as he entered the room. She was on her knees, cleaning up the broken cup and spilled tea while both Con Colbert and Des Ryan made ineffectual efforts to help her. "Perhaps a nice boiled egg? And there are creamed kidneys on the sideboard; I made them special. My Little Man is so fond of creamed kidneys."

When Ned knocked at the study door the headmaster opened it at once. "Is it time to go?"

"It is, sir."

"I shall just be a moment."

They gathered in the entrance hall. Margaret was on the verge of tears; Mrs. Pearse was pale but composed. Two sets of military kit were piled by the front door. Ned, Con Colbert, and Des Ryan already had theirs strapped to their backs.

Emerging from his study, Pearse handed some last-minute business letters to his mother. "You are not to worry. Everything will be fine."

Mrs. Pearse forced her lips into a lopsided smile that threatened to slide off her face. "Now Pat, don't do anything rash."[7]

"No, Mother," he replied submissively. He bent his head for her kiss.

Five bicycles were waiting at the foot of the steps. Con Colbert was still unhappy about having returned the Ford. Ned consoled, "Don't moan about it, we're probably safer on our bikes anyway."

"I'm a good driver!"

"I never said you weren't."

Pádraic and Willie cycled side by side with their greatcoats bulging over their kit and provisions.[8] The commander-in-chief was carrying a Browning automatic pistol and had completed his uniform with a sword, which was awkward to manage on a bicycle.

The brothers did not speak much during the journey, though once Willie remarked, "There are some who will condemn us, I suppose. They'll say we were arrogant. Or mad."

"We cannot live our lives according to what others may think," his brother reminded him. "We are answerable only to God. He knows that every motive is not suspect, nor every passion impure."

"Does Mother understand, really?"

"I believe she does," Pearse replied. "She asked me to write a little poem for her, something that would sound as if she said it herself. I have it with me in my wallet so I can finish it. I am trying to put into words what I know is in her heart.''

The poem lay in the wallet he carried in his inside pocket; over his own heart.

THE MOTHER
by P. H. Pearse

I do not grudge them: Lord, I do not grudge
My two strong sons that I have seen go out
To break their strength and die, they and a few,
In bloody protest for a glorious thing,
They shall be spoken of among their people,
The generations shall remember them,
And call them blessed;
But I will speak their names to my own heart
In the long nights;
The little names that were familiar once
Around my dead hearth.
Lord, thou art hard on mothers:
We suffer in their coming and their going;
And tho' I grudge them not, I weary, weary
Of the long sorrow—And yet I have my joy:
My sons were faithful, and they fought.

Chapter Forty-eight

B<small>Y</small> Monday morning Neville Grantham was a troubled man. The previous night he had attended a conference in the Viceregal Lodge at which the decision had been taken to arrest the rebel leaders and disarm the Dublin Volunteers.[1] Although Sir Matthew Nathan was reluctant at first, Baron Wimborne was adamant.

"There must be no clemency; we have to make an example of traitors," he insisted. "In the light of his past service to the Crown, Sir Roger's treachery is particularly abhorrent. Consorting with the Germans, indeed! Further, I want to implicate as many Sinn Féiners as I can in this . . . this *invasion* of Great Britain by the king's enemies. Arrest them all; we have an internment policy in place now. If we just stir up the hornet's nest and leave the hornets we may have serious trouble."

The viceroy dictated a letter to this effect which he sent in haste to Secretary Birrell in London.[2] If it proved necessary, he was confident pressure from Birrell would force Nathan to move against the rebels.

As they left the Phoenix Park late that night, Grantham tried to voice his own concerns to the under-secretary. "I don't think Baron Wimborne has a full grasp of the situation."

Nathan sat stony-faced beside him. He did not like being

summoned to the Viceregal Lodge on Sunday night and accused of incompetence. He had been patient with the Irish in
an effort to dispel what he felt was an unfortunate reputation
for British obduracy. Wimborne, however, said he had vac-
illated when he should have been uncompromising. Wimborne said the job of a colonial administration was to weed
out dissidents and undesirables. Wimborne said a lot of things,
all of them highly critical of Sir Matthew Nathan.

"The republicans are acting against the interest of the
Crown, that's what we have to remember," Nathan told Grantham now.

"Are you going to order arrests?"

"We have a little time; tomorrow's the Easter bank holiday.
The viceroy will want a report on his desk immediately, however, so tonight I want you to go through our files and draw
up that list of known troublemakers for him.[3] He wants at
least sixty and would prefer a hundred. If you can't find
enough evidence to justify arresting them, talk to the DMP.
See what sort of police records they can come up with."

It was Monday morning by the time Neville Grantham finally left Dublin Castle. He felt exhausted . . . and dirty. But
he did not go to his apartment off Merrion Square for a bath
and a few hours' sleep. Instead he wandered through the city,
trying to square his conscience with his duty.

He had come to know the Irish as Baron Wimborne never
would, and try as he might, he could not condemn the rebels
for wanting independence from a foreign power that had
served them so badly for so long. He found himself wondering
how he would feel if Germany won the war and reduced England from a prosperous country to an impoverished one; if
the English language was forbidden and German substituted;
if English people were driven out to make room for Germans.
Would he not fight back? Of course he would—to the death
if necessary. Nor would he hesitate to take any advantage he
could.

Grantham loved his country and was uncomfortable with
the image of her as oppressor. If the Irish wanted to be free,
let them! his conscience cried. The desire did not spring up

overnight, it had been there for centuries, surfacing again and again, as indestructible as this island.

But they are traitors, a different voice within him argued. Traitors to the very Great Britain of which this land is a part. They must be punished; it is our duty to punish them to protect the empire.

Neville Grantham found himself standing outside the building that had once housed the Irish Parliament, staring at a citadel of lost dreams.

"What is the answer?" he murmured to himself.

An old woman with a black shawl over her head and a broken shopping basket on her arm pushed past him. Her chilblains were burning like fire, some soldier had got her youngest daughter pregnant, and she did not have enough money to feed her family. The well-dressed toff blocking the footpath infuriated her.

"Yer blockin' me way," she snarled.

APRIL 24, 1916; almost eleven o'clock. In luxurious townhouses around elegant Georgian squares, Ascendancy Dublin slumbered in the twilight of an Edwardian dream. The Great War was being fought on distant shores. The empire seemed invulnerable.

In a radiantly blue sky seagulls swooped and soared over the Liffey, indifferent to the affairs of men. Like the occupants of the teeming tenements, survival was their preoccupation.

As he cycled through the city, Ned thought it strange not to be going to work on a Monday morning. Although this was a bank holiday, the *Independent* would go to press just the same. He wondered what they would make of his absence. He might well lose his job, but that was unimportant now. He was on his way to fight for Ireland.

The streets of Dublin were thronged with people enjoying the glorious weather. Many of them were country families who had come into the city for the day, taking the place of the soldiers and city dwellers who had gone into the country for the races. They did not even glance at the four Volunteers

cycling past them. That too seemed strange to Ned. People
should be cheering. They should be throwing their hats in the
air as the commander-in-chief passed by.

OVER Liberty Hall floated the green flag of Ireland, emblazoned with the harp without the crown.[4] Bicycles were parked
a dozen deep in some places around the building. Some two
hundred and fifty members of the Citizen Army were formed
into a double column in the open square in front of the hall.
James Connolly was giving the company commanders their
final orders. His uniform fitted badly, emphasizing his pot-
belly; his bandy legs were accentuated by polished leather
leggings. He was no classic Gaelic chieftain, yet there was
something indomitable about him.

As Pearse and the others dismounted from their bicycles
the first company of thirty-six was preparing to move out. An
elderly man and a boy no older than twelve hurried up to
them. ''Here's my lad,'' the old man said. ''Will you take
him with you? I'm too old for the job myself.''

When the company—including the twelve-year-old—
moved off toward Eden Quay, James Connolly beckoned to
Pádraic Pearse, then went into Liberty Hall.

But Pearse was surrounded by Irish Volunteers asking
questions. Less than a quarter of them had heather-green uniforms. The rest wore work clothes or their Sunday suits, with
identifying yellow armlets around their left sleeves and Sam
Browne belts tightly fastened over their jackets. Those who
did not have Sam Brownes had attached their equipment with
mazes of straps and string. Ned observed a few modern Lee-
Enfields and Sniders and a couple of Martini rifles smuggled
in from Italy, but the majority of firearms consisted of the
obsolete Howth Mausers. Some men had a rifle on one shoulder and a shotgun on the other.

Some had no firearms at all.

As he waited for Pearse's orders, Ned listened without comment to the conversations around him. Some of the Volunteers
were still expecting routine maneuvers, a 'route march'

through the city. Most knew better by now, however. How could they not know? The air was sparking with excitement, unmistakable as the tang of salt from the sea.

Thomas MacDonagh joined Pearse and they stood talking together for a minute or two. As Ned watched, Pearse caught his underlip with his teeth and shook his head slowly from side to side. MacDonagh put one hand on his shoulder and the two old friends gazed into one another's eyes. Then Commandant MacDonagh snapped a crisp salute and went to join his men.

Next Pearse had a few words with Seán T. O'Kelly, a captain in the Volunteers who had helped organize the gunrunning at Kilcoole. As a result of The O'Rahilly's apparent defection, Pearse asked O'Kelly to be his aide-de-camp. "I would be honored," O'Kelly replied.

"Halloran here is my personal courier. He will help you in any way he can." Pearse then hurried up the steps and into Liberty Hall. His new aide-de-camp and his brother, Willie, followed him.

Minutes later fifty-six uniformed Volunteers came marching up, led by Joe Plunkett's brother George. The company, which proudly called itself Pearse's Own, had taken the tram in from Kimmage.[5] Not far behind them was a motor cab accompanied by Joe's youngest brother, Jack, on his motorcycle. The cab nosed its way to the steps of Liberty Hall, and Joe Plunkett himself, looking very ill but determined, got out.

Pearse's Own gave him a crisp salute.

Plunkett's throat was still wrapped in bandages, but he had dressed for the occasion in a custom-made officer's uniform complete with saber, highly polished riding boots, and spurs. He also wore a filigreed silver bracelet on one wrist, and his fingers glittered with rings.

Two other Volunteers had been in the cab with him.[6] One helped him up the steps to Liberty Hall; the other followed. Joe smiled at Ned with his eyes but did not speak; he was hoarding his strength. The man supporting his arm was big and handsome, with a good-humored face. His nose was long and fine, his jowls full, his gray eyes set wide apart. He gave Ned a friendly nod as they passed.

"Who's that?" asked Con Colbert.

"Mick Collins. I met him last time I was at Larkfield. He's Joe Plunkett's aide-de-camp; he'll be in headquarters with us."

"Is Madame Markievicz going to be there, too?"

A uniformed Citizen Army officer overheard. "Not likely! Madame thinks headquarters will be too tame. See her over there, just driving off with Dr. Lynn?[7] They have that car packed with medical supplies. They're taking some to City Hall first for Seán Connolly's company, then the rest to Michael Mallin in Stephen's Green. The best of the action will be on that side of the river, you know. Our crowd is going to march on Dublin Castle."

Des Ryan gave a low whistle. "Mr. Pearse calls Dublin Castle Ireland's Bastille.[8] Do you have enough men to take it?"

"There are always too many soldiers inside, I'm afraid.[9] But Mr. Connolly's plan is to seal up the Castle by seizing the guardroom and gates in the Upper Yard. We'll have snipers in City Hall and the other buildings facing the gates, and hold the government penned inside the Castle like rats in a trap."

Ned and Ryan looked at one another. "It might work," Ryan said hopefully.

The Volunteers were also beginning to leave for their posts. As Thomas MacDonagh marched away at the head of the Second Battalion he turned his head slightly and looked in Ned's direction. For a moment their eyes met across the distance between them. The little professor raised two fingers to the brim of his hat.

Then he was gone.

WHILE he waited for Pádraic Pearse to come out of Liberty Hall, Ned studied the scene around him. He had the vague idea that he might write about it some day.

After the Rising.

Off to one side he observed two horse-drawn drays piled high with pitchforks, shovels, pickaxes, crowbars, and the favorite weapon of rebels of a bygone era: pikestaffs. Pearse's Own had helped themselves to some of the pikes to augment their other weapons. In addition to the drays there were a couple of large wickerwork hampers holding oak batons, and a closed cab that Ned assumed contained Connolly's grenades and homemade bombs.

Everything was ready—and nothing was ready, Ned thought to himself. For once he was sorry he knew as much as he did.

James Connolly emerged from Liberty Hall alone and stood gazing thoughtfully at the remaining men, assessing numbers. When someone spoke to him, Ned was just close enough to hear him reply, "Bill, we're going out to be slaughtered."

"Is there no hope?"

"None whatever," Connolly said cheerfully. He clapped his friend on the back and strode down the steps.

Ned turned to Con Colbert. "Have you plenty of ammunition?"

"A hundred rounds, why?"

"Stay close to Mr. Pearse. I don't think headquarters is going to be so tame."

Colbert nodded. When Pádraic Pearse and Joseph Plunkett came out of the hall together he quietly moved into place behind the commander.

As Connolly had done before him, Pearse surveyed the troops. From his vantage point Ned had the same view. Including those who had already left, the insurgents totaled only around twelve hundred. Either the officers had not been able to get word to enough of their men, or the rank and file had been confused by the contradictory orders. Perhaps some suspected what was about to happen and had simply lost their nerve.

Whatever the cause, the result was the same. The army upon which so much depended was decimated.

A dusty De Dion Bouton turned into Beresford Place and

The O'Rahilly emerged to loud cheers. Through the open car door a load of additional rifles was plainly visible.

He's given up on MacNeill, Ned thought. It seemed a good omen. "Perhaps more will still come," he remarked to Con Colbert.

The O'Rahilly ran up the steps to shake hands with Pearse and Plunkett. For the first time that day Pádraic Pearse smiled. "I'm glad to see you, Michael. I was afraid we'd lost you."

"I've helped to wind up the clock," came the jaunty reply. "I might as well hear it strike!"[10]

The officers were holding a last-minute strategy conference when Mary Brigid Pearse came running up with her hair flying and her face flushed. She flung herself at Pádraic Pearse and to his intense embarrassment cried, "I've just heard! No one ever tells me anything. Come home, Pat, and leave all this foolishness!"[11]

He patted her awkwardly and whispered something. She took half a step backward, looking around as if disoriented. "Will Cumann na mBan see that my sister gets home safely?" Pearse requested. "I must tend to the business of the day."

PROMPTLY at noon a bugle blew. James Connolly bellowed a command to form ranks, and Pearse and Plunkett joined him at the head of the combined force destined for the G.P.O. The commander-in-chief took the center position. Any trace of the gentle schoolmaster had vanished; in that penultimate moment Pádraic Pearse looked both stern and noble.

James Connolly, Commandant-General of the Dublin forces, was on his right, with Joseph Plunkett, Chief of Staff, on his left—a triumph of willpower over mortality. As he marched forward, Joe Plunkett unsheathed his saber and held it up to catch the sun.[12]

The rest followed, Irish Volunteers and Citizen Army mingling together. They were scarcely a hundred and fifty in total but one body now, the advance guard of a new republic.

Perhaps more will come.

Tom Clarke, President of the Provisional Government, walked to one side of the column with Seán MacDermott, who was limping badly and leaning on a cane. Seán O'Kelly, Michael Collins, and The O'Rahilly stayed close to the leaders. Farther back was Winifred Carney, James Connolly's devoted secretary and the only woman in the company. She was armed with a large Webley pistol. Beside her was Connolly's fifteen-year-old son, Roderic, better known as Rory.

The parade included the loaded drays, The O'Rahilly's De Dion Bouton with its cargo of rifles, the closed cab, two motorcyclists, and the company from Kimmage guarding the rear[13]—followed by several grubby street urchins and a yapping dog.

The column stepped out briskly, moving with certainty of purpose as they proceeded from Liberty Hall down Lower Abbey Street. There were no soldiers in evidence. A few civilians stopped to watch the march go by, but most were as indifferent as always. It did not matter. Nothing mattered now but the doing of it.

In the middle of the column, Ned walked with his shoulders back and his chin held high. *Marching in the company of men, with the golden sunshine pouring over them like a blessing.*

After the Great Famine the political theoretician James Fintan Lalor had written, "Somewhere and somehow, and by someone, a beginning must be made, and the first act of armed resistance is always premature, imprudent, and foolish."[14]

Sometimes you have to make things come right or die trying!

Chapter Forty-nine

THE column reached Sackville Street. People stepped back from the curb to give them room and one or two, recognizing the uniforms, even cheered. Traffic halted enough to allow the parade out into the boulevard. They swung right and marched in the direction of Nelson's Pillar.

Revving the motor of his cycle, Jack Plunkett called, "I hope we see some action today, lads!"

Several of the older men smiled.

The classical facade of the General Post Office was serene in the brilliant sunshine. In spite of the bank holiday the post office was doing a brisk business. Upstairs was the telegraph office, where soldiers were posted to guard the switchboard for the duration of the war.

The column halted at the G.P.O. George Plunkett began issuing commands to the men from Kimmage.[1] "Into line— turn left." They drew up in two lines facing the front entrance. "A Section—right wheel!" A section trotted off toward Henry Street. "D Section—left wheel!" D Section set off toward O'Connell Bridge, and B and C Sections stood firm, waiting.

People passing in and out beneath the portico were unaware that anything was amiss until suddenly James Connolly's strident voice rang out, ordering the entire column, "Left turn, the G.P.O.—Charge!"

A wild cheer burst from the throats of the little army. Seventy men ran for the main entrance while the rest raced off to take up positions nearby.

The O'Rahilly led the charge into the building with his drawn pistol in his hand, safety catch off.[2] A young female customer gave a shriek as if she had seen a mouse and Con Colbert paused to apologize to her.

At the sight of an armed mob invading the post office the staff behind the counters froze. The customers milled around in confusion until the voice of James Connolly rose above the clamor, ordering them to leave peacefully. A lieutenant in the uniform of the Royal Fusiliers who was interrupted in the act of writing out a telegram to his wife in England protested. Michael Collins promptly yanked the telephone cord out of the post office call box, heaved the startled lieutenant onto one of the large glass-topped tables in the center of the room, trussed him with the phone cord, then laughingly dumped him for safekeeping into the same call box.

There were several other British officers in the post office. The O'Rahilly informed them they were political prisoners of the new Irish Republic and would be treated with all due courtesy. Considering the fate of their fellow in the phone box, however, they looked dubious.

A policeman who had been waiting his turn to send a telegram found himself facing an insurgent holding a leveled rifle. "Don't shoot me," he pleaded in a northside Dublin accent. "I've done ye no harm."

"We don't shoot prisoners," Collins assured him.[3]

"I'm not leaving until I have my stamps!" an indignant matron cried. But there was no one to sell them to her. After a few moments of bewildered disbelief the post office staff had decided to abandon ship. Some even vaulted over the counters in their hurry to get outside. They joined the gathering spectators in the street in spite of a jocular invitation from Seán MacDermott: "Stay and accept our hospitality. This is going to be the safest place in Dublin soon!"

While the ground floor was being secured, a squad of men was sent in search of the telegraph office on the floor above. Ned joined the party that ran up the wide stairs, only to be met on the landing by seven soldiers holding rifles. Someone nervously snapped off a pistol shot that grazed the forehead of one of the soldiers. The sound echoed alarmingly in the marble interior. Blood pouring, the wounded man staggered backward.

The others immediately dropped their weapons and threw up their hands. "Our guns aren't loaded!"

Within minutes the squad located the telegraph office. When they burst through the door shouting for everyone to put up their hands, they found only the female supervisor on duty. The other telegraphists had already fled, but the sturdy middle-aged Scot refused to abandon her post. "I have to send out yesterday's death notices," she insisted. "The next of kin must always be informed when—"

"We can do that for you."

"Ye wouldn't know how to—"

"I assure you we have someone who does. Halloran, take her downstairs and see her safely out of the building, will you?"

There was a crash of glass below. James Connolly was ordering the men to smash the windows in the lobby and barricade them.

The Rising had begun.

By the time Ned returned to the main hall it was chaotic. Writing desks and heavy glass-topped display tables had been pushed against the walls. Men were standing on them to knock out the upper panes of the windows with their rifle butts. Others were busy stuffing the emptied window frames with everything they could lay their hands on, including the post office files. Some men were already bleeding from broken glass.

A detail had been assigned to carry the arms in from outside, and everything was being piled together on the floor of the post office. Rifles, pickaxes, grenades, pikes, oak batons, and cases of gelignite—which the men handled with a fine disregard for its potential until Tom Clarke shouted at them, "Blow your heads off if you want to, but wait until we've won!"

Joe Plunkett unfolded a map and spread it out on the parcel counter. "The element of surprise made all the difference," he jubilantly declared. His strength was spent, though; he had to lean on the counter for support.

Seán MacDermott bent over the map. "Here are our positions," he said, pointing. "If everything's gone as well elsewhere as it has here, we have a ring around the city by now. We'll know as soon as dispatches start coming in."

Michael Collins, who claimed he could decode British messages, was sent to the top floor to take charge of the telegraph office.

One of the Fianna came trotting in to announce, "We have snipers installed in buildings all around the Pillar. There's riflemen in Kelly's Gun Shop at the corner of Bachelor's Walk,[4] and three Volunteers with shotguns on O'Connell Bridge.[5] Two of the Fianna are helping cover the bridge from Hopkins Jewellers." He added with a laugh, "The clerks didn't want to let us in because they thought we'd come to steal watches!"

James Connolly remarked, "With so many Volunteers not showing up today, it's a good job we have Con's Fianna. They're going to do more than carry dispatches. Some of them are brilliant marksmen."

"Some of them are just boys," Joe Plunkett pointed out disapprovingly.

"Ah, Joe, a boy from the slums is a man at twelve."

From the distance came an ominous crackle of rifle fire.

Somewhere in Dublin, someone was fighting back.

Ned heard Pearse say to James Connolly, "Should we not be raising our flag—the one Madame Markievicz made for us?"[6]

Connolly stared blankly at him for a moment, then banged

his fist against the nearest table. "We went off and left the damned flags at Liberty Hall!"

Pearse turned to Ned. "Please ask my aide to fetch them."

Seán O'Kelly was leaning against a counter with his hands in his pockets, idly watching Winifred Carney, who had located a typewriter and was typing out Connolly's constant flow of orders. Although he was a captain in the Volunteers, O'Kelly was no more a military man than Pádraic Pearse. He seemed at a loss for something to do and was glad of the assignment. "If Pearse can spare you, do you want to come with me?" he asked Ned. "Everything seems pretty well under control here, and it won't take us long."

When the two left the building they found a rather bewildered crowd still gathered in the street, gazing up at the riflemen who were looking down at them from windows and rooftops. A man complained, "Bloody Volunteers, shutting down the post office so decent folk can't even buy a stamp. What do they think they're playing at?"

"It's a Rising at last," countered an old woman with a lilting Cork accent. She clasped her hands together over her bosom. "God be with them."

Someone else said, "It's a bloody freak show! Clatther of idiots spoiling the holiday for their own amusement, if you ask me."

A man in a top hat interjected, "The soldiers will put a stop to it as soon as they get here."

"Where are the soldiers?" asked an anxious young woman with a baby in her arms. "Aren't they coming?"

O'Kelly told her, "They'll be here soon enough, I expect."

A man called Peter Ennis was closing up Liberty Hall. Tall and bony, with a long neck and bad teeth, Ennis had worked there for most of his life and knew every inch of the building. "The Citizen Army's already evacuated the place and taken out all the arms and supplies," he told Ned and O'Kelly. "I'm just staying here as caretaker until Mr. Connolly beats the British. We'll have some good times then!"

Ennis helped them find the brown paper parcel marked "Flags" and the two men hurried back to the G.P.O.[7] Ned was among those who went outside to watch the first flag go up. A few people cheered as the banner was raised to the top of the pole on the Prince's Street corner of the building. With a lump in his throat, Ned raised one hand in salute.

Against a green background the words "Irish Republic," painted in white and gold, stood out brave and true.

Chapter Fifty

A tricolor of green, white, and orange—reminding Ned of Katty Clarke's ribbon badges—was subsequently flown from the flagpole at the Henry Street corner of the G.P.O. Flags were going up all over the city. Another tricolor was raised over Jacob's Biscuit Factory, where Thomas MacDonagh's Second Battalion was settling in. At the Four Courts, Edward Daly was flying a professionally made green flag with a plain gold harp, while at the Mendicity Institute Seán Heuston had a tricolor with horizontal bands of color. Eamonn Ceannt had a tricolor for the South Dublin Union; James Connolly flew the Plough and the Stars over the Imperial Hotel as a tribute to Jim Larkin and the working man.

It did not matter which flag was used; all proclaimed freedom.

ONCE the flag of the Republic was raised, Pádraic Pearse emerged from Government Headquarters to address the Irish people. James Connolly went with him. Ned, Con Colbert, and Des Ryan proudly formed the escort.

The postal clerks had either gone home or into their locals. The crowd remaining in Sackville Street was composed mostly of tenement dwellers looking for any sort of free diversion. The seizure of the post office had offered some excitement at first, but nothing much seemed to be happening now.

They were growing bored.

Standing under the massive portico, Pádraic Pearse settled his pince-nez on his nose and unrolled the Proclamation. As he began to read aloud, his voice held none of the fire and passion it had contained at Glasnevin. The power was in the words themselves—if anyone cared to listen.

His audience was amused and hostile by turns. A half-grown boy sniggered and made faces. A man shouted, "Ye louser, why don't ye go back where ye came from?" Others simply lost interest and walked away. When Pearse finished reading the words meant to set Ireland free there were a few cheers from lads who saw the whole thing as a bit of *craic*, a bit of fun.

But Dubliners for the most part did not care.

For a moment Pádraic Pearse looked old.

James Connolly impulsively reached out and grasped his hand. "Thanks be to God, Pearse, that we've lived to see this day!"[1]

Pearse gave him a grateful smile.

A trickle of new recruits, including members of the Hibernian Rifles, began arriving. They all requested to be given orders. After a brief conference with Connolly over maps of the city, Pearse assigned Con Colbert to lead a squad to Watkins' Brewery near James's Gate and establish a post there.[2]

"But I'm your bodyguard, Commander!"

"I am surrounded by my army and perfectly safe," Pearse assured him. "As an experienced officer you will be a great deal more useful in the field. We are spread too thin; we have to try to cover ourselves."

As he left the G.P.O. Colbert threw a rueful glance at Ned.

A group of almost forty women reported for duty. They were neatly dressed, neatly coiffed, with an air of well-drilled efficiency. "Cumann na mBan is going to run a canteen for us," Connolly told the men, "so we need to keep them well supplied. They'll give us hell otherwise." Foraging parties were organized to go in search of tea, sugar, milk, anything edible that would not spoil, and bedding.

"Leave chits for whatever you take and be exact about the money due," Pearse ordered sternly. "We shall settle up with the shopkeepers later. There is to be no stealing and no taking advantage."

Ned and Des Ryan joined one of the foraging parties, but just as they were leaving the G.P.O. a company of Lancers on horseback came charging down Sackville Street with their sabers drawn. When they reached the Pillar they were met with a hail of bullets from roofs and windows. Four of the Lancers and two of the horses fell. The rest of the troop wheeled around and galloped back the way they had come.

Ned ran to the nearest man, who though still alive was groaning and clawing ineffectually at his blood-soaked shoulder. "Help me!" he pleaded. Ned darted into the G.P.O. and returned with stretcher bearers to help carry him inside.

The other Lancers lay dead at the foot of Nelson's Pillar. High above them the admiral stood impervious, though his nose was freshly nicked by a rifle bullet.

Bystanders gawped at the bodies. A shawlie who had had too much to drink seated herself on the shoulder of a dead horse and patted it solicitously, then burst into raucous song.

Inside the post office the skirmish was hailed as a victory until James Connolly reminded the others, "Those buckos are just the tip of the iceberg."

His choice of words sent an involuntary shiver up Ned's spine.

Some of Cumann na mBan had begun brewing tea and cooking meals on the first floor, while others who were Red Cross nurses prepared an infirmary in one of the large sorting rooms at the rear of the building. Their first patient was the wounded Lancer.

The O'Rahilly expressed a concern that someone might help himself to the money the postal clerks had abandoned in their flight.[3] He sent his nephew, Dick Humphries, around to all the wickets to collect the cash and postal orders. He then turned them over to one of the captured British officers to count, record, and put into the fireproof safe in the basement. There was almost seven thousand pounds.

"We'll return every penny of this to the British government," The O'Rahilly stressed. "This is going to be the new Irish government, not a band of rabble."

Joe Plunkett produced a packet of stamps designed for the fledgling republic and passed them around for everyone to admire. Ned bought one and tucked it into his notebook. The tiny, beautifully designed bit of gummed paper made the future tangible. Someday I'll put this on a letter to Kathleen, he promised himself.

A tardy detachment of militia was challenged by the sentries outside. When they identified themselves as members of the Rathfarnham Volunteers a sniper in one of the windows shouted down, "Mr. Connolly says there are no Volunteers and Citizen Army anymore.[4] We're all the Irish Republican Army now!"

CONNOLLY was proving an able military leader. He could hold half a dozen situations in his head at once and assess them with cold-eyed realism. His sturdy, tireless figure seemed to be everywhere, checking the defenses, giving encouragement to the men, examining weapons, issuing orders, asking questions.

Ned saw Connolly stiffen with dismay at the answer to one of his questions. "Get someone down to Crown Alley to cut those wires at once!" he shouted at the man.

He caught Ned watching him. "Did you hear that?"

"I did, sir—just a bit. I can forget it if you like."

Connolly pulled a handkerchief from his pocket and mopped his face. "I wish I could. We have control of the telegraph here, but . . ."

"But not the Central Telephone Exchange," Ned finished. "I heard."

"We didn't have enough men show up, damn it! The ones who knew what to do . . ." He shrugged his meaty shoulders as if it did not matter.

It did matter, and vitally.

Work within the post office continued. Connolly ordered
an internal phone line rigged up so he could communicate
with the snipers on the roof. An armory was organized to
repair damaged rifles, fill empty shotgun cases with lead pel-
lets, and prepare bombs.

One of the bombs exploded prematurely, leaving a man
streaming blood from face and hands. His best friend wanted
to take him to the hospital in Jervis Street but he refused.
"I'm here to see the fight to the end," he insisted.

PÁDRAIC Pearse had been shaken by the reaction of the
crowd during the reading of the Proclamation. "I have always
believed the poor of Dublin would realize what we are risking
for them and rise up and follow us," he told Ned, "but now
I am not so certain."

"With respect, sir, you haven't spent much time among the
poor of Dublin. My friend Henry Mooney said the instinct for
survival overrides every other consideration for them, and
he's right. Abstract ideas like republicanism don't mean anything to them; they're just worried about where the next
meal's coming from."

Pearse stared into space for a few moments, then said, "I
have to do something useful. Find me pens and paper and a
quiet place to write, will you?"

THE atmosphere outside the G.P.O. changed. The rattle of
gunfire sounded closer; coming from somewhere along the
quays. The crowd in Sackville Street was growing. The Abbey
Theatre had canceled its matinee performance, and disappointed theatergoers were adding to the crush. The mood
turned ugly when soldiers' wives began lining up outside the
post office to collect their British army separation allowance,
only to be told that the building was now official Government
Headquarters of the new Irish Republic.

"Ye friggin' Fenians!" one shouted, shaking her fist.

"Wait till the Tommies blow yer bloody heads off!"

Thin strands of barbed wire were run out from the columns of the portico, and a space was cleared in front of the building to become a miniature no-man's-land.[5] In the lanes around Sackville Street barricades were being erected using whatever came to hand: cart wheels, rolls of linoleum, sacks of coal, beer kegs, packing cases, broken furniture.

The slum dwellers began stealing anything useful the moment the barricade builders turned their backs.

DISPATCHES were reaching headquarters only sporadically; there was a distressing shortage of information. What did come through was bad. Thanks to the failure to destroy telephone service, the police had informed Military Headquarters at Parkgate that Dublin Castle was under attack. Trinity College had been secured against the insurgents by members of the Dublin University Officers' Training Corps. British reinforcements were being mobilized at the Phoenix Park, as well as at Portobello Barracks, to the south, and Richmond Barracks, to the west of the city. The sixteen-hundred-man Mobile Column at the Curragh was being sent from Kildare to Dublin with all haste, as were the soldiers garrisoned at Athlone.

"What's happened at the Castle?" Connolly demanded of each new messenger. "For God's sake, tell me what's happened at the Castle!"

SÍLE Duffy had been flattered when Dr. Lynn asked her to join the women who would be serving as support staff for the Rising, but she was also nervous. The good ladies of Cumann na mBan were respectable wives and mothers. How would they react if they knew Síle had been a whore?

"You're not one anymore," Katty Clarke had said firmly. "Scrub your face raw and wear something plain and they'll never know the difference."

Síle had decided not to tell Ned about her assignment. If

being a revolutionary meant being secretive . . . well, she could be secretive, too.

On Monday morning she arrived outside City Hall well before eleven o'clock. None of the other women were there yet, and the medical supplies had not been delivered, so she went over to have a look at the Upper Yard of Dublin Castle. There was not much to see. The castle gates were open and a member of the DMP was on duty beside them. He eyed her appreciatively, but when she did not respond he began picking at his fingernails.

Síle went back to wait in front of City Hall, where she was soon joined by several of Cumann na mBan. They accepted her without question and offered to share their flasks of tea. Madame Markievicz and Kathleen Lynn arrived and unloaded boxes of medical supplies, then Dr. Lynn remained with the group while the countess drove the doctor's car toward Stephen's Green.

At around noon fifty members of the Citizen Army approached the Upper Castle Yard.[6] A gray-haired policeman walked toward them with his hand raised to warn them back. They tried to push past him, he slammed the gates in their faces, and the leader of the company shot him.

The attackers forced open the gates and rushed in. Racing to the guardroom, they overpowered the six soldiers they found there and tied them up with their own puttees.

Someone began firing on the yard from an upper window.

Seán Connolly decided it would be prudent to withdraw to City Hall. Otherwise they would surely be overrun and captured by the numerically superior soldiers inside the Castle. He led his company from the Upper Yard and locked the gates behind them, pocketing the key. There was no resistance at City Hall, which was closed for the bank holiday. They established a command post with ten members of the Citizen Army while the rest of the company was sent to occupy nearby buildings and set up snipers' nests aimed at the Castle.

The women entered City Hall with the insurgents. Seán

Connolly's sister had been part of the company that attacked the Castle; she seemed almost despondent. "I would have given anything if we could actually have captured the Castle," she said. "This feels more like a defeat than a victory."

Her brother tried to console her by promising to raise the Irish flag over City Hall, "for the whole world to see."

Dr. Lynn busied herself setting up a first aid station, but for the other women there was nothing to do. "Could I not be of more use somewhere else?" Síle asked the doctor. "I'll go mad simply sitting here."

Kathleen Lynn, a big, powerful woman with short-cropped hair, gave her a measuring look. "You're young and fit, why don't you go up to Stephen's Green? Tell Countess Markievicz I sent you and ask if she needs more nurses."

Carrying a first aid box tucked under her arm, Síle set out. She felt like one of the "angels of mercy" at the front lines of the war in Europe. It was her first experience of a sense of personal worth. In the republic being born this day she was no longer a whore; she would be fresh and new as the nation would be fresh and new.

As she turned into Grafton Street she noticed people standing in the doors of shops, gazing in the direction of the Green with expressions of bewilderment. Then there came the unmistakable crack of rifle fire. Síle broke into a run.

When she reached Stephen's Green the iron gates were closed.[7] Some of the insurgents were barricading them with park benches and wheelbarrows, while others with rifles on their shoulders were peering out through the bars. Civilians in the street were staring back at them.

A bystander warned her, "The Sinn Féiners are overrunning the town. That's them inside. You better get away from here, miss."

She whirled on him. "I'm a Sinn Féiner myself!"

"Then if you're any bloody good, come in and fight for Ireland!" cried one of the men at the gates.[8] He forced them open enough to allow her to squeeze through.

For a moment she feared he recognized her, even without makeup and plainly dressed. She knew his face, had seen it grunting and wheezing above her in Mrs. Drumgold's. He blinked; the moment was gone. Seen out of context she was just another pretty girl, and he had no time for pretty girls at the moment.

The original plan had been for Michael Mallin's company to occupy Stephen's Green. The dense planting of trees and shrubbery in the park would make it all but impossible for the enemy to assess their exact location and troop strength. Using the park as a command center, a mixed company of Volunteers and Citizen Army would then seize the Shelbourne Hotel; take up strategic positions in nearby buildings; control Grafton Street, Harcourt Street Station, and Leeson Street; and guard the approach from Portobello Barracks.

Given the large turnout expected, the plan had been sound.

With only a fraction of that number it was suicidal.

There were women in the Citizen Army contingent that marched toward Stephen's Green that sunny morning, plus a squad of the Fianna to carry dispatches. Altogether they comprised scarcely a hundred troops. When they encountered Thomas MacDonagh on his way to Jacob's Factory he cast a worried glance at their small numbers and advised, "Above all, avoid unnecessary bloodshed!"[9]

When they reached the Green a policeman was lounging against the iron railings of the fence, smoking a cigarette. He mistook them for just another militia parade until they marched past him into the park. The policeman was armed with only a baton, but he thought his authority was sufficient. He shouted at them to move on and not cause a disturbance.

Tense, untried, and expecting the worst, they shot him.

As soon as she left the first load of medical supplies at City Hall, Con Markievicz had driven Dr. Lynn's car to Stephen's Green with the remainder.[10] There she stayed on as Michael Mallin's second-in-command.

Mallin still hoped that more men would show up to secure the buildings around the Green. In the meantime, he ordered the company to make camp and set up a command post, which, in the style of European armies, meant pitching tents and digging defensive trenches. The trenches would become death traps if someone was firing down on them from a height such as the upper storeys of the Shelbourne Hotel across the street, but no one seemed to realize this. This was their first war.

Covered by the rifles of their companions inside the fence, men began setting up barricades in the streets surrounding the Green. Everything portable was seconded to the cause, including delivery carts and fittings from nearby shops. One very young lad strutted out into the street with a large revolver in his fist and commandeered the first motorcar that passed by on its way to the Shelbourne.[11] Within moments the three astonished occupants were retreating to the hotel while their car was added to the nearest barricade.

Bystanders began hurling insults at the company in the park.

Off-duty army officers in the nearby United Service Club started taking potshots at the insurgents from the windows of the club.

The men in the park shot back. "Got one!" a voice crowed gleefully. Rifle fire spattered off the front of the gracious Shelbourne Hotel.

Members of the Ascendancy inside the hotel were accustomed to taking their tea at this hour and in this place, and had no intention of interrupting tradition because of the illogical behavior of a band of rabble. Two or three men and a woman in a flowered hat came to the windows to look. Others simply moved to tables at the rear of the room.

In Stephen's Green, Síle was looking for Countess Markievicz when a gunshot ricocheted off a tree trunk and spattered her with bark. Startled, she dropped her first aid box. *Someone's trying to kill me. Damn them anyway!*

She snatched up the box and ran farther into the park. A thin, fierce-eyed young woman in a Citizen Army uniform stepped into her path. "Here, come help us." Eliza Goggins

held out a battered shovel. "We took these from the garden-
ers. We're digging trenches like the soldiers do in Belgium."

A score of people were already at work. When Síle tentatively poked her shovel into the ground, a freckled boy gave
her a wink. "It's easy, miss. These are flower beds anyway."
He hefted a shovelful of dark loam. "See? Not even heavy."

Síle told him, "I'm not afraid of hard work." The earth
smelled rich and sweet.

On Síle's other side, Eliza Goggins was smiling as she dug.
She felt no fear, only a manic exhilaration. "We're as good
as any of them now," she muttered to herself. "As good as
any of them!"

A flurry of shots from the Shelbourne tore holes in the
shrubbery. Eliza threw down her shovel and ran to the fence.
Drawing a pistol, she began returning fire through the railings.
Suddenly she whirled around like someone doing an intricate
dance step, threw out her arms, and fell backward. Her legs
twitched violently.

By the time Síle got to her, Eliza Goggins was dead.

She was still smiling.

Síle picked up the fallen Luger.

The pistol was heavier than she expected; she had to use
both hands to hold it steady. "Can someone show me how to
shoot this?" she asked.

Chapter Fifty-one

SHORTLY after midday a junior officer on a bicycle managed to slip past Eamon de Valera's men and reach Kingstown, seven miles south of Dublin. The telegraph at the G.P.O. was under the control of the insurgents, but a naval vessel in the harbor at Kingstown had a wireless.[1]

Within minutes news of the Rising was flashed to London.

The staff of the *Irish Independent* was informed of the Rising by the sound of gunfire. Henry Mooney ran out to stand on the quay, eyewitness to history.

There was not much history to be seen; not at first. Some boys were scrambling onto the parapets of O'Connell Bridge for a better view, but otherwise the Sackville Street area seemed almost normal.

Almost. Henry watched as a squad of armed men fanned out along the quays, running low. Others stationed themselves along the bridge.

A portly man in a brown suit and a bowler hat was standing nearby, smoking a cigar. Henry asked him, "What's this all about?"

The man barked a laugh. "Those boyos, those Volunteers, have seized the G.P.O. and proclaimed a republic. A republic! Didja ever hear anything so daft? They'll be flushed out as soon as the soldiers come."

Henry stood very still. All the way to his core was stillness, a great pool waiting to be filled.

It's now. Today. The Rising.

Without conscious thought he began to walk across the bridge in the direction of the post office. The men on the bridge had shotguns, but they did not challenge him. They just watched him. He felt as if the whole world were watching.

When he reached the north end of the bridge he noticed the snipers watching, too, from windows and doorways. One called to him, "I wouldn't come any farther if I was you."

"I'm a reporter."

"Och, that's all right then." The man waved him on.

As he proceeded up Sackville Street Henry could hear a low hum like the sound of swarming bees. A crowd was milling in front of the G.P.O. Men with rifles looked down at them from windows and rooftops. A boy near the Pillar blew a paper bag full of air and clapped it to create a sudden bang. There was a shout, a curse, derisory laughter.

Standing in front of a drapery shop was a member of the DMP, armed only with the regulation baton. Henry went over to him and took out his notebook. "I'm a reporter for the *Independent*. May I ask how you're going to handle this situation?"

"Handle it? Not me; I have my instructions. I'm not to interfere, I'm to go back to my barracks at once—and that's where I'm headed."[2] The policeman turned and walked away.

So there *are* orders in the event of an insurrection, Henry said to himself. Perhaps the Castle Document was genuine after all.

Someone threw a brick. A shop window smashed. Two ragged boys began seizing merchandise and passing it out to others in the street. One of the riflemen on the post office roof yelled at them and they scampered away, but the broken window remained an open invitation.

Henry knew the poor people of Dublin. Once looting began it could swell far beyond Sackville Street. Ducking into the nearest laneway, he took a shortcut to Louise Kearney's boardinghouse.

He found the house unlocked; there was no sign of his cousin. From the direction of Sackville Street came a sudden burst of rifle fire. Henry pounded up the stairs to his room and rummaged under his mattress for his valuables. He dispersed these through the pockets of his trousers and jacket, threw a change of linen and a clean shirt into a paper bag, put his good topcoat over his suit and his other pair of shoes in the topcoat pockets, then took a long look around the room to see if he had overlooked anything.

On Ned's locker was the book of Thomas MacDonagh's poems. He took it with him as well. For safekeeping.

AFTER locking the door of the house behind him, Henry searched the neighborhood for his cousin. If there was going to be trouble he did not like the idea of a lone widow woman in the thick of it. The proprietor of the corner shop told him, "Mrs. Kearney was in here earlier, God love her, looking for bread soda, but we're out of it. I think she said she was going into town anyway."

"Into town" meant she could be anyplace.

Henry hurried back to Sackville Street. While he was gone the rebels had strengthened their position. He saw barricades going up and more armed men patrolling. Two horses wearing military saddles lay motionless at the foot of Nelson's Pillar.

"Took the dead 'uns away just now, so they did," volunteered a bystander.

"Dead 'uns?"

"Lancers. Our boys inside shot 'em down. Mucky British; they shoulda stayed where they belonged."

Henry stared at the fallen horses.

His mouth was dry. He edged his way through the crowd and headed for Meagher's Public House, where there was an announcement on the door. He bent closer to read,

> *Irishmen and Irishwomen:*
> *In the name of God and of the dead generations from*

which she receives her old tradition of nationhood, Ire-
land, through us, summons her children to her flag and
strikes for her freedom.

Henry tried to read the rest but his eyes had misted over.

There were copies of the Proclamation pasted everywhere, even on the base of Nelson's Pillar. He carefully took down two, one from a postal pillar box and one from a shopfront, folded them neatly, and put them in his pockets. He would take one back to the *Independent,* but he just might keep the other for himself.

Then he took out his notebook and began working his way back toward the bridge, filling pages with his impressions as he walked. No one spoke to him, no one stopped him.

"Dublin today is alive with hope and dead with apathy," he wrote, "but the scales will tilt soon. It is not an even contest."

When he got back to the Carlisle Building he was eager to start writing, but there was no time for a leisurely feature article—news was coming in hot and fast. Everyone in the city room was desperately trying to keep up, to sort out ver- ifiable fact from wildest rumor. According to who told the story, Dublin was ringed with insurgent strongholds; Profes- sor MacDonagh had personally captured Dublin Castle; Cork, Kerry, and Limerick had risen in revolt; Jim Larkin was fight- ing his way across Ireland with fifty thousand men; the Irish regiments were deserting their garrisons to join with the Vol- unteers; the Turkish navy had landed at Waterford in support of the rebels . . .

At the same time there were stories of mutiny in the ranks of the Citizen Army; appalling defeats in the country; whole- sale desertions by the Volunteers; crushing triumphs on the part of a massive British force said to be landing all up and down the coast.

There was no way of knowing what to believe.

Henry Mooney hurled his pencil across the room and shouted, "I wish to God I was in the G.P.O. so I'd know what was going on!"

INSIDE the G.P.O., the new Provisional Government was receiving equally confused reports. During the earlier part of the afternoon things appeared to be going according to plan. Nothing had been heard from North County Dublin, but dispatches reported the other battalions in place. Edward Daly had seized the Four Courts; Seán Heuston was at the Mendicity Institute. Thomas MacDonagh had successfully occupied the Jacob's Biscuit factory and Eamon de Valera had Boland's Mills. A squad of Fianna had set the powder magazine in the Phoenix Park ablaze; skirmishing was reported at Portobello Barracks.

There was shooting in many parts of the city.

"Shots fired for freedom," exulted Tom Clarke as he made the rounds, personally congratulating the other members of the Military Council.

Later in the day the dispatches began to tell a different story.

When a messenger reported the retreat from Dublin Castle, Seán MacDermott lost his temper. "Damn it to hell! Damn it to friggin' hell! Didn't they realize? On a bank holiday there'd only be a skeleton staff at the Castle. A few civil servants maybe; a couple dozen soldiers. A *handful* of our lads could have captured the entire place!"

James Connolly looked appalled. Obviously he had not known that crucial detail; had not taken it into account in his plans.

MacDermott cried in frustration, "I should have been there! I should have been with them!"

Joe Plunkett remarked sorrowfully, "We all should have been with them."

"We were," said Pádraic Pearse. "We are."

THE bad news continued.

The telegraph office intercepted a message to the effect that General Sir John Grenfell Maxwell had been appointed

Commander-in-Chief of His Majesty's forces in Ireland. Maxwell was on his way to the rebellious island with a huge number of troops. In addition, he had been granted plenary powers to reward treason with firing squads.

MacDermott's response was, "The British expect us to intercept their messages. They're just trying to intimidate us."

Meanwhile the crowd in Sackville Street surged this way, then that, broke up, re-formed, lost interest, swelled again. Women began crowding into shops in a wave of panic buying. For many Dubliners, however, the insurrection remained a holiday diversion, and as the afternoon wore on they took to the streets to share in the fun. Men who had firearms brought them out and fired off "a few potshots for the new Irish Republic." When they tired of the game they went home.

Others found a different game to play.

Noblett's Confectioners, near the Pillar, was broken into and the sweets thrown into the street to be trampled underfoot. Small boys scrabbled through shards of glass to seize a bit of toffee. Shawlies broke the window of the Cable Boot Company and helped themselves without bothering about the fit. As the frenzy spread, families of tenement dwellers began rushing from shop to shop, smashing and grabbing whatever they could. A filthy street urchin came prancing out the doorway of Brady's in a pair of high-heeled satin slippers meant for a bride.

The looters fell to squabbling over their prizes; eyes were blacked and noses broken.

Pearse told Ned, "Go up to the snipers' command post and ask Michael O'Rahilly to do something about this. We cannot have Irish people behaving like savages on the first day of the Republic."

Willie Pearse went with Ned. When the message was delivered they paused to watch from the highest windows. The O'Rahilly had his men hurl water down on the looters, but it was ignored. The door of Lawrence's Toy Shop was forced open and people came running out with dolls and toy rifles. A small girl dragged a wooden rocking horse into the street.

The horse was almost bigger than the child; one of its rockers was already broken.

Ned pointed. "See that girl, Willie? I know a little girl just about her age. You met her; I brought her to Saint Enda's for Christmas."

Willie smiled. "Of course I remember. We were all very taken with your Precious."

"She could have been one of those down there, not knowing right from wrong."

"Those things have to be taught, Ned. When we were children we wouldn't have stolen so much as a shoe button. We thought our parents were dreadfully strict, of course."

"Precious doesn't have any parents."

"She has you."

Looking down, they saw Seán MacDermott emerge, limping, from the G.P.O.[3] He held his hands above his head and cried out in a passionate voice for the people not to disgrace the fight for Irish freedom by their behavior.

Someone jeered him; someone else threw a rock. To Ned's relief, a man ran out of the post office with orders from Connolly for MacDermott to come back inside.

The O'Rahilly had a couple of his riflemen load their weapons with blank shot and fire over the heads of the looters. They ran for cover, leaving plunder strewn behind them. Some shouted curses at the republicans as they ran.

Within minutes fire broke out—first in one of the looted shops, then another.

The fire brigade arrived with a great clanging of bells. They left their engine parked at the curb of Henry Street and ran into the burning buildings. The watching republicans speculated that the fires might be a ruse by the British to get their men into the area.

By nightfall the occupants of headquarters were exhausted. The tensions of the day had taken their toll. "We'll be under siege by tomorrow," James Connolly said as calmly as if he were predicting rain. "But don't worry, we'll do just fine." When a man asked him about the British chances he replied, "Oh, they are beaten!"[4] His dauntlessness was a welcome source of strength. Ned longed to tell him so, but it was not the sort of thing one man said to another.

Every possible precaution had been taken against the counterattack to come; there was nothing to do but wait. Waiting was more exhausting than anything else.

At eleven o'clock a fresh round of sentries was posted. The leaders were supplied with mattresses placed on the floor behind the main post office counter. No one expected to be able to sleep much. Joe Plunkett refused even to lie down. Coughing, sometimes gasping painfully, he went from blocked window to window, peering out through the small loopholes that had been left for the riflemen. At last one of the women took him by the arm and forcefully marched him to bed, then brought him a sleeping draught.

Ned spread his blanket and lay down on his side with his head cushioned on his bent arm. All around him men were trying to make themselves comfortable in unfamiliar and unyielding surroundings. He heard the constant shuffle of feet carrying nervous bladders to one of the toilets. There was the rattle of cigarette packets, the strike of matches.

Someone farted explosively. Someone else laughed.

Ned's overstimulated mind raced off on a tangent, arranging words and phrases to describe the scene.

When he finally fell asleep he dreamed of the child in the street.

ALONG the quays the night crackled with gunfire.

April 25, 1916
IRISH REBELS STAGE DUBLIN UPRISING

Chapter Fifty-two

KATHLEEN Campbell stared at the third page of the *New York Times*. Amid news devoted to the war in Europe, the brief article about rebellion in Ireland was almost lost. Yet to her it seemed the only story on the page.

She wanted to scream with joy. She wanted to seize someone and caper about in a circle, but she was alone except for the housemaid. Alexander had long since gone out, leaving the newspaper flung carelessly across the breakfast table.

Even if he were there, Kathleen could not have shared her excitement with him. He would give her that censorious stare and say, "Kate, you are an American now. Control yourself. I expect decorum of my wife."

My wife. My property. Never again physically attacked, but punished for her transgressions in a hundred subtle, cruel ways. Criticized and belittled. Day after day after day.

She put down the newspaper and went to stare out the window into the street. New York was outside; energetic, prosperous, fashionable. Everything she had once dreamed about.

I want to go home, Kathleen thought. Ned was right to return when he did.

Oh dear sweet Jesus, I want to go home too, and . . .

And what? Fight for Ireland?

She had never shot a gun in her life. She could not possibly kill a man.

She stared down at her soft white hands. Once they had been strong and useful, helping with the washing, doing the mending, even digging in the vegetable patch. Now they were . . . ornamental.

Jumping to her feet, Kathleen began to pace the room like a caged animal. Her mind was racing.

How can I get back to Ireland? I have no money for the passage and Alexander would never give it to me. There is no one I could ask. Besides, we don't borrow, we Hallorans. *We Hallorans.*

She considered the life she had rushed into so willingly. America. Wonderful America. To be honest, she knew she could still be happy here . . . if she was happy.

But she would never be happy with Alexander and there was no way out, no way, no way . . . !

With a sob of despair, Kathleen Halloran Campbell admitted defeat.

She thought her heart would break.

DAWN revealed lowering clouds and sullen skies. When Síle first awoke she did not know where she was. Rubbing her eyes, she sat up and the world swam into focus. She had spent Monday night sleeping in the Stephen's Green bandstand with the rest of the women, while two male republicans stood guard.

One of them noticed Síle was awake and gave her a rueful shake of his head.

"What's wrong?" she asked.

"Just about everything. Before dawn a hundred soldiers and a machine gun unit came up Kildare Street and took over the Shelbourne and the Service Club.[1] It looks like we don't have much chance of getting out of here alive now, but some of our men are trying to organize an escape route."

I'm getting out of here alive, Síle Duffy thought with grim determination. I have Ned waiting for me.

Oh Ned! Where are you? *How* are you?

Beyond the sheltering roof of the bandstand the rain began to fall.

Gunfire, which had been sporadic throughout the night, intensified dramatically with daylight. To the report of rifles was added the vicious stutter of the machine-gun. Casualties were mounting. Across from the Shelbourne a badly wounded republican lay stretched out against the fence railings in the falling rain.[2] From time to time he moved a little, or raised his hand as if calling for help. No one could get to him. Remorseless gunfire from the hotel and the Service Club thwarted every rescue attempt.

The barrage pouring into the park increased. Despite the screen of trees and shrubbery, bullets were finding targets. Hampered by their narrow skirts, Síle and the other women crouched close to the earth and walked on their knees, trying to get to the fallen men. They were relieved when a sentry just outside the Grafton Street gate shouted that a Red Cross ambulance had reached the barricade. The uniformed nurses were eagerly welcomed into the park to help care for the wounded.

Moments later the same sentry was shot. When Michael Mallin ran out to carry him inside the park he took a bullet through his hat, missing death by inches. Mallin took off the hat and showed it to Con Markievicz.

She turned it over in her hands and poked a finger through the bullet hole. ''We're going to have to retreat now or we'll all be cut down,'' she said grimly, ''and I'm not willing to see my Fianna slaughtered.''

''We've got some men installed in the College of Surgeons,'' Mallin replied, referring to a solidly built three-storey building on the far side of the park from the Shelbourne.[3] ''If we can get the rest of our people over there we'll at least be in a defensible position. If necessary we can break through the walls into the adjacent buildings.''

Madame's face was bleak. ''I hate giving in to them. God, I hate having them see us run!''

Partially shielded by a barricade of carts, wicker baskets,

and an open motorcar, the beleaguered company began scurrying across the street in small groups.[4] Their flight was not unobserved. Riflemen targeted them; bullets sent chips flying from the cobblestones they ran across.

When he reached the middle of the street a young lad panicked. He threw down his rifle and looked wildly around, his eyes those of a terrified animal with the hunters closing in. "I want to go home!" he wailed.

Síle Duffy felt a great and tender pity. Picking up his rifle, she handed it back to him. "We're all far from home now," she said gently.

In the G.P.O. the long night passed somehow. People began stirring, moving about. Several new prisoners were brought in. Ned heard The O'Rahilly say, "One of them, Lieutenant Mahony, is a surgeon and a damned good one, he claims."

Connolly replied, "Bully for him. The other side will need him more than we will."

Ned got to his feet and adjusted his rumpled clothing. He desperately wanted a cup of hot tea but first he had to know what was happening.

He found James Connolly peering out through one of the loopholes.

"What's out there, sir?"

"It's beginning to rain. I'm afraid we've seen the last of the good weather for a while. The only people in the street right now are looking for abandoned loot from last night, the poor sods. It's hard to blame them. Pearse thinks they could do better, be more like his vision of the noble Irish, but he's asking too much of human nature."

"Have you seen Mr. Pearse this morning?"

"Got away from you, has he? Oh, don't look so worried, Halloran, he's all right. He's on the first floor in one of the staff offices, writing something or other."

When Ned knocked on the door he heard the familiar *"Failte isteach."* Pearse rose to shake Ned's hand in the old formal way. His eyes were hollow from lack of sleep, but his uniform looked as crisp as if he had just put it on. "I was about to come looking for you," he said. "I've spent much of the night composing our first official newsletter."

He showed Ned a handwritten communiqué entitled "Irish War News." It was full of optimism in spite of the fact that there was no word of a Rising in the south and west. Pearse wrote as if victory were a foregone conclusion, and repeatedly urged the rest of the country to stand with the rebels at this critical moment in Irish history.

"Ned, run over to Liberty Hall and ask them to make the printing press ready. I should have this finished by lunchtime, and I shall want at least five hundred copies printed."

"Yes sir!"

Pearse unholstered his Browning automatic pistol.[5] "Here, take this with you. I have never fired a shot in anger and do not intend to, but on assignments for me it will be handier for you to carry a pistol than a rifle. Just bring it back to me safely." He added with a smile, "I cannot replace either one of you."

WHEN Ned ventured into Sackville Street he was aware of an eerie stillness, as if he moved inside a bubble. Beyond the skin of the bubble was a battlefield. Even the rain could not wash away the smell of smoke and gunpowder. The republicans had worked through the night, tightening their defenses. They were using burnt-out trams for barricades now, and the entire contents of a motorcycle shop blocked one approach to the boulevard.

Ned had to pound at the door of Liberty Hall for several minutes before Peter Ennis finally responded. His hair was tousled and his fly only partially buttoned. Ned had to explain his mission twice before making him understand. "How long will it take to get the printing press running again? Do you know how to do that?"

"Oh, I know how, all right. But it won't be easy, Halloran, I'm here on my lonesome. It's half six now; call back in a couple of hours and I'll see what I can do for you."

Ned did not go straight back to the G.P.O. His curiosity was getting the better of him and this seemed the perfect opportunity to see what was happening south of the Liffey.

He was almost across the Swivel Bridge when he heard the unmistakable rattle of machine-gun fire coming from the direction of College Green. It could only be the British; the republican forces had no such weapons. Machine guns at Trinity would practically cut off the south city—including the Second Battalion and Thomas MacDonagh.

Had they been warned?

He trotted off the bridge and turned right, onto Burgh Quay.

As he approached the Carlisle Building he muttered, ''Making history, Henry,'' under his breath. To his surprise he saw that the doors were tightly closed. Normally at this hour the newspaper offices would be a hive of activity.

But this was no normal morning.

Ned wrapped his topcoat more tightly around himself to hide his Volunteer uniform, then joined several men in suits and bowler hats who were crossing D'Olier Street. In spite of the upheaval in the city some Dubliners—angry, contemptuous, amused, or oblivious—were attempting business as usual.

Yesterday there had been almost no soldiers in the streets, but today was different. Tense-faced men in British khaki were everywhere; there seemed to be hundreds of them. Ned tried to appear harmless. I'm just an ordinary bloke going to work, he instructed himself, recalling his playacting days at Saint Enda's. I'm a newspaperman covering a story; there's nothing suspicious about me.

He went farther down the quays to avoid whatever was happening in College Green.

A British officer coming out of the Clarence Hotel looked at him very hard, as if he could see the pistol beneath Ned's coat. Ned tossed the man a cheery wave. ''Busy today, are you?'' he asked as casually as he could, as casually as an innocent person might.

The man blinked but did not answer. Ned's smile froze on

his face and he walked on. He could feel eyes boring into the back of his neck.

As he followed the river he could hear gunfire from the direction of Dublin Castle. There was no direct route to Jacob's Factory that would not take him close to the government compound, so he went as far as Winetavern Street, skirted Christchurch, and began working his way back to Chancery Lane and thence to Whitefriar Street.

He was nearing Jacob's when he came upon a detachment of soldiers marching in the same direction. Ned did a sharp about-face and entered the nearest open door, which proved to be the hallway of a private house. A woman sweeping a strip of carpet gave him a startled glance as he slammed the door behind him.

From an inner room came the fretful wail of an infant. "You've woken the babby!" the woman accused him.

The tramp of hobnailed boots in the street drowned out the cry of the child. The woman darted into the room and came back holding it tightly clutched against her bosom. Her eyes were huge with fear. When the soldiers had passed Ned apologized and left in a hurry.

He had only gone a short distance when several soldiers coming out of Wood Street challenged him. His hand instinctively slipped inside his coat for Pearse's pistol. In that moment his uniform was plainly visible. One of the soldiers leveled a rifle at him. "Hold up, you!"

Knowing he was hopelessly outnumbered, Ned began to run. He dodged into the narrow laneway called Whitefriar's Place and fled toward Stephen's Green. He was just in time to see a group of people running across the street from the Green toward the College of Surgeons. A man threw down a rifle; a woman paused long enough to pick it up and hand it back to him.

The woman was Síle Duffy.

When Ned shouted her name Síle turned toward him. At that moment a bullet struck the pavement close beside her. Her first thought was not for herself but for Ned, who was running toward her as if unaware of the danger.

* * *

In the G.P.O. they could hear continuous rifle volleys along the quaysides and the hammering of the machine guns south of the river. James Connolly exuded a reassuring confidence, however, and Joe Plunkett remained convinced that his plans were sound.

In spite of what he had written in the "Irish War News," Pádraic Pearse was less sanguine. As he worked on his newsletter in the hours before dawn he had been unable to ignore the constant report of rifles. They seemed so much louder at night. People were being wounded; people were dying. Gunfire made real what had been an abstraction.

Ned ran toward Síle through a hail of bullets. She had her arms out, waving him back, but he could not leave her. He made a dive and caught her around the waist, throwing her to the pavement. Even as she fell she twisted in his arms so that her back was shielding him.

At the G.P.O. a foraging party went into Moore Street in search of some fresh fruit and returned to report, "There's full-scale censorship now. Today's early edition of the *Irish Times* had details of the Rising, but it was bought up as soon as it hit the streets. Every copy has disappeared. Other papers went to press late and made no mention of anything unusual. Some don't seem to be printing at all."

"The authorities don't want us to know we're winning," said James Connolly.

Dispatches confirmed that the republicans were holding their positions around the city. The British army was concentrating on the rebel outposts and failing to make much progress toward Sackville Street itself. "We have enough men posted around headquarters to hold off the enemy for days," Connolly declared.

In anticipation of a siege, Pearse gave instructions to begin rationing the food.

The garrison in the post office was growing. As fighting intensified elsewhere, men who were forced to retreat from their positions made their way to headquarters for redeployment.

They brought badly needed firsthand information.

· The area around Dublin Castle had been cleared, although the republicans were still holding City Hall and resisting the most determined attempts to dislodge them. "Seán Connolly was shot dead yesterday when he went up on the roof to raise the flag," an eyewitness reported.

College Green was under constant fire from Trinity College, where the cadets in the officer training program were getting firsthand experience as they worked alongside seasoned troops. Soldiers under the command of Brigadier-General Lowe were attempting to set up a cordon from College Green to Kingsbridge Station to cut the rebel forces in two.

There was skirmishing throughout the south city, as well as around the Four Courts on the north side of the river. MacDonagh's Second Battalion were acquitting themselves well at Jacob's Factory. Ceannt's men in the South Dublin Union had fought fiercely to establish their position and, though undermanned, were well entrenched.

"If we can hold out for a week the British will negotiate," Connolly assured the others.

Tom Clarke said, "We have to hang on. If we don't win independence now the best we can hope for is Home Rule— someday. Maybe. And even if we get it, Carson and his Unionists will make damned sure it includes partition. The mutilation of Ireland."

Pádraic Pearse retired to his office to begin work on a new pronouncement, a manifesto intended to rally the good people of Dublin while making the looters feel shame for their actions.[6] After a while he came to the door to ask Seán O'Kelly, "Has Ned Halloran returned yet?"

"Haven't seen him," O'Kelly replied.

•   •   •

WHEN they hit the pavement Ned rolled with Síle locked in his arms. He was not thinking anything; his mind was as cool and blank as a sheet of paper. His muscles remembered the Fianna drill he had once practiced for "being under fire" and took over.

Then he was up on his feet, still holding her. Bending over, running, zigzagging along the street, dragging the protesting girl with him. "I have to go back, Ned! They need me."

"I need you, damn it." He kept running.

It was not the Dublin he knew, not anymore. Pedestrian traffic that had made the streets appear normal earlier had disappeared. People who had reported for work had turned around and gone home again.

Rifle fire and rain. Cobbles gleaming and slippery underfoot, doors and windows resolutely locked and shuttered. The smell of cordite was acrid on the back of the throat.

A company of soldiers came out of a laneway and opened fire at the fleeing pair without bothering to find out who they were.

Ned hated the soldiers for making him run. They were trying to kill him and Síle—kill Síle!—and he hated them. They were not the British, not the government, not anyone in particular anymore, just the enemy—and he hated them. If it had not been for Síle, in that moment he would have turned around and fought them all, damn them, fought them to the death and gone down screaming his contempt for them. The enemy.

"Where are we going?" Síle gasped as they ducked from doorway to doorway, from one uncertain shelter to the next.

"Headquarters." He could think of no place else to take her where she would be safe. Besides, Mr. Pearse was expecting him to come back.

Getting across the Liffey would be the hardest part. No matter which bridge they used they would be exposed. As they fled toward the river Ned mentally reviewed their options. The south end of O'Connell Bridge would be a death trap if the British had control of the area between Trinity and the river. If they went farther west they might be able to get across Grattan Bridge, but it would be a long, dangerous way back to the post office.

"I can't run anymore, Ned," Síle panted.

"Just until we cross Dame Street." Leading from College Green, Dame Street was swept by gunfire. They held hands, kept low, and raced across. Ned expected to feel the shock of a bullet at any moment. He was almost surprised when they arrived on the other side of the street unhurt.

Between Dame Street and the river lay Temple Bar, a run-down area that had once contained the chambers and offices serving the Irish Parliament. In its narrow laneways Ned slowed to a walk and allowed Síle to catch her breath.

They came out of Crown Alley close to the Ha'penny Bridge.

In the midst of nightmare the delicate beauty of the foot-bridge appeared as insubstantial as a dream.

Ned and Síle began to run again.

Gunfire flashed from Wellington Quay.

Had they been on one of the broad spans built for carriage traffic they might have been cut down, but the Ha'penny's fanciful design saved them. Shots spanged harmlessly off cast-iron railings and arches as they sped across the bridge and turned into Bachelor's Walk.

The snipers in Kelly's cheered them as they ran by.

Ned and Síle did not stop until they reached the monument to Daniel O'Connell at the foot of Sackville Street. Sheltered behind the Great Emancipator, they stood gasping for breath and looking at one another.

Ned expected Síle to be faint with terror. Instead she shook her head and told him, "You're mad, Ned Halloran. Barking mad, did you know that? Perhaps it's why I love you."

She had never spoken those words before. They sank into the marrow of his bones.

There were new volleys of gunfire in D'Olier Street.

Ned caught Síle's hand. "Let's go. I'll feel better when you're safe inside headquarters. Then you can tell me again."

She lifted one eyebrow teasingly. "Tell you what?"

"You know." Once more he was in a bubble, with the war outside. But this time Síle was with him.

As they went up Sackville Street she stared at the detritus littering the boulevard. Broken crockery and swaths of torn cloth lay sodden in the rain. Clery's, the largest store in the street, had been thoroughly looted. Every shop had shattered windows, but the smashed doors had been taken away to add to the barricades. Farther on, two dead horses lay at Nelson's Pillar. They smelled very dead.

A number of sentries were patrolling the headquarters area and on the roof were more riflemen, including Des Ryan. Ryan shouted down to Ned, "Been on holiday, have you?"

"Went south for my health," Ned called back. "Decided I was a northsider after all, so I've come home."

One of the sentries cautioned Síle, "Mind the wire, miss."

Ned asked him, "Has there been trouble here this morning?"

"Just looters, but they've moved on now. Frank Skeffington was here for a while, waving his walking stick at them and scolding them. He's as odd as three ears on a fish but he means well. You should have seen them swanning around in fancy clothes. Toddlers in women's hats and greasy old washerwomen in evening dresses with their tits hanging out—" The sentry blushed. "Pardon me, miss. I forgot myself; that's not fit talk for ladies."

Síle allowed herself a private smile. As they entered the post office she paused long enough to pull Eliza Goggins's revolver out of the waistband of her skirt and show it to Ned. "This is what sort of a lady I am," she said.

Inside headquarters James Connolly was busily dictating orders for reinforcing threatened positions. He stopped long enough to question the couple. The news from Stephen's Green obviously troubled him, but he greeted Síle warmly. "I remember you; you took first aid lessons in Liberty Hall. We have a few nurses but we can always use more skilled hands." He gave her a searching look, then added wistfully, "You put me in mind of my Lillie at your age."

"Is your wife safe, sir?"

"Thanks for asking, Halloran. She's at Madame's cottage in Balally looking after Poppet, Con's spaniel. The countess could hardly wait to get a gun in her hand and go to war for Ireland, but first she had to be certain someone was looking after that damned little dog! Women. They're wonderful."

"I agree," Ned told him.

Seán MacDermott and a pallid Joe Plunkett, his forehead bedewed with sweat, were again poring over maps of the city while Tom Clarke supervised the weapons' repair. Pearse was completing a manifesto he would read to the populace later in the afternoon. A constant stream of men was being sent to erect and repair barricades, break through walls for access routes, fortify sentry positions.

Michael Collins walked by munching a sandwich that exuded a pungent odor of sardines. Síle's eyes followed the sandwich.

"Are you hungry?" Ned asked.

"I've had nothing since yesterday morning. I could eat a horse."

Collins laughed. "We may all come to that. Good job we shot a couple yesterday."

"It isn't funny, killing horses."

He sobered at once. "It wasn't meant to be, miss."

Ned asked one of the women to give Síle some bread and bacon, then went to report to Pádraic Pearse. Pearse looked up with obvious relief as Ned entered the little office. "I was beginning to despair of you."

Ned gave a nonchalant shrug. It was easy to be brave now, in Pearse's company. "I had a bit of an adventure but I'm all right, and I'm returning your pistol with thanks. It hasn't killed anybody."

"Thank God for that." Anyone who did not know Pearse might think it a strange remark for the leader of an army. "And what of your mission, Ned?"

"The press should be running at Liberty Hall soon."

"Good. We still have heard nothing from the south or west, but we assume the British must be having trouble there because they have put the whole country under martial law. Meanwhile they are bringing in artillery and beginning to cordon the north suburbs.'' Pearse's expression was grave. ''At least five thousand troops will be in Dublin by nightfall. Connolly expects an attack on the post office at any time now.''

Chapter Fifty-three

Shortly after noon word reached the G.P.O. that City Hall had been taken. The fate of the defenders was not known.

Mallin was holding out in the College of Surgeons, as was MacDonagh at Jacob's. Daly had his hands full at the Four Courts, and there was no word from de Valera. Fighting was intensifying everywhere, with the numerical superiority of the British being met by such determination that sometimes they were forced to fall back.

Cumann na mBan were doing more than cooking and nursing now. James Connolly was sending them out as dispatch carriers. They also helped build barricades and even went as far as the quays to bring back the ammunition and explosives that had been removed from Liberty Hall and hidden nearby. With no military status, they worked shoulder to shoulder with the men.

Once Ned had been afraid for Pádraic Pearse to meet Síle, as if those all-seeing eyes would know her history at a glance and condemn her. But since then Ned had learned there were worse things to fear than what someone else—even Pádraic Pearse—might think.

He went to the infirmary and drew Síle aside. "Can you spare a few minutes?"

"Is it important?"

"Very. There's someone I want you to meet." Taking her hand, he led her to a small office and tapped on the door. At Pearse's invitation he and Síle went in together.

LATE in the afternoon the artillery fire began. Sullen thunder shook the city.

Ned had been sitting with Joe Plunkett, talking about writing. When Plunkett remarked that he was keeping a journal of events Ned admitted he was doing the same. "In bits and pieces," he added, pulling the dog-eared notebook out of his pocket to show his friend.

At the sound of the guns he tensed. "What are they firing at, can you tell? Do you think they're anywhere near the North Circular Road?"

"There aren't any strategic targets in that direction," Plunkett replied. "I imagine they're trying to destroy the buildings between us and them so they can get at us."

A chill ran through Ned. Precious might be safe at the orphanage, but he had brought Síle into the very heart of danger.

WITH censorship in full operation the newspapers all but closed down. Henry Mooney spent Tuesday in a state of simmering frustration. Unlike the army, the government officially chose to pretend the Rising was not happening. Yet it could not be ignored; it was blooming all around them like a dark flower.

Late in the day one of the reporters at the *Independent* learned from an informant that Francis Sheehy-Skeffington had been arrested and taken to Portobello Barracks. Henry was baffled. "That harmless little man? What could he possibly be guilty of?"

"It seems he was trying to organize bands of citizens to stop the looting. He was in Rathmines when some British soldiers came along and arrested him. He was simply in the wrong place at the wrong time," the informant said.

The story made no sense, but its aftermath would make even less.

That evening when Henry returned to Middle Gardiner Street he was relieved to find Louise Kearney alive and well, though badly frightened. "Go away until it's over," he advised her. "You have friends who live in Balbriggan; go to them."

Her eyes flashed indignantly. "What, and leave my property! Soldiers or Volunteers it's all the same to me, none of them bowsies is going to take over my house."

SíLE spent Tuesday night in an improvised dormitory on the first floor with the other women. On the ground floor, the men kept watch for the anticipated British attack. Few were able to sleep. Joe Plunkett finally lost the battle to stay awake, but his wracking cough did not rest with him. The sound haunted the G.P.O. like a death rattle entombed in marble.

WEDNESDAY morning Henry Mooney arose early and hurried downstairs for a quick cup of tea before he went to the newspaper office.

"There's no milk for the porridge," Louise Kearney complained. "No milk, no newspapers, no anything. Everything's upside down. Oh, Henry, why are they doing this to us!"

He stepped from the house into brilliant sunshine. Gunfire had become the norm—he hardly heard it anymore—but he could not ignore the sound of distant artillery. Not so distant as he would like, coming closer.

Knots of people stood on street corners nervously exchanging rumors. The knots broke up; re-formed. "Two eighteen-pounders opened fire on Liberty Hall a while ago," a man told Henry. "The soldiers have them set up in Tara Street and are firing across the river. They haven't hit the Hall yet, but all the windows in the neighborhood are smashed."

"There's soldiers everywhere," a woman complained, "and they all have guns. I don't know how I'm going to get any food for my family. I'm afraid to walk down the street.''

"Don't bother," another woman advised. "The shops are out of everything anyway."

"Jaysus, this is a right pain in the arse!"

After considerable deliberation, Henry decided to chance O'Connell Bridge. There were republicans entrenched on the north end and British soldiers patrolling the south, but he held his hands above his head and both sides let him pass.

From outside, the Carlisle Building looked closed. A skeleton staff was on duty in the newspaper offices, however. "Might as well take off your hat and sit down, Henry," his editor advised him. "It's going to be a long day."

"Has Ned Halloran come in yet?"

"The copyboy? Haven't seen him in days. He'll be fired if he ever does come back; we can't have people taking off with no . . . I say, where are you going?"

"Out. There's a revolution, in case you didn't know, and I'm a reporter. I can cover it better out there than in here."

"But we can't—"

As he emerged from the Carlisle Building Henry paused to jot down in his notebook, "No traffic on the Liffey today." How strange, he thought, to see the river idle. The gunfire was daunting to the south and west, so he began walking east, curious to see what effect the insurrection was having on the docks.

He was almost opposite the Custom House when a single vessel came up the Liffey, a gray fisheries' patrol boat with the name *Helga* painted on its bow. Henry stopped to speculate on its purpose on a day when no one else dared the river. As he watched, it tied up on the south quays not far from where he stood.

Then the crew whipped the cover off a large gun mounted on the deck and opened fire on Liberty Hall.

The gunners were nervous; the first shell hit the Loop Line railway bridge instead. The metallic clatter was almost as loud as the explosion itself.

The crew adjusted their sights and fired again.

This time the shell sped unerringly across the river to ex-

plode on the roof of Liberty Hall. With a tremendous crash
the roof collapsed inward.

A man burst from the building and loped awkwardly down
the quay with his elbows flapping. British snipers opened fire
on him. "Run you poor bastard, run for your life!" Henry
shouted. To his relief the man dodged into an alley and disappeared.

Suddenly a bullet whined over Henry's head and he
crouched instinctively. He wanted to protest "I'm just a reporter!" but no one was listening.

The crew of the *Helga* had been told Liberty Hall was filled
with rebels. They were taken aback to have flushed only one
man. They continued to fire over the railway bridge, frequently hitting their target but also demolishing a number of
buildings nearby. After an hour of thunderous noise they cast
off and sailed back up the Liffey.

Behind them the shell of Liberty Hall stood abandoned in
the sun.

JAMES Connolly had listened to the bombardment with
white-lipped anger. He had been proved wrong; the "capitalists" had no hesitation about destroying property. But it was
worse than that. The destruction of Liberty Hall was like an
attack on his family; in a way, that building represented to
the labor leader what Saint Enda's represented to Pádraic
Pearse.

Yet he reassured his men by saying "Don't be alarmed.
When the British government is using artillery in the city of
Dublin it means they're in a hurry to finish the job. Probably
the Germans are coming to help us."[1]

News came down from the telegraphy office: Maxwell and
his British troops had landed at Kingstown. The advance force
alone consisted of two full battalions. Connolly dispatched
warnings to the outpost garrisons.

•   •   •

IT was almost noon when two men arrived with an urgent request from Seán Heuston for more reinforcements. "We sent some of the Volunteers from Swords down there yesterday," Seán MacDermott said.[2] "What's happened to them?"

"Dead or wounded," was the reply. "There are only fifteen men still holding the Mendicity Institute and the British have them surrounded. They're raking the building with machine-gun fire."

Connolly, now visibly upset, agreed to send a relief party. Upon examining the roster he found that every able-bodied man was already deployed. Eventually he seconded a few sentries, including the ever-eager Jack Plunkett, but as they assembled near the entrance they were a pitifully small band.

Ned told Síle, "I can't stand this. Seán Heuston is my friend." He was striding toward Connolly to volunteer when a Fianna messenger, flushed and near exhaustion, announced that the garrison had fallen. "Captain Heuston and his men have retreated across the river to the Four Courts. Toward the end the British were lobbing grenades in through the broken windows and Heuston's men were catching them and hurling them back!"[3]

In the G.P.O., men knelt to pray.

STRETCHER bearers returning from quayside reported that the *Helga* had found a new target. "It sounds as if they're shelling the rear of Boland's Mills."

James Connolly erupted. "Does anyone know what the bleedin' hell's going on with the friggin' Third Battalion?" he roared.

No one did.

With the tightening of the British cordon, news from the outpost garrisons was almost nonexistent. The telegraph was only useful for intercepting British messages. There had been no report from de Valera in a long time. If he was driven out of Boland's Mills the way would be open for British troops landing at Kingstown to march straight into the city.

Connolly summoned a hurried conference.

"You could take some of the Kimmage lads off sniper duty and send them down there," Michael Collins suggested.

The O'Rahilly scowled. "Wait a minute; I need every one of them just where he is."

"I won't commit any men until I know what the situation is," Connolly said flatly.

Seán MacDermott surveyed the post office. "There's no way of communicating with de Valera for a while; all our dispatch carriers are out."

"What about Ned Halloran?" asked Tom Clarke. "Pat doesn't give him very much to do, and he's been across the city under fire already. He knows how to handle himself out there."

Connolly nodded. "Good idea." He waved Ned over. "If Pearse will give you leave, I have an assignment for you."

"I'll ask him immediately."

Collins volunteered, "I saw him upstairs with his brother. He's going around the building trying to raise morale with poetic phrases when what we really need is a good . . ."

Ned was running for the stairs.

Although Michael Collins found Pearse's oratory inappropriate under the circumstances,[4] for many in the G.P.O. his words were a source of strength. He was no warrior and did not try to be; in military matters he invariably deferred to the commandant-general. But he could inspire men when their hearts were faltering, and that was no small gift.

Ned caught up with the brothers on the top floor. As he explained, Pádraic Pearse listened with bowed head and folded arms. "The young woman you introduced to me, your fiancée—is she willing for you to go?"

"She understands."

"And if you do not come back?"

Ned met Pearse's eyes. "She will understand that, too."

"Ah." Pearse gazed at the floor for a moment. When he spoke his voice was very soft. "She is a good woman, your Síle."

Those visionary's eyes did see through her after all, Ned thought. They saw all the way to the spirit.

· · ·

THIS time Ned took his rifle. Síle walked as far as the door with him. They did not say anything to each other. The moment was more intense for being silent. Just as he started to go, she laid the palm of her hand over his heart.

INTENSE sunshine was turning the day sultry. Sweating, Ned made his way by a circuitous route that avoided the main streets. The worst moment was crossing the Liffey. Fortunately, a crowd had gathered to stare at the demolished Liberty Hall, and no one paid any attention to a man walking alone across the Swivel Bridge.

On the south quay he saw someone he recognized as a member of the Third Battalion and called out to him, "What word from Boland's Mills?"

The other man strode toward him. He was disheveled and grimy, and there was a long tear in the sleeve of the suitcoat he wore. But he had a Sam Browne belt and a yellow armlet.

"A gunboat came along the river to shell us," he told Ned, "but Dev raised our flag over an empty building and they turned their guns on that instead."

"Dev?"

"De Valera; we don't call him Dev to his face, of course. Not him! He likes everything just so; very precise man. Knows to the inch where we all are. Anyway, our garrison was damaged a bit but not too badly. We have a signaler up on the roof sending out all sorts of phony semaphores about German troops and airplanes; that should scare them off. I'm on my way to report to headquarters now."

"That's all the news you have?"

"Hardly! At nine this morning a scout brought word that British troops have landed at Kingstown. They're almost here by now. They've split into three groups, so I guess a lot of them will get through, but Dev's had men in position since Monday, waiting for them. There's a concentration of our best marksmen at Mount Street Bridge. If any soldiers come up

Northumberland Road they're not going to get past that bridge!''

Ned could have taken the news to Connolly himself, could have let the other man go back to Boland's Mills while he returned to the dubious safety of headquarters. He would never know why he did not, unless it was the memory of Síle's face as she put her hand over his heart.

She was proud of him. The way Mary Cosgrave would have been proud of him if he wore a British uniform.

The thought was unsettling.

"Go on to headquarters as fast as you can," Ned advised the other man, "and tell them what you've told me. And for God's sake put that armlet in your pocket, will you? There's no point in drawing fire if you're just carrying dispatches. Do you need reinforcements?"

"Do we! There's thousands of British soldiers on the way. If you could see how few men we really . . . Hold on, where are you going?"

"Mount Street Bridge," Ned called over his shoulder. He did not wait to see whether the man removed the yellow armlet.

Mount Street Bridge spanned the Grand Canal. A total of thirteen men under the command of Michael Malone, de Valera's aide-de-camp, had taken up positions in Clanwilliam House, a substantial three-storey residence overlooking the bridge from the city side, and in the Haddington Road Parochial Hall and a house at 25 Northumberland Road, on the far side of the canal.[5]

They had given their word to the departing occupants not to do any more damage than necessary. No furniture had been taken out to build barricades and the scene looked deceptively peaceful.

Ned ran up the steps of Clanwilliam House and pounded on the door. A young man in a Volunteers' tunic opened the door at once, then peered past him with a look of profound disappointment. "Are you alone? We were hoping for reinforcements."

"I've just come from headquarters," Ned replied, "and if you need—"

"They're coming!" shouted a voice from upstairs.

Ned was seized by the arm and dragged into the drawing room. "Look what they sent us from headquarters!"

"All donations gratefully accepted," remarked a sandy-haired man who was carefully positioning his rifle on a windowsill facing the bridge.

THE British army came marching down Northumberland Road. In this particular column there were only a few hundred, but to Ned they looked like all the soldiers in the world.

"Do you know how to shoot that rifle or is it just an ornament?" the sandy-haired man asked him.

"I can shoot."

"Then get over here by me."

Ned crouched down by the window and sighted along his rifle barrel. His heart was thundering in his chest. This was what war came down to, kill or be killed. Isn't that what Tom Clarke had said?

The head of the column reached number 25. Gunfire exploded. The advance guard halted abruptly, taken by surprise, and a few of them dived for cover.

"Now us," said the sandy-haired man beside Ned. A volley of shots rang out from both Clanwilliam House and the Parochial Hall.

The column fell back in disarray.

After a moment's hesitation the British officers drew their swords and shouted confused orders. Soldiers rushed at number 25 with fixed bayonets, then reversed their rifles when they reached the door and hammered on the wood with their gun butts. Firing down from upstairs windows, the men in number 25—there appeared to be only two of them—drove their attackers back with a display of deadly accurate revolver fire. There was a cacophony of officers bellowing, men yelling, angry curses, screams of pain, more gunfire.

The officers tried to lead the column past the house, but the men inside were such good marksmen it was impossible. One soldier after another fell and lay in the road, dead or dying.

In Clanwilliam House, Ned had fired his first shot almost before he realized it. The old Howth Mauser had a vicious recoil, and the shot went wide. "Steady on," he muttered to himself. He held his breath, sighted carefully, and fired again.

This time his aim was true. He watched a soldier stagger and go down on one knee. The man made feeble, waving gestures with his hands and blood gushed from his mouth. He fell over and did not move.

I've killed a man, Ned thought. I should feel something. But there was no time to feel. Only to shoot.

The soldiers kept coming.

British snipers managed to get into the belfry of the Haddington Road Church and opened attack on the republican positions. Bullets whistled through the open windows of Clanwilliam House. "Keep your head down!" someone shouted.

Bullets were pouring into the drawing room, splintering paneling and gouging holes in plaster. "Keep down I said!" the voice cried again.

The air was alive with a swarm of hornets that hummed and stung and left a moment's white-hot pain in their wake.

The army began lobbing grenades through the windows and into the basement of number 25. Smoke billowed from the house, but the men inside kept shooting.

The republicans set up a deadly crossfire that turned Mount Street Bridge into a bloody nightmare.

The noise was deafening. Ned's head began throbbing intolerably. Every time he fired the Mauser he felt as if he had been hit on the skull by his own rifle.

There was a terrible explosion from number 25. Cartridges stored in a bedroom had fallen victim to a grenade tossed in a rear window. But the men inside somehow survived, somehow kept firing with the full fury of the British army turned against them.

The republicans in Clanwilliam House redoubled their efforts. The focus of the attack shifted to them. The sandy-haired man shouted encouragement to the others as he fired round after round from his window. Successive waves of soldiers rushed the bridge, led by officers brandishing swords and cheering their men on. They would have been a gallant sight had they not been the enemy, Ned thought.

He held his breath, sighted, fired.

Time ceased to have meaning. The light glinting on the canal changed as the afternoon wore on, and still the defenders of the bridge had not let the army pass. Every inch of ground was bitterly contested. There was a rhythm to battle, Ned discovered; fighting was not as random as it looked. A wave of energy hurled men forward and then subsided, and in its trough they gathered themselves and prepared to go again. The trick was to take advantage of the cresting wave.

He was sweating profusely. The salt stung his eyes and he wiped them with his forearm, then glanced at the sandy-haired man beside him. He was slumped into the window recess with his face turned away. There was something boneless about him.

"Are you hit?" Ned asked.

Silence.

He did not want to touch the body. He did not want to think about it at all.

Hold your breath, sight, fire.

No reinforcements arrived. The man he had sent to Connolly must not have got through, then. Ned breathed a prayer for him.

There were more grenade explosions. The concussions sent white lights skittering painfully along Ned's optic nerves. His head wanted to explode too, to open up and let the throbbing, tortured brain escape.

A sea of khaki-clad figures was snaking its way along the bridge, finding cover wherever it could. Each of the three republican positions was isolated now, fighting on its own.

Hold your breath, sight, fire.

Someone shook his shoulder. "Did you say you're from headquarters?"

"I am."

"Then for God's sake get back there and ask them to send us some help, will you? Or go to Boland's Mills and tell Dev. He has damned few men himself but he can spare us some if he knows how bad it is here."

"I can't leave you like this."

"If you don't we'll all die surely. We may die anyway, but it would be a comfort to think help might be coming. You can get out the back of the house if we create enough diversion in front. Go, man; it's our last chance!"

April 26, 1916

ROYAL NAVY SHELLS DUBLIN

April 26, 1916

UNIONIST MPS DEMAND ALL REBELS BE SHOT

Chapter Fifty-four

Henry Mooney sat slumped at his desk. He was defeated. Faced with the mounting violence of revolution he had retreated to the newspaper office, and now was staring at a stack of copy that held no meaning for him.

Evening was coming. Soon it would be time to go home. If he still had a home. He looked up at the clock on the wall and discovered it had stopped.

Of course it has, he thought with a mirthless chuckle. We're frozen in time and the shooting will go on forever.

"What's so funny?" asked a fellow reporter, handing him yet another sheet of paper. "It can't be this."

Henry glanced at the page. "Dear sweet Jesus!"

That morning Captain J. C. Bowen-Colthurst, the army officer who had arrested Francis Sheehy-Skeffington the previous evening, had taken Skeffington and two others into the yard at Portobello Barracks and shot them in cold blood with neither trial nor hearing.[1] The other two men were journalists who had no connection with the nationalist movement. Their arrests were as arbitrary as that of little Frank Skeffington, who passionately believed in pacificism and the equality of women.

Henry was dumbfounded. "This doesn't make any sense."

"The man who brought me the information says Skeffington was a witness when Bowen-Colthurst shot an unarmed boy in Rathmines earlier.''

"How does your informant know?"

"He's stationed at Portobello, actually. Says the captain's quite insane, they're all afraid of him down there. Colthurst's killed several innocent men since the Rising began. Blew off one lad's head while he was kneeling in the street signing the cross. My contact called to tell me about Skeffington, then scarpered away to find a pub that's still open.''

"What will happen to Colthurst?"

"Probably nothing, Henry. He has a lot of influence in the Castle, he was aide-de-camp to Lord Aberdeen at one time.''

"We can't use this story, you know that.''

The other man nodded. "I know. But maybe someday . . .'' He left the thought unfinished.

"I'd like to find that pub myself,'' said Henry Mooney.

RUNNING, walking, dodging, desperate, Ned Halloran left a neighborhood littered with the dead and dying. Mount Street Bridge was clogged with the victims of bungled orders whose officers had sent them into the republican crossfire like sacrificial victims. They crawled, they groaned, they died in the broiling sun, and still more waves were sent after them to die and fall across their bodies. It was incredible to think that so few were doing so much damage to so many. It could not last.

We may die anyway, but it would be a comfort to think help might be coming.

His head was pounding so savagely he could not think. He forgot about Boland's Mills and de Valera. He had to return to Mr. Connolly; to Mr. Pearse; to Síle.

Ned could no longer tell if anyone was shooting at him; his ears were continually ringing. Reality was tenuous. He turned a corner and everything looked normal; he clearly saw well-dressed men and women walking about on a balmy spring afternoon. He turned another corner and there were nothing but khaki uniforms and men lying on their bellies, aiming guns.

Somehow he crossed the Liffey. He would never remember how or where.

Later he came upon British soldiers lined up in front of a barricade in Talbot Street, smilingly having their photograph taken.[2]

SÍLE was kept busy in the infirmary on the first floor of headquarters. A doctor, a medical student, and a captured British surgeon were in attendance.[3] Stretcher bearers brought a stream of wounded men. The original stock of medical supplies was exhausted. Raiding parties replaced what they could from nearby chemists' shops—and left signed promissory notes.

Síle was sent to the ground floor to someone to request more morphia, if there was any to be found. The leaders were sitting together on stools and boxes, talking. She wanted to scream at them, "Where's Ned? Find Ned for me, that's all that matters!" But she knew it was not all that mattered.

An exhausted figure came staggering into the G.P.O.

Síle felt time stop for a moment.

God, she thought. Just the one word. God. And then, Thank you.

She ran to meet Ned.

His eyes were glazed; he hardly seemed to see her. He had lost his rifle someplace, and his uniform was stained. "Where's Mr. Connolly?" he said several times.

"Over there with the others. Give me your hand and I'll take you to him."

In a voice that shook with emotion Ned recounted the battle of Mount Street Bridge. "You have to send reinforcements, sir," he told Connolly. "You have to send everything we've got."

Seán MacDermott gave a hollow laugh. "Everything we've got? Do you know how little that is, and how thin it's spread already?"

"But they have nothing! A dozen men have been holding out against hundreds of British soldiers all afternoon! Didn't a messenger get through from them earlier, asking for help?"

"No one's come from there," Connolly told him. "Looking at you, I would say it's a miracle you did."

"What about the reinforcements?" Ned persisted. "I promised them."

"There's no way right now, Halloran; there's just no way. Maybe if they can hold out until tomorrow and we get more men coming in here . . ."

Ned swallowed hard. "I see, sir."

Joe Plunkett said in a hoarse whisper, "If it would make you feel better to talk to a priest, Ned, Pat just told me he's sent to the Pro-Cathedral for a curate. Someone to hear confessions and grant absolutions."

Ned slumped onto the floor with his back propped against one of the counters. Síle brought him tea. He could not drink. He could not see her face. He could only see the Mount Street Bridge.

Well after dark, a three-man squad who had been pinned down near Merrion Square reported the outcome of the battle as they had heard it from an ambulance driver. Over two hundred British soldiers had died at the bridge that afternoon. Eventually the defenders in the Parochial Hall had been forced to retreat and were captured. One of the two men who had held out so long and so valiantly in number 25 was thought to have escaped. The other was dead.

Clanwilliam House had been bombed into a blazing ruin, incinerating everyone inside.

THAT night Ned had a dream. Penned beneath the overturned bowl of a hard, unyielding sky, he crouched on the smoking earth.

The extinguishing tide rose inexorably.

•   •   •

SOMETIME later he awoke to hear Pádraic Pearse having a low-voiced conversation with Des Ryan.[4] Pearse was sitting on a barrel, Ryan standing beside him. A sullen red glare seeped into the post office from fires now burning throughout the north side. With gunfire punctuating his words, Pearse asked, "It was the right thing to do, was it not?"

Ryan was astonished at the question. "Yes!"

"And if we fail it means the end of everything, Volunteers, the Republic, all?"

"I suppose so, sir."

"Tonight there are countless brave men fighting for this city, Des. Countless women too, even carrying gelignite in spite of every danger. No matter what happens now, someday people will speak of Dublin as one of the splendid cities, as they speak of Paris.

"When we are all wiped out at first they will blame us, condemn us. However, but for this protest, the war would eventually end and still nothing would have been done." Pádraic Pearse drew a long, slow breath. "After a few years they will see the meaning of what we tried to do."

He arose, collected his brother, and the two of them went on one of their rounds, visiting with the men at their posts, inspiring them through the darkest hours of the night.

THURSDAY morning dawned on an increasingly grim and devastated Dublin. The artillery was doing its work. The rubble was piling up.

The British infantry was drawing steadily closer to the republican stronghold as the various outpost garrisons were no longer able to prevent them. Both artillery and machine-gun fire were beginning to make their presence felt in the Sackville Street area. James Connolly led numerous sorties to reinforce old positions or establish new ones. However, he admitted to The O'Rahilly that the post office would not be able to hold out much longer.

• • •

NED had passed from sleep into that amorphous state where nothing is quite real. He tried with all his might to imagine himself solidly in his own narrow bed at Saint Enda's with the dawn chorus outside his window, and when that failed he wished himself into the room in Gardiner Street, and Henry humming as he shaved. Henry used cocoa butter shaving soap. Ned could almost smell it.

Then he heard the guns. Artillery. Very close.

He gave a violent start.

"You were shattered when you came in," said Willie Pearse, bending over him, "so we let you sleep. But I guess you'd better get up now. Mr. Connolly thinks they'll be shelling us very soon."

Groggily, Ned got to his feet. Someone was pounding a drum somewhere. Perhaps inside his head.

The defenders in the post office were strengthening their defenses yet again, while the women worked stoically beside them. Síle told him the secret. "We talked about it amongst ourselves last night. If we show fear it might infect the men and we don't want to do that."

She needed a bath and her hair was stringy and matted, but he thought she looked beautiful. They all looked beautiful.

AT precisely ten o'clock the British began shelling Lower Sackville Street. One building after another caught fire. Kelly's Gun Shop, which had become known as "Kelly's Fort," was abandoned. The men retreated to the G.P.O., where George Plunkett criticized their decision. "You could have held out," he kept saying.

His older brother remonstrated with him. "Don't blame them for being human, George." As the situation worsened, Joe Plunkett was forcing himself to walk up and down the post office, waving his saber and encouraging the men with little jokes and a gently mocking smile. In his elegant uniform and gleaming jewelry, with death upon his face, he was a bizarre figure. But the men responded to his valiant spirit. He was digging deep into himself to give them all the strength he had, a gift bestowed through a superhuman triumph of will over weakness. In those desperate hours, Joe Plunkett was greatly loved.[5]

As he made the rounds of the republican positions that morning, James Connolly found a curious little squad gathered on the top floor of the Metropole Hotel. He subsequently reported to Pearse with a tone somewhere between anger and amusement, "There's a dozen of your Saint Enda's lads up there with our snipers, Pearse.[6] They're too young to be Volunteers, they're not even Fianna, yet they say they want to join the fight. What am I to do with them? The streets are too dangerous to try to send them home."

"Since they are there, I suggest you provide them with weapons. They may have to defend not only their ideals but themselves."

The day grew hotter. Had there been no women in the G.P.O. the men might have stripped to the waist. As it was, they simply suffered. The fires burning throughout the center of the city were increasing too, beyond the ability of the fire brigades to cope.

A thick cloud of black smoke hung over Dublin.

From the first time the sounds of gunfire had reached the orphanage in the North Circular Road, the little girl called Ursula Jervis slept very little and was unable to eat. A new head matron had recently arrived at the orphanage. She assured the little girls, "Some men are hunting out in the fields, that's all. There's no need to be frightened." Most of the children accepted what she said. They were accustomed to believing authority figures.

But Precious had heard the unmistakable sound of rifles being fired in city streets before. Although she was terrified, she also was contemptuous of the woman for lying.

No organism can sustain a high level of terror indefinitely, however. As time went on and the sound must be endured,

Precious dug into the gritty corners of her soul for courage.

Then on Thursday morning she looked out a window and saw an amorphous dark shape crouched over the city. Occasional red sparks gleamed like angry eyes. Terror returned in full measure.

Precious ran to the back hallway, where she found the staff sorting through haphazard piles of foodstuffs, the evidence of frantic hoarding. Precious tugged at the matron's sleeve. "Dublin's on fire!" she cried.

The woman pushed her away. "Not now, child, can't you see I'm busy? I know about the fire; it's just someone burning rubbish. I promise you there's nothing to worry about."

Precious flicked her eyes from the matron's face to the hoarded supplies and back again. Then she turned on her heel and trotted off.

When she next looked out the window, the smoke cloud was larger than before.

Precious quietly began to gather her few treasures. They consisted of the toys Ned had given her, including a bear that banged a drum when you pulled its string, and a tiny bisque baby doll from Síle. There was also one beloved picture book that Mrs. Pearse had given her the previous Christmas at Saint Enda's. Methodically, the little girl stripped the pillowcase from the one flat pillow on her bed and carefully packed her treasures inside. Then she tied a knot in the top of the pillowcase. From that moment, she did not let the bundle out of her sight.

"There are things you may want beyond mere subsistence," Ned had once said, "so you'll need to make plans."

Precious listened to everything Ned told her.

TOWARD the middle of the afternoon the post office took its first direct hit from an artillery shell. There was no panic, but a pall of choking dust filled the building.

Pádraic Pearse praised the republicans for their courage in the face of danger. They answered his words with a heartfelt cheer that made them all feel, briefly, better.

James Connolly's response to the attack was different. He led a squad to set up additional defenses in Liffey Street, an area already infiltrated with British snipers. On the way he stopped to help repair a damaged barricade and his left arm was grazed by a bullet. Without calling any attention to the injury he quietly returned to the infirmary in the G.P.O. to have it dressed, then rejoined his men in Liffey Street.

When he was satisfied they were well dug in, he started back toward headquarters.

In Middle Abbey Street a sniper's bullet smashed James Connolly's leg just above the ankle.

He fell to the cobblestones and lay without moving. Eventually, in agony, Connolly began dragging himself toward the G.P.O. When he came within sight of the sentries Dick Humphries ran inside to summon stretcher bearers.

Connolly was hoisted onto an iron-framed bed with casters that had been found rusting in the basement. No one could imagine why such a piece of furniture was in the post office. While the doctors examined him he lay sweating and swearing and demanding news of the battle. His leg was all but destroyed; an immediate operation was necessary to save it. The only anesthetic available was chloroform.

Makeshift screens were put around the bed, and the British surgeon worked as devotedly on the rebel leader as on one of his own. Following the operation Connolly was given an injection of morphia, but he refused to be taken to the Jervis Street Infirmary.

After dark a messenger arrived with news of a furious battle at the South Dublin Union. The fight had ended in a stalemate. The British could not overcome the defenders but they had the position surrounded.

DUBLIN was a sea of flames.

THE interior of the G.P.O. was hellish. Throughout Thursday night men continued to crowd into the building as they fell

back before the British assault. They could not be redeployed;
they were caught in a tightening noose. The atmosphere was
stifling. Food was in short supply and the two toilets in the
building, overwhelmed by numbers they were never meant to
serve, stopped up.

There was no pretense of sleep now. British machine-gun
fire was raking the area from the quays to the Rotunda. The
republicans were kept busy lubricating their overheated firearms with sardine oil. A bucket brigade was formed to keep
inflammable material saturated with water.

Sometime during the night the men began singing.

By dawn Friday the British were pumping artillery shells
into Upper Sackville Street, demolishing the buildings opposite the post office. It was an act of wanton destruction. The
O'Rahilly commented, ''They just want to show us how little
they think of us and our city.''[7]

Ned still had his headache plus a nagging nausea that found
no relief in vomiting. He tried to ignore both. When Pearse
sent him to the infirmary to inquire about the condition of the
commandant-general, he was thankful for the distraction.

Síle told him, ''Mr. Connolly had an uneasy night but he
seems better now. We gave him a book.''

''You did what?''

''We found a detective novel hidden under one of the counters. Now you know what postal clerks do on a slow day.''

James Connolly was lying in bed with his lower leg in
splints. Pale from loss of blood, he was propped up on his
folded blanket, reading. When he saw Ned he grinned. ''A
good book, rest, and an insurrection all at the same time!
Why, this is revolution *de luxe*!''[8]

A little while later he summoned Winifred Carney and dictated a stirring but almost totally fictional pronouncement that
he had The O'Rahilly read out to the garrison. It was filled
with glowing descriptions of victories that had never happened. Although the listeners knew better, they were touched
by the effort he was making to keep their spirits high.

The speech concluded: "Courage, boys, we are winning, and in the hour of our victory let us not forget the splendid women who have everywhere stood by us and cheered us on. Never had man or woman a grander cause, never was a cause more grandly served."

From outside came the crash of a burning building collapsing in Sackville Street.

During a brief lull in the gunfire, the leaders decided to evacuate the women and the wounded. James Connolly, of course, refused to go.

Síle told Ned, "I won't do it, I won't leave you."

"You can argue with me but you can't argue with Seán MacDermott. Now that Mr. Connolly's out of action he and Tom—"

"I can argue with anybody! Winifred Carney is staying and I'm staying too. The other women feel the same way."

MacDermott appealed to Pearse. "Connolly has every right to stay, but if the women refuse to go, Pat, what can we do? They argue that since we wouldn't let them be soldiers, they don't have to take our orders."

"I'll speak to them."

In the hot, dusty, pungent main hall of the post office, Pádraic Pearse addressed the thirty-four women who had shared the last four days. He expressed his intense admiration for their courage and made a point of shaking each by the hand. "We ask you to go now," he told them, "because once this is over we will need you more than ever. It will give us strength, knowing you are waiting to help build the new Republic. We cannot do it without you."

In the end they could not resist him. All but four agreed to leave: Winifred Carney and two nurses, Julia Grenan and Elizabeth O'Farrell, who were also members of Cumann na mBan—and Síle Duffy.[9]

Ned was at the point of despair. He knew without anyone having to tell him that the defenders of the post office were doomed. The British meant to pound them to a pulp. He had one argument left to offer.

"I'm not asking for myself," he told Síle, "but for Precious. You said Precious was ours and promised that if anything happened to me you would take care of her.''

"Och, Ned, that's not fair!"

"I know how you feel about honesty, and you know how I feel about promises. I'm holding you to yours. Get out of here while you have the chance, sweetheart, and go to Precious. Keep her safe for me, for both of us.''

He watched, helpless to do more, while the battle raged within Síle. At last her shoulders slumped and he knew he had won. "All right, Ned, I'll go. But I ask a promise of you in return. Stay alive.''

He forced a grin. "I'll do my best.''

And then she was gone. Gone, and the light gone with her.

FROM the day he first saw Kilmainham Jail, Father Paul O'Shaughnessy had hated the place. It was built to be hated, he thought. Originally intended as a debtors' prison to accommodate a hundred men and women at the most, it had contained ten times that number during the height of the Great Famine, in conditions that the priest could not imagine.

Kilmainham's principal function had become the housing of "political prisoners," however; men whose crime was resistance to British rule. Seeped into its gray stones was the pain and passion and desperate thwarted longing of generations of rebels. They were kept apart from the ordinary miscreants housed in the county jail in order to avoid contaminating them with the dangerous seeds of nationalism.

So Paul was told by Reverend Eugene MacCarthy, the prison chaplain. "We minister to these unfortunates as best we can," Reverend MacCarthy explained. "They are not bad men, most of them; just misguided.''

Kilmainham comprised an open, four-tiered area ringed with cells that could be seen at all times from a central position, and an older wing where cells lined murky corridors. Built according to Victorian penal principles, the newer part of the prison attempted to provide some degree of light and air.

The old wing was a nightmare from another age. Its narrow, vaulted corridors were like catacombs beneath a dead city. Cramped stone cells were damp and frighteningly dark. Furnishings consisted of a thin mattress on the floor and a slop bucket in the corner.

In an attempt to gain empathy with the prisoners, Paul went into an empty cell in the old wing and closed the solid oak door. The sense of isolation was stifling.

It was like being in one's own coffin.

When insurrection broke out on Easter Monday, Kilmainham Jail was put on alert immediately. Army officers came and went; cells and supplies were inspected, but no new prisoners arrived. On Wednesday morning as Paul set out from Ringsend he was stopped in the street by two British soldiers who demanded to see his pass.

"I'm a priest. I'm on my way to Kilmainham to assist the chaplain."

"We'll have plenty of Catholics in Kilmainham soon," one of the soldiers laughed.

The other said more kindly, "Please turn around and go back, Father. You can visit the jail in few days, I promise you, and your services will be needed by then. We're going to fill the jails with Sinn Féiners."

Reluctantly, Paul returned to the Cahill house. Thursday morning he tried again, only to find himself still restricted to Ringsend. The army had partitioned Dublin into segments and was insisting that civilians remain in their own districts.

On Friday, with the flames of the inner city plainly visible, Paul made another attempt to reach Kilmainham. This time the soldiers at the barricade told him, "Cheer up, Father, the rebellion's almost over."

Chapter Fifty-five

THE air in the post office was unbreathable. Men were coughing and choking, their eyes streamed from the smoke that infiltrated every part of the building. Joe Plunkett suffered terribly until Ned thought to wring out a wet handkerchief and give it to him to breathe through.

Plunkett managed to make a little joke. Holding up his wrist with its filigree bracelet, he said, "All this smoke is going to tarnish my bangle. Grace gave it to me; I wouldn't want anything to happen to it." He broke off, fighting for breath. "We're going to be married, you know. Just as soon as this is over. It'll be the first marriage in the Republic of Ireland."

"I know," said Ned. "I'm coming to the wedding."

SOME of Cumann na mBan accompanied the wounded to the hospital in Jervis Street. So did the British surgeon, Lieutenant Mahony, and Father Flanagan, the curate from the Pro-Cathedral, although Mahony subsequently returned to the G.P.O. to look after James Connolly.

Other women were determined to try to reach their homes. Their men were fighting, their children were being cared for by relatives, but their homes held irreplaceable treasures accumulated over a lifetime. Grandmother's delph plates on the dresser, their own wedding pictures in the bedroom. The children's first drawings, lovingly brought home from school. Home was the world they had created in a larger world that was being destroyed. If necessary, they would make their last stand there.

With only Eliza Goggins's Luger for company, Síle Duffy set out for the orphanage in the North Circular Road.

IN the G.P.O., Pádraic Pearse issued a final pronouncement in which he lavished praise on his fellow revolutionaries. He described James Connolly as "the guiding brain of our resistance."[1] With characteristic generosity, he even credited Eoin MacNeill with always having acted "in the best interests of Ireland." He also gave an accurate assessment of the current situation and promised to hold out as long as the building lasted.

Connolly had himself carried into the main hall on a stretcher so he could be at the heart of the action. Although he was holding his emotions under tight control, Pádraic Pearse looked grief-stricken. By contrast, Connolly was regaining his old verve. He was never so tough as when fighting against impossible odds.

The day wore on. Men at the outer barricades were being forced to retreat to the post office as the British forces advanced slowly but inexorably, sweeping the streets with machine-gun fire.

Exhausted, Pearse took a sleeping draught and asked O'Kelly to wake him after an hour. But before the soporific could take effect a new fire broke out in the building and Joe Plunkett made a valiant effort to fight it himself. For the first and last time that week Pearse lost his temper. "Lie down in the name of God, Joe!" he roared, "and let healthy men do the work!"

"THE roof's burning!" yelled Michael Collins from the head of the stairs.

The O'Rahilly led a party up to fight the flames and Pádraic Pearse ran after them, heedless of danger to himself. An incendiary shell had ignited part of the top storey. British snipers were pouring gunfire into the area. A bullet crashed against the wall inches from Pearse's head as he helped the men who were battling the blaze.[2] When they got it under control a new one broke out elsewhere.

PEARSE, MacDermott, Clarke, Plunkett, and The O'Rahilly gathered around the stretcher where James Connolly lay.[3] The ground floor was barricaded with sandbags; buckets of water stood ready to hand. Incredibly, they had held out until darkness fell, but they knew the post office was doomed.

"Connolly's quite ready to stay right here and fight it out to the bitter end," Willie Pearse confided to Ned. "A gun battle to the death, no quarter asked or given."

"Is that what Mr. Pearse wants?"

"Merciful hour, Ned! That's the last thing he wants. He's arguing now to move the garrison while we still have a chance. We can set up the government headquarters elsewhere; it isn't the building that matters." Suddenly both men flinched. There was a terrific crash overhead as the upper floors collapsed, followed by the thunder of ammunition stores exploding.

THE O'Rahilly called the last men in from their snipers' posts. The thirteen British soldiers who had been taken prisoner during the previous days were led to safety at the rear of the building and released. Through cracks in the collapsing walls of the G.P.O., those inside could see the smoldering ruins of Sackville Street. And still the artillery thundered.

Pádraic Pearse calmly rationed out what was left of the food and, like a schoolmaster instructing his pupils, made sure each man filled his water bottle and took his haversack with him. Then he explained the plans the leaders had agreed upon for evacuating the garrison. "We shall leave by the Henry Street entrance, make a dash up Moore Street, and take up a position in the William & Woods factory in Parnell Street. From there we may be able to get through enemy lines to Commandant Daly in the Four Courts.''

At the end of Moore Street was a British barricade, the only apparent obstacle between the republicans and the factory. But it was a crucial one—and well defended. The O'Rahilly organized a squad of a dozen men to storm the barricade and open the way for the rest. He did this as discreetly as possible, but by now Ned Halloran had become a past master at observing everything that went on.

Ned went to Jack Plunkett. ''Did you know The O'Rahilly's taking an advance party to clear the way?''

''Not without me he isn't!'' cried Jack.

He and Ned went to The O'Rahilly and asked to be included. ''You only have twelve,'' Jack observed.[4] ''Would you not like another twelve?''

''You stay with the others, both of you. Any more men would only draw fire.'' The O'Rahilly turned and told his friend Desmond Fitzgerald, ''Good-bye, Desmond. This is the end for certain. I never dreamed it would last so long.''[5] Then suddenly he grinned. ''But fancy missing this and then getting killed running for a tram or catching cold!''

As The O'Rahilly was about to lead his men out the Henry Street exit his eye fell on Father Flanagan. Taking off his hat, he knelt in front of the priest. ''I don't suppose, Father, that we will ever meet in this world again,'' he said soberly. ''Please give me your blessing.''

With tears in his eyes, the priest complied.

Ned and Jack watched anxiously as the squad set off, then went back inside.

PÁDRAIC Pearse and James Connolly remained in the post office, refusing to leave until the last man had gone. Only Ned, Willie Pearse, Winifred Carney, and two Fianna stretcher bearers were allowed to stay with them. As the others filed past, Pádraic Pearse said, ''Go out and face the machine guns as if you were on parade.''[6]

Leaving the G.P.O. for the last time, they began to sing a song they had sung many times:

Soldiers are we, whose lives are pledged to Ireland;
Some have come from a land beyond the wave;
Sworn to be free, no more our ancient sireland
Shall shelter the despot or the slave.
Tonight we man the bearna beoghail
In Erin's cause, come woe or weal;
'Mid cannon's roar and rifle's peal
We'll chant a soldier's song.[7]

They had almost reached Moore Street when a man came running back to tell them The O'Rahilly had been shot down. A hail of bullets pursued him.

Consternation swept through the company. Some ran one way, some another. Tom Clarke and Seán MacDermott tried to rally them; Joe Plunkett held up his saber and cried in a voice of surprising strength, ''Don't be afraid! Don't be cowards, any of you! On! On!''

Through a descending dusk lit by flames and gunfire, the garrison struggled to find a brief haven.

THE time had come for the last defenders to leave the G.P.O. Connolly's stretcher bearers lifted him and headed for the door. He grimaced with pain but said nothing. As they passed out of the building into the range of enemy snipers, the boy at the head of the stretcher bent forward to use his own body to shield James Connolly. ''How old are you, lad?'' Connolly asked hoarsely.

''Fourteen, sir. Be easy now, we'll have you safe soon.''

PÁDRAIC Pearse made a hasty tour of inspection to be certain everyone was out while Ned and the others waited for him just outside. After an unbearable few minutes he appeared in the doorway alone, covered in soot, his face swollen and blistered from the heat. He gave a curt nod. To the sound of crashing beams they left the G.P.O. to its fate.

The fire roared triumph.

As if indifferent to the bullets, Pearse walked around to the front of the building. Ned followed him. From this angle they could see that the entire post office was now an inferno. But Pearse was not looking at the blaze. His eyes were lifted to the flag flying above it, whipped by the wind from the fire. The lettering was badly scorched, but the words IRISH REPUBLIC were still discernible.

The two men saw the flagpole collapse. Slowly the green banner sank across the parapet and slumped toward the rubble in the street.

Chapter Fifty-six

I N the offices of the *Independent*, Henry Mooney stubbornly kept to his post. Other newspapermen did the same, though no one dared cross the Liffey for firsthand information on Friday. Nothing seemed to dampen the avid curiosity of some Dubliners, however, who wandered dangerously close to the battle raging in Sackville Street just to gawk.

The reporters mostly contented themselves with smoking cigarettes, pacing the floor, going to the door to stare toward the flames of Sackville Street and then going back to their desks to stare at their folded hands.

And wait.

Friday night they slept on their desks.

Saturday morning information began to trickle in. One by one, the rebel positions around the city had fallen. Some garrisons were still holding out, however. The Four Courts and Jacob's Biscuit Factory remained in republican hands.

Upon arriving in Dublin on Friday, General Sir John Maxwell had issued orders to quell the rebellion at once by whatever means necessary. A frontal attack on a republican position in North King Street turned into an exceptionally bloody battle that lasted until Saturday morning. In frustration at not being able to defeat an enemy for whom they had nothing but scorn, some of the British troops ran amok. They smashed their way into the tenements in the area and vented their anger on the inhabitants. Fifteen innocent men had been shot and bayoneted to death in front of their terrified families.

"I'll need someone to confirm this," Henry's editor said.

"Why? You know we won't print it."

A smoke-stained, filthy figure stood in the doorway of the Carlisle Building, looking around as if dazed. Henry Mooney jumped to his feet. "Ned, is it you?"

"It is me," Ned replied in a ravaged voice. He sounded as if he were not quite sure. "Henry. Thank God you're here. I thought you might be. Have you . . . is there any water?"

Henry gestured, and one of the other reporters ran to bring a tumbler of water. They all gathered around Ned as he drank.

"Do you need to see a doctor?" Henry asked worriedly.

"Not now. I have to go back."

"Go back? What are you talking about, you can't go back!"

"I must, Henry. I have to be with them. I just . . . Mr. Pearse . . ." He swayed in the chair and put one hand to his head. "It hurts so bad."

Henry moved Ned's hand and replaced it with his own. Beneath the matted black curls he felt a crust of dried blood.

"We'd better get that doctor," his editor said.

"No!" Ned's eyes were suddenly clear. Clear, green, and very cold. "No doctor! Listen to me. I've come to deliver a message and then I'm going back. I'm headquarters staff, you see."

Henry told the others, "There's no arguing with this fellow when he's determined." We'll let him talk it out, he thought to himself, and then we'll get help for him. At least he'll be calmer by then. "All right, Ned; what's the message? And where is it you're going back to?"

"After the G.P.O. was destroyed we hid out in a grocery in Moore Street.[1] The woman who lives over the store helped us. This morning we tunneled through into the back of Hanlon's Fishmongers but we can't go any farther. There's British artillery at the corner of Parnell Street and machine-gun nests everywhere.

"We have seventeen men who were wounded leaving the post office, plus a British soldier George Plunkett found lying in the street and wouldn't leave out there to die. It was the strangest thing . . ." Ned's eyes briefly came unfocused. "The soldier kept saying, 'I want to speak to the big man over there.'[2] We told him that was Mr. Pearse, and he said, 'Yes, I know, I want to speak to him.' Mr. Pearse went over, and the soldier said, 'Put your arms around me and lift me up,' and Mr. Pearse did. The soldier relaxed then as if all the pain went out of him, and in a few moments he was asleep. It was the strangest thing."

The men in the newspaper office looked at one another. One of them shook his head.

With an effort, Ned recalled himself to the present. "There are three women with us, too. James Connolly's badly injured and in a lot of pain, and Joe Plunkett's dying, though he won't admit it. Mr. Pearse sent a scouting party to find a way to get them out so the rest of us could go on fighting, but the scouting party never came back."

"If it's that bad up there, how in the name of God did you get out yourself?"

Ned gave a vague smile as he repeated the words of his friend Dan Duffy, drowned so long ago. "Och, I have me little ways. I've had plenty of practice ducking and dodging." The smile vanished as quickly as it had come. "Not everyone was so lucky, though. A squad of volunteers tunneled out through a rear wall. They were going to set up a diversion so the rest of us could get to the Four Courts and establish headquarters there. When they came back they reported seeing Michael O'Rahilly's body lying in a laneway. As he was dying he had dipped his finger in his own blood and written 'Here Died The O'Rahilly R.I.P.' "

One of the reporters moaned, "Dear sweet merciful Christ."

"Mr. Pearse was so moved he couldn't speak. He looked out the window instead. A man, a woman, and a young girl were running along Moore Street waving a white flag. Suddenly Mr. Pearse put his hands over his face. He'd just seen the British shoot all three down."[3]

There was silence in the room.

Ned was panting.

"Help me get this tunic off him," Henry said, "and loosen his collar. Can't you see he's feverish?" He turned to his editor. "Do you still want to fire this man?"

"I never said that. As far as I'm concerned he has a job here for the rest of his life."

"I hope he lives that long," said Henry. "Go on, Ned."

"The heart seemed to go out of Mr. Pearse then. He decided to negotiate a surrender. The other members of the government argued about it at first; it's very hard for them. But Mr. Pearse said the Rising must end now so no more lives are lost.

"He's going to surrender as commander-in-chief and submit to whatever punishment British justice demands—on condition that the rest of us are granted amnesty and no more civilians are hurt.

"Mr. Pearse says he will trust the British to act honorably, but Tom Clarke's afraid they'll shoot the commander on sight without giving him a chance to . . ." Ned was fighting to stay conscious. "That's why I'm here. Mr. Clarke sent me to make sure the truth gets out. He thinks they'll accuse us of all sorts of things to justify . . . Look in my tunic, Henry. My notebook's in the pocket. I've been writing down . . ." A faraway look came into his eyes. Before anyone could catch him he toppled over.

IN the slanted eyes of the woman holding the pistol was a look of unshakable determination. The new matron stared at her. "What is it you want? We don't have any money here; this is an orphanage."

"Amn't I speaking the King's English?" Síle gave a harsh laugh. "'Course I'm not, I'm speaking republican English now."

This woman's hysterical, thought the matron. She might do anything.

"I've come for our little girl; you have to give her to me."

"Ah now, you wouldn't want to be taking a child out today. There's a rebellion going on, don't you know?"

"I've seen it," Síle said tersely. "I've seen it all, the bombs and the flames. They're destroying Dublin. What makes you think they would spare an orphanage if the humor took them? She'll be much safer with me, I can protect her. I promised I would. So bring me Ursula Jervis, please. *Now*."

The pistol pointed unwaveringly at the matron's heart.

A few minutes later Síle was holding Precious by the hand and the two were hurrying away from the orphanage. In her other hand the little girl clutched a cloth bundle.

"Where are you taking me, Miss Síle? To your house?"

"I can't take you there, the place is probably being watched by now. We have to find someplace safe."

They ran on.

A rattle of rifle fire sounded only a few streets away and Precious flinched. "Is there anyplace safe?"

"I don't know," Síle answered grimly. "We may have left it too long."

They came to a narrow laneway and she turned in. At least the buildings on either side would provide some protection, Síle thought, while she decided which way to go.

At that moment there was a whistle followed by a thunderous roar. The wall beside them exploded into a deadly rain of bricks and mortar.

THERE was no way of telling how badly Ned was hurt without a doctor's examination, and doctors were in short supply in Dublin that morning. Casualties throughout the city were demanding attention.

"He's unconscious," Henry said as they stretched him out on a couch in the editor's office. "It's a mercy of God. Otherwise I haven't a doubt in the world he'd go back and end up like the rest of them."

"You don't think the British will agree to Pearse's terms?" asked a reporter with a fringe of gray hair around his bald head.

"Do you?"

"They will if they have good sense. Right now people are sick of the fighting and the destruction and just want it to be over, and they're perfectly willing to blame everything on the rebels. But if the British are foolish enough to give them martyrs . . . Remember Pearse's oration at the Rossa funeral?"

Henry nodded. "I remember. I was there." He thought for a moment, then reached for his hat.

"Where are you going?"

"I think it's time I went back to covering the news."

THERE was still gunfire in various parts of the city, but the worst was over. Armored cars improvised from boiler tanks mounted on flatbeds had begun sweeping through Dublin, knocking down barricades. They were followed by squads of infantry flushing out snipers and taking prisoners. Mopping up.

Already the Dubliners were beginning to reclaim their city. Scavengers were scrambling over the rubble of buildings like ants on an anthill. A few of the more respectable citizens were cautiously sightseeing.

If Pearse was going to surrender, Henry reasoned, he would either have to send an emissary to Dublin Castle or go there himself. Instructing his colleagues at the *Independent* to look after Ned and find him a doctor as soon as they could, he set off for the Castle.

The seat of government was solidly, almost flagrantly, in British hands. The Union Jack flew from every flagpole and was hanging from windowsills and draped over doorways. Getting inside was an exhaustive process of showing his identification and press pass to one guard after another, each of whom eyed Henry with the gravest suspicion when they heard his Limerick accent. At last he was handed over to a very low-level flunky who apologized for keeping him waiting, then showed him to a room at the back of the building and forgot about him.

After an hour a second functionary arrived, tut-tutted, and promised to speed him along. He was left in various corridors and offices, then shown along to other corridors and offices. People appeared agitated and desperately busy, but Henry could not see that much actual work was getting done. The afternoon dragged on. As he waited, he chatted with the soldiers and civil servants and found what he had expected: everyone claimed to know what was going on and no one did.

Henry Mooney was a patient man. Eventually he managed to work his way to Neville Grantham.

Grantham was sequestered in a tiny cubicle well out of the main traffic area. When he saw the journalist in the doorway he stood up from his desk and rubbed the small of his back with his hands. He was gray with fatigue, and the pouches under his eyes were bloated. "I thought you'd be along sooner or later," he told Henry. "Did you have any trouble getting in?"

"I've been kept waiting all afternoon."

Grantham shook his head. "Typical. I'm sorry, Henry."

"I'm sorry, too."

"Are we talking about the same thing?"

"I think so."

"Yes. Well. Take a seat, will you?"

"Do you know what the situation is, Neville? Is there a surrender?"

"I know some of it. I don't think anyone will ever know all of it. Is this for the record?"

"Not if you don't want it to be."

In the light from the window beside his desk, Grantham's face was somber. "I don't suppose it matters, Henry. The rebel leaders evacuated the G.P.O. yesterday and retired to Moore Street. Around noon today they sent out a nurse—her name's Elizabeth O'Farrell, for the record—under a white flag. It was a bloody brave thing for her to do; there's been a lot of civilians shot. And that's not for the record."

Henry nodded.

"She was taken to the British command post in Parnell Street,[4] where she told the officer in charge that the commander-in-chief of the Irish Republican Army wished to negotiate with the commander of the British forces in Ireland. The officer—a colonel, you don't need to mention his name—insisted she meant the Sinn Féiners. Miss O'Farrell insisted right back at him that the name was the Irish Republican Army. 'And a good name it is too!' she said."

Henry suppressed a smile.

"The colonel detained her until General Lowe arrived. He was very courteous to her, but made it plain that only an unconditional surrender would be accepted. She was to go back and tell Pearse and the others that without one the hostilities would resume in half an hour. General Maxwell was prepared to show no mercy.

"At about three-thirty Miss O'Farrell accompanied Patrick Pearse to General Lowe in Parnell Street. Pearse formally surrendered his sword, then they took him by motorcar to General Maxwell at Parkgate."

"Did Pearse make any statement about his reason for surrendering?" Henry asked, watching Grantham carefully.

The other hesitated. "What do you mean?"

"I think you know. I've already been told the reason by an unimpeachable source, and I have witnesses. If the government doesn't make it public, I will."

"There's no need to threaten me, Henry. As a matter of fact, at Parkgate Pearse did write out a statement. I'm not certain we intended to . . . give me a few minutes, will you?"

While Grantham was out of the room Henry got up and went to look out the window. The view was of a cobbled courtyard, without a trace of green.

Grantham eventually returned with a single sheet of paper. "The under-secretary has agreed that we'll release this ourselves. To show good faith. Formal surrender orders are being printed up for the various rebel command posts, but you can copy this if you like. Just allow the Castle to publish it first."

The handwritten statement read:

> In order to prevent the further slaughter of Dublin cit-
> izens, and in the hope of saving the lives of our followers
> now surrounded and hopelessly outnumbered, the mem-
> bers of the Provisional Government present at Head-
> quarters have agreed to an unconditional surrender, and
> the Commandants of the various districts in the City and
> Country will order their commands to lay down arms.
> (Signed) P. H. Pearse
29th April, 1916
3:45 p.m[5]

· · ·

ON SATURDAY, Father Paul found himself still prevented
from reaching Kilmainham. "We'll have all this cleared away
soon, though," he was informed by the soldiers at the first
roadblock he came to. "We just don't want to let any of the
rebels escape in this direction."

Paul turned away, trying to decide what to do while he
waited.

All at once he remembered. By an exhaustive, rambling
route that skirted the ruined heart of northside Dublin and
avoided a number of British barricades, he at last reached the
North Circular Road.

The matron of the Orphan House for Destitute Females
surveyed the priest with an air of frank curiosity. "Months
and years can go by without a living soul caring a ha'penny
for any of these children," she said. "Then in the same
week—a week when the whole city's in an uproar—two of
you show up wanting the same child."

"The same child. Ursula Jervis?"

"Indeed."

"Is she here, then?"

"She was, but a woman took her away last night. A woman
with a pistol," the matron added as if she still could not quite
believe it.

· · ·

HENRY did not return to the *Independent* until long after dark, by which time he was confident he knew as much as any reporter in Dublin. The knowledge did not make him happy.

Before he even took off his hat he asked about Ned.

"He's gone," someone told him.

"Gone? Gone where? And how could he—he was hurt!"

"We kept him here all afternoon; never could get a doctor. Mostly he just slept. After teatime he seemed to come 'round a bit and asked where you were. Then he drifted off again. We figured the best thing was to let him sleep. We were keeping an eye on him; he was quite safe.

"Next thing we knew, though, he was simply . . . gone."

Henry was dismayed. "How could you let him leave? They're all being arrested! Pádraic Pearse has been taken to Arbour Hill; James Connolly's in the military hospital in Dublin Castle. The garrison remaining from the G.P.O.—less than two hundred altogether—marched into Parnell Street and laid down their arms. They're being held under guard in the grounds of the Rotunda for the night. If Ned tries to rejoin them he'll get what they get, and it's not going to be very pleasant."

HIS ears were still ringing. His head was still throbbing. But like Joe Plunkett he resolved to hold his consciousness elsewhere, outside his body.

When he emerged from the alley behind the Carlisle Building, Ned was surprised to find that darkness had fallen. He was in shirtsleeves. No rifle. No pistol. No Sam Browne belt.

It seemed to take hours to get across the Liffey without attracting attention to himself.

In one of the laneways he stumbled upon a pub that was still open and took a seat in the corner. He asked no questions, merely listened. Until he knew.

It was over, then. Heartbreakingly over.

He wanted to put his aching head down on the table and weep. Instead he made himself get up and walk through the flame-lit night to the Rotunda. He was careful that no one should notice him, dodging from doorway to doorway, melting into shadows. "Och, I have me little ways," he murmured feverishly once or twice.

He found the remnant of the post office garrison herded together onto the grassy forecourt of the maternity hospital, within sight of the monument to Charles Stewart Parnell and not fifty yards from Tom Clarke's shop, which was now being used as an operations center by the British. Unnoticed in the darkness, Ned squirmed along the wall until he came to an angle only a few yards from the prisoners. There he flattened himself against the stone.

A British officer was flashing lamps in the faces of different men to identify them.[6] "I know this bastard. Hullo, Pigface!" When he came to Seán MacDermott he said contemptuously, "I see you have cripples in your army."[7]

MacDermott replied, "You have your place, sir, and I have mine. And you had better mind your place," he added with bared teeth.

"How the hell do you expect to fight, beat me over the head with your stick?" The man snatched MacDermott's cane away from him and laughed when he staggered.

Meanwhile the officer in charge took some of the prisoners to the foot of the hospital steps and stripped them.[8] Poor Tom Clarke, robbed of his clothing and his dignity, stood with his scrawny, shriveled flesh humiliatingly exposed to the women staring down at him from the windows above.

Michael Collins growled to the man beside him, "We'll get that fellow's name. Pass the word."[9]

Ned could stand no more. He stepped forward to draw the attention of the guards.

"Ho there, here's another rebel trying to run off! They're all cowards. Come 'ere, you! Get over there with the others where you belong."

It felt good to be back with Headquarters Company. Nothing else made any sense.

They spent twelve hours crowded together on the strip of grass. They were allowed to sit, but not to stretch out their legs far enough to touch the pavement. Their muscles cramped from inactivity.

Ned wanted to report to Tom Clarke that his mission had been successful; he had told someone . . . something. But he could not think clearly. He could not get to Clarke anyway; he and the other leaders were too closely guarded. Ned contented himself with sitting on the grass and trying to get comfortable. He thought vaguely of his tunic, which would make a pillow. Where was his tunic?

Where was his rifle? He leaned toward the man sitting next to him. "Did you see my rifle? I think I left it in Moore Street."

"You couldn't have, we took everything out of there."

"Everything?"

"Just everything that was ours. The commander was very particular about that. If we had picked up anything that didn't belong to us, even so much as a pin, we had to put it back before we left so we couldn't be accused of looting."

"I've lost my rifle," Ned said sorrowfully.

"Ah sure, we've all lost our rifles, lad."

EARLY next morning they were marched down Sackville Street and across O'Connell Bridge, surrounded by soldiers with bayonets at the ready. Dubliners turned out to laugh and jeer. "Serves ye right, ye shitehawks, ye bowsies!" "Them Tommies'll put some manners on yiz!"

But one Dublin fireman, hosing down the smoking rubble near the bridge, called out, "God bless you, lads!"

As they were marched through the city people threw rotten vegetables at them, and they were spat upon by women who cried, "Ye treasonous gobshites! Why aren't yiz fightin in Flanders like daycent men?" Others shouted, "Bayonet them! Bayonet them!"

"Don't take a blind bit of notice," George Plunkett advised his companions. "Those shawlies are married to men in the British army; as far as they're concerned we've betrayed their husbands."

For the weary men, the long walk to Richmond Barracks was an ordeal. At first the sun was a comfort, but it soon became a torture. Twice Ned was overcome by nausea but he was not allowed to stop. He had to trudge along, racked by dry heaves, while the world spun and swooped around him.

When they finally reached the army barracks they were herded into an open square and made to stand in the sun without water. After almost an hour of this, Joe Plunkett finally collapsed. It was incredible he had made it that far. Two of the soldiers took him by the arms and dragged him into the shade.

HENRY Mooney blamed himself for Ned's disappearance. Instead of going back to Mrs. Kearney's—provided the house was still standing, which he did not know for certain—he set out to find his missing friend. He had a strong suspicion Ned would be with the others from the G.P.O., but when he went to the British post in Parnell Street to inquire about him the officer in charge turned him back. "No one's allowed to talk to the prisoners."

"I don't want to talk to him; I just want to know if he's here."

"I can't give you that information."

Henry fumbled in his pocket for his press pass. "But I'm a reporter and—"

"I can't give you *any* information! Go on, get away from here. This area's off-limits to civilians."

Frustrated, Henry went home. Number 16 was still there. He dragged himself upstairs and sat down on his bed, staring at the empty bed across the room. With a sigh, he took Thomas MacDonagh's book out of his pocket and put it back on Ned's locker.

Then he opened the notebook Ned had given him and began to read.

Chapter Fifty-seven

W HAT do you mean, they're not here and you can't tell me anything?'' Henry Mooney gave the duty officer a look like thunder. ''I'm not just anybody, you know! I have a pass signed by Neville Grantham at Dublin Castle, giving me permission to enter government facilities. I've come to inquire about Edward Halloran. I demand to know if he was brought here yesterday.''

The duty officer was trying to be polite. Richmond Barracks was usually quiet on Sunday morning; a chap could read the papers and tidy up his kit if he had a mind to. But this particular morning was most hectic. Everyone wanted to know the fate of the rebels, not least of all the angry reporter standing in front of him waving a pass from the Castle.

''Be careful with the press,'' the duty officer had been warned. ''Keep them on our side.'' He was doing his best to comply.

He told Henry, ''The rebels from the post office and those who surrendered from the Four Courts were taken down to the quays last night, sir, and put on the boat.''

''What boat? Going where?''

''England, for internment. They're perfectly all right, I assure you. They were even given food before they left. I expect thousands more will be deported before we have this cleared up.''

''But you can't send Ned Halloran to England!'' Henry knew he was being illogical; the British could do what they liked. ''He's very ill, I saw him myself yesterday. He may have a bullet in his head.''

''Why didn't you say so? Just a tick, I have a list . . .'' The officer riffled through papers on a clipboard. ''Yes, here they are. Special category prisoners. Detectives from the DMP were here last night identifying suspects for court-martial. They had files on about a hundred men and went through the prisoners several times, picking out the ones they wanted held back. Anyone too ill to travel was also detained, and will be—''

Henry snatched the clipboard and ran his eyes down the list. Joseph Plunkett, described as ''son of alleged Count Plunkett.'' George and Jack Plunkett, ditto. John MacDermott, cripple. Michael Collins. Name after name; some familiar, some not.

Toward the bottom, Edward Halloran.

Henry breathed a sigh of relief. ''Where is he?''

''In the infirmary, I suppose. But you can't see anyone on this list. I'm sorry, sir, but I have my orders.''

You're lucky to find me in the Castle this morning,'' Grantham told Henry. ''If it were any ordinary Sunday I wouldn't be here. Did the pass I gave you get you inside any faster?''

''It did, but I need a different sort of pass now. I need to get a prisoner out of Richmond Barracks.''

Grantham sat back in his chair and looked at Henry in astonishment. ''You must be joking, old fellow.''

''I assure you I'm not. My friend Ned Halloran—your friend too, I should point out—is in Richmond Barracks this very minute, held with the special category prisoners.''

''Special category? Are you trying to tell me that young man's one of the rebel leaders?''

"I'm trying to tell you just the opposite, damn it!" Henry braced his arms on Grantham's desk and leaned across, almost into the other man's face. "His arrest was a mistake! Ned works for the *Independent*. He must have been after a story last night when he sneaked into that group being held at the Rotunda." Henry forced a smile he did not feel. "That's just like Ned, eager as a hound puppy. I don't know why they mistook him for one of the Volunteers; he certainly wasn't wearing a uniform. He was in shirtsleeves and a pair of serge trousers."

Henry paused, then said reflectively, "Those trousers might be mistaken for part of a uniform, I suppose, since he wore puttees over them to keep them from getting caught in his bicycle chain. That's what he had on when I last saw him yesterday. He'd been out and about the city writing down his impressions.

"At some time during the day he got too close to the fighting and took a head wound. When he came back to the newspaper office he was bleeding and badly concussed. We made him lie down until we could get a doctor to look at him. By the time I got back to the office last night he had gone. I figure that's when he went to the Rotunda and was mistaken for one of the rebels. In his dazed condition he couldn't explain who he was, or if he could, they didn't believe him."

Neville Grantham was looking very hard at Henry. "Quite an incredible tale," he said with no inflection in his voice.

"It's true and I can prove it. Look here." Henry held out Ned's notebook, opened to a selected page. "See? Read that. His impressions of the fighting on the north side. He can *write*, you see that yourself. And here's his press pass identifying him as a staff reporter for the *Independent*. Same as the one I carry, except Ned left his behind the last time he went out. He would not have done that if he was in his right mind. He's badly hurt, Neville. You have to help me get him out of Richmond Barracks before a dreadful mistake is made."

Henry kept his face impassive while Neville Grantham examined the little pasteboard press pass. He turned it over several times in his fingers.

"You claim he's a reporter?"

"Like the two journalists Captain Bowen-Colthurst shot down in cold blood in Portobello Barracks," Henry said.

Grantham blinked. "How did you hear about that?"

"You know better than anyone what good sources I have. And I assure you, Neville, the full weight of the press will be brought to bear against any government official misguided enough to allow one of our people to be mistaken for a rebel leader."

Grantham was looking at the press pass again. "Incredible," he repeated.

FATHER Paul O'Shaughnessy had been following events the way most people were in Dublin that Easter week, by word of mouth. Rumor was as unreliable as ever, but by Sunday evening some facts were beginning to filter through. After receiving orders from Pearse, Edward Daly reluctantly had surrendered the Four Courts garrison on Saturday evening. The surrender was negotiated by two priests, and the rebels were marched off to Richmond Barracks, although pockets of resistance continued to hold out for another day.

On Sunday morning the leaders of the North Dublin County men and of a company of Volunteers from Wexford had called on Pádraic Pearse in Arbour Hill. Pearse verified their orders to surrender and thanked them for their service.

Eamon de Valera had begun the fight with only a fifth of the Third Battalion, and seen that number drastically reduced as the week progressed and his men bore the brunt of the attack from the south. The pressures they were under drove one Volunteer to the breaking point; he ran amok and shot a comrade through the heart.[1] A sentry shot him in return, leaving the garrison badly shaken. Late on Friday, de Valera had evacuated Boland's Mills as an untenable position, only to find that all Dublin appeared to be in flames. He had returned

his men to the bakery, where they remained until Pearse ordered them to surrender.

On Thursday the British had undertaken their most concentrated attack on Eamonn Ceannt and the South Dublin Union.
Cathal Brugha, with five bullets and several bomb splinters in
him, had single-handedly defended a barricaded position for
over two hours.[2] Thinking him long since dead, his comrades
shared a last cigarette and vowed to fight to the end.

Then they heard someone singing, very weak and far away:

God save Ireland say we proudly,
God save Ireland say we all.
Whether on the scaffold high or the battlefield we die
Oh, what matter when for Ireland dear we fall.[3]

Eamonn Ceannt led the rescue party that found Cathal
Brugha still alive, sitting in a pool of his own blood and singing.

The enemy had withdrawn.

From Thursday night on, the Fourth Battalion remained surrounded but was left in relative peace until Sunday. When
Pearse's orders were received the garrison surrendered.

In the well-fortified Jacob's Factory garrison, Thomas
MacDonagh had seen little fighting since Tuesday, though on
Wednesday some of his outposts were fiercely attacked and
had to be abandoned. On Thursday he had tried to send food
and supplies to the hard-pressed Third Battalion at Boland's
Mills, but the relief party could not get through. MacDonagh
managed to stay in contact with Michael Mallin and Con Markievicz in the College of Surgeons, however, keeping up the
spirits of that beleaguered garrison throughout their ordeal and
supplying them with food and ammunition. Then on Sunday
afternoon, and only on orders from his commander-in-chief,
a weeping Thomas MacDonagh lowered the tricolor.

There was still gunfire here and there throughout the city,
but the Rising was over.

I'LL have to go to Kilmainham in the morning," Paul told Ina Cahill as they were having their tea on Sunday night. "The police and the army are arresting everyone who has any connection with the rebels . . . or who they think might have. They're going to be sending prisoners to Richmond Barracks and Kilmainham Jail by the hundreds. God alone knows what will become of them, but they'll need me."

The old woman's eyes had become much brighter since her husband's death. She gave Paul a broad wink, laid her forefinger across her lips, and went to the a small chest where she kept her few valuables. Making a great show of turning her back to hide what she was doing, she rummaged in the chest until she found a huge, rusty key.

"You take this key," she told Paul, "and when none o'them Britishers is lookin' you let our lads out, hear me!"

The priest examined the key with amusement. It would fit no lock he had ever seen. "Where did you get this, Ina?"

"Never you mind now, just do as I say."

Paul had no difficulty reaching Kilmainham the following morning. The military patrols that had kept civilians penned in their own districts were being withdrawn; traffic was beginning to move again.

At Kilmainham the priest was greeted with relief by Reverend MacCarthy. "We shall need all the clergy we can get, I'm afraid."

The anticipated flow of prisoners was already arriving. Some were civilians who seemed genuinely baffled as to why they had been arrested. The actual rebels were tired, dirty, grumbling with the complaints of fighting men everywhere. But most of them had a look in their eyes Paul had never seen before. He could not think of a name for that look; it was just a certain expression he would remember all his life.

When he had the chance he surreptitiously tried the key in the locks of several cells, but found, as he had expected, that it would open none of them.

• • •

"How many times do you expect me to put my head on the block for you?" Neville Grantham asked Henry on Tuesday.

"This isn't a big favor, just a pass to cover the court-martial whenever they begin. Today's the second of May, so I should think that will be within a week or so, am I right?"

Grantham sighed. "I've been very patient, Henry, and I've done all I possibly could. Grant me that. But you must remember, I represent His Majesty's government. It is General Maxwell's opinion that British interests would not be served by allowing civilian spectators to observe what is essentially a military matter."

"Are you saying no reporters?"

"I'm afraid so. The trials are being held in Richmond Barracks and facilities there are limited. The accused, the witnesses against them, the various detectives whose evidence is required, the guards, the three officers of the court-martial and the prosecutor will all be in the same room. There's no space for nonessential personnel."

"Nonessential horseshite!" Henry exploded. "You're going to try those men in secret!"

"The trials are closed, yes. For security reasons."

"And the verdicts—are they going to be secret, too?"

"I understand the men will be told of the verdicts shortly after the court-martial, but the public at large won't be informed until later. After . . . it's all over," he added meaningfully.

Henry sank back in his chair and wiped his hand across his forehead. "Good God Almighty. That's barbaric. But wait a minute. Didn't you just say 'The trials *are* being held in Richmond Barracks?' "

"I did."

"They're going on right now? I don't believe it! Tell me what's happening, Neville."

"You can't print it yet. You do understand that, don't you?"

"Of course I do, I'm no fool. Have I ever printed anything you asked me to hold back? Just tell me."

"Yesterday all the accused received written copies of the charges against them. They are the same in every instance, I believe: 'Rebellion with the intent of assisting the enemy.' "[4]

"You think Pearse and the others staged the Rising for the benefit of *Germany*?" Henry asked incredulously.

"Whether or not that was their intent, it could have had that effect by weakening Britain. Consider how many soldiers we've had to reroute to Ireland, men we desperately needed at the front."

"Oh yes, you certainly needed twenty thousand soldiers to beat twelve hundred Irishmen!"

"There's no need to be sarcastic, Henry. Besides, who gave you those figures?"

"Are you denying them?"

Grantham said stiffly, "I am not officially confirming them."

"I understand that the number of people who've been arrested already exceeds the total number of men who fought in the Rising.[5] I also know that the chief secretary came hurrying back to Ireland last week to confer with Maxwell and report to Asquith. Now both Birrell and Nathan are resigning, isn't that true?"[6]

It was Neville Grantham's turn to slump in his chair. "My, you have been busy."

"Just doing my job."

"Then get out of here and let me do mine, will you? I have to clean out my desk."

"What?"

"I'm afraid I've been recalled."

"Oh. Oh, I am sorry, Neville. I hope it wasn't anything I—"

"No, no, I brought this on myself. It's probably time I went home anyway; one should never serve on a foreign posting for too long. There's always the temptation to go native."

"Foreign posting?"

Grantham gave a sardonic smile. "It is, isn't it? Ireland

isn't England and never will be. But before I go I would like to know something, Henry.''

"Ask away."

"Ned Halloran. How is he?"

"He's still alive—so far," Henry said guardedly. "Can I ask you something in return?"

"So long as it's not a pass to the court-martial."

"Just tell me who's being tried this morning."

Neville Grantham picked up a sheet of paper from his desk. "The first three are P. H. Pearse, Thomas Clarke, and Thomas MacDonagh."

PEARSE was brought from Arbour Hill on Tuesday morning. The night before, he had written a letter to his mother and composed a tender poem for his brother. Poetry was his solace during long hours of solitary confinement.

WITH the exception of James Connolly, the rest of the leaders had spent the time in Richmond Barracks. They were crammed into a small room with other republicans awaiting court-martial. Seán MacDermott—affectionate, warmhearted, handsome Seán MacDermott—was trying to keep up everyone's spirits with jokes and banter. Joe Plunkett lay gasping for breath on a quilt another prisoner had brought all the way from the College of Surgeons. Tom Clarke sat in a corner with a faint smile on his lips. Perhaps he was thinking of Katty, and his garden.

On Monday night Seán MacDermott fell into a restless sleep with his head pillowed on Tom Clarke's shoulder. Near them Willie Pearse tossed in his own troubled dreams, mumbling, "The fire! Oh, get the men out, the fire, the fire!"

ON Tuesday morning Pádraic Pearse was the first to face court-martial. The presiding officer, General Blackadder, listened gravely to the evidence presented, then allowed the accused to make a statement.

Pearse told the court, "My object in agreeing to an unconditional surrender was to prevent the further slaughter of the civilian population of Dublin and to save the lives of our gallant fellows who, having made for six days a stand unparalleled in military history, were now surrounded and without food. I fully understand now, as then, that my own life is forfeit to British law, and I shall die very cheerfully if I can think that the British government, as it has already shown itself strong, will now show itself magnanimous enough to accept my single life in forfeiture and to give a general amnesty to the brave men and boys who have fought at my bidding.

"When I was a child of ten I went down on my bare knees by my bedside one night and promised God that I should devote my life to an effort to free my country. I have kept that promise.

"I assume that I am speaking to Englishmen who value their own freedom and who profess to be fighting for the freedom of Belgium and Serbia. Believe that we too love freedom and desire it. If you strike us down now we shall rise again and renew the fight. You cannot conquer Ireland; you cannot extinguish the Irish passion for freedom. If our deed has not been sufficient to win freedom, then our children will win it by a better deed."[7]

His statement was not taken down or made public.

He wrote it down himself, however, and put it with his letters and poems for delivery to his mother.

Pádraic Pearse was taken from Richmond Barracks to a dark, dank cell in the old wing of Kilmainham Jail. There he would await the verdict of the court. He still hoped that his request for amnesty for the others might be granted; that Willie and the rest would be spared.

He had no idea that his brother was also being court-martialed and would soon be in the same prison.

•   •   •

FATHER Paul O'Shaughnessy stood in the narrow passage-way and peered through the peephole into the cell. It was so dark inside he could hardly make out the man leaning against the wall. "Can I bring you anything?"

"Enough light to write by would be welcome, Father," Pádraic Pearse replied. The priest brought a lamp, then lingered outside, offering the small comfort of his presence.

"Do you like poetry, Father?" Pearse eventually asked.

"I suppose so."

"Shall I read you what I've written?"

"Please do."

The beauty of the world hath made me sad,
This beauty that will pass;
Sometimes my heart hath shaken with great joy
To see a leaping squirrel in a tree,
Or a red lady-bird upon a stalk,
Or little rabbits in a field at evening,
Lit by a slanting sun,
Or some green hill where shadows drifted by
Some quiet hill where mountainy man hath sown
And soon would reap; near to the gate of Heaven;
Or children with bare feet upon the sands
Of some ebbed sea, or playing on the streets
Of little towns in Connacht,
Things young and happy.
And then my heart told me: These will pass,
Will pass and change, will die and be no more,
Things bright and green, things young and happy,
And I have gone upon my way
Sorrowful.[8]

General Blackadder, President of the Court-Martial, dined that evening with the countess of Fingal. He had no appetite and was unable to take part in the usual lively dinner table conversation. Eventually he confided to his hostess, "I have just done one of the hardest tasks I have ever had to do. I have had to condemn to death one of the finest characters I have ever come across. There must be something very wrong in the state of things that makes a man like Patrick Pearse a rebel. I do not wonder that his pupils adored him.''[9]

LATE on Tuesday, Pearse asked for a Capuchin priest, Father Aloysius, to hear his confession and give him Holy Communion. That night he wrote two final letters. One was for ''Dear old Willie,'' and said, ''No one can ever have had so true a brother as you.''

The other was addressed to ''My Dearest Mother.'' In it Pearse wrote, ''I hope and I believe that Willie and the St. Enda's boys are safe.''

The letter went on:

I have just received Holy Communion. I am happy, except for the great grief of parting from you. This is the death I should have asked for if God had given me the choice of all deaths.

May God bless you for your great love for me and for your great faith, and may He remember all that you have so bravely suffered. I hope soon to see Papa, and in a little while we shall all be together again.

Wow-wow, Willie, Mary Brigid, and Mother, good-bye. I have not words to tell of my love of you, and how my heart yearns to you all. I will call to you in my heart at the last moment.

Your son, Pat[10]

At 3:30 A.M. on the third of May, 1916, Pádraic Pearse was taken from his cell in Kilmainham Jail. The last thing he did before leaving the cell was to tuck his pince-nez carefully into his pocket.

In the Stonebreakers' Yard the chill of night was trapped within stone walls so high no escape was possible. Neither was any glimpse of the Ireland that lay beyond.

Electric light illumined the scene, casting harsh shadows.

The firing squad was waiting.

Just before the bandage was tied across his eyes, Pádraic Pearse threw back his head and looked up.

The starry sky was free.

Chapter Fifty-eight

THE chaplain tried to arrange for Willie Pearse to see his brother before Pádraic's execution.[1] Under heavy guard, Willie was halfway to his brother's cell when they heard the rifle volley.

His guards looked at one another. "Too late," one said.

PEARSE was followed to the Stonebreakers' Yard by Tom Clarke, who had been allowed a brief visit with his wife in his cell the night before. "I'm glad it's a soldier's death I'm getting," he told Katty. "I've had enough of imprisonment."[2]

She would not let him see her cry.

THOMAS MacDonagh had also had a visitor that last night. He was not told until midnight that he would be shot at dawn, and shortly thereafter his sister, a nun, was shown into his cell. She brought him their mother's rosary to put around his neck. "I hope they will give me this when it's over," she said.

"Ah no, they will shoot it to bits," her brother replied.

He met the bullets with his head high.

"They all died well, but MacDonagh died like a prince," said a British officer who witnessed the executions.[3]

MR. Stoker was relieved that his jewelry shop in Grafton Street had escaped damage during the rebellion.[4] By Tuesday he felt it was safe to open for business again. That night, as he was about to lock up, a motor cab stopped outside and a slender young woman came into the shop. A heavy veil hid her features, but he could see her trembling as if she was fighting back tears.

"What's wrong, my dear? Can I offer you a glass of brandy?"

She shook her head and held up one hand. "Just give me a moment. It's my nerves, that's all. I would like to look at a selection of wedding rings, please. The best that money can buy. You see, I'm about to be married to a remarkable man."

While the jeweler watched solicitously, she selected a heavy gold ring and asked to have it engraved. "I shall call for it tomorrow." She gave him her calling card and left the shop. Mr. Stoker held the card up to the light. The name on it was Miss Grace Gifford.

FATHER Paul O'Shaughnessy was so tired he did not think he could go on, yet he could not leave Kilmainham. He did not want to leave Kilmainham. His pastoral skills would never be as badly needed as they were in that appalling place.

The first three executions had taken place in rushed secrecy, but by Wednesday night a crowd of women had gathered outside the prison and begun chanting prayers.

"They're Cumann na mBan," explained the chaplain. "The women's auxiliary for the Volunteers."

"How did they know?"

"You Americans wouldn't understand, but Ireland's a very small country."

The women were kneeling in the road, holding up candles. "They won't change General Maxwell's mind," one of the guards remarked. "Nothing would. He's in total charge now, and he's determined to crush the rebellion once and for all and make such an example of the leaders that no one will ever try this again.''

Paul stared out at the candle flames flickering in the twilight. ''How brightly they burn,'' he said.

He lay down on a cot in the chaplain's office to try to get a few hours' sleep, only to be awakened in the dead of night by Reverend MacCarthy. ''Sorry to disturb you, Father.''

Paul sat up. The room was in darkness; the only illumination came from a candle in the chaplain's hand. ''We've had a power failure. Candles are the only light we have tonight; perhaps it's for the best.''

Puzzled, Paul followed Reverend MacCarthy to the prison chapel.

Twenty soldiers with fixed bayonets lined the walls of the chapel. A young woman stood beside the altar with her eyes fixed unwaveringly on the doorway. Reverend MacCarthy went to her and spoke softly, but she did not respond.

She saw nothing but the man who was being led into the room in handcuffs.

Joe Plunkett still wore his dashing uniform, though it was filthy and minus its saber. In the candlelight blood glistened on his lips. ''White dove of the wild dark eyes,'' he greeted her as if no one else could hear.

For them there were no bayonets, no soldiers. No yesterday and no tomorrow.

They were not allowed to touch except for the exchange of wedding rings. The ceremony was brief, yet all the more beautiful for its simplicity. Do you promise this woman? Do you promise this man? In sickness and in health. Until death us do part.

Kathleen. Oh, Kathleen!

When the ceremony was over, Grace Gifford had to stand and watch while her husband was led away. There was no kiss.

Shortly before dawn, however, she was allowed ten minutes with him in his cell. Ten minutes, while fifteen soldiers crowded in with them to stand guard, and the time was measured to the second by an officer with a watch.

Afterward, Paul O'Shaughnessy returned to the prison chapel. For a few brief minutes death and all its terrors had been held at bay by love, and the sweet ghost of that love lingered in the flickering candlelight.

The priest was profoundly moved.

If God *is* Love as we are taught, he thought to himself, then truly I have seen tangible evidence of God tonight.

Kneeling, Paul bowed his head over his clasped hands and tried to formulate a prayer. The words of Ned Halloran filled his head instead: "If you really care for Kathleen, you'll go back to her. Don't leave her to Alexander Campbell. Go back and fight for her yourself."

He looked up, startled. The echo of those words seemed to ring in the chapel.

AT dawn on the fourth of May, Joe Plunkett was shot. With him that morning died Edward Daly, Michael O'Hanrahan, and Willie Pearse. Willie would have escaped the death sentence, as he was neither a commanding officer nor a member of the Military Council, had it not been for the fact that he insisted on stressing his own involvement. During the last confusing days he had signed several orders as "acting chief of staff," a fact he proudly pointed out to the court. He thus signed his own death warrant.

Surprised witnesses at his execution reported he seemed almost eager to go, as if someone was waiting for him.

Major John MacBride, MacDonagh's second-in-command at Jacob's, died on May 5. On the same day the death sentence that had been pronounced on Constance, Countess Markievicz, was—to her fury—commuted to life imprisonment because she was a woman.

As one execution followed another and became known, a feeling of revulsion set in. People began urging clemency for the rebels. George Bernard Shaw was but one of many writing letters to the government. The United States Senate also expressed the hope that Great Britain would show mercy.

ON the eighth of May, Eamonn Ceannt, Michael Mallin, Seán Heuston, and Con Colbert were shot.

On the eleventh, the death sentence of Eamon de Valera was commuted to life imprisonment out of deference to his American citizenship.

Surely, people thought, there would be no more executions.

Then on Friday, the twelfth of May, Seán MacDermott was shot. MacDermott had fought hard for his life, arguing every point at the court-martial. But the sentence had already been decided.

He did not die alone. James Connolly, feverish and in great pain, was brought by ambulance to Kilmainham. He was carried into the Stonebreakers' Yard on a stretcher and tied seated in a chair because he was too ill to meet his fate standing on his feet.

The last bullet was his.

Chapter Fifty-nine

GENERAL Maxwell took his mandate seriously. He had been sent to crush the rebellion and punish the rebels, and crush and punish he would. Ninety-seven other prisoners were also condemned to death. There would have been more, but sympathetic policemen refused to identify some and helped a few others escape.

As the presses began to roll again Henry was kept busy. "There's plenty of blame to go around," his editor told him, "and everyone's pointing the finger at someone else. See if you can find out what the government's feeling is about all this."

Dublin Castle had been startled by the speed and severity of Maxwell's actions, but made no official protest. They seemed paralyzed.

Another for whom indecisiveness was a problem was Eoin MacNeill. During Easter Week he had dithered about joining his old comrades while his family and Bulmer Hobson sought to dissuade him.[1] In the end, when it was much too late, he had put on his Volunteer uniform and declared himself—only to be arrested and court-martialed without ever having struck a blow for freedom.

. . . .

In Dublin seven hundred and sixty-three prominent supporters of the union with Britain signed a formal protest against any interference with General Maxwell's policies on the grounds that it would weaken governmental authority. But in the House of Commons, John Redmond, who initially had expressed abhorrence of the Rising, began exerting pressure on Asquith to stop the executions in spite of Unionist objections.

On the eleventh of May, John Dillon, the nationalist M.P., said in Commons, "I know they were wrong, but they fought a clean fight and they fought with superb bravery and skill. No act of savagery or act against the usual customs of war has been charged against any leader or any organized body of insurgents."[2]

In Dublin, Captain Brereton, a British prisoner who had been held by Ned Daly's men in the Four Courts, told the *Irish Times*, "The Sinn Féiners observed all the rules of civilized warfare and fought clean. They proved they were men of education, incapable of acts of brutality."

Balanced against the King Street massacre, the senseless murder of Francis Sheehy-Skeffington, the secret trials and hasty, unnecessarily cruel executions, the behavior of the Irish Republican Army was exemplary.

"Our lads did us credit," people said to one another with slowly surfacing pride. The mood of the country began to shift.

At first Asquith had merely expressed surprise at Maxwell's "drastic action," but as opposition mounted he made it clear to the general that his hard line was losing support at the highest level.

When Maxwell telegraphed Asquith to notify him that MacDermott and Connolly were going to be executed, he reluctantly added that they would be the last to suffer capital punishment "as far as I can now state."[3] The death sentences of the other ninety-seven—including Eoin MacNeill—were commuted to penal servitude.

In spite of a strong plea from Mrs. Pearse and the other families to have the bodies of their loved ones returned for burial in consecrated ground, the executed men were buried in quicklime, without coffins, in the grounds of Arbour Hill Prison.[4]

HENRY found that last insult particularly cruel. As he climbed the stairs to the quiet room in Sandymount, he tried to imagine them wrapped in sheets of burning lime, the flesh eaten from their bones . . .

Ned looked shrunken in the bed. His tall body was reduced to skin and bone, but his eyes were clear at last. "What news, Henry?"

"It's over. There aren't going to be any more executions. A Volunteer officer called Thomas Kent was shot in Cork and poor Roger Casement will probably be put to death in England, but the republicans who've survived this far will go on living for a while."

"Until the next time."

"There may not have to be a next time. The same people who spat on you are beginning to wear tricolor ribbons and sing 'The Soldier's Song.' The executions have affected them as nothing else could."

"I'd love to go out and see."

"You don't put your head outside that door until things cool down more, Ned, and I don't mean the smoldering rubble. You're safe here; no one knows where you are. This place belongs to friends of mine who're under orders not to breathe your name. I didn't get you out of Richmond Barracks just to have the British take you."

"I still don't know how you managed it."

Henry chuckled. "Blackmail. Intimidation. A bit of forgery. I used their own methods against them through poor Neville Grantham. It's really him you have to thank."

"I will when I can."

"That won't be possible. He's already gone back to London."

Ned looked surprised. "Why?"

"They've all gone back in disgrace—Birrell, Nathan, and

a lot of their staff. The resignation of Baron Wimborne was also suggested; he refused. Then the cabinet demanded it and the viceroy gave in, though I understand he'll stay on until his replacement arrives—if there is to be another viceroy, which looks doubtful. Asquith's coming to Ireland personally to reorganize the entire governmental structure from the top down.''

''We did all that?'' Ned said wonderingly.

''It's too soon to know just what you have accomplished, but Ireland will never be the same.''

''What about the Volunteers down the country? Did they rise with us after all?''

''Many did, once they learned what was happening in Dublin. They fought brilliantly in Galway and actually held Wexford, but it was too late and not enough. The confusion about the orders had already done its damage. Speaking of damage, a lot of Dublin's in ruins, several thousand men and women are being deported to internment camps and prisons . . . and how's your head?''

''It still hurts.''

''You had a serious concussion. For a while we thought there was a bullet lodged in that thick skull of yours, but it was just a fragment.''

Ned was quiet for a time. Henry thought he was asleep until he said, ''Have you found her yet?''

''Have you forgot what I told you yesterday? I went to the house where she'd been living but it's locked up tight. Tom Clarke's wife has been arrested, and no one in the neighborhood could tell me what's become of your Síle.''

Ned closed his eyes. ''She's all right. She has to be. I'm going to buy a cottage in Howth and she's going to plant flowers in the garden.''

''Don't set your heart on it, boy. That last day was hell. People are still missing. Caught under rubble, trapped in fires—some of them may never be found. If she tried to get back to you after the G.P.O. was destroyed . . . well, anything could have happened to her.''

Ned stirred restlessly on the bed. "The little girl I told you about . . ."

"Lie still, you're supposed to keep quiet. I'm sure she's fine. When I went to the orphanage to ask for Ursula Jervis, the caretaker told me they'd evacuated the children and staff to the country temporarily. It's going to take a while before things return to normal, though. In the meantime, you're not the only person worried about loved ones. Many of those shipped off to internment had no time to notify their families."

"How many people were killed?"

"Counting both sides, several hundred are known dead. We haven't been given exact figures yet. Total casualties are estimated at less than three thousand countrywide, including injuries and related accidents."

"The Rising of 1798 killed thirty thousand," Ned said with his eyes still closed, "and didn't accomplish a thing."

"Historians won't be able to say that about this one," Henry assured him. "Pearse and Connolly and the others made sure of that. They got shag-all help when they needed it, but now that they're gone, I don't think this country's going to be willing to go back to where it was. People from every walk of life have faced British guns for the freedom of *this* small nation. Men we knew, men we saw in the streets or in the classrooms or even in the pubs, have been executed for trying to give us a republic. People who didn't give a toss one way or the other, before, are beginning to talk about them. And about independence."

Ned opened his eyes and stared at the ceiling. "Perhaps this is how it has to be, Henry. In Ireland the living are vilified while the dead are sanctified. Mr. Pearse promised me we would win, one way or the other. And we will." His green eyes brimmed with tears. *"But oh God, suppose my Síle isn't here to see it!"*

Chapter Sixty

On a timeless afternoon, beneath a forgotten sky, Ned Halloran returned to Saint Enda's. He was surprised to find it unchanged in a month that had changed his world forever.

He was still subject to spells of dizziness. Henry had argued that Ned should stay out of sight for a while longer to be safe, but he was too restless.

He paid off the motor cab and asked the driver to return for him in a couple of hours. Then he stood gazing at the familiar building with its embracing forecourt.

Mrs. Pearse and Margaret were hoping to reopen the school in September.

He could not go in, not yet. He would have to steel himself for the sight of Mrs. Pearse. If his grief was terrible, what of hers?

Turning away from the house, Ned began to walk through the grounds.

The fine weather that had marked Easter Week had given way to rain, and the rain to sunshine again. Saint Enda's was lush with the promise of summer to come.

Such beauty could inspire reams of poetry.

He walked slowly, carrying pain like a brimming chalice.

They had gone to their deaths, the three poets; each to a mortal termination that fitted him like the last stanza of one of his own works. For flamboyant, romantic Joseph Mary Plunkett, a heroic death was far preferable to the devastation of disease. Thomas MacDonagh, the perfectionist, had finally found the total commitment that even his beloved family had not demanded, but which his soul required.

And Pádraic Pearse? The gentle headmaster of Scoil Eanna, who could not bear to see the smallest, weakest creature harmed, had offered in full and complete measure his own blood sacrifice.

For Ireland's sake they had lost their lives, those men who loved life so well.

Not lost. Laid down willingly, almost gladly. They had accepted death as a price that must be paid for the idea of a free and sovereign nation. Yet such concepts as nationhood were man-made and could by man be unmade, while the bodies made by God were eaten by quicklime.

How, Ned wondered, could God allow such things? But even as he asked the question, he could hear Pearse gently scolding him for demanding that God justify Himself.

God is. No more answer was required. Or perhaps all the answers were implicit in that simple fact. God is.

Surrounded by blossoming summer, Ned recalled the love of nature that illumined the work of his lost friends. Like most Irish poets, Pearse, Plunkett, and MacDonagh had seen the natural world as metaphor for creation, combining construction and destruction in equal measure.

If there was an answer perhaps it lay there, more than in any human words of comfort.

Ned followed the meandering paths where Robert Emmett once strolled with Sarah Curran. They had been young and in love. They had seen leaves wither and fall to the earth, decay and nourish strong new growth. They had lived and died and the world went on.

Pádraic Pearse had wandered these pathways, too. Had he recalled them that last night in his dark cell? In his mind had he traveled back to the leaf-dappled woods and the clear cold lake and the meadows fragrant with golden hay? Had he listened one last time to the shouts of boys racing up and down the playing field, enjoying to the fullest the life he had worked so hard to provide?

As Ned walked on, a kind of understanding came to him.

Human beings are sensory organs through which God appreciates the physical world. God is continually creating such organs, allowing them to suffer and be glad, to love and hate and fear and exult, each according to its own unique nature, then ultimately taking them back to Himself. To enrich that which we call God. To live forever in Him.

Thus the best men that Ireland had produced in their generation were shot to death in Kilmainham yard by other men. In those terrible moments, each had a unique experience of mortality.

Was that what God sought? The experience? "It is God's will," the old people said fatalistically of any tragedy. Perhaps it was. Perhaps men and women did not die for Ireland or for Britain or for any human concern, but to add to the sum total of the wisdom of a divine intelligence beyond their understanding.

The dark sea, waiting.

Pearse must have foreseen and accepted everything that day long ago when they spoke of the *Titanic*. From that moment the man had gone forward without hesitation, although he knew where it must end. Yet he had not been afraid, and his fearlessness had given the others courage.

In 1915 Pearse had written:

> . . . *the wise have pitied the fool that hath striven to give a life*
> *In the world of time and space among the bulks of actual things,*
> *To a dream that was dreamed in the heart, and that only the heart could hold.*
> *Oh wise men, riddle me this: what if the dream come true?*[1]

Still brimming with pain, Ned retraced his steps to the house. He was ready to face Mrs. Pearse now. He would put his arms around her and they would cry together for all they had lost.

Halfway up the steps his head began to swim. There was a roaring in his ears like the roar of the fire in the G.P.O. Perhaps this had not been such a good idea. Perhaps he should go back to Dublin.

But the motor cab would not return for a while yet. He waited until the dizziness passed, then opened the door.

The entrance hall was the same as it had always been, complete to the portrait of the radiant child with arms extended.

''Ned-Ned!'' the child cried.

Precious was locked in his embrace before he knew it.

Then over the top of her head he saw Síle Duffy standing in the doorway of the drawing room.

''We've been searching for you everywhere,'' she said.

November 22, 1916

H. M. S. *BRITANNIC*, SISTER SHIP OF *TITANIC*, SINKS IN THE AEGEAN

RINNEADH AISLING DÚINN

I nDORChACht an éaDÓChais RINNeaDh aisLING DÚINN. LasaMAR soLas AN DÓChais. agus NÍOR MÚChaDh é. I bhfásACh an LaGMhisNIGh RINNeaDh aisLING DÚINN. ChuIReaMAR CRAN NA CRÓGAChta. agus tháinIG bláth AIR.

I NGEIMhREADH NA DaoIRse RINNeaDh aisLING DÚINN. MheiLeaMAR sNeAChta NA táIMhe. agus RIth abhAINN NA AthbEOChANA as.

ChuIReaMAR áR N-aisLING AG sNáMh MAR eaLa AR AN abhAINN. RINNeaDh fíRINNe DEN aisLING. RINNeaDh saMhRADh DEN GheIMhREADh. RINNeaDh saoIRse DEN DaoIRse. agus D'fhágaMAR AGAIbhse MAR oIDhReACht í.

A GhLÚNta NA saoIRse CUIMhNÍGÍ ORAINNe, GLÚNta NA haisLINGe . . .

WE SAW A VISION

In the darkness of despair we saw a vision. We lit the light of hope. And it was not extinguished. In the desert of discouragement we saw a vision. We planted the tree of valour. And it blossomed.

In the Winter of bondage we saw a vision. We melted the snow of lethargy. And the river of resurrection flowed from it.

We sent our vision aswim like a swan on the river. The vision became a reality. Winter became Summer. Bondage became Freedom. And this we left to you as your inheritance.

O Generations of Freedom remember us, the Generations of
the Vision . . .

Liam Mac Uistín, 1976

Inscription in the National Garden of Remembrance
Dublin, Republic of Ireland

Notes

CHAPTER ONE

1. Cocoanut: This is the spelling actually used on the *Titanic* menu. *A Night to Remember*, p. 29.

CHAPTER TWO

1. *These My Friends and Forebears*, p. 132.

CHAPTER THREE

1. *A Night to Remember*, p. 159.

CHAPTER SEVEN

1. *The Liffey in Dublin*, p. 230.

CHAPTER EIGHT

1. *Patrick Pearse: The Triumph of Failure*, p. 24.
2. Prospectus: Scoil Eanna.
3. *Patrick Pearse: The Triumph of Failure*, p. 116.

CHAPTER NINE

1. *Patrick Pearse: The Triumph of Failure*, p. 47.
2. Saint Enda's Museum collection.

CHAPTER ELEVEN

1. *Patrick Pearse: The Triumph of Failure*, p. 14.
2. *Patrick Pearse: The Triumph of Failure*, p. 14.
3. *Patrick Pearse: The Triumph of Failure*, p. 132.
4. *Patrick Pearse: The Triumph of Failure*, p. 119; also *The Complete Works of P. H. Pearse: The Man Called Pearse*, p. 215.
5. *The Complete Works of P. H. Pearse: St. Enda's and Its Founder*, p. 55.
6. *The Easter Rebellion*, p. 41.
7. From "I Have Not Gathered Gold," by Pádraic Pearse.
8. *Patrick Pearse: The Triumph of Failure*, p. 119.
9. *"Dear, Dirty Dublin,"* p. 152.
10. *The Story of Monto*, p. 2.
11. *The Story of Monto*, p. 6.
12. *The Damnable Question*, p. 142.
13. *The Newspaper Book*, p. 107.

CHAPTER TWELVE

1. *In the Footsteps of Big Jim*, p. 32.
2. *"Dear, Dirty Dublin,"* p. 149.
3. *Ireland: A Cultural Encyclopedia*.
4. *Leaders and Men of the Easter Rising*, p. 195.

5. From *Of My Poems*, by Thomas MacDonagh.
6. *An Barr Buadh* (*The Trumpet of Victory*).
7. *Terrible Beauty: A Life of Constance Markievicz*, p. 23.

CHAPTER FOURTEEN

1. *Terrible Beauty*, p. 118.
2. Family papers, Jim Larkin IV.
3. *The Complete Works of P. H. Pearse: The Man Called Pearse*, p. 242.
4. *The Irish Republic*, p. 75.
5. *The Irish Republic*, p. 75.
6. Excerpt from *Uniforms of the 1916 Period*, by F. Glenn Thompson.
7. *Patrick Pearse: The Triumph of Failure*, p. 119.
8. *The Complete Works of P. H. Pearse: The Man Called Pearse*, p. 186.
9. *The Newspaper Book*, p. 122.
10. *Leaders and Men of the Easter Rising*, p. 127.
11. *Terrible Beauty*, p. 98.
12. *The Irish Republic*, p. 95.
13. *Dublin Views in Colour*, plate 16.
14. *The Irish Republic*, p. 96.
15. *Patrick Pearse: The Triumph of Failure*, p. 118.
16. *The Irish Republic*, p. 96.
17. *Patrick Pearse: The Triumph of Failure*, p. 1.
18. *The Irish Republic*, p. 909.
19. *The Irish Republic*, p. 98.

CHAPTER FIFTEEN

1. *Elegant Times*, p. 28.

CHAPTER SEVENTEEN

1. From *The Complete Works of P. H. Pearse: Political Writings and Speeches*, p. 206.

CHAPTER TWENTY

1. Family papers, Jim Larkin IV.
2. *The Irish Republic*, p. 98.
3. *Patrick Pearse: The Triumph of Failure*, p. 113.
4. *Irish Freedom*, July 14, 1914.
5. From "On the Strand of Howth," by Pádraic Pearse.

CHAPTER TWENTY-ONE

1. *Dublin Pub Life & Lore*, p. 38.
2. *Enchanted by Dreams*, p. 47.
3. *Arthur Griffith and Non-violent Sinn Féin*, p. 9.

CHAPTER TWENTY-TWO

1. *Terrible Beauty*, p. 111.
2. *Eamon de Valera*, p. 6.
3. *The Irish Republic*, p. 113.

CHAPTER TWENTY-FIVE

1. *Thoms Official Directory*, p. 1415.
2. *Terrible Beauty*, p. 109.

CHAPTER TWENTY-SIX

1. *The Irish Republic*, p. 115.

CHAPTER TWENTY-SEVEN

1. *Patrick Pearse: The Triumph of Failure*, p. 224.
2. *The Irish Republic*, p. 123.
3. *The Life and Times of James Connolly*, p. 360.
4. *The Easter Rebellion*, p. 32.
5. *Uniforms of the 1916 Period.*
6. *Where They Lived in Dublin*, p. 138.
7. *The Easter Rebellion*, p. 38.

CHAPTER TWENTY-NINE

1. *The Irish Republic*, p. 133.
2. *Modern Ireland*, p. 472.
3. *The Story of the Irish Race*, p. 610.

CHAPTER THIRTY

1. *Leaders and Men of the Easter Rising,* pp. 104, 246.
2. *The Rising,* p. 66.
3. From *1916 Poets,* "New Love."
4. *Survivors: Nora Connolly-O'Brien,* p. 197.
5. *The Newspaper Book,* p. 114.
6. *A History of Irish Flags,* p. 204.
7. *Leaders and Men of the Easter Rising,* p. 157.
8. *The Complete Works of P. H. Pearse: The Man Called Pea* p. 142.
9. *Roger Casement,* pp. 271–273.
10. *Leaders and Men of the Easter Rising,* p. 170.
11. *Leaders and Men of the Easter Rising,* p. 168.

CHAPTER THIRTY-THREE

1. *Revolutionary Woman*, p. 54.
2. *Revolutionary Woman*, p. 53.

3. *Revolutionary Woman,* p. 55.
4. *The Irish Republic,* p. 134.
5. *The Irish Republic,* p. 133.
6. *The Irish Republic,* p. 134.
7. *The Rising,* p. 61.
8. *Leaders and Men of the Easter Rising,* p. 195.
9. *The Life and Times of James Connolly,* p. 394.
10. *Roger Casement,* p. 307.
11. *Patrick Pearse: The Triumph of Failure,* p. 245.
12. From ''Barbara,'' by Thomas MacDonagh, written in June 1915.

CHAPTER THIRTY-FOUR

1. *Revolutionary Woman,* p. 56.
2. *Revolutionary Woman,* p. 56.
3. *Dublin Castle & the 1916 Rising,* p. 11.

CHAPTER THIRTY-FIVE

1. *The Irish Republic,* p. 135; and *Revolutionary Woman,* p. 57.
2. *Portrait of a Rebel Father,* p. 243.
3. Rossa souvenir program, National Library of Ireland, p. 19.
4. *Dublin 1916,* photograph on p. 65.

CHAPTER THIRTY-SEVEN

1. *Patrick Pearse: The Triumph of Failure,* p. 239.
2. *Patrick Pearse: The Triumph of Failure,* p. 240.
3. *Leaders and Men of the Easter Rising,* p. 196.
4. *Terrible Beauty,* p. 114.

CHAPTER THIRTY-EIGHT

1. *Ireland This Century,* p. 53.
2. *Chronicle of the Twentieth Century,* p. 210.

3. *Revolutionary Woman*, p. 61.
4. *The Damnable Question*, p. 143.
5. *The Damnable Question*, p. 143.
6. *Leaders and Men of the Easter Rising*, p. 196.

CHAPTER THIRTY-NINE

1. *The Irish Republic*, p. 143 (erroneously calls paper the *Irish Worker*); *Patrick Pearse: The Triumph of Failure*, p. 246.
2. *The Irish Republic*, p. 146.
3. *Patrick Pearse: The Triumph of Failure*, p. 246.
4. *Terrible Beauty*, p. 125.
5. *The Life and Times of James Connolly*, p. 369.
6. *The Rising*, p. 268 (Appendix VII).
7. *The Rising*, p. 47; *The Life and Times of James Connolly*, p. 387; *Patrick Pearse: The Triumph of Failure*, p. 247.
8. *Survivors*, p. 197.
9. *Terrible Beauty*, p. 23.
10. *Terrible Beauty*, p. 122.
11. *The Liffey in Dublin*, p. 59.
12. *The Life and Times of James Connolly*, p. 388.
13. *Terrible Beauty*, pp. 123–124.
14. *Portrait of a Rebel Father*, pp. 249–252.

CHAPTER FORTY

1. *The Irish Republic*, p. 139.
2. *Revolutionary Woman*, p. 67.
3. *Chronicle of the Twentieth Century*, p. 212.
4. *Revolutionary Woman*, p. 88.

CHAPTER FORTY-ONE

1. *The Life and Times of James Connolly*, p. 396.
2. *Dublin Castle & the 1916 Rising*, p. 66.

3. *Dublin Castle & the 1916 Rising,* p. 66.
4. *Chronicle of the Twentieth Century,* p. 212.
5. *Survivors: Nora Connolly-O'Brien,* p. 196.
6. *Dublin Pub Life & Lore,* p. 53.
7. From a letter from Pádraic Pearse to John Devoy, held in the Carmelite Order's archives in St. Albert's Priory, Middletown, New York.
8. *Chronicle of the Twentieth Century,* p. 213.
9. *The Irish Republic,* p. 148.

CHAPTER FORTY-TWO

1. *Michael Collins,* p. 37.
2. *The Irish Republic,* p. 147.
3. *The Modernisation of Irish Society,* p. 154.
4. *Dublin Castle & the 1916 Rising,* p. 70.
5. *The Complete Works of P. H. Pearse: St. Enda's and Its Founder,* p. 98.
6. *Dublin 1916,* p. 356.

CHAPTER FORTY-THREE

1. *Roger Casement,* p. 310.
2. *The Irish Republic,* p. 153.
3. *The Rising,* p. 73.
4. *Patrick Pearse: The Triumph of Failure,* p. 287.
5. *The Rising,* pp. 64–70; also *Leaders and Men of the Easter Rising* and *Dublin Castle & the 1916 Rising.*
6. *The Rising,* p. 67.
7. *The Irish Republic,* p. 159.
8. *Leaders and Men of the Easter Rising,* p. 171.
9. *Revolutionary Woman,* p. 68.
10. *Revolutionary Woman,* p. 68.
11. *The Rising,* p. 76.

12. *The Rising*, p. 76.
13. *Revolutionary Woman*, p. 70.

CHAPTER FORTY-FOUR

1. *Where They Lived in Dublin*, p. 139.
2. *The Irish Republic*, p. 155.
3. *De Valera*, p. 67.
4. *Patrick Pearse: The Triumph of Failure*, pp. 277, 295.
5. *Winding the Clock*, p. 83.
6. *Revolutionary Woman*, p. 71.
7. *The Irish Republic*, p. 169.
8. *The Rising*, p. 155.
9. *The Irish Republic*, p. 156.
10. *The Rising*, p. 90; *Patrick Pearse: The Triumph of Failure*, p. 268.
11. Excerpted from "From a Hermitage," an essay by P. H. Pearse.
12. *The Rising*, p. 92.

CHAPTER FORTY-FIVE

1. *The Rising*, p. 69.
2. *The Irish Republic*, p. 154.

CHAPTER FORTY-SIX

1. *Patrick Pearse: The Triumph of Failure*, p. 269.
2. *The Irish Republic*, p. 162.
3. *Where They Lived in Dublin*, p. 139.
4. *Patrick Pearse: The Triumph of Failure*, p. 270.
5. A semiautomatic weapon manufactured by the Deutsche Waffen and Munitionsfabriken of Berlin in 1900.
6. *The Rising*, p. 93.
7. *The Irish Republic*, p. 160.

8. *The Irish Republic*, p. 163.
9. *Patrick Pearse: The Triumph of Failure*, p. 273.

CHAPTER FORTY-SEVEN

1. *The Rising*, p. 98.
2. *Michael Collins*, p. 37.
3. *Patrick Pearse: The Triumph of Failure*, p. 273.
4. *Terrible Beauty*, p. 132.
5. Oxford English Dictionary.
6. *Dublin 1916*, p. 70.
7. *Patrick Pearse: The Triumph of Failure*, p. 273.
8. *Patrick Pearse: The Triumph of Failure*, p. 275.

CHAPTER FORTY-EIGHT

1. *The Rising*, pp. 99–100.
2. 1916 Commission, Minutes of Evidence.
3. *Dublin Castle & the 1916 Rising*, p. 86.
4. *A History of Irish Flags*, p. 208.
5. *Enchanted by Dreams*, p. 24.
6. *Dublin Burning*, p. 33.
7. *Terrible Beauty*, p. 140.
8. *The Complete Works of P. H. Pearse: The Man Called Pearse*, p. 245.
9. *The Rising*, p. 117.
10. *Winding the Clock*, p. 207.
11. *Patrick Pearse: The Triumph of Failure*, p. 278.
12. *Patrick Pearse: The Triumph of Failure*, p. 278.
13. *Enchanted by Dreams*, p. 25.
14. *Terrible Beauty*, p. 133.

CHAPTER FORTY-NINE

1. *Enchanted by Dreams*, p. 26.
2. *Winding the Clock*, p. 207.

3. *The Rising,* p. 125.
4. *Dublin 1916,* p. 52.
5. *Enchanted by Dreams,* p. 26.
6. *Terrible Beauty,* p. 130.
7. *A History of Irish Flags,* pp. 209–217.

CHAPTER FIFTY

1. *Patrick Pearse: The Triumph of Failure,* p. 279.
2. *Terrible Beauty,* p. 142.
3. *Winding the Clock,* p. 208.
4. *The Rising,* p. 130.
5. *On Another Man's Wound,* p. 34.
6. *The Rising,* p. 117.
7. *The Insurrection in Dublin,* p. 7.
8. *Terrible Beauty,* p. 143.
9. *The Rising,* p. 120.
10. *Terrible Beauty,* p. 143.
11. *The Insurrection in Dublin,* p. 19.

CHAPTER FIFTY-ONE

1. *Terrible Beauty,* p. 144.
2. *The Rising,* p. 134.
3. *The Rising,* p. 138.
4. *The Rising,* p. 139.

CHAPTER FIFTY-TWO

1. *Terrible Beauty,* p. 144.
2. *The Insurrection in Dublin,* p. 26.
3. *Dublin as a Work of Art,* p. 198.
4. *The Easter Rising,* photograph on p. 18.
5. On display in the National Museum of Ireland.
6. *Patrick Pearse: The Triumph of Failure,* p. 290.

CHAPTER FIFTY-THREE

1. Eyewitness report taken from the *Gaelic American*, "Inside Story of the Easter Week Rebellion," July 29, 1916.
2. *The Rising*, p. 160.
3. *Terrible Beauty*, p. 146.
4. *The Rising*, p. 296.
5. *The Rising*, pp. 193–202.

CHAPTER FIFTY-FOUR

1. *The Irish Republic*, p. 192.
2. *The Easter Rising*, photograph on p. 24.
3. *The Rising*, p. 147.
4. *The Complete Works of P. H. Pearse: The Man Called Pearse*, p. 188.
5. *Enchanted by Dreams*, p. 49.
6. *Enchanted by Dreams*, p. 40.
7. *Winding the Clock*, p. 216.
8. *The Rising*, p. 147.
9. *Dublin 1916*, p. 206; account of Elizabeth O'Farrell.

CHAPTER FIFTY-FIVE

1. *Patrick Pearse: The Triumph of Failure*, p. 299.
2. *The Rising*, p. 152.
3. *Patrick Pearse: The Triumph of Failure*, p. 301.
4. From the private memoir of Jack Plunkett.
5. *Winding the Clock*, p. 220.
6. *Patrick Pearse: The Triumph of Failure*, p. 302.
7. "The Soldier's Song," which later became the Irish National Anthem.

CHAPTER FIFTY-SIX

1. *Patrick Pearse: The Triumph of Failure*, p. 304.
2. *The Rising*, p. 251; *Dublin 1916*, p. 207; account of Elizabeth O'Farrell.
3. *Patrick Pearse: The Triumph of Failure*, p. 304.
4. *The Rising*, p. 254.
5. *The Irish Republic*, p. 176.
6. *Enchanted by Dreams*, p. 76.
7. *Patrick Pearse: The Triumph of Failure*, p. 309.
8. *Michael Collins*, p. 44.
9. Captain Lee Wilson, later an RIC inspector in Wexford, who was mysteriously killed in 1920.

CHAPTER FIFTY-SEVEN

1. *The Rising*, p. 191.
2. *The Rising*, p. 184.
3. "God Save Ireland," traditional rebel song, *The Rising*, p. 185.
4. *The Rising*, p. 258.
5. *The Irish Republic*, p. 183.
6. *Dublin Castle & the 1916 Rising*, p. 113.
7. Suppressed; not published until 1946, by the *Irish Press*.
8. "The Wayfarer," by Pádraic Pearse.
9. *Patrick Pearse: The Triumph of Failure*, p. 319.
10. Letter in Pearse Museum, Saint Enda's.

CHAPTER FIFTY-EIGHT

1. *Patrick Pearse: The Triumph of Failure*, p. 322.
2. *Dublin 1916*, p. 262.
3. *A Dictionary of Irish Biography*, p. 197.
4. *Dublin 1916*, p. 264.

CHAPTER FIFTY-NINE

1. *Patrick Pearse: Triumph of Failure,* p. 298.
2. *Patrick Pearse: Triumph of Failure,* p. 324.
3. *Dublin Castle & the 1916 Rising,* p. 126.
4. *Dublin Castle & the 1916 Rising,* p. 131.

CHAPTER SIXTY

1. Excerpt from "The Fool," by P. H. Pearse.

Select Bibliography

Ballard, Robert D. *The Discovery of the Titanic*. London: Hodder and Stoughton, 1987.

Bartlett & Jeffery, editors. *A Military History of Ireland*. Cambridge: Cambridge University Press, 1996.

Boyce, D. G. *Englishmen and Irish Troubles*. London: Jonathan Cape, 1972.

Boylan, Henry, *A Dictionary of Irish Biography*. Dublin: Gill and Macmillan, 1978.

Brennan-Whitmore, W. J. *Dublin Burning*. Dublin: Gill and Macmillan, 1996.

Buckland, P. *The Origins of Northern Ireland*. Dublin: Gill and Macmillan, 1980.

Catholic Bulletin. *Easter Week and After: Eyewitness Accounts Biographies*. 1916.

Caulfield, Max. *The Easter Rebellion*. London: Frederick Muller, 1964.

Clarke, Kathleen. *Revolutionary Woman: An Autobiography*. Dublin: O'Brien Press, 1991.

Colum, Pádraic. *The Irish Rebellion of 1916 and Its Martyrs*. New York: Devin-Adair, 1916.

Connolly, James. *Labour in Irish History*. Dublin: 1910.

Connolly-O'Brien, Nora. *Portrait of a Rebel Father*. London: Rich and Cowan, 1935.

Coogan, Tim Pat. *De Valera*. London: Hutchinson, 1993.

———. *Michael Collins*. London: Hutchinson, 1990.

Cooke, Pat. *Scéal Scoil Éanna*. National Parks and Monuments Service. Ireland, 1986.

Cowell, John. *Where They Lived in Dublin*. Dublin: O'Brien Press, 1980.

Daly, Mary E. *Dublin: The Deposed Capital*. Cork: Cork University Press, 1984.

Dangerfield, George. *The Damnable Question. A Study in Anglo-Irish Relations*. London: Constable, 1977.

Davis, Richard. *Arthur Griffith and Non-violent Sinn Féin*. Dublin: Anvil Books, 1974.

de Breffny, Brian, editor. *Ireland: A Cultural Encyclopedia*. London: Thames & Hudson, 1983.

deCourcy, J. W. *The Liffey in Dublin*. Dublin: Gill & MacMillan, 1996.

Dinan, Brian. *Clare and Its People*. Cork and Dublin: Mercier Press, 1987.

Doherty & Hickey. *A Chronology of Irish History since 1500*. Dublin: Gill and Macmillan, 1989.

Ní Dhonnchadha, Máirín, and Dorgan, Theo, editors. *Revising the Rising*. Dublin: Field Day Publishers, 1991.

Edwards, Ruth Dudley. *Patrick Pearse: The Triumph of Failure*. New York: Taplinger, 1978.

Ellis, Peter Beresford. *A History of the Irish Working Class*. London: Gollancz, 1972.

Farmar, Tony. *Ordinary Lives: Three Generations of Irish Middle-class Experience*. Dublin: Gill and Macmillan, 1991.

Fianna Handbook. Dublin, 1914.

Finegan, John. *The Story of Monto* (paperback). Dublin, 1978.

Foster, R. F. *Modern Ireland, 1600–1972*. London: Allen Lane, Penguin Press, 1988.

Good, Joe. *Enchanted by Dreams*. Ireland: Brandon Books, 1996.

Gorham, Maurice. *Dublin Old and New*. West Yorkshire, England: EB Publishing, 1975.

Granville, Gary, editor. *Dublin 1913: A Divided City*. Dublin: O'Brien Educational, 1989.

Gray, Tony. *Ireland This Century*. London: Little, Brown, 1994.

Greaves, C. Desmond. *The Life and Times of James Connolly*. London: Lawrence & Wishart, 1986.

Haverty, Anne. *Elegant Times*. Dublin: Sonas, 1995.

Hayes-McCoy, G. A. *A History of Irish Flags*. Dublin: Academy Press, 1979.

———. *The Making of 1916*. Dublin Stationery Office, 1969.

Hobson, Bulmer. *A Short History of the Irish Volunteers*. Dublin, 1918.

Inglis, Brian. *Roger Casement*. London: Hodder & Stoughton, 1973.

Irish American Cultural Institute. *Éire-Ireland*. Various issues.

"Irish War News," *The Irish Republic,* Vol. 1, No. 1, Dublin, Tuesday, April 25, 1916.

Joyce, Weston St. John. *The Neighbourhood of Dublin*. Hughes & Hughes, 1994.

Kearns, Kevin C. *Dublin Pub Life & Lore*. Dublin: Gill & Macmillan, 1996.

———. *Dublin Tenement Life*. Dublin: Gill & Macmillan, 1994.

Kenny, Michael. *The Fenians*. National Museum of Ireland publication, 1994.

Kiely, Benedict. *Counties of Contention*. Cork: Mercier Press, 1945.

Kierse, Seán. *Education in the Parish of Killaloe*. Killaloe: Boru Books, 1987.

Larkin, Jim. *In the Footsteps of Big Jim*. Dublin: Blackwater Press, 1995.

Lee, Joseph. *The Modernisation of Irish Society, 1848–1918.* The Gill History of Ireland Series. Dublin: Gill & Macmillan, 1973.

Le Roux, Louis M. *Tom Clarke and the Irish Freedom Movement*. Dublin: Talbot Press, 1926.

Lincoln, Colm. *Dublin as a Work of Art*. Dublin: O'Brien Press, 1992.

Lord, Walter. *A Night to Remember*. New York: Henry Holt, 1955.

Lovett, Richard. *Ireland 100 Years Ago*. London: Bracken Books, 1995.

Macardle, Dorothy. *The Irish Republic*. Dublin: Irish Press, 1951.

Mac Eoin, Uinseann, editor. *Survivors* (updated edition). Dublin: Argenta Publications, 1987.

McHugh, Roger. *Dublin 1916*. London: Arlington Books, 1966.

MacKenna, Stephen. *Journals and Letters of Stephen MacKenna*. London: 1936.

MacLoughlin, Seán. *Memories of the Easter Rising*. Dublin: 1948.

MacManus, Seamus. *The Story of the Irish Race*. New York: Devin-Adair, 1944.

McRedmond, Louis. *Ireland: The Revolutionary Years*. Dublin: Gill and Macmillan & Radio Telefis Eireann, 1992.

Malton, James. *Dublin Views in Colour*. Dublin: Dolmen Press, n.d.

Marreco, Anne. *The Rebel Countess*. London: Weidenfeld and Nicholson, 1967.

Martin, F. X. *MacNeill on the 1916 Rising.* Dublin: Irish Historical Studies, 1916.

———. editor. *Leaders and Men of the Easter Rising: Dublin 1916.* London: Methuen, 1967.

Maxtone-Graham, John. *The Only Way to Cross.* New York: Macmillan, 1972.

Mercer, Derrik, editor-in-chief. *Chronicle of the Twentieth Century.* London: Longman Chronicle Communications, 1988.

O'Malley, Ernie. *On Another Man's Wound.* Dublin: Anvil Books, 1979.

Norman, Diana. *Terrible Beauty: A Life of Constance Markievicz.* London: Hodder & Stoughton, 1987.

O'Brien, The Hon. Grania R. *These My Friends and Forebears.* Co. Clare: Ballinakella Press, 1991.

O'Brien, Ivar. *O'Brien of Thomond.* London: Phillimore, 1986.

O'Brien, Joseph V. *"Dear, Dirty Dublin": A City in Distress, 1899–1916.* Berkeley, Calif.: University of California Press, 1982.

O'Broin, Leon. *Dublin Castle & the 1916 Rising* (revised edition). London: Sidgwick and Jackson, 1970.

O'Buachalla, Seamus, editor, *The Letters of P. H. Pearse.* London: Colin Smythe, 1980.

O'Connor, Ulick. *A Terrible Beauty Is Born.* London: Hamish Hamilton, 1975.

O'Rahilly, Aodogán. *Winding the Clock: O'Rahilly and the 1916 Rising.* Dublin: Lilliput Press, 1991.

Oram, Hugh. *The Newspaper Book.* Dublin: MO Books, 1983.

Pearse, Mary Brigid. *The Home Life of Padraig Pearse.* Dublin: 1935.

Pearse, Padraic H. *The Complete Works of P. H. Pearse: The Man Called Pearse* and *St. Enda's and Its Founder* (two volumes). Dublin: Phoenix Publishing Co., 1924.

Royal Commission. *On the Rebellion in Ireland*. London, 1916.

Ryan, Desmond, editor. *The 1916 Poets*. Dublin: Gill & Macmillan, 1995.

————. *The Rising*. Dublin: Golden Eagle Books, 1949.

Nic Shiubhlaigh, Maire. *The Splendid Years*. Dublin: Duffy, 1955.

Sinn Féin Rebellion Handbook. Compiled by the *Irish Weekly Times*. Dublin, 1917.

Stephens, James. *The Insurrection in Dublin*. Dublin and London: Maunsel, 1916.

Thompson, F. Glenn, "Uniforms of the 1916 Period," *AA Motoring*, Dublin, 1992.

Thoms Official Directory. Dublin: Waterworks Committee, editions 1912–1916.

Wallace, Martin. *One Hundred Irish Lives*. New Jersey: Barnes & Noble, 1983.

Walsh, Caroline. *The Homes of Irish Writers*. Dublin: Anvil Books, 1982.

ARCHIVES CONSULTED
(including unpublished material)

Dublin Civic Museum, Dublin
Dublin University (Trinity College)
Irish Bureau of Military History, Dublin
Kilmainham Jail Museum, Dublin
National Library of Ireland, Dublin
National Museum of Ireland, Dublin
Pearse Museum, Saint Enda's Park, Rathfarnham

Turn the page for a preview of

1999

Morgan Llywelyn

*Available now in paperback
from Tom Doherty Associates*

FORGE®

A FORGE PAPERBACK   ISBN 978-0-8125-7799-0

Chapter One

Like candles blown out by a celestial wind, the last stars vanished.

The beam of headlamps swung wildly as the Austin Healey skidded on a patch of black ice. Barry Halloran turned into the skid and kept his foot on the accelerator. The green car fishtailed; teetered on the brink of a ditch; recovered and raced on.

Barry's anger was unstoppable.

He hardly saw the road. Other images clouded his vision like a double exposure. Unarmed civilians being shot down in the street. An injured man shot in the back at point-blank range as he lay writhing on the pavement. An old woman battered to the ground with the butt of a rifle. British soldiers sniggering while the still-bleeding bodies of their victims were tossed into trucks like sides of beef.

On the screen of Barry's mind the cinematic horror ran over and over again.

His knuckles were white on the steering wheel.

He had taken advantage of the better roads in Northern Ireland by driving south from Derry through Tyrone and Fermanagh. Avoiding the manned border crossing west of Enniskillen, he had entered the Republic of Ireland by a neglected byway, then angled southward again across Leitrim and Roscommon. Even when he reached County Galway very few lights were visible from the road. Much of the region was all but deserted. In the west of Ireland unemployment was endemic. Thousands of young men and women had 'taken the boat' to England in search of jobs.

Signposts were notoriously unreliable. With nothing better to do, the local youngsters who remained behind often turned road signs to point in the wrong direction. The unwary driver could go miles out of his way before discovering his mistake.

Finbar Lewis Halloran needed no signposts to County Clare. The map was imprinted on the marrow of his bones.

By the time he turned into the country lane leading off the Ennis Road dawn was breaking. A sullen crimson dawn for the last day of January, 1972. "Red sky at night, farmers' delight," Barry muttered to himself. "Red sky at morning, farmers take warning."

Take warning, his tired brain echoed.

Ancient hedgerows of furze and whitethorn rose like walls on either side of the laneway. Deep ruts held automobile tyres to the track. Once committed, a driver had no choice but to follow the lane to the end.

After a few hundred yards it came to a substantial farmhouse flanked by barns and outbuildings. Within easy sight from the house a large paddock waited to receive the broodmares, heavy with foal, who would be turned out later in the morning.

Everything looks the same. Thank God, it always looks the same. Barry could feel knots loosening in the pit of his stomach.

Built of local stone in the eighteenth century, the original tiny cottage had been altered repeatedly by successive generations of Hallorans. The house now comprised two full storeys with a steeply pitched slate roof bracketed by brick chimneys. In a rare fit of domesticity, Ursula Halloran had built an extension off the kitchen to hold an array of modern appliances such as a washing machine and a freezer chest. She never got around to buying them. The space had become a catchall for muddy boots and haven for orphaned farm animals.

Ursula referred to it as 'the nursery.'

Barry slammed on the brakes and hurled himself from the

car like a giant spring uncoiling. He was very tall and the leg space beneath the dashboard was insufficient. The long drive had caused his damaged leg to stiffen. When he stood upright a spear of pain shot through the muscles.

A swift intake of breath. A momentary closing of eyes. Then it was over.

Two long strides carried him to the house.

A light was burning in the parlour to the left of the hall. As he ran past, Barry glimpsed the huddled figure of his mother in her favourite armchair, where she sometimes fell asleep listening to the late news on the radio. He took the stairs three at a time. Raced to his room, flung open the door. Threw himself on his knees beside the bed and fumbled beneath the mattress. Inhaled the dusty scent of feathers and ticking, and linen bleached in the sun.

Grasped the polished stock of Ned Halloran's old rifle.

A woman said from the doorway, "Thank God you're all right! When I rang your house in Dublin Barbara told me where you'd gone. What just happened in Derry is all over the news, RTE even interrupted its regular programming. I've been terrified."

The haggard man stood up with a rifle in his hands. "You've never been terrified in your life, Ursula." His deep baritone voice was hoarse with weariness.

"That's all you know. What happened?"

"I don't think I can talk about it, not yet."

"Please, Barry."

Reluctantly, he dragged out the words that made it all real again. "When the civil rights march formed up in the Creggan I was there with my cameras. A great opportunity for photojournalism, I thought. Images of hope in Northern Ireland after all these years. People came in their thousands, even from in the Republic. Men and women, boys and girls; it was more like a huge picnic than a protest rally. They brought food, their children, even their dogs. There was a lot of laughter and optimism. By the time they moved out the marchers were singing."

His voice dropped to a harsh whisper. "When they reached the Rossville Flats area the British soldiers trapped them in those narrow streets and shot them down like dogs. At least thirteen were killed then and there. Scores of others were wounded. I saw it; I saw it all." Barry closed his eyes for a moment; swayed where he stood.

Ursula put out a hand to steady him. He brushed it away. "I'm all right," he insisted.

His mother sat down on the bed. Running up the stairs after him had left her short of breath. "They're already calling it Bloody Sunday," she panted. "Like the original Bloody Sunday in 1920, when British forces machine-gunned Irish civilians at a football match. That incident was pretty well hushed up, but what happened yesterday is a different story. Television around the world is carrying scenes from Derry."

"Bless the telly," rasped Barry. "For once the Brits can't pretend one of their atrocities never happened."

He leaned the rifle against the wall and slumped onto the bed beside his mother. Ursula waited. Slowly, inch by inch, his spine straightened. When he spoke again his tone was that of a professional observer. "When I went to Derry I didn't expect a massacre, Ursula, though maybe I should have. Maybe we all should have. Surely by now we know the imperial mentality.

"Remember when Martin Luther King gathered a quarter of a million people at the U.S. Capitol in support of civil rights for his people? What a splendid day that was. The whole world seemed new, as if chains were finally being broken and anything was possible. The Catholics in Northern Ireland took King's message to heart. They believed the same non-violent protest could work for them.

"They were wrong.

"Yesterday they staged a peaceful march for their civil rights, and were shot in cold blood by the very army that was supposed to protect them. That's justice in the United Kingdom. In 1960 the American people elected a Catholic president. In 1972 Catholics in Northern Ireland can't even get a decent job." Barry's voice remained steady. Yet tremors of outrage ran through his body.

His mother longed to take him in her arms and comfort him. Theirs had never been that sort of relationship, however. His rumpled hair was the same red-gold it had been when he was a boy, but the sleeves of his coat were stained with someone else's blood.

He drew a long, deep breath. Exhaled slowly. Drew another. Sought the quiet pool at the centre of himself, which alone could armour a man against the shocks of life.

When he got to his feet, Ursula tilted her head back to look up into his face. Jutting cheekbones and quiline nose; a wide, mobile mouth. Sharply etched lines that made him appear older than his thirty-three years.

In his deep-set grey eyes she glimpsed the flash of swords.

Barry Halloran looked dangerous.